I0552950

Cold Feet Fever

The Fever Series, Book 2

(A Romantic Crime Mystery with Tons of Humor)

Maureen Fisher

Secrets and Crime Have Never Been So Much Fun
— or So Romantic!

A bad boy gambler with a lazy streak and commitment issues:

Owning Kinki, Atlantic City's first paranormal nightclub, isn't as easy—or as much fun—as Sam Jackson had anticipated. Someone's trying to shut him down before he opens, he's on the verge of bankruptcy, and his matchmaking granddaddy has hired a sexy event planner with a mysterious background, bossy disposition, and criminal ties.

A mortician-turned-event-planner with big secrets:

A job as event planner offers single mom, Katie Deluca, her last chance to escape her past. Turns out party planning is more difficult than organizing funerals. Plus, the nightclub owner, although perfect for awakening her sensuality, couldn't be more wrong for the stability she craves.

Forced to collaborate, they overcome obstacles and fight crime:

Katie is the one person who can salvage Kinki—and heal Sam's emotional wounds. Together, they tangle with a goofy dog, exploding trucks, an unfortunate synchronized swimming episode, homicidal thugs, a corrupt building inspector, disappearing corpses, a kidnapping, and the threat of live cremation, all to deliver a kick-ass grand opening.

Praise for Maureen Fisher and Her Novels

"The story rattles along at a cracking pace, witty, exciting, cheeky and very, very sexy. Not just the action, but the dialogue itself sizzles. I was hooked from the beginning. A wonderful mix of action, humor, sex and suspense." ~ *Alan Hardy (Goodreads.com)*

"Maureen combines action, adventure, romance, mystery, and an often LOL sense of humor in her page-turning novels. They are the perfect additions to your electronic libraries, like da rum and da coconut in your piña colada." ~ *Amazon.com*

"Maureen Fisher is a very talented writer and I'm glad to have found my way to her books!" ~ *Amazon.com*

"It is well written and skillfully plotted. Well done Maureen Fisher." ~ *Amazon.com*

"Maureen Fisher is an excellent author and I would read and recommend her books." ~ *Amazon.com*

"an awesome writing and storytelling talent." ~ *Amazon.com*

"I will be reading Maureen Fisher again, for sure." "Ms. Fisher has a deft hand at incorporating wit & humor." ~ *Amazon.com*

Cold Feet Fever
by Maureen Fisher

Copyright © 2016 Maureen Fisher

ISBN 978-0-9877902-6-2

Edited by Stacy Juba
Cover by The Killion Group Inc.
Formatted by MarksEbookFormatting.com

All Rights Are Reserved.

Except in the case of brief quotations embodied in critical articles and reviews, no part of this book may be used or reproduced in any manner whatsoever without prior written permission from the author.

This is a work of fiction. All of the characters, organizations, and events portrayed in this story are either products of the author's imagination or are used fictitiously, and any resemblance to actual events, locales or persons, living or dead, is entirely coincidental.

Discover more about Maureen Fisher
http://www.booksbymaureen.com

Cold Feet Fever

Maureen Fisher

Chapter 1: New Job

"Darlin', that feels real good. Hoo-eee, you surely do have magic fingers." The masculine voice, Southern with a twist, was clearly audible over the commotion.

Katie Deluca backed away from the closed office door. It would be just her luck to march inside, eager to start her new job as event planner for *Kinki*'s grand opening, only to find the junior partner in a compromising position.

She reined in her imagination. No one, not even a player like Sam Jackson, had the gall to pull a nooner during his own hiring blitz. Someone nearby must have spoken the words she'd overheard. There were plenty of potential culprits.

Job applicants were lined up along the corridor. Several sprouted vampire teeth, while others dripped gore from neck wounds. Many uttered howls, wails, or moans. Katie had never experienced anything so bizarre in the workplace, and as a former undertaker, she'd seen some doozies. Then again, *Kinki* was hiring staff for its unveiling as Atlantic City's first paranormal nightclub, a far cry from its previous fetish club status.

She smoothed her skirt. Confident of her professional appearance in a black suit, white blouse, and smart pumps, she squared her shoulders and rapped on the door.

Inside, a clicking noise grew louder, then stopped. No one answered.

Chalking up the sound to antiquated office equipment, she opened the door (not locked, thank you, God), and froze at the sight of a German shepherd hurtling toward her. She recognized the dog as belonging to Hiram Jackson, the senior partner who'd hired her three hours earlier.

"Down, Rex."

With a joyous yelp, Rex reared up and placed both front paws on her shoulders, enveloping her in fur and dog-breath. Her knees threatened to buckle under the weight of eighty-plus pounds of eager canine. She staggered backward, propelled across the corridor until plastered against the opposite wall. After a tussle, she managed to dislodge the massive paws. Rex dropped to the floor, circled twice, and licked her ankles.

She made a grab for his collar. The dog danced away. Sighing, she opened her Gucci knockoff. Vetoing a bran muffin for the fiber overload it packed, she extracted her sandwich.

Rex froze. His nose twitched. He pointed his muzzle at the ceiling and gave a prolonged howl that caused several vampires and one semi-rotted zombie to stare, possibly expecting a werewolf.

Tearing off the wrapping, she lobbed the sandwich into the office. Rex chased after it with Katie close on his heels.

While the dog gulped down her chicken-with-tomato-on-whole-grain, she shut the door and leaned against it, composing herself. A surprising amount of noise, including the occasional groan from a ghoul or goblin, filtered through an air vent above the door.

Feeling calmer, she looked around. The office was unoccupied (thanks again, God). Either the junior partner had forgotten her arrival, or word of her hiring hadn't filtered down. Three hours wasn't much lead time.

After doing her due diligence on the Internet, she wasn't ecstatic about sharing an office with the junior partner. According to a chat group discussion, Sam Jackson was a player with a fondness for gambling, booze, and women, not necessarily in that order. Sadly, she didn't have the luxury of declining the first job offer she'd received since leaving the family business. Apparently, no one wanted to hire a former mortician as their party planner.

Determined to make the best of a bad situation, she examined her new workspace with interest. The sun-drenched office was L-shaped and huge, the main area easily big enough for two matching desks, several visitor's chairs, and multiple filing cabinets. In the adjoining space, she glimpsed a gleaming conference table lined with chairs.

A moment later, her nose twitched. Pepperoni. Garlic. Cheese. On top of the highest filing cabinet sat a pizza box, takeout coffee, and jumbo bottle of painkillers. Sam Jackson had obviously stepped out knowing Rex couldn't reach the pizza.

Rex, apparently an optimist, paced beneath the food, as if willpower alone could topple the box to the floor.

With the dog occupied, Katie slung her purse over her shoulder and headed for the conference area to check it out. She didn't get far. Rex clamped his jaws around her purse. Apparently, raisin bran muffins were easier prey.

The dog released another quavering howl, ending in a sharp bark.

A man's voice yelled, "Quiet or I'll return you to Animal Services."

Crap, crapity crap. Time to leave. When she tried to tip-toe away, Rex disagreed.

Glancing over her shoulder, Katie panicked. At the other end of the conference area was an alcove she'd overlooked. A pair of cowboy boots lay on the floor. A garment dangled from a chair. The couch's back mercifully hid the occupants, but the top of a woman's head was visible, bobbing in a rhythmic movement.

She appeared highly focused on the task at hand.

With growing desperation, Katie managed to pry her purse from Rex's jaws. He registered his disapproval with another howl ending in an eerie, wolf-like falsetto.

She prayed the couch's occupants were far enough along in their bliss to ignore the interruption. Purse to chest, she backed away. She'd reached the main office when a man's drawl flooded her entire body with apprehension. "Much as I hate to break the mood, darlin', I'd better check up on Rex. I don't trust him near the pizza."

Before Katie could flee, or dig a hole for herself, or better still, throw herself out the window, Sam Jackson, playboy and, if she believed the Internet gossip, all-around heartbreaker strolled out of the alcove. Buttoning an amber silk shirt the same color as his eyes and wearing a Stetson, he halted and scrutinized Katie across the gleaming expanse of conference table.

The grainy newspaper photos she'd studied online didn't come close to doing justice to his masculine glory. Everything about him screamed sexy, from that chiseled jaw and those sculpted lips, to his streaky blond hair framing a face that belonged on the big screen.

Fortunately, pretty packaging didn't interest her in the slightest. Nope. No way. The man was a degenerate of the highest order.

As he closed in, his gaze took a long, leisurely tour of her body before settling on her mouth. He exuded a hint of cologne, all woodsy and spicy and delicious, not that she cared. Was it her imagination, or did his expression hint at amusement?

"Howdy, ma'am. I apologize if my dog scared you, but I'm afraid you've got the wrong office." His voice was a little raspy, steeped in moonlight and magnolias.

Katie cleared her throat. "I'm in the right place, thank you."

One side of his mouth kicked up a notch. "You must be here for our job fair. Try Room 204. That's our HR department. In that outfit, you'd make a perfect *Dracula's Lair* attendant." A broad grin creased his cheeks, causing the corners of his eyes to crinkle.

"No, but thank you anyway." Katie studied his face. "It's obvious you didn't touch base with your boss this morning."

"Really? And all this time I believed I was the boss."

About to point out his error in thinking, Katie lost her train of thought at the sight of a woman emerging from the alcove. She wore a Meatza Pizza uniform with a pizza logo emblazoned on her chest, also the shortest pair of booty shorts in the world. Face averted, she scurried along the opposite side of the conference table toward the door.

Sam caught up with her. "Thank you, darlin'. You did a superb job of curing my headache." Ignoring Katie's presence, he had the nerve to reach into his pocket, pull out several bills, and tuck them into the woman's hand, saying, "This is for the pizza, and a little something extra for your help. I want you to remember you're one fine-looking woman. Your moron boyfriend is lucky to have you." More whispered words triggered a giggle.

For a split second, Katie imagined she detected kindness in his voice, but she must be mistaken. He'd just indulged in office sex with a vulnerable young woman.

The woman left the office, and Katie found herself alone with Sam, minus his killer grin. She eyed him warily.

Ever-so-gently, he pressed the door shut. "Cupcake, we need to have a long chat about privacy, but first things first. My headache's screaming for a painkiller or three." He tossed his Stetson onto the desk and sauntered over to the filing cabinet in the main office area.

Katie marched after him and planted her feet. "You told her she cured you."

His eyes sharpened, displaying both irritation and lively intelligence. "Little white lie. She gave it her best shot." He reached for the painkillers and extracted two red pills.

"I'm sure she did." Knowing she had to speak up, Katie gripped her purse tighter. "Do you always use your office to indulge in *that* sort of … activity?"

The painkillers disappeared along with a swallow of coffee. He grimaced before answering, "It was a win-win. She needed an ego-boost, I needed TLC." He shook out another pill and dry-swallowed.

"What? You had pity sex with her?"

An aggrieved expression crossed his face. "Who said anything about sex?" He rubbed the bridge of his nose again. "She gave me a massage to cure my headache. All I did was listen as she poured her heart out about how her idiot boyfriend ignores her. Claims she's not sexy enough. She left here a whole lot richer and prepared to rip him a new one. Her exact words."

Restraining an eye-roll, Katie held her ground. "You're a prince among men."

His eyebrows shot up. "I am. I really am, aren't I?"

"I hope you realize if she mentions your, uh, massage to her boyfriend, you'd better watch your back."

"Won't be a first."

"You sound proud of the fact." Katie locked her hands together. Her reservations about sharing an office with him were growing by leaps and bounds. Hey, he might put the couch to use again, next time with a goth groupie for the real deal.

Note to Self: Purchase disinfectant wipes.

He picked up his hat and slapped it onto his head. "Well, now, this has been more fun than playing in traffic. I'll escort you to the door."

"I'm staying until after the grand opening." She was contemplating the most tactful way to explain her presence when, without apparent provocation, he yelled, "Stop."

Her pulse shot into the red-alert zone. At this rate, she'd better place an order for a portable defibrillator as well. Once she unglued her tongue from the roof of her mouth, she asked, "Are you always this explosive?"

Sam smiled, revealing a double row of gleaming white teeth. "I hope you don't have food in your purse."

She yanked her purse to safety while Rex flopped to the floor beside her. "Why would you care?"

"Rex is a fur-encased stomach with four paws, a gullet, and a sniffer. He howls whenever there's food around. We call it the food alarm." Without warning, he bellowed again. "Down. Don't even think about it."

A throaty grumble alerted her to the wet black nose snuffling her purse again. "Thanks for the warning." She clutched her purse to her chest. "Rex ate my lunch. Now, he's after my bran muffins. Did you know raisins and bran provide vitamins and plenty of fiber? The healing power of fiber is such an important factor in maintaining—" She broke off in mid-sentence. "Sorry. I swear I only babble when I'm stressed."

This time his smile looked genuine. "You must be uber-stressed to be discussing fiber. Why don't you tell me why a pretty little thing like you is paying me a visit?" His voice was as smooth as warm caramel.

She had a feeling he wouldn't do a happy dance when she explained how Hiram had given her carte blanche to organize *Kinki*'s grand opening, along with instructions to share the junior partner's office. Since her duties included keeping Sam in line, she assumed he'd be reporting to her.

Katie drew herself up to the full five foot four inches her smart pumps provided. "You might want to sit down for this," she suggested, gesturing to a chair.

Chapter 2: Sam Toys with Katie

Sam stood stock still, staring at the determined jut of the woman's chin as she indicated a visitor's chair. Everything about her was restrained and tidy. He was unable to tell if her black hair was curly or straight because she'd scraped everything into some sort of sleek twist. Her plain white blouse was buttoned up to the chin and the black business suit would be right at home in a funeral parlor.

A wave of amusement washed away his financial woes. He decided to have some fun. Prim, bossy, and more than a tad uptight, this wisp of a woman was exactly the distraction he needed to forget his troubles. She needed his help to loosen up. Fortunately for her, he was a giver.

For starters, he slouched away in the opposite direction, concentrating on moving slower than a sloth on Valium. Out of the corner of his eye, he noted her impatient foot tapping. Yeah, he was getting under her skin.

"Let's sit down and chat, shall we?" she suggested in a strained voice.

He offered a grimace followed by a hard-done-by sigh, not difficult given the severity of his hangover. His mouth felt as though he'd spent the better part of the night licking a shag carpet.

"Be right with you," he mumbled.

He inched over to the filing cabinet to retrieve the pizza box and coffee. Next, he shuffled to his desk and deposited everything there. With great ceremony, he cracked open the box.

Rex circled the desk, his plumy tail whipping up a small gale. He licked his chops and pointed his nose to the ceiling. Recognizing a looming food alarm, Sam hollered, "Rex. Quiet."

The dog subsided with a baleful glare and a grumble.

Sam inspected the pizza, turning the box this way and that, examining the contents from every angle.

"May I help you choose a slice?" she asked, desperation crackling in her voice.

"No thanks. I'm good."

When he figured an explosion was imminent, he focused on his visitor, letting vague surprise cloud his face, as if he'd forgotten her presence. "Pizza? Best thing in the world for hangovers. It's a Meat-Lover's Special, extra sausage, bacon, and meatballs, double cheese."

"Absolutely not. I try to avoid animal fat whenever possible. Do you have any idea what it does to the arteries? According to last month's

Healthier You, cholesterol plaque builds up. Sooner or later—" She broke off with an eye-roll. "Forget it. Eat whatever you want."

Priceless. "Thank you for the very wise nutritional advice." He pulled a scrap of paper and a pen from his pocket and scribbled. "A reminder," he explained, flashing her a guileless grin. "Switch to veggie pizza, extra broccoli, hold the cheese."

The muscles around her jaw tightened. She bared a mouthful of very white, very sharp teeth. "Nearly ready?"

He wrinkled his forehead. "This is too important to rush." Examining the pizza, he pretended to hunt for the perfect slice.

"Take your time," she said in a strained voice.

After more deliberation, he tore off a slice and placed it on a napkin, aligning it precisely in the middle of the desk.

"Make sure Rex doesn't go near my pizza." Sam closed the box and returned it to the filing cabinet at the same leisurely pace. While there, he straightened some file folders and a stack of paper before sauntering back. With an innocent glance in her direction, he ignored the chair she indicated and parked himself in his swivel chair. With a satisfied sigh, he picked up his pizza.

She sat across from him, looping her purse over the chair back. All prim and proper, she folded her hands in her lap.

Her unruffled act didn't fool Sam. Her body vibrated with tension.

He took a huge bite, chewed, and swallowed. "Ahhhhh. Grease, carbs, and caffeine. Perfect." After lowering the pizza and dabbing his lips with a napkin, he leaned back. Propping his feet on the desk's glossy surface, guaranteed to capture her attention, he slurped his coffee.

She merely folded her arms and clamped her lips together, likely to prevent breakthrough babble.

He hit her with his most potent weapon, the sexy grin that more often than not resulted in afternoon delight. Not that he expected—or wanted— bed sports from a woman whose expression broadcast that she considered him a weevil she wanted to crush underfoot.

When she failed to respond, he dialed back the grin. "Why do I think I won't like whatever it is you're twitchin' to tell me, cupcake?"

Her chest rose and fell as she inhaled a deep breath. "Please don't call me 'cupcake'. My name is Katarina Deluca. People call me Katie." She regarded him as though she expected a reaction.

"Should I know you?"

"Of course not."

A lesser man might have missed her subliminal relaxation. Reading body language was a mandatory talent for skilled gamblers, and he considered himself one of the best. She'd hoped he didn't recognize the name. Making a mental note to Google Katie Deluca, he stuck out a hand. "Sam. Sam Jackson."

She shook his hand with surprising firmness. "I know all about you."

"I get that a lot."

"If we're to hit it off, I have one request." She fixed him with melted chocolate eyes, which, on closer study, sparked with disapproval.

"Do tell." He picked up his pizza.

"Since we're sharing an office until after the grand opening, I must ask you to refrain from entertaining female guests on your couch."

Sam froze, the pizza halfway to his mouth. "Say what?"

"I won't tolerate more 'massages' while we're sharing the space."

"Sweet baby Jesus," he moaned. "I've gotta lay off bourbon."

"Excellent idea. Do your body a favor. Nevertheless, your senior partner, Hiram, engaged me to plan and coordinate *Kinki*'s grand opening. He also mentioned the only available space was in your office, and indicated that he expected me to supervise you."

An arrow of pain speared Sam's skull. The wily old man's powers of persuasion obviously worked fine in spite of major impulse control issues. Smelling another of his granddaddy's matchmaking attempts, he set down the last of his pizza. "Hiram's my granddaddy. He calls himself the senior partner because he's older, not because he's my boss. He has no hiring authority."

"Hiram warned me you'd say that." Katie's voice brimmed with compassion. "He also promised that after you got over your snit, you'd be happy to comply." Under her breath, she muttered, "It would have been a nice touch if he'd warned me about the casting couch."

Sam lowered his feet to the ground with great care. Leaning forward, he spoke softly, emphasizing every word. "It's not a casting couch. I should know. It's my office, my couch." For some reason, it mattered what she thought.

"Believe it or not, I find this situation as difficult as you do."

"I doubt it." He gulped a fortifying swig of coffee, wishing with all his heart he could lace it with something stronger. "What else should I know?"

He watched with reluctant amusement as she whipped out a notepad and flipped the pages. Who used a notepad in this era of tablets and other electronic devices?

She must have found the nugget of information she wanted because she stopped flipping. "Ah, yes. Here it is. Hiram informed me you won a lot of money in the casinos, enough to buy *Kinki* and renovate it too, with plenty left over for a grand opening. His words were, and I quote, 'The sky's the limit'."

Sam choked on his coffee. Katie passed a napkin, which he accepted. When he stopped coughing, he asked, "How did you two meet?"

She studied her notepad as if hunting for inspiration. Or to avoid looking at him. "I was leaving an early morning job interview today when I saw an elderly man trying to catch a large German shepherd." Still refusing to look up, she jotted something down.

Yeah, she was hiding something. What deep, dark secrets could she possibly have? After a prolonged silence, he said, "My granddaddy told me Rex managed to escape during their pre-breakfast constitutional. He didn't mention meeting anyone."

She squirmed a little. "Must have slipped his mind." After a moment, her eyelashes swept up. "I helped catch Rex by bribing him with cheese."

"Do you always carry food in your purse?"

"The cheese was part of my lunch. Did you know those twisted cheese snacks provide long-lasting energy because—" The look she gave him was sheepish. "Forget it. After we collared Rex, I gave them both a lift back to *Kinki*. Long story short, we hit it off, Hiram offered me a job, I accepted, end of story."

Sam settled deeper into his chair, his curiosity growing. She was kinda cute—in a delightfully earnest and intense sort of way. He nodded. "I imagine he had a convincing explanation."

"He said his young partner needed a lot of help, but nothing about how you're his grandson." She hit him with her velvety dark gaze. "I'm extremely grateful for this opportunity. You'll both be happy with my results."

Her enthusiasm caught Sam off-guard. He liked her sincerity. He liked it a lot. But he couldn't ignore her insistence that she had a job here.

Her voice penetrated his thoughts. "If we're finished with the preliminaries, I suggest we get started. Three weeks isn't long, and I have exciting ideas I'm sure will impress Hiram."

Guilt ripped through Sam. It was his own damn fault. After every casino in town had closed its doors on him because they'd caught on to his card counting, he'd let his granddaddy believe money was no issue. It was a whole lot easier than admitting he'd blown through the better part of six-point-eight million dollars. Hell, as if losing his own money wasn't bad enough, he'd also lost Granddaddy Hiram's retirement savings.

"I'm sure you'll love my ideas, too," Katie assured him, apparently unaware of his dark thoughts. "I'm thinking complimentary buffet, free Vampire Martinis, a live rock band." She paused, then rattled on, "Oh, let's go all out, shall we? Make that three bands. We'll have one techno-rock, one alternative-rock like a goth revival band, and a classic rock band for the older generation."

A choking sensation gripped Sam. Everything she suggested would cost a fortune. He snapped out of it only to realize she was staring at him with concern.

"You look disturbed. Do you think Hiram wants splashier ideas? Let's see. Hardacid will be in town. I met him last year at his cousin's funeral. He owes me a favor."

Sam leaped from his chair, sending it spinning sideways. "Enough." Did she have a clue how much Hardacid charged?

"Did I say something wrong? If not Hardacid, I could try for Red Hot Thunder."

In desperation, he executed a few of the lightning-fast mental calculations that were as natural to him as breathing before reaching a painful conclusion. His granddaddy had no idea how close to bankruptcy they were. An event coordinator with grandiose spending ideas was out of the question. Katie had to go.

No sooner had it crossed Sam's mind that he should find out if Katie Deluca had signed a contract, when a voice boomed out, "I see you've met my grandson."

Speak of the devil. All gussied up in his go-to-bingo suit and string tie, with his white hair and beard neatly trimmed and cowboy boots polished, Granddaddy Hiram stood in the doorway. His million-dollar smile lit the room. Sam hoped his own teeth looked that great when he, too, reached 83.

Katie smiled back. "Hi Hiram. Yes indeed. We were discussing—"

Sam spoke over Katie's pleasantries. "Granddaddy Hiram. You and I need to have a long and serious talk. Now." Rude, yes, but the situation was urgent.

It was as if he hadn't spoken. Granddaddy Hiram focused all his attention on Katie. "I hope Sam's treating you well."

Katie flushed a bright pink. "As well as can be expected."

As the pair chit-chatted, Sam noted that his granddaddy studiously avoided looking in his direction. Jesus, the old matchmaker had hired a cutie and thrown them together in the hopes of a happily-ever-after and a handful of great-grandchildren. Hell, Katie, probably had no credentials to organize a birthday party, never mind the grand opening.

"I'm right here," Sam reminded his granddaddy, waggling his fingers.

Granddaddy Hiram looked at Sam for the first time. "I know. You're hard to miss, boy. Take good care of Katie, or you'll answer to me. Gotta run. I'm off to the Senior Center. My ride's waiting. See you later." And with a cheery wave, he hightailed it out of the office.

"Wait," Sam shouted at the now-empty doorframe. "We need to talk, then I'll drive you."

Katie's forehead wrinkled. "He's in a hurry, isn't he?"

Sam leaped to his feet. He had to corral Granddaddy Hiram for a little heart-to-heart. There might be grounds to fire Katie.

Through a tight jaw, he said, "I need to talk to my granddaddy before he leaves. I'll be right back."

Feeling Katie's puzzled gaze on his back, he sprinted into the corridor. His conscience twitched at leaving her alone. Then he relaxed, remembering she had Rex for company.

What could possibly go wrong?

Chapter 3: Sam Makes a Decision

There was no sign of Granddaddy Hiram. He was likely hiding out until the dust settled. It didn't matter. Sam had reached a decision. He must find a hiring loophole in order to fire Katie Deluca without costly repercussions.

Hurrying back to his office, the clatter of his cowboy boots ricocheted inside his skull. Prepared to deliver the unhappy news, he sauntered inside. "Ms. Deluca, I'm afraid we, uh—" He froze in mid-sentence. "Sweet lord a' mercy."

Smack dab on the middle of his office floor was a sight a man didn't see every day.

Pinned by two plate-sized paws, a woman squirmed, spread-eagled on her back in a patch of early afternoon spring sunshine. She clutched a leather handle, which had parted company with the purse. A large furry body prevented Sam from getting a good look at her face, but he knew who she was.

Katie Deluca. The woman he planned to fire.

Apparently Rex had hit pay dirt in the form of raisin bran muffins. The fear of lawsuits jump-started Sam's vocal cords. "Rex. Off."

Rex swung his head in Sam's direction. The German shepherd appeared blissful. His jaws worked rhythmically, munching on a brown paper bag. The bag disappeared with a gulp, a ribbon of drool, and a couple of dry retches. His snack consumed, Rex collapsed on top of Katie's body.

"Urk!" she said in a muffled voice.

Sam tilted his head to examine Katie's legs, which were all he could see of her beneath the mountain of fur. Being an excellent judge of legs, he deemed hers to be premium quality, slender and nicely shaped, curvy in all the right places. When confronted with amazing legs, a smart man made allowances for regrettable black pumps.

Unbelievably, she raised her knees, thighs spread, and wriggled in an effort to break free. All rational thought flew out the window.

Except for a garter belt and stockings, Katie was buck naked under the businesslike skirt.

After one heart-stopping moment, Sam realized his mistake. Not naked. She wore lacy peach panties, which, come to think of it, was the next best thing.

His heart was thumping heavily by the time she twisted her lower body sideways in an attempt to dislodge Rex. All it did was block his view. Rex remained sprawled across her chest.

Sam knew he should help, and that ogling was all wrong, but hey, he was a guy. He sidled a little to the left of center, hoping a different perspective would improve his view.

Releasing a stream of fluent Italian, she snapped her knees together and tugged at her skirt, which had bunched around her waist in a delightful way. A series of wriggles had Sam's heart thundering with hope for another panty sighting.

His blood flow returned to normal when she succeeded in dragging the black wool down.

Rex gave a canine grin, as if expecting an approving scratch for finding a friend with such fabulous legs and flimsy underwear.

Sam smiled back. Katie's dismissal could wait.

"Comfy?" he asked, unable to resist. "Personally, I prefer a chair, but there's no accounting for taste."

"Don't stand there gawking. Do something."

"A pillow, perhaps?"

"Not funny. Fix this."

She sounded exactly like his high school librarian, who hadn't been his biggest fan either, especially when she'd caught him reading a *Playboy* inside a geography textbook.

He grinned. "Would you look at that? We're bonding already. Adorable."

She let fly with more lethal-sounding Italian.

Rex licked his jaws. Sam was sure the dog would wink if he knew how. Realizing he'd pushed his luck to the max, he issued an order. "Rex. Come." When nothing happened, he braced himself, got a good grip on the collar, and tugged.

It was like trying to dislodge an elephant. Rex merely stretched his neck and licked Katie's fingers, releasing slobber into her hand.

"What are you waiting for?" she demanded, shooting Sam a glare. "Lift him off."

Sam hesitated. If he lifted Rex, he'd have to reach under the dog's middle, which was positioned smack dab across her chest. Obviously, she was unaware of his chivalrous attempt to avoid an inadvertent grope.

"Not a great idea, cupcake."

"The name's Katie, and now rather than later would be good. That is, if you've finished having your fun. I hate to deprive a man of his entertainment."

Sam was torn between guilt and amusement. She was right about one thing. He was having more fun with a woman outside the bedroom than he'd enjoyed in years.

"Yes, ma'am. I live to please."

She replied with a muffled snort.

Rolling up his shirt sleeves, he positioned himself just so, straddling both dog and woman. He went at it from both sides, snaking his hands underneath Rex's body. His hands brushed against the swelling of breasts. Turned out Katie possessed the type of breasts he adored—firm, beautifully shaped without being enormous, and judging by their enticing softness, all her own. He resisted a little detour of discovery, moving past them to wrap his arms around the dog's chest. Then, taking care to avoid slobber, which tended to stain silk, he hauled like crazy.

His exertion merely dislodged a burp.

Filled with remorse, Sam let go. It was no longer funny, never was. Moving faster than he had in a long time, he got to the pizza and opened the lid. The perfume of garlic, five meats, and double cheese filled his office. He snagged a slice and waved it at Rex.

"Bad idea," Katie said, a note of warning in her voice.

"It's all I've got."

Rex moaned his approval. The black nose twitched as he sniffed the air. In a single bound he was off Katie. The pizza made a fast disappearance.

While Rex licked his chops, Sam snapped on the leash and tied it around a desk leg to prevent another incident. Reaching out to assist Katie, he discovered she'd already scrambled to her feet.

How had he not noticed her height? The top of her head barely reached his collarbone. He tried to assess the breasts he knew lay hidden beneath the jacket. Fabric concealed her figure better than a tent. A gooey mess comprised of saliva and what appeared to be crumbs coated the front of her suit.

While she straightened herself out, he rescued the purse with two fingers. Using a Meatza Pizza napkin he mopped off the slime before handing it over.

She dabbed her chest with another napkin. "My best suit's ruined."

Sam wisely refrained from voicing his relief. Hypnotized, he focused on the napkin's rhythmic motion as it reached the spot where her breasts surely nestled. "I'm truly sorry about Rex's manners. Naturally, I'll pay for the dry-cleaning bill and a new purse."

The napkin dabbing stopped. A still-functioning sliver of his brain alerted him to trouble. He dragged his gaze away from the danger zone.

"It's always the owner's fault, not the dog's." She didn't bother waiting for an answer. "You and Rex would both benefit from obedience training."

She looked so prim and cute, Sam couldn't help grinning. "You're right. Our actions were inexcusable." His smile faded when he remembered he was about to fire her.

Rex distracted him by flopping onto the floor with another burp.

A worried frown crinkled her brow. "I'm afraid you're in for a rough afternoon."

"Is there a problem?"

"On top of the twisted cheese and my lunch, Rex ate all six muffins, the muffin liners, the paper bag, and a slice of pizza."

He was close enough to take note of her eyes. They were eyes to get lost in—almond-shaped, slightly slanted, long-lashed, and a deep, velvety brown. He snapped out of it. "Aren't you being alarmist?"

"They're called Powerful Bran Muffins for a reason. Please pay attention. What I'm about to tell you is essential."

Sam fought the urge to snap his heels together, salute, and say, "Yes, ma'am."

She waved a finger under his nose. "This animal needs plenty of water to hydrate the massive amount of fiber he ate. If not, he'll be blocked for a week. Either way, it won't be pretty."

His headache made a quick return. It was easier to agree. "Right. Water. Bran blockage." He located Rex's water dish under the conference table and nudged it closer.

She didn't exactly smile, but a cute dimple appeared in one cheek. Immediately, her face lost its graveness and transformed into one of extraordinary appeal, brimming with warmth, friendliness, and kindness. And why hadn't he noticed her mouth earlier? His hangover must be worse than he'd thought. Those full, pink lips were shockingly tempting once she stopped pinching them together.

He hardened his heart against the attraction. Hell, he was about to fire the woman.

He'd barely opened his mouth to let her down gently when she demonstrated a spooky mind-reading ability. "Hiram and I discussed my remuneration. Since the assignment is short-term, I will receive a single payment upon successful delivery of the grand opening." She named a pricey dollar figure.

Hope flared. Money was no longer an issue. He didn't need to worry about draining the bank account before the opening. The only remaining question was whether she could accomplish the impossible—organize a kick-ass grand opening in less than three weeks and on a limited budget. In his experience, the direct approach always worked best.

"Do you mind answering a couple of questions?"

***

Sam chose to sit behind his desk to conduct the interview, with Katie opposite him, facing the window. He wanted to absorb every facial expression, every twitch, every gesture she made in order to come up with an accurate reading. He kept the questioning brief, mainly "what-if" scenarios involving hypothetical problems.

When they finished, he said, "All done. I need to think for a few minutes, so pretend I'm not here."

She gave a decidedly unladylike snort, but held her peace.

Pacing the office, he ignored her frown and put his seldom-used Harvard MBA to work. Applying his ability to read people, a useful skill he'd perfected in casinos, he re-wound a mental tape of the interview.

Three things were obvious. Katie was hiding a shitload of secrets, her quick thinking was impressive, if not out-and-out genius, and she was highly motivated, one might say desperate, to tackle the assignment.

It was a no-brainer. She had the job. And sooner or later he would learn her secrets.

As he approached to deliver the good news, he eyed her lush, sweet mouth. It occurred to him that if he cut back on his nightlife, he'd have more money to throw at the grand opening. And more time to spend with his new event planner.

She stood up and faced him, arms folded, foot tapping. "So? Did I pass the test? Not that it matters because Hiram already hired me."

He'd expected apprehension or wariness. Belligerence was an unanticipated curve ball. He smiled to show there were no hard feelings. "With flying colors. Congratulations." He enfolded her hand in his, anticipating a warm response. "Welcome on board."

"Right. I'm glad you approve. It makes my job easier. I imagine it must be demoralizing having no voice in the selection of the management team." All business, she gave his hand a strong shake and disengaged with unflattering speed.

Clearly, she was not feeling the gratitude. What in God's name had Granddaddy Hiram told her about him? Then again, she had no clue how close she'd come to being fired, or that he was her boss. It would be fun to chip away her starchy exterior.

He plunked himself down in his chair. To loosen himself up, he opened a drawer and extracted a deck of cards.

Alerted by the clip-clop of sensible shoes, he looked up to find her leaning over his desk. From her earnest expression, he assumed she was trying to look all boss-lady. He gave the cards a one-handed shuffle.

A tiny line appeared between her eyebrows. "We have under three weeks until the grand opening. I hope you're willing to work closely with me."

The opening was too easy. "Yes, ma'am. Your wish is my command. I'll work as close to you as you want, and that's a promise." He executed a one-handed cut.

She clasped her hands together in a tight knot of whitened knuckles. "Oh. Well. I'm glad you feel that way."

He made a slow and thorough study of her lips. "I'm looking forward to providing you with all the input you need."

She narrowed her eyes at him. "In that case, I suggest you put away your toys, and get busy."

Bustling over to the other desk, she sat. From the same purse that had yielded cheese, the sandwich she'd fed Rex, bran muffins, and a notebook, she dragged out a laptop. After turning on the computer and pecking away at a few keys she cleared her throat.

"Thank you for sharing your office."

"I'm happy to accommodate you. It's more than big enough."

A darker pink stained her cheekbones. Ignoring his comment, she ducked her head and resumed typing, faster than before. Cute. If he spent a little more quality time with her, he was certain he could sweet-talk her into some afternoon delight.

He was in the middle of a world-class fantasy when door flew open.

Rooster, *Kinki*'s bouncer, bodyguard, and all-around muscle burst inside, his crimson Mohawk quivering.

Katie took one look and appeared to shrink, scrunching down in her chair until she was barely visible.

Rooster skidded to a halt in front of Sam. "I don't believe it. Hiram told me he'd hired someone called Katie Deluca, but I had to see for myself."

Sam hoped his reassuring nod would erase Katie's shocked expression. Rooster tended to make most folk wary, what with his gangly height, shocking red crest of hair on a shaved pate, and a barrel chest straining against a black leather vest. Industrial boots proclaimed this was a man who could kick serious ass.

"Rooster." Sam nodded at his bouncer. "You're looking fine today."

"Thanks, Boss. You, on the other hand, look like shit."

"Bourbon shooters."

"Been there, done that, fell into the sack with a condo salesman from Manhattan." Rooster appeared to notice Katie for the first time. His breath hitched and tears trickled down leathery cheeks. "Katie," he wailed "It really is you."

After a brief hesitation, Katie stood and opened her arms. "It's okay."

Sam felt his eyeballs bug out of his head when all six-and-a-half feet of rugged bouncer flew into Katie's arms. He leaned his chin on top of her head and sobbed in earnest. Soon, the howls were ear-splitting.

"I assume you two know one another," Sam yelled.

They ignored him. Or, more likely, the racket drowned out his question.

Between sobs, Rooster said, "S-sorry. Seeing you reminded me of the funeral."

Sniffing a little herself, Katie patted Rooster's back. "Don't worry. This happens to me all the time."

"You were wonderful. That eulogy ..." Rooster's voice broke.

Sam noted the wary glance Katie slanted at him before she lowered her voice to a comforting murmur. "There, there. Get it all out, baby. *Bene. Perfetto.*" When the torrent subsided, she dug into her purse and handed Rooster a tissue.

"Blow," she ordered. Once the deed was done, she murmured, "Let's not bother Sam with our history. We'll catch up later."

Rooster seemed to understand sort of secret message she'd sent. "Sure thing. I'd better get back to work." He gave her a watery smile. "Do I look like I've been crying? I'm a bouncer. I gotta appear intimidating."

"You look very fierce," Katie assured him.

"*Grazie.*" After one more hug, Rooster told Sam, "I'd better patrol the job fair. I noticed a couple of drunks in the lineup, and I don't trust the HR bitch to weed them out." His gaze flew to Sam. "Shit. Sorry. Deanna Sweeney's a friend of your politician buddy, isn't she?"

"No problem. Go do your thing." For some reason, womenfolk and gays took an instant dislike to Deanna.

Once Rooster disappeared, Sam asked Katie, "What was that about a funeral and eulogy?"

She didn't answer immediately. He had no problem letting the silence stretch out.

Katie caved first. "A shared friend passed away. I gave a eulogy."

"You know a lot of people from funerals."

"Italians are a close-knit community. Some die."

Sam smelled evasion and hoped he hadn't made a mistake keeping her on. He had more questions, a lot more, but Rex gave a mournful moan and a burp before scrambling to his feet. He yipped, as if to say, "Get the lead out, buddy, or else."

A frown crinkled Katie's brow. "Uh-oh. Don't say I didn't try to warn you about those bran muffins. Better hurry. And take doggy-do bags."

Sam recognized Rex's potty-dance. The dog's timing sucked.

Moving quickly, he grabbed the necessities and clipped on the leash. Letting Rex drag him out the door, he said, "In case I don't see you later, be here bright and early tomorrow. I want to give you a hands-on indoctrination."

"I hope your indoctrination doesn't involve the casting couch," she said to his back, then raised her voice. "I need your staffing plan, Sam. In the meantime, I'll develop a preliminary project proposal, including entertainment suggestions, a promotion strategy, menu ideas, a detailed schedule, preliminary budget figures, another ..."

He grinned until he was out the building.

Chapter 4: Katie With Her Family

It was six thirty by the time Katie parked behind *Paradise Gate Funeral Haven & Crematorium*. She was an hour and a half late. Good job Ma was always happy to babysit Josh. How did other single moms do it without help from their families?

Katie hurried along the path to the wood-and-clapboard addition sprawled against the mortuary. Dubbed The Annex by Pop, the structure provided living space for the Deluca family. It used to be her home, but not anymore. On learning of her brother's continuing flirtation with crime, she'd taken her son and moved out, also resigning as funeral director of *Paradise Gate*. Now, only her brother and Ma lived there.

Katie's rental house, which was draining her bank account in an alarming manner, was three blocks from *Paradise Gate*, close enough for Ma to babysit, but far enough away to preserve her privacy. Hey, if she met a man, she might indulge in the occasional sleepover—not that she anticipated getting lucky, but anything was possible now that Luigi Guglione was behind bars. For the first time in years, she'd felt a rush during Sam's accidental grope. Her fun parts were still in good working order.

She unlocked the front door of The Annex and stepped into the vestibule. Her mouth watered at the scent of garlic and cheese.

"Anybody home?" she called, kicking off her shoes. "Sorry I'm late."

Sneakered footsteps thumped down the narrow hallway. A moment later, Josh launched himself at her, wrapping skinny arms around her waist in a display of small boy excitement.

"Hi Mom."

She pressed a kiss onto her son's silky black hair. The fruity smell of bubble-gum, a forbidden treat, clung to him. She was too tired to make an issue of it. "How's my little *polpetta*?"

"Aw, Mom. Don't call me a meatball. That's for babies. I'm nine years old."

She ruffled his hair. "You *are* my baby and I think you're good enough to eat."

He pulled away. "Nonna Francesca wants us to stay for dinner? Can we? Huh?"

"Not tonight, Sweetie. It's been a long day, and I'm frazzled." The creation of Sam's project proposal had taken twice as long as it should have, and it still wasn't finished.

Josh gave her a piteous look. "But—"

"Another time, Josh. Promise. You've got your homework, and I have to do laundry, fix your school lunch, change the kitty litter, maybe even get to bed before midnight. I started a new job today." Her imagination promptly jumped to a vision of Sam, lean, golden, and mostly unclothed, beckoning to her from a couch for the hands-on indoctrination he'd promised.

Bad imagination.

"But Nonna Francesca made lasagna, the kind I like, with no mushrooms and lots of sausage, and there's cake, and ice cream too, with sprinkles. There's gonna be a party for Aunt Bella." Josh paused for breath. "Ple-e-e-ease?"

Katie blinked her way back to reality. "Bella? She's back? You're kidding, right?"

Josh's dark eyes gleamed with excitement. "Nope. Aunt Bella's home, and I like her a lot. I've gotta go help set the table." He dashed off, leaving Katie standing in the vestibule.

Two years younger than Katie, Bella was the wild child, gorgeous, willful, spoiled by the whole family. At age eighteen, she'd headed for the bright lights of Manhattan to become a top model. At least she'd had the decency to wait until after Josh's birth before taking off. Soon after gracing the cover of *Feminine Flare*, she'd married an admirer, moved to suburban Connecticut, and severed all family ties. Although the family figured Bradley was behind the estrangement, Katie resented bearing the brunt of Ma's grief and depression, which had abated over the years, but never fully disappeared. It was so like Bella to return home without warning, the same way she'd left nine years ago.

Yeah, Katie didn't know whether to be happy or pissed off about her sister's abrupt reappearance. She leaned her forehead against the velvety flocked wallpaper until hesitant footsteps caused her to turn around.

Two crystalline tears trickled down Bella's perfect cheekbones. Once vibrant, this woman was a ghostlike imitation of the sister Katie remembered.

A surge of emotion made speech difficult. Katie held out her arms. "You're the only person in the world who can cry and still look beautiful. I ought to hate you."

Bella brushed the tears away. Stooping a little due to the height difference, she wrapped her arms around Katie in a warm, fragrant hug. "I deserve it. I turned my back on my family."

"Once you got married, you never answered my emails or phone calls," Katie whispered. "I was frantic."

Bella let go first. "I know. Please forgive me."

"It appears I already have."

"Oh, Katie, if only you knew how many times I thought about calling you. But it was too dangerous." Bella changed the subject. "Josh is adorable. He was a tiny baby when I left."

"Thanks. He's a good boy."

"I tried to get home for Christmas a couple of times, you know, but I couldn't get away because Bradley ..." Her voice trailed off.

"It's okay. We figured out it was his fault. Rico went up to Connecticut to make sure you were okay, but neighbors said you'd moved to Florida."

"My husband, soon-to-be-ex, told me he wanted to be closer to his family, but he lied. He only wanted to isolate me. I'm still too raw to talk about it."

"It damn near killed Ma. She would barely let me out of her sight for the first four years. Even now, she insists I stay nearby, claims she'll die if she loses another child."

Bella turned her face away, as if ashamed. After a long silence, she said, "Ma told me you'd quit *Paradise Gate*, and you and Josh have moved out of The Annex. Is that true?"

"Yeah. Rico's into some stuff that worries me. I'll explain later, once Josh is in bed."

"Sure. But why a brand new career? Why not join another funeral home."

Again, Katie gave the short answer. "I tried but couldn't find anything local. Word of Luigi's obsession with me has spread. Worse, some people remember the rumors surrounding the death of Josh's father."

"Yes, I can see how that might be a couple of strikes against you. But surely you could have found something out of town."

"I got job offers in Seattle, Houston, and Phoenix, but I couldn't take them. Ma freaked out at the thought of losing Josh and me."

Bella sat on the velvet-covered bench, which matched the forest green wallpaper, and hid her face in her hands. "Oh, God. I really screwed up didn't I?"

A burst of compassion her sister surprised Katie. "Not you. Bradley. But you're back now. That's what counts. Besides, everything worked out for me. I have an event planning business called *Galas Unlimited*. It was a slow start for all the reasons I mentioned, plus I'm guessing no one wants to hire a former mortician as a party planner. But today, I got lucky and snagged my first contract. The owners are out-of-towners who haven't heard about my sordid baggage."

And hopefully never would. She had to make a go of it at *Kinki*, not only for the money, which she needed to avoid eviction, but also to establish credentials in her new career path.

Bella's voice cut through Katie's worries. "But party planning? Seriously?"

"Why not?" Katie checked over her shoulder to make sure they were alone before lowering her voice. "Right from the start, I knew the mortician profession wasn't for me, but at the time, I had no choice. It wasn't so much the blood, guts, and bodily fluids." At Bella's skeptical snort, Katie felt herself flush. "Okay, so they didn't help, but mainly it was dealing with the bereaved. The sadness and grief got to me. Then it struck me that planning a kick-ass party requires the same skill-set as organizing a funeral, except the focus is on fun rather than death."

Bella's perfectly-tweezed brows drew together a fraction of an inch. "So if you've reinvented yourself as a fun-filled event planner, why are you still wearing mortician clothes?"

"Hey, this is my best business outfit."

"Please tell me you're joking."

Katie looked down at her severe black suit. Bella had a point. "Okay, so maybe I could use some fashion advice. I should warn you, though— I'm broke."

Bella examined Katie from head to toe. "This is a fashion emergency. I'll help you find your sexy, no problem. The right shade of red will perk up your complexion, and I'll find you a good consignment store. It won't cost much."

"Just like old times." Katie sank down beside Bella, wrapping one arm around her sister's shoulders, shocked to feel every bone. "God, how I missed you," she whispered.

She sensed the moment when Bella relaxed. "Me, too. You have no idea how much."

Ma's voice, laced with a touch of panic, floated into the vestibule from the kitchen. "Bella, Katarina. Where are you?"

They both sprang to their feet.

"Coming, Ma," Bella shouted back. She said to Katie, "I hope you're staying for dinner."

Katie shoved her exhaustion aside. "Wouldn't miss it."

She followed Bella into the kitchen, where they found Ma stirring a large pot. Her hair, once as dark as Katie's, was threaded with white. She raised her head at their entrance. Seeing who it was, the shadow of anxiety around her eyes disappeared.

"Here you are, both my beautiful daughters." Her brilliant smile caused the years to drop away. "My family is together again." Her smile faded as alarm filled her eyes. She grasped Bella's hand. "This time, you're staying, aren't you? You can't leave again. I won't let you."

Bella's eyes glistened with unshed tears. "It's okay, Ma. I'm home, and I'm not going anywhere."

"But what about that husband of yours? He likes you under his thumb."

"He'll never get the chance to hurt me again. I've filed for divorce. The bastard spoiled my life for too many years. I won't let him spoil my homecoming too."

"Good." Ma turned her attention to Katie and held out her arms. "Katarina. You were so late, I was worried about you."

Katie hugged her mother. "My new job is more demanding than I ever imagined. How was Josh today?"

"*Perfetto*. My grandson, he's a little angel sent from Heaven."

Katie had her doubts, but she wasn't about to argue. Apparently Josh didn't act out for Ma the way he did at home. "Ma, you're the best. I have no idea what I'd do without you. I don't thank you often enough."

"I'm the lucky one. Each day I get to see my little *bambino*. I hope you're both staying for dinner because I made enough for everyone. Your brother Rico, he's like a starving wolf." Using oven mitts, Ma grasped the plate of lasagna and sailed toward the dining room, adding over her shoulder, "I nearly forgot. Rico told me Luigi Guglione phoned this afternoon."

A sense of impending disaster washed over Katie.

***

The dining room chandelier cast a warm glow over Katie's family, leaving the corners shadowed. As usual Ma sat at the head of the table, urging everyone to eat. Tonight, with Bella's return, she was beaming from ear to ear.

Josh, Bella, and Rico, obeyed eagerly. Katie, not so much. The news of Luigi's phone call had stolen her appetite. Even from behind bars, the bastard poisoned her happiness. If Josh knew Luigi had phoned from prison, his feeling of safety would vanish. Hers certainly had.

Toying with her food, Katie studied Rico, wondering if she could trust him. Her brother's hazel eyes twinkled as he threw back his head and laughed at something Ma said. No doubt about it, he was one attractive man with his wavy dark hair, olive skin, and brilliant smile.

She caught Ma's worried frown. To conceal her agitation over Luigi's phone call, Katie described her first day on the job. Rico contributed anecdotes, most of them morbid. Nothing rocked a dinner party like mortician humor, but it beat discussing Luigi. So she gritted her teeth and listened to her brother describe how, in the middle of Marco Antonelli's funeral, somebody's phone started playing *Stayin' Alive* and how the widow pulled out a gun and tried to shoot the phone's owner. Luckily, she'd forgotten to load it.

Katie wasn't amused, especially when her son's giggle joined Rico's roar of laughter, but it was too late to do anything about it. Again, she congratulated herself for removing her son from an unhealthy environment.

Once dinner ended, Josh scooted off to the den, ostensibly to do his homework, but more likely to sneak in some video games. No one else made a move to leave.

Ma glanced at the door, presumably to make sure Josh wasn't listening. Her furrowed brow and tight lips indicated Katie's reprieve was over. Sure enough, she said, "I don't like it when a murderer calls my daughter from prison." An Italian hand gesture intended to ward off evil accompanied her words.

Realizing Ma had her best interest at heart, Katie took a steadying breath and softened her voice. "I can't control who calls me, Ma."

Bella raised one eyebrow. "I don't believe Luigi's still sniffing around you."

"Gotta hand it to him. He's persistent." Rico snagged the cake plate and placed it in front of him with his usual self-indulgent assumption that no one else wanted more. It was time he grew up.

Katie whirled on her brother. "You mean he's called here before?"

"Sure." Her brother grabbed the cake knife, sliced off a hunk of cake, and cubed it. "Luigi and I go way back. I don't ignore a friend, even one in prison." He used the knife to pop a chunk into his mouth.

Katie's chest tightened into a ball of anxiety. "What did he want?"

"He said he needed to talk to you about something real important. He'll call later. I told him he was wasting his time, but he insisted. You know how he is."

"Yeah, only too well. He's the reason I got an unlisted number and new cell phone."

Ma set her cup down, sloshing coffee into the saucer. "Luigi is a bad man. I don't like him."

"Me neither," Bella agreed. "I never understood what any of you saw in him."

Hey." Rico waved the cake knife to emphasize his point. "Luigi saved our family's collective asses time after time. Whenever Pa needed help, especially after he got sick, Luigi lent us money. In exchange, all he wanted was some free cremations."

Under the table, Katie' nails dug into her palms. "You can't believe for one minute those midnight cremations were above-board and legal."

Rico gave his phony grin, the one he used whenever he was lying. "Sure they were."

"Dammit, Rico. We've had this discussion several times. Luigi wanted those bodies to disappear without a trace, and you know it."

Under her breath, Bella said to Katie, "I'm beginning to understand why you left the business, especially with Josh to think about."

Ma reached over the cake platter and twisted Rico's ear. "How did I not know about free cremations? Is this the truth?"

"Ouch," he yelped. "Okay, it's true. But in my defense, I trusted Luigi."

"But Luigi, he's in prison now. Everything's okay again, yes?"

The anxiety in her mother's voice prompted Katie to back off. "There's nothing for you to worry about, Ma."

Ma released Rico's ear, leaving a red mark behind. "That's good."

Katie sensed Rico wanted to rub his ear. Instead, he leaned over and kissed Ma's cheek, saying, "Yes, everything's okay."

Katie couldn't help appreciating Rico's spontaneous gesture of affection, but it wasn't enough. Refusing to let him off the hook, she pointed two fingers at her own eyes in a V-sign, then one at him, to inform him she knew he was lying. "You. Me. Later."

Lies, white and otherwise, obviously ran in the family. After Luigi's incarceration, plenty of other clients needed a discrete disposal service, and were willing to pay. Rico had continued the midnight specials. Katie knew this because she'd accidentally walked in on one. There were several long and acrimonious chats with Rico before she resigned from *Paradise Gate* and moved out of The Annex with Josh.

As if reading her mind, Rico smirked back. "Katie tends to overreact."

Not allowing herself to get sidetracked, Katie returned to her main concern. "Luigi terrifies me. Look what happened to Josh's father."

"That was terrible," Bella said to Katie. "You were devastated when Joey died, and just after you learned you were pregnant."

Ma looked bewildered. "But Joe Farnogli was killed in a hit and run accident. They never found the driver. That had nothing to do with Luigi."

"I'm not so sure about that." Katie grabbed her glass, and chugged some Chianti. "When Luigi learned I was dating, he was so furious, I thought he'd explode. Everyone, including the cops, thought Luigi was responsible for Joey's death. I truly believe he was."

Joey, her first love and, as it turned out, her last, was a student she'd met at university when she was twenty. Four weeks later, he was dead. Although over nine years had elapsed since that fateful night, Katie still felt guilty about his death.

Ma, who'd been remarkably silent given the bombshell dropped on her, drilled Katie with a penetrating stare. "Why am I just hearing of this now?"

"You were anxious enough about Pop's health. There was no point worrying you without proof."

Rico cut another chunk of cake and grinned at Katie. "You haven't had a date since you were pregnant with Josh, and by my calculations, you're now thirty."

"Thank you for reminding me of my dismal social life. After Joe died, I was still in school and pregnant. Soon after I graduated, I found myself with both a baby and a job at *Paradise Gate*. Whenever anyone asked me for a date, and very few did, I was terrified he'd end up like Joey, dead in some sort of 'accident'. I couldn't take that chance. Luigi was still stalking me."

Always single-minded on the marriage front, Ma asked, "Luigi's in prison now. You can accept dates again, yes?"

Katie's thoughts flew to Sam. Surely Luigi was no longer keeping tabs on her from prison. Besides, he might find God. Or take a knife in the ribs. Hey, miracles happened, didn't they? She pinned Rico with a meaningful glare. "Yes, I can. And if and when I do decide to date, I would prefer to keep my private life a secret from Luigi, if that's okay with Mr. Big-Mouth."

Rico licked frosting off the knife and waved it in the air. "No problem, Sis. He won't hear a word about you from me. But if you're so worried, you should return to *Paradise Gate*. You'd be safer, surrounded by family."

Katie pretended to stir her coffee. Rico loved her, she knew that, but returning to *Paradise Gate* with Josh was out of the question. Rico's midnight specials weren't exactly the wholesome environment she wanted for her child.

She raised her head and smiled sweetly at him. "Thanks, but I'm good."

Rico swallowed the last of the cake. "You might want to reconsider. Last I heard, Luigi's lawyer was raising an appeal."

Refusing to let her brother see how much his news rattled her, she kept her voice calm. "Evidence proved he committed murder. I seriously doubt his appeal will get off the ground."

As if mocking her, the business line shrilled. She gulped her wine.

"Answer that," Rico advised her. "It might be Luigi."

Her lasagna threatened to make a return visit. If Luigi's appeal resulted in the overturn of his conviction, she wouldn't hesitate to take Josh and flee, even if it meant breaking Ma's heart again. She'd have no choice. Subjecting Josh to a man who terrified him was out of the question. Her child came first.

The phone rang again.

Unable to stand the tension, Katie dashed for the phone and checked call display. Her heart thundered in her ears. "It's the New Jersey State Prison."

Rico said, "Pick up. He'll only call again. You might as well hear him out."

Her hands shaking, Katie took the phone and sped from the room. To prevent her family from eavesdropping, she entered the hall closet and closed the door before answering. Over the sound of blood thundering in her ears, she said, "Hi, Luigi."

"My lovely Katarina. It's so good to hear your voice. I think of you constantly."

That was downright creepy. At a loss for words, she finally said, "I hope you're comfortable."

"Comfortable enough. I have everything I need—except you."

After exchanging more pleasantries, he got to the meat of the matter, beginning with, "We belong together," and going downhill from there.

She listened in growing disbelief. Luigi's call had nothing to do with his appeal. It was worse than that. He'd called to claim her as his fiancée. He couldn't do that. But he had.

Knowing the call was being recorded, he didn't spell out his expectations in so many words. But she'd known him long enough to understand the subtext. He left no doubt in her mind that he expected her to marry him. He also hinted that he wanted her to return to *Paradise Gate*, presumably because it was unlikely that men would hit on Katie-The-Mortician. Although she rejected both marriage or a return to *Paradise Gate*, it was obvious he assumed she'd fall into line.

Finally, his time was up, and he disconnected. Using one hand, she swept aside a coat that threatened to choke her. Only then did she sink slowly to the floor, pushing shoes aside and wrapping her arms around her knees.

She shouldn't be surprised. Ever since Luigi's mother had died three months ago, Katie had half-expected him to make a move. He'd idolized his mamma, and Signora Guglione had done her best to keep him in line. She'd frowned on the way he stalked Katie and occasionally tried to coerce her into marriage. Now that Signora Guglione was gone, so too was the protection she'd provided. Clearly, in his grief, Luigi had crossed the fine line between sanity and madness.

Bottom line? Anyone dumb enough to hire her or, worse, date her, wouldn't fare well. Even if Luigi's appeal failed, he had contacts on the outside and offshore accounts to pay for anything he wanted. He could force her to marry him. She was trapped as long as he was alive, behind bars or not. She needed money to escape, and *Kinki* was her ticket to freedom. With Bella home again, she could only hope that Ma would survive the loss of another daughter.

She considered her job situation. Chances were excellent Luigi wouldn't learn about her short-term contract. She refused to consider the unthinkable—that one of Luigi's spies would track her to *Kinki*. Assuming she took precautions, Sam and Hiram should be safe enough, at least for now.

In the meantime, she would focus on delivering a grand opening the goth and vampire wannabes of Atlantic City would never forget.

Chapter 5: The Grand Tour

On Katie's second morning at *Kinki*, Sam entered the office to find her hard at work, a pencil tucked behind her ear. Today's dark gray suit, he was happy to note, was less funereal than yesterday's. She looked adorably serious, poring over what appeared to be a project proposal for his grand opening. But it was the sight of her tiny frown as she gnawed her lower lip that sealed the deal. Then and there, he made it his mission to demolish her iron control with the hands-on indoctrination he'd promised.

He opened with an apology for yesterday afternoon's no-show at work, pleading a bad case of potty fatigue. At her puzzled expression, he described how, over the course of a three hour walk, Rex had managed to fill six deluxe doggy-do bags, after which, they'd both returned to the apartment, where Sam had given the dog a bath and taken a scalding shower himself.

Certain one corner of her mouth had lifted for an instant, Sam gave himself a mental high-five. Pulling up a chair, he joined her behind the desk. A faint whiff of coconut and vanilla tantalized his nostrils. Lordy, but she smelled delicious, all fresh and sweet.

Settling on a cerebral approach to win her over, he focused his attention on the project proposal she'd prepared. Her work was thorough, accurate, and logical. Before long, he got caught up in it. After an hour of casual shoulder brushing during which he asked questions, commented, and made adjustments, he sensed a lowering of her guard when she suggested a grand tour of *Kinki*.

Hands-on indoctrination, here we come.

They started out with Katie striding ahead in her usual take-charge manner. Using a light touch here, a gentle stroke there he delivered a spiel he hoped was both entertaining and informative. So far, she'd appeared impressed, exclaiming over *Inferno*, admiring *The Undead Zone*, and requesting a drink in *Decom-Posers Tavern*.

He studied the cocktail menu before flagging the bartender over. "A Zombie Fizz for the lady, please, and I'll have something called Vampire Punch."

"Please make that a Virgin Zombie Fizz."

Apparently the masterful approach was wasted on her. Something to remember.

They sat on skull-shaped bar stools in *Decom-Posers Tavern* to wait for their drinks. Her questions about his security system gave him an opening. Leaning closer, he let his arm brush hers while he launched into a description of his handiwork. "I installed cameras in every room, then linked them to various electronic gizmos."

"Impressive. By yourself?"

The drinks arrived. She picked up her cloudy green drink and wrapped her lips around the straw while examining him with what he hoped was admiration.

"Yeah, by myself. At the risk of appearing immodest, I have an aptitude for technology. Watch." He pulled out his smartphone. "I can select any location and see what's happening." Surrounded by her feminine scent, he punched some buttons and selected their current location. He handed her the phone and leaned closer. "I never show this to anyone. I'll make an exception for you."

She edged away before setting her drink down and studying the images from the camera feed. After a few seconds she returned the phone. "Ingenious. In fact, brilliant."

He fought a gratified grin and lost. Next to gambling, bar-hopping, and his own personal favorite, charming women, he excelled when it came to technology. "I also installed motion sensors in every room. After locking up at night, we verify all interior doors are closed before activating the alarm system."

"Remarkable."

"Then there's my guard dog."

She laughed. "You can't possibly mean Rex."

"I do." Sam's grin widened. "At night, Rex runs loose in the public areas. But if an intruder gets past him, the slightest motion inside one of the rooms triggers a camera, sends a message to my smartphone, and sounds an alarm in the apartment I share with my granddaddy. We live here, right down the hall from the office, so I can be downstairs in seconds." He draped his arm around her shoulders. "*Kinki* is a fortress."

A tiny vertical line formed on her forehead. She wriggled away, forcing his arm to drop. "Let me see if I've got this straight. You only activate your security system at night."

"Yeah. The place is too busy during the day. The alarms go off every five minutes. I hired rent-a-cops for the front desk. They notify me of visitors. Of course, the job fair makes it difficult to screen visitors, but they're supposed to verify the purpose of their visit."

"What company do you use?"

"Breakaway Security." He didn't mention they were the cheapest he'd found.

"Big mistake."

"Why?"

She was silent so long, staring at the graveyard mural behind the bar, he thought she wouldn't answer. Apparently the opportunity to display her knowledge trumped silence because she said, "Never trust a company with the initials B.S. Although organized crime in Atlantic City has shrunk, B.S. is connected with the remaining pockets. You might as well leave the door open and hang out a welcome sign."

He hoped like hell it wasn't true. "How would a pretty little thing like you know that?"

"Common knowledge."

Hardly. He sensed Katie knew more than she was saying, but this was the wrong time to press her. If what she said was true, he'd have to terminate B.S. and beg his brother for help.

He forced an easy grin. "Thanks for the tip. But so far, so good. No one enters *Kinki* without my knowing."

"And yet, I did. The guard at the front desk didn't notice me as I walked past. He was too busy studying a centerfold. You need to hire a more diligent firm." Disapproval radiated from her in waves. She set her drink down and slipped off the stool. She shot her nose into the air and marched away, her back ramrod straight, her shoes making indignant clacks.

Catching up, he walked beside her in silence until they reached the main bar, where they halted. Inside, the walls, carpet, even the ceiling were navy. The eerie flicker of tiny ceiling lights and one wall consisting of a backlit aquarium left the vast space in moody darkness, accented by mirrors and touches of stainless steel.

"Welcome to *Mermaids*." He moved to one side, letting her absorb the aquatic atmosphere, hoping she'd snuggle closer.

No such luck.

"After you," he said. It was shocking how much he wanted to trace the delicate, sensual curve of her neck with his finger. Instinct warned him to back off.

She met his gaze, her eyes dark and mysterious. "I'm not dumb enough to enter a dark room with you." Her voice resonated with mistrust.

His hopes for a happy ending crashed and burned. He found the dimmer switch and brightened the room. "Better?"

"Much." She stalked inside.

A gleaming sweep of mahogany enticed customers to linger at the bar. Shelves glittered with bottle upon bottle of every type and color of alcohol known to man. Tables surrounded the dance floor, which would do double duty as auditorium seating during live performances.

Which brought him to the room's focal point. The colossal martini glass, custom-crafted of molded acrylic, towered over one side of the stage. Weighing over two tons, the engineering miracle had set him back a tidy fortune. It was *Kinki*'s ticket to success.

He hoped.

Sliding behind the bar, Sam selected a bottle of Dom Perignon from the walk-in refrigerator. There was nothing like expensive champagne to loosen inhibitions. Carrying the bottle and two glasses, he led Katie to a table and held a chair for her.

"Why the giant glass? Will this be part of a show?" She ignored the chair and wandered over to smooth her hand along the glass's massive base.

Four steps took him to her side. "It's *Kinki*'s brand new water feature. During a Vegas junket, I caught Cirque du Soleil's 'O' show." Noting her puzzled expression, he elaborated, "The aquatic performance at Bellagio. It gave me the idea. There will be a nightly aquatic show, complete with mermaids and Celtic music." He saw no reason to drop the word "topless" into the conversation.

"Nice idea. Original and classy. Mermaids add the perfect paranormal flash. Did you know they're often associated with perilous events such as floods, storms, shipwrecks and drownings?" She warmed to the subject. "In some folklore, they can be unlucky omens, both foretelling disaster and provoking it. They can also be benevolent, falling in love with humans. I always loved the legends, especially ..." She flushed.

Sam felt the urge to smooth over her embarrassment. "I'm glad you like it." He led her to the table, where he opened the champagne and poured.

The clatter of high heels accompanied by excited shrieks announced he had company.

"Oooooh, Sammy. You're a hard man to find."

"This is gonna be crazy fun."

Sam did a double-take. Literally. Two identical young women bounced inside and darted toward him. They wore identical ass-baring shorts with identical skimpy red tops, barely concealing identical eye-popping boobs.

Beside him, he caught Katie downing her champagne.

One of the women said, "Remember us, Sammy? We're the stripper twins from *Happy Hustler Bar & Grill* two nights ago. I'm Mango, she's Tango. You said we were cuter than two speckled pups. We're here to deliver your private lap dance."

"Oh, thank the Lord," he breathed. "I thought I was seeing double." Noticing Katie's disapproving frown, he forced himself to remain calm. Truth be told, the episode was a blur of pounding music, bourbon shooters, and nubile bodies.

To buy time, he said, "How did you get past security?"

"These puppies did the trick." Tango unfastened her top button. A pair of triple-Ds sprang to freedom.

Look away, his brain screamed. His eyeballs ignored the warning. Hypnotized by Tango's bouncing rack as it escaped captivity, he snapped out of it when Mango embraced him and ground her pelvis against his ass.

Using his finely-tuned peripheral vision, a skill he'd honed to preserve his hide from pissed-off husbands, he caught Katie pouring herself another glass of champagne. He thought she muttered, "Nice fortress you have here."

His hopes for impressing her fizzled. It looked bad, especially when Mango climbed him as if he were a stripper pole, wrapping one leg around his calf tighter than a python.

Noting Katie's scowl, he responded with a rueful shrug intended to project innocence. Disengaging from Mango without hurting her feelings was a challenge. He started by unpeeling one surprisingly strong arm from his waist. "Easy there, sugar."

Mango responded by clamping her other arm around him and purring, "Let's you and me get comfy in a chair for your special treat."

"Sorry, ladies." Making a point of not staring at any boobs, he tried to hide his desperation. "I'm afraid you're interrupting an important business meeting."

"Aw, baby," Tango rubbed her booty against his leg before unzipping her shorts, "Chillax. You were tons more fun two nights ago."

Katie interjected, "I bet he was a laugh a minute."

Mango loosened her grip a fraction. Sam managed to break free. Breathing hard, and not in a good way, he retreated three paces.

While Tango shimmied out of her shorts, she scowled at Katie. "Who's the undertaker bitch?"

"Hey." Katie slammed down her glass. "Who are you calling an undertaker? I own a successful event planning business."

Tango's lips twisted in a sneer. "What kind of events do you plan? Wakes? I swear that suit would turn Morticia green with envy."

Katie's eyes narrowed to dangerous slits as she advanced on Tango. "Don't. Call. Me. Morticia."

Sam slung an arm around her waist. There was plenty of fire and flash beneath the prim exterior. She struggled like a wild kitten. It took some muscle to plaster her against his side.

Keeping a tight grip on her wriggling body, he announced, "Sorry, ladies. I've reformed. No more strip clubs, no more lap dances for Sammy. My new event planner says those shenanigans are bad for my image." He winced as a black pump tromped on his instep.

Tango pulled up her shorts. "Morticia's a real downer."

Katie's indignant hiss was audible over her renewed struggles. "Let go of me, you baboon. We Italian girls learn to rumble before we hit the schoolyard."

Both twins edged away from Katie. Mango said, "Fine. Don't get your granny panties in a twist. We're leaving."

Tango stuffed her boobs back inside and buttoned up. "This was a waste of time."

Sam's conscience kicked in. Holding Katie with one hand, he fished a handful bills from his pocket and handed them over. "Sorry for the mix-up, ladies. Take this for your trouble. I'll send you free tickets for the grand opening."

One of the twins pocketed the money and they departed, all hostility forgotten. Their footsteps faded and silence descended.

Katie quit squirming. He was surprised at how much he liked the way she felt, all soft and warm, her back pressed against his body. She must have read his mind because she struggled again, wriggling her cute little ass against him. Suspecting she hadn't intended it as a turn-on, he released her.

But it had *so* been a turn-on.

She turned to face him. "Does that happen to you often?" Her gaze travelled to his package and jerked to his face. "I mean the whole lap dance thing."

He grinned to let her know he understood where her thoughts had wandered. "Women go above and beyond to get a piece of Sammy. They can't help themselves."

"I adore modesty in a man, but that's not what I meant."

Sam sighed. "Do tell."

Katie's clinical assessment of him raised a warning flag.

She took him at his word. "Based on the information Hiram provided, coupled with my observations, you fit into the womanizer category." She started walking.

He caught up at an intersection of corridors. "Turn left. What did my granddaddy say?"

"That you needed help That's why he hired me. He's worried you're wasting your life on booze, gambling, and loose women. I hope you appreciate the fact that he loves you so much, he's willing to hand you a job."

Shock over her assumption of nepotism damn near caused Sam to trip over his feet. "Don't listen to him. He runs off at the mouth all the time. Can't help himself." How much had his granddaddy told her?

"The background check I did supported everything he said.

"Background check?" Sam echoed faintly.

She marched on. "You might be surprised to learn how helpful social media is. Do you realize there's a chat room full of your ex-girlfriends?" She didn't wait for an answer. "I also did extensive research on the subject of womanizers. Are you interested in hearing what I learned?"

"Don't hold back."

"Womanizers have something they need to prove, either to themselves or others."

"I did not know that," he said through a tight jaw. "Nor do I want to analyze my behavior with women. Not today, not tomorrow, not ever. I

like women and they—at least most women—like me, end of story."
Seeing as how the best defense was a good offence, he said, "I'll ask you
the same question. Do things like that happen to you often?"

"Things like what?"

"Your anger management issues."

"Okay, so I might have over-reacted. It won't happen again."

"Jealous?"

The answer came in an unflattering hurry. "Hardly."

He let the silence stretch out. The only sound was the clatter of her
sturdy shoes.

"Okay, so I hate being called 'Morticia'. It's a thing."

"Care to talk about your thing?"

"Nope."

"Then we're even."

***

All too aware of Sam at her side, Katie sped up. Without apparent effort,
he kept pace, maintaining a running chatter in a slow Texas drawl,
intended, no doubt, to lull her into a false sense of complacency before
launching another question about her background. She eyed the chiseled
profile, the easy smile. The man possessed an overabundance of charm and
good looks. Interesting how he'd diverted the conversation away from his
secrets.

A large, warm hand pressed into the small of her back. He smelled
amazing, all clean and woodsy. The sizzle, when it shot through her, left
her breathless.

Sex had been off her radar for years. While he pointed out more
highlights, she toyed with the idea of jumping his bones. On the plus side,
he was gorgeous, charming, had plenty of carnal experience, and based on
the number of irate husbands who'd tried to take him out, didn't mind
risking death to have sex, always an important consideration when it came
to men she dated.

On the down side, the list was lengthy. First and foremost, she had an
impressionable and vulnerable son who could easily get his heart broken
when Sam walked out of their lives. Plus, as a single working mom, she
had neither time nor energy for a dalliance. Not to mention Sam's drinking,
gambling, and womanizing. Oh, yeah, and Luigi might kill anyone she
dated. Hooking up with Sam was a recipe for heartache on so many levels
she lost count.

You know you wan-na, her inner bad girl chanted.

Moving faster, she pushed the thought away. She couldn't live with
herself if Luigi learned where she was working and hired a hitman to kill

Sam. Tempting though Sam was, and he was very, very tempting, she couldn't date him. Not that he'd asked.

His voice interrupted her internal battle. Something about Rooster. How was that for an ego-deflator?

His eyes, sharp with curiosity, blazed on her face with laser-like intensity. This good ol' boy wasn't as laidback as he wanted the world to believe.

"Sorry. I was wool-gathering. Would you mind repeating that?"

"What is it you're hiding about Rooster?"

Her face radiated heat. Rooster knew her story. A murderous fiancé was a sure-fire contract terminator and a former career as a mortician was generally a turn-off. She had no intention of coming clean.

She waited until a pair of giggling vampires disappeared before answering, "You're imagining things."

A quirked eyebrow rewarded her evasion. "Really?"

Giving a light laugh, she feigned wide-eyed innocence. "Don't be ridiculous. I know Rooster because we're both Italian, plus we've lived in Atlantic City all our lives. There's all kinds of connections."

No need to mention those connections were either thugs or clients of *Paradise Gate*, often both. Or that a crazed crime lord might try to kill him. Not that he'd actually killed any of her dates, at least, none that could be proven.

"I'll find out sooner or later." Apparently they'd reached another destination because Sam halted. "There's one last theme room I want to show you—*Dracula's Lair*."

He flipped a switch, which did little to illuminate the room, and held the door open, as if expecting her to lead the way.

Chapter 6: Vandalism

For fear his presence might be distracting, Sam lingered in the corridor while Katie ventured inside. She stood there, unmoving and silent, no doubt speechless with wonder.

Dracula's Lair was his brainchild. He'd spent many hot, dirty hours, not to mention a good chunk of his dwindling cash, on ensuring a crypt-like appearance. He'd used faux mud to simulate mold on the walls, stalactites dripped from the ceiling, and high-end slate paved the floor. Soon, the used coffins would arrive, each containing a dummy corpse.

After a prolonged silence, she faced him, her hands fisted on her hips. "Is this a joke?"

He was pretty sure her voice dripped with irritation, not awe.

Forgetting to adopt his customary amble, he charged inside. At the sight of his shattered dream, his tongue stuck to the roof of his mouth. A chunk of the loose rock damn near flung him on his ass. Regaining his balance, he turned in a slow circle, unable to comprehend the devastation. The fancy slate floor was a heap of rubble surrounding a hole large enough to hold an elephant. Gashes in the walls revealed underlying studs.

"Son of a bitch," he whispered. "What did they use? Sledgehammers?"

Tugging out his smartphone, he forced his shaking fingers to push some buttons while he studied the display to see if his cameras had caught something. "Nothing," he muttered. "Not a damn thing. The vandalism must have happened this morning, after I de-activated the cameras."

"Did your cameras malfunction?"

"Nope. My technical work never fails." His computer skill was something he took for granted, much like breathing.

He was a fool. When he'd bought *Kinki*, he'd been dumb enough to imagine that this time—this once—he'd found a way to succeed in his father's eyes. But nope. The old man's scathing remarks about buying a fetish club had worn him down, and he'd pretty much stopped trying. Then Katie burst into his life, breathing new life into his impossible dream.

It seemed his father was right after all. He would never amount to a hill of beans.

"I'm out of business before I open."

He must have spoken aloud, because Katie said, "But you must open. There's too much at stake to cancel the opening."

With an effort, he willed his panic to subside. "I have eighteen days to repair this room, also find out who did it, and why, otherwise I can't open

Kinki to the public." And if he failed, he and his granddaddy would lose everything and end up living together. Permanently.

"Don't develop cold feet so close to the finish line."

If the urgency in Katie's voice hadn't snapped him out of it, her grip would have. She clutched him so hard, pain shot up his arms.

Liking her concern, if not the pain, he said the macho thing. "Don't worry. I'll sort it out."

Her grip tightened around his biceps, as if she wanted to shake sense into him. "You have a phone. Call the police."

"An investigation would delay the grand opening." True enough, especially if a certain jealous detective learned of his troubles. But hell, the cop's woman hadn't mentioned a boyfriend, never mind a fiancée.

Katie pursed her lips. "I didn't think of that." She squeezed his arm harder. "So no cops, no investigation. Now what?"

"First, stop cutting off the circulation in my arm."

She let go. "Sorry."

The sight of bright pink creeping into her cheeks took his mind off the throb of blood returning to his fingers. He stroked her arms in a soothing motion. Too bad the warm, creamy skin was inaccessible, hidden under gray fabric. Injecting his voice with reassurance, he said, "I have a solution."

"What?" She actually tapped her foot.

In spite of the worry gnawing his innards, his lips twitched with amusement. Rather than reveal how much her bossiness entertained him, a wise man, especially one who wanted to get into those nice lacy panties, would humor her.

"My brother, Nick, owns a private security firm. Among other things, they provide rent-a-cops." A service Sam couldn't afford unless Nick agreed to delayed payment.

"Why didn't you hire him in the first place?"

He wasn't about to tell her he'd rejected Nick's high-priced services in favor of an active social life. He settled on, "I prefer not to lean on family."

Her eyes softened. "That's commendable. But preventing crimes like this," she waved her hand, "requires specialized expertise. You should call him immediately."

Seeing no escape, Sam called Nick, wondering how to convince his brother. Admitting he'd screwed up again wouldn't cut it. When Nick's voicemail kicked in, Sam blew out a silent breath of relief, and left a message to return his call.

Katie nodded her approval. "Excellent. And I'll do everything in my power to help find the vandals."

This time, Sam couldn't prevent a bark of laughter from escaping. "A little bitty wisp like you?" He stopped laughing long enough to say, "'Course as they say, size doesn't matter."

"Oh, please. That's what all the under-endowed say."

Sam was amazed to discover he was having fun in spite of his worries. "Glad to hear you're considering my endowments," he said with a perfectly straight face. "But I digress. What makes you think you can help figure out who's vandalizing my club?"

"Don't underestimate me. I think outside the box, I have skills you can't begin to imagine, I'm tricky, and best of all as far as you're concerned, you're not the only one with connections."

"Do tell." He folded his arms across his chest and leaned against the wall.

She nodded. "My contacts may be a little … uh … unorthodox in their methods, but they have their ears to the ground."

"Tell me more."

"I'd rather not."

He was starting to think she might be on speaking terms with Atlantic City's seedier element. He was good with that. Pushing away from the wall, he sidestepped some loose slate to move closer. "Okay. I would love your help."

She backed away, putting some distance between them. "In that case, I'll make inquiries." She dug into her purse for her notebook and pen. "Any idea who might be vandalizing your club?"

"Not a clue." Best to avoid mentioning the pissed-off cop.

She scribbled in her notebook before resuming her interrogation. "Has anyone asked for protection money or shown interest in buying *Kinki*?"

"Nope." He hit her with a question. "Do you think organized crime's behind the vandalism?"

"It's possible."

"What do you know about the protection racket?"

"Not much. Businesses refusing to pay for protection often find their place damaged or their kneecaps smashed. Of course, racketeers are only offering protection from themselves." Her voice was casual. Too casual.

"For an event planner, you know a lot about criminal operations."

"It's common knowledge." She scribbled something in her notebook.

He stopped pressing her for answers and tried to lighten the mood. "I hope I haven't pissed off the mob. I'd hate to find a dead horse's head dripping blood on my satin sheets."

Tension left her body in visible waves. "I'm sure you've pissed off thousands of people. But look on the bright side. Decapitations, at least of horses, happen mainly in movies."

Sam grinned. "You're a hard woman."

"I've had to be. I'll put out feelers."

More determined than ever to learn her secrets, he plucked the pen from her fingers. "It's not your problem, cupcake. It's mine."

"Katie," she reminded him, "and now it's mine too."

"Katie, let's grab lunch, my treat, since Rex ate yours yesterday." He headed for the door, relieved to hear her follow. "I'll deal with this later. In the meantime, *Dracula's Lair* stays locked. The vandalism is our little secret." He smiled to conceal the fact that his brain was working overtime, scheming how to stretch his money to cover repairs.

"Okay, but if the vandalism happened this morning, whoever did it might still be in the building."

"No one would be dumb enough to stick around."

"You'd be surprised. The vandals could use the job fair as cover. We should check your office."

Sam couldn't remember whether or not he'd locked his office, but he wasn't giving up on lunch with Katie. "Great idea. We'll order in."

Chapter 7: Intruders

On discovering that Sam had, indeed, remembered to lock their office door, Katie breathed a sigh of relief. While they ate, she pretended to ignore him by scanning her notes. Had he been coming on to her during the tour? Being sadly out of practice, she wasn't certain.

She forked up a mouthful of kale salad and ignored him some more, which was more difficult than she'd anticipated. Her brain whirred. The man was a mass of contradictions. On the one hand, he was full of small kindnesses, like the gentle way he'd handled Pizza Girl and the seductive twins. On the other, he was a player of the highest order.

Immersed in thought, she jumped when his chair creaked. But he'd only tipped into a reclining position and closed his eyes. It was likely his favorite hangover posture.

She stopped all pretense of indifference and feasted her eyes without fear he'd catch her drooling. His chest rose and fell with slow, rhythmic breaths. She took in in the perfectly shaped jaw, the firm, sensual mouth, the impossibly long lashes fringing golden eyes.

Golden eyes?

Sam was staring back, his eyes full of mischief and not the least bit sleepy. Leaning forward, he clasped his hands on the desk. "Who'd have guessed I'd awaken to find you ogling me?"

"There's no ogling happening. None." She snapped her notebook shut. "You'd sleep better in bed."

"Is that an invitation?"

"Of course not. I'm about to contact my sources to determine if they've heard rumors about *Kinki*."

"What sources are we talking about?"

Better to tell the truth whenever possible, right? "Mostly arsonists who enjoy torching properties for cash. They may have inside knowledge." She held out one hand, palm up. "I'll need working capital for bribes."

"You're joking, right?" He looked wary, but handed over some cash.

She stuffed the money into her purse before he changed his mind. "That's more than generous. I hope you're not too hung over to answer questions."

"You'd be surprised at my recuperative powers, given the right incentive." A lazy smile creased his cheeks, as if he knew a secret joke.

"Did I say something funny?" she asked, genuinely wanting to know. Her brother complained she was too stiff and serious, conditions she was trying to remedy.

"Nope." His smile widened into a badass grin revealing a double row of gleaming white teeth. "Something about you is different today. Different good. Can't put my finger on it."

Yeah, he was flirting. The room seemed to grow warmer, her suit scratchier. Contacting her sources could wait. As casually as possible, she unbuttoned her jacket and shrugged it off, first from one shoulder, then the other, and draped it slowly over her chair back.

Glancing down, she reminded herself that Bella had helped her find her sexy, and dammit, she intended to put her discovery to good use. The filmy blouse, her sister's, was semi-sheer. The maximum-boost push-up bra (also a loner) added another cup size or two. Deciding to experiment with the flirting techniques Bella had taught her, Katie straightened her shoulders to emphasize the new uplift.

Sam made a small, hungry sound, his gaze riveted on her boobs. "Thank you, sweet baby Jesus, for a lovely surprise. Who knew grey ugliness could hide so much glory?"

It was working. "You're criticizing a good suit." Katie leaned forward to display more cleavage, elated to discover she finally had some. She was enjoying herself with a man for the first time in a decade. She felt safe, at least for now. It was refreshing, even liberating, to flirt without fear of a mobster on a mission discouraging any man showing interest in her.

She dialed her expression to fake-concerned. "Are you sure you're feeling okay? You're flushed. In my experience, men don't function properly with a hangover, and I need your best performance."

His eyes, hot and full of sensual promise, raked her face. "I'm ready, willing, and able. All you have to do is crack the whip."

His purring tone sank into Katie's bones, turning her knees to jelly. "I've never used a whip." She made a practice sweep of her lashes. She'd lengthened and thickened them with fiber-loaded mascara (again, Bella's idea).

"You should try one." He settled deeper into his swivel chair, long legs crossed, as if he had all the time in the world to do nothing at all, simply eye her as if she were a tasty morsel he intended to devour. "Might loosen you up, dislodge those secrets you're hiding."

Was Sam toying with her or flirting? "No secrets." It was true. Almost. Her stomach gave a guilty flip. The entire Italian community knew she was a former mortician with criminal connections. The new twist was that the biggest criminal connection of all had proclaimed himself her fiancé and demanded she return to the family business.

His smile faded. "Oh, we all have secrets."

Heart racing, she studied Sam's face. Yeah, he had secrets too, the kind that didn't bear discussion. Just as well. Hers were more than enough to handle.

It must be lovely, for example, to experience a normal date, maybe a pasta dinner accompanied by a fragrant Valpolicella, without danger of Luigi's minions lurking nearby, ready to discourage her date in a highly unpleasant manner. Not that she believed it would happen.

Seriously.

She flicked another surreptitious glance at Sam, who grinned back. The heat in his eyes made her toes curl. Not good. After trying to imagine introducing him to Josh (and failing dismally), she busied herself with fake-typing.

Next thing she knew, the office door crashed open. Two men stumbled inside, along with a cloud of liquor fumes.

Both visitors were short. Both wore gobs of black eyeliner. Matching black lipstick gave their teeth a yellowish tint.

For someone reluctant to exert himself, Sam moved with deceptive speed, pushing away from his chair and positioning himself in front of the drunks. Katie's heart gave a squeeze when she realized he was shielding her.

"Easy there, asshole." The skinny one's pinstriped suit bagged over white and black shoes. A black shirt, white tie, and black Fedora completed the caricature of a Goth racketeer. "What the fuck—"

The plumper thug elbowed his buddy. "The broad at the job fair said the can was down the hall." Beady eyes and a pointy nose made him resemble a ferret. He wore a six-button black jacket, baggy pants, and a shirt made of shiny fabric.

Certain she should recognize the pair, Katie got a bad feeling. Trying for inconspicuous, she stood up, but couldn't get a good look because of Sam's broad back.

"Y'all must be here for the job fair," he drawled. "You boys are in no shape for an interview, so beat it before I lose my temper."

His air of authority took Katie by surprise. She tried to catch another glimpse of the men without drawing attention to herself. Sam blocked her view by placing his hands on his hips and shifting his body. She was too short to see over his shoulder, so she solved the problem by peeking under his left bicep.

The taller drunk took a healthy swig from his hip flask before nudging the other with his elbow. "Let's get the fuck outta here." His whisper was loud enough to rattle windows. "I told you a million times this was a piss-poor idea."

Katie scooted to the other side and peeked again.

The ferret-faced Goth glared at his companion. "Shut up, moron." His right eye gave a series of rapid twitches.

Alarm bells jangled in her head. The twitch was unmistakable. She ducked behind Sam. With any luck, the drunks hadn't seen her face. If they blew her cover, her days as *Kinki*'s event planner were over.

Enzo and Ralphie Allegretti were two of Luigi's thugs, unpredictable, especially when drunk, utterly ruthless, and undoubtedly packing heat. As kids, their backpacks always contained switchblades or, for variety, slingshots.

It wouldn't surprise her to learn the pair had vandalized *Dracula's Lair*. They were arrogant enough to commit a daylight crime. But she didn't dare reveal her suspicions to Sam. He'd go ballistic and become the guest of honor at his own funeral. Pissing off the Allegretti brothers would be a terrible mistake.

Her heart sank when Sam stuck his thumbs in his belt. The gesture trumpeted male dominance. He had no idea he was playing with fire.

"Time to say goodbye, ladies," he said, all smooth and icy. "Y'all can leave one of two ways. Under your own steam or with my assistance."

Ralphie got in Sam's face and flipped him the bird. The gesture caused him to stumble.

A growl rumbled deep in Sam's throat. Katie hadn't pegged him as an alpha male, but apparently the Y chromosome ran strong and true. Standing on tip-toe, she whispered in his ear, "I'm good with drunks. Let me handle this."

Sam's response was to spread his legs wider and demand, "Move it."

She nudged Sam's calf with her toe. When that didn't work, she kicked him. "Listen up, Macho-Man," she whispered. "I recognize these guys. Let me talk to them."

She should have saved her breath. As Sam addressed the brothers, the note of menace in his voice was loud and clear.

"You need help finding the door?"

Ralphie bestowed a bleary glare on Sam. "This moron," he jabbed a thumb at Enzo, "couldn't find his own asshole using both hands and a shovel."

Enzo scowled. "Hey, watch your fuckin' mouth. There's a lady present." The eye twitched, as if to emphasize his point.

Oozing testosterone and hostility, Sam bared his teeth in a snarl.

To prevent a reckless act, one which might well be Sam's last, Katie did what any fast-thinking woman in her position would do. Aiming for the waistline, she wrapped both arms around his middle. Her fingers landed on an interesting bulge beneath his zipper.

Flustered, she barked out an order. "I'll handle this."

He released a ragged breath. "You're already handling things real nice."

Duh! She'd misjudged the position of his waistline by a good eight inches. Came from being vertically-challenged. She detected a faint stirring beneath her fingers. If she didn't take action before blood returned to Sam's brain, this would end badly.

As if grabbing a man's package was an everyday event in her life, she whipped her hands away. Sidestepping Sam, she trotted forward with a bright smile and an outstretched hand. "Enzo, Ralphie. I didn't recognize you at first."

The pair gaped at Katie. Enzo recovered first, and pumped her hand. The entire right side of his face jerked so fast, he reminded her of a demented ferret. "Katarina, as I live and breathe. Long-time no see. You look so good, I didn't recognize you at first." His grin broadened, displaying a pair of twisted incisors.

Too bad Luigi didn't offer his gang members bad free dental work as a perk.

Ralphie shook her hand, too. "Whatcha doin' here, babe? Someone die or what?"

Sam approached, interrupting the exchange of pleasantries. "Do you know this pair?" His voice was a soft growl.

"Little bit," Katie admitted, hoping Luigi hadn't hired the brothers to trash the place. If word of her new job leaked out, he'd stop at nothing to take *Kinki* down. She had to hustle them out before they revealed too much. Or killed Sam.

"Hey, we were at *Paradise Gate* last week, but I gotta tell you, things sure ain't the same without you." Ralphie's words came out slurred, but recognizable.

No doubt, another Allegretti had met his Maker. Hey, crime was a risky business. And there, in a nutshell, was the reason she couldn't return to *Paradise Gate* with her son.

"What's *Paradise Gate*?" Sam asked. "A church?" His voice brimmed with suspicion.

"Sort of." The funeral parlor did, after all, contain a chapel. "I, uh, organized some special functions there."

Close enough.

Ralphie stuck a cigar into his mouth. Sam's scowl deepened. He yanked it away and tossed it in the trash. "No smoking."

Katie's uneasiness grew when Sam addressed her. "These two aren't the type to attend special functions anywhere. Or job fairs, for that matter. Who are they?"

She didn't dare let them speak, so she raised her voice. "Ralphie and Enzo Allegretti, former business acquaintances of mine."

Gospel truth.

To distract Sam, she ended the introductions with a round of meaningless chit-chat. Every time he opened his mouth to quiz Enzo or Ralphie, she interrupted with another inconsequential question about mutual acquaintances. She sensed Sam was ready to explode, and heaved a sigh of relief when the phone rang.

He answered it, keeping the brothers in the crosshairs of his vision. He listened, then straightened in his chair. "What's wrong? ... Aw, I plumb forgot. I'll be right there ... lobster rolls, sure thing ... Slasher flicks? Nope, too much violence."

While Sam argued on the phone, she made the most of his momentary distraction. "Leave before he calls Security," she whispered to the brothers, hoping they'd leave quietly.

Enzo rewarded her with a smirk. "Sure thing, babe." He grabbed Ralphie's arm and dragged him out of the office.

Katie breathed freely again. Ten to one, she'd saved Sam's life, not to mention her career. Besides, for all she knew, they were telling the truth about attending the job fair.

Hey, it could happen.

Sam ended the call and looked around for the brothers. "They're gone?" He sucked in a deep breath, telegraphing the exact moment his suspicions centered on her. "You let them go."

"There wasn't much I could do to stop them. Don't you have an appointment?"

"Yeah. The first Tuesday of every month is a special lunch date with Granddaddy Hiram. I can't believe it slipped my mind."

"You already ate lunch," she pointed out. "Overeating has a lasting impact. It—"

"I only ate one burger. As annoying as my granddaddy is, I wouldn't dream of standing him up. We always watch an afternoon movie, so I may not be back before you leave."

Her heart melted a little. Although Sam might not admit it, he obviously cared deeply for the elderly man. And she'd taken shameless advantage of his momentary distraction, letting the Allegretti brothers escape.

All she wanted to do was come clean. Well, half of her wanted to come clean. The other half wanted to hide the truth as long as possible.

His voice dragged her back to the moment. "We'll continue our discussion first thing tomorrow. You have some serious explaining to do."

His rigid back disappeared as he stomped out.

Chapter 8: Request for Help

To make the most of his afternoon with his granddaddy, Sam placed his concerns on hold. Although he needed to stay close in case his phone monitoring revealed anything suspicious, his granddaddy was good with ordering in two lobster rolls and a jumbo clam bucket accompanied by melted butter, coleslaw, and crusty bread. After two back-to-back slasher flicks on Netflix, they called it a day with more takeout—cheesesteaks, fries, and chocolate shakes. Granddaddy Hiram crashed early, bitching about acid reflux and cheesesteak blockage.

After tidying up, Sam scanned the club again. Everyone, including Katie, had left for the day. For once, the notion of a strip joint held no appeal. With the security system activated and Rex at his heels, he conducted a walkaround. They found nothing suspicious.

An early night wouldn't hurt. That way, he'd arrive at work clear-headed and primed to interrogate Katie about her deep, dark secrets.

Sleep didn't come easy. He'd barely crawled into bed when a chill shot down his spine at his recollection of how Katie had suggested the tour of *Kinki*. He didn't want to believe she'd been buying time for her buddies to trash the place. Looking back, he saw how she'd prolonged matters by asking questions and initiating a fight with Tango, both excellent delaying tactics calculated to capture a red-blooded male's attention. But the kicker was she'd let the two Allegretti brothers escape while he talked to his granddaddy.

Yeah, he had plenty of questions.

After another walkaround, exhaustion overtook Sam. Much later, his phone jolted him from a troubled doze. After three tries, he punched the right button. "Whazzat?" he mumbled.

His brother's hearty morning voice boomed in his ear. "You hung over again?"

Sam raised himself on one elbow, suddenly wide awake. "No. You get my message?"

"Yeah. I have to stick around my office today, but in the interest of brotherly love, I'll squeeze you in for ten minutes. Be here at 10:05."

Sam checked the time. "That's in thirty minutes."

"Better get your ass in gear." The phone clicked in his ear.

If he hadn't needed Nick's help, Sam would have called back to unload a piece of his mind. Cursing, Sam rolled out of bed. As soon as his feet hit the floor, something cold and wet nudged his bare knee. He pushed Rex's nose away. "Business meeting. You're staying put. Sorry, boy."

Undeterred, Rex wagged his tail.

Sam ruffled the dog's ears. "Hell, no. What was I thinking? You're a chick magnet and Nick's receptionist is smokin' hot. Better still, my brother objects to big, bouncy dogs in his office. Of course you're coming." Two birds, one furry and very boisterous stone.

Ten minutes later, he and Rex hopped into the shiny black Dodge Ram he'd won in a poker game. The twin longhorn hood ornaments drove Nick crazy, an added bonus. They made good time, Rex with his head out the window, tongue lolling, and Sam singing along with Billy Ray Cyrus. The truck rumbled to a halt in his brother's parking lot with two minutes to spare. As a small act of defiance, Sam leaned on the horn, blasting out the first few bars of *The Yellow Rose of Texas*. A childish gesture for a thirty-three-year-old, he knew, but it made him feel better.

For a glorified bodyguard, his brother was doing okay. Last year's takedown of *Kinki*'s homicidal owners had put him on the map as Atlantic City's top personal security firm. It had also reunited Nick with an ex-girlfriend, now his wife.

Acknowledging a twinge of envy for Nick's success, both business and personal, Sam crammed his Stetson onto his head and attached Rex's leash. Together they rode the elevator to the tenth floor, home of *Jackson Protective Services*.

The receptionist's forward-lean while petting Rex presented the Grand Canyon of cleavage. Sam felt no twinge of interest. Zero. Nada. Something was badly wrong. All he could think of was Katie's slender hands cupping his dick as she'd tried to restrain him. It took intense concentration, but he averted a hard-on. Tipping his hat with an apologetic smile, he let Rex lead the way into Nick's office.

Behind an acre of desk, Nick glanced up from his sheaf of papers. Not for the first time, Sam reflected on their differences. Nick's Armani suit, designer tie, and neatly combed brown hair all screamed business, while his own attire reflected individualism and non-conformity.

Nick gave a brief nod, his gray eyes unsmiling. "Sam. I have an urgent appointment, so we have to make this real quick. What's up?"

"Nice to see you, too, big brother." Sam unclipped Rex's leash and parked himself. Pretending didn't have a care in the world, he stretched out his legs, ankles crossed and announced, "I changed my mind. I want to hire you. Here's what happened." And before Nick could interrupt, he described the vandalism.

Silence.

"You hear me?"

Nick's gusty sigh was deafening. "Thunderation, Sam. Okay, so you're a computer genius and rigged up your own security cameras, but then you went and hired a security firm that isn't worth a pinch of coonshit. No wonder you're in trouble."

Sam recognized that if he wanted his brother's help, he'd better suck up. He started with a contrite expression. "You're right. I figured heavy-duty security measures could wait until *Kinki* was up and running." He gave the modest smile that usually achieved the desired result. "Guess I was wrong, huh?"

Nick pressed harder. "You also promised to handle the nightshift yourself. Looks like you skipped some patrols."

Sam plopped his hat on Nick's desk. No way was he admitting how often he'd rolled in at dawn after unwinding with a willing woman and a few shots—okay, a bottle of Jack Daniels. "Nightshift had nothing to do with it. The vandalism happened during the day, after I switched off the security cameras."

"In that case, I assume you called the cops."

"Nope. A police investigation would delay the grand opening."

Nick's gaze raked Sam's face. "You're broke," he stated with uncanny perception.

"Hell, no," Sam lied. And he would have been fine, except as how every casino within striking distance had banned him.

Nick's eyes were colder than a polar bear's ass. "You've gone and blown all your winnings and most of Granddaddy Hiram's retirement fund too, haven't you?"

Damned if he'd admit anything of the sort. "Give me credit for having common sense."

"For your sake, hope you're telling the truth."

"Shit-on-a-stick!" Sam yelled, but immediately, dialed down the volume. This wasn't the time to piss his brother off. "Like I said, I want to hire you to get on top of this security breach."

More silence.

Sam did the one thing he vowed he would never do. He swallowed his pride and groveled. "Okay, you were right, I was wrong. I need your expertise. Please help."

After a long pause, Nick said, "Sorry, Sam. I hate to tell you, but I'm not taking on any new assignments at this time, even for you. I didn't want anyone to know yet."

Great. His brother was teaching him a lesson. "I'll pay double your regular fee, hell, make that triple, but payment after the grand opening."

Nick raked his fingers through his hair, destroying his pulled-together image. "I told you. No new cases. I'm real sorry."

Unprepared for the blast of bitterness sweeping through him, Sam shook his head. Although he and Nick gave one another a hard time, they'd always been there for one another. That is, until today.

As if sensing his master's mood, Rex padded over and laid his huge head across Sam's knee. Feeling the warm weight, he ruffled the dog's fur. "Fine. I get it. You've given up on me. You're exactly like our daddy."

"I will never, ever give up on you, no matter what. Good God, Sam. You're my brother. What's going on in my life is too personal to discuss right now, even with you."

Sam jerked his head up and held his brother's gaze. "Is everything okay? You're not sick are you? Is Gracie divorcing you?"

Nick's contagious smile transformed his face. "Nothing like that. We're both fine. I'll fill you in as soon as everything's settled."

A wave of relief washed over Sam. "In that case, don't worry about me. I'll figure it out."

There was someone else who might be willing to delay payment until after the grand opening, but the price tag would be steep. If possible, he'd rather hang tight. Existing security measures, augmented with a tad more vigilance on his part, especially night surveillance, should do the trick.

Rex slobbered into his hand before wandering off to sniff at the contents of the trash can, no doubt hoping for a snack.

Nick changed the subject. "Our daddy's coming for a visit. He wants me to invite you to a family barbecue. Said I shouldn't take no for an answer."

"Hell, no."

"He asked specifically for you to be there."

"I'm busy that night," Sam muttered, his gut twisting. His father hadn't given a good rat's ass about him while he was growing up, so why pretend to care now?

"You don't know when he's coming."

"Doesn't matter. Don't care. I'm busy." So what if he sounded childish. Some things were too painful to discuss.

"Think it over. I'm inviting our granddaddy, too. You'll have to drive him anyway."

"Doesn't mean I have to come in. I have nothing to say to our father, bless his heart."

"I hate to see resentment eating you up, Sam. It's time for forgiveness."

"Yeah. And the next time you hear wings flapping, it'll be a pig flying past the window." Sam stood and plopped his Stetson on his head. "I'll be in touch. Give your beautiful wife a big, sloppy kiss for me."

He marched out with Rex at his heels. Katie's interrogation was about to begin.

Chapter 9: The Explosion

The day after the vandalism, Katie was too jittery to concentrate on work. Sam was late, even for him, and the impending interrogation loomed like an executioner's axe. For the tenth time, she wandered over to the window and scanned *Kinki*'s parking lot. There were vehicles of all shapes and sizes, everything but Sam's black pickup. Her gaze rested on a jumbo tow truck, mainly because it towered above other vehicles and occupied two parking spots. Huge tires and a lifted suspension elevated the frame several feet from the ground. The truck contained two people. The driver flicked an inch of cigar ash out the window.

An unladylike word popped out of her mouth. The Allegretti brothers had returned, but not, she suspected, for the job fair.

Buttoning her jacket, Katie hustled downstairs. She felt obligated to learn what the brothers were doing at *Kinki* and, if possible, thwart their plans. They wouldn't hurt her in broad daylight. She'd drop Luigi's name if necessary.

A minute later, she stepped into the early May sunshine. The tow truck was on the move, gathering speed as it lumbered between rows of parked cars. Squealing tires preceded a metallic crash. She hiked up her skirt and jogged to the end of the row. The truck's front bumper was embedded in a tree at the far end of the lot.

"Dumbass!" Enzo's voice yelled from inside the truck. "Ya stalled this fuckin' shitbox again, Ralphie. Get us the hell outta here before the cowboy dude tacks us up by the balls."

"It wasn't my fault. Driving a standard's a bitch."

"You're smoking a cigar, for chrissake. Standards need two hands." Enzo's voice rose to full throttle. "I *told* ya stealin' a truck was a lousy idea."

"Hey, we needed new wheels. Your shitbox died."

"And this one ran outta gas. You shoulda checked the fuel gauge."

"And you shoulda remembered to bring lock-picking tools."

"We wouldn't of needed them if the muscle at the front desk hadn't demanded ID. And who knew they would lock the delivery door today? Our client's gonna kill us."

Katie gnawed her lower lip. Sam had obviously increased security. She needed to find out what the Allegrettis wanted. Gravel crunched underfoot as she marched toward the tow truck. The brothers continued bickering, oblivious of her presence. Standing on tiptoe, she rapped on the door. "Open up, boys."

Silence.

"I know you're in there. Don't make me hurt you."

"Katarina?" Enzo's head popped out the passenger side. "Hell, someone your size couldn't hurt a flea." Without Goth makeup, his eye twitch was more noticeable.

She would have jiggled the door handle, but it was too high. "What's up? Did you forget something yesterday?"

Enzo nodded in Ralphie's direction. "This was my dumbass brother's idea."

"Hey, hey, hey. Who're you calling dumbass?"

Enzo ignored Ralphie and addressed Katie. "I told Ralphie we should wait until tonight, but he said our client was in a big, fucking hurry."

Ralphie used the heel of his hand to whack Enzo across the back of the head. "Watch your language, asshole."

She repeated her question. "Why are you guys here? I want the truth. Don't try to lie. I'll know if you do."

A smirk creased Enzo's face. "It's a special assignment."

"Wow," she chirped. "What's the job?"

"Our client wants us to—"

Enzo interjected, "Shut up, Ralphie. It's a secret."

"We can trust Katie. She's an old friend."

Hoping Luigi hadn't hired them to save her from Sam's clutches, Katie checked over her shoulder to make sure no one was listening. "Let me in." When Enzo hesitated, she tapped her foot. "Open up. Now."

"Okay, okay." Enzo unlocked the door, leaned his seat forward, and extended a hand to hoist her up. She scrambled inside and squeezed past Enzo to sit in the back seat.

Ralphie puffed out a cloud of smoke and twisted around. "We can trust you, right?"

She crossed her fingers. "Absolutely."

If anyone belonged behind bars, it was this pair. She figured the best way to coax them to spill their guts about their mysterious assignment was to stroke their egos.

"This must be an ultra-sensitive job."

Ralphie grinned. "Damn straight. Our client's into deals worth millions. That's why he warned us to keep our mouths shut." He jammed the cigar into his mouth. Ashes hit the floor.

She suppressed the urge to cough. "You're making a mess, Ralphie."

Ralphie's grin broadened. "Don't worry, babe. It ain't our truck." He aimed his cigar in the general direction of the ashtray and flicked.

"So this big client—"

"Shit!" Enzo yelled. "You lost the entire fucking cherry."

"So what?"

"So you missed the ashtray. The damn burger wrappers are catching fire."

Acrid smoke wisped up. A second later, flames flared. Katie's mouth went dry. "Put the fire out," she shouted around the terror clogging her throat. She scrunched her eyes shut, hoping when she opened them again, the flames would be gone.

They weren't. If anything, they'd shot higher. She was living her recurring nightmare of live cremation. Within seconds, she'd die a horrible, fiery death, and Josh would be an orphan.

By then, the food wrappers were blazing. Ralphie grabbed a rag and pounded the flames. The rag ignited and sparks shot up. He dropped it onto the floor where the carpet promptly smoldered.

"Moron!" Enzo yelled, stomping the smoldering floor. "That rag's covered in oil. I used it to wipe the gas can."

"Watch out!" she shrieked, staring in horror at the red, plastic gas container. "It's melting. Move it away."

"Nothin' to worry about. The container's empty." To prove it, Ralphie removed the lid and shook the container. Gasoline sloshed and a few drops soaked into the upholstery. Fumes saturated the cab. "Oops, I forgot. I was in a hurry, so I only used half of it." He fumbled with the lid. It slid off his lap and disappeared into the flames.

"Idiot!" Enzo shrieked. "Shift the can away from the fire."

Ralphie deposited the container on the console, steadying it with one hand.

"That thing's gonna blow," Enzo yelled.

"Hey, t-trapped here in the back seat," Katie reminded them, her voice breaking. "What's my son going do without his mom, huh? He's just a little kid."

Ignoring her frantic plea, the brothers each opened a door. Enzo turned to Ralphie. "Shit on a stick. It's too far. I'm gonna break something if I jump."

"You'll be fine so long as you land on your head. Quit bitchin' and jump."

They leaped, leaving Katie in the back seat. Frantic now, she fumbled for the seat release but couldn't find it. She was trapped.

A draft from the open doors encouraged flames to shoot through the oily smoke. From its perch on the console between the front seats, the open gas can mocked her.

Gasping for air, Katie leaned forward to clamp a shaking hand over the spout. Comprehension slapped her in the face. If she removed her hand to make a break for it, fumes would escape. If she stayed put, flames would jump to the upholstery and melt the plastic. Either way, she hoped the explosion would kill her outright, before the greedy fire charred her flesh.

This wasn't the way she wanted Josh to remember her. It would haunt him for the rest of his life.

"Hey!" she screamed at the brothers as they limped away. "You can't leave me here to fry." She hated the quaver in her voice, but she couldn't help it. "I have a son. H-he's only nine." She coughed, then resumed, "I want to watch him grow up, go to his first prom. I always dreamed he'd get married, have children. Please help me." She started to hyperventilate.

They both turned their heads. Ralphie shouted, "Get the hell outta there, babe."

Enzo added helpfully, "Be careful when you jump. Gravel's a bitch." They turned and sprinted out of sight.

***

On his return trip, Sam glanced at the sky. Clouds of black, oily smoke billowed from the vicinity of *Kinki*. He floored it. Tires squealed as he screeched into the parking lot. Smoke streamed from the open doors of a tow truck in the far corner. Flames curled inside the cab.

"Stay," he ordered Rex before hopping out.

He took a few steps and stopped. The damn thing was ready to blow. Only an idiot would get closer. He was reaching for his phone to dial 9-1-1 when movement in the back seat made him stiffen. The truck contained an occupant. He figured he must be seeing things until he remembered he wasn't hung over today.

A puff of wind cleared the smoke. For one second Katie was clearly visible, her pale face staring out the rear window was contorted with terror. His gut cramped at the sheer horror of the situation.

He didn't stop to analyze, simply acted on instinct, and raced across the parking lot. He hoisted himself up to the cab with shaking hands. A billow of smoke hit him in the face, and he coughed.

"W-what took you so long?" she asked through chattering teeth.

"What in God's name are you doing? Get out."

She shook her head. "C-can't. If I take my hand away, it'll blow."

The smoke parted long enough for him to see she'd clamped one hand over the mouth of a plastic fuel container.

"Jesus!"

"My sentiments precisely."

The carpeted floor in the front was ablaze. Flames had spread to both sides of the seat, and were converging at the base of the fuel container.

"It's too late," she said between clenched teeth. "Leave."

"I have an idea." Sam patted his pocket and breathed a sigh of relief. The deluxe doggy-do bag he always carried since he acquired Rex was still there. He dug it out.

"I see no point in both of us dying."

His fingers were clumsy with fear. "Are you always this bossy?"

"I p-prefer to think of myself as a-a-assertive."

Next, he shrugged his jacket down one arm. He'd read that real leather didn't burn. With the sleeve covering his hand, he reached through the flames for the seat lever. It took several precious seconds to find it. Even through six hundred dollars-worth of the world's finest leather, he sensed the metal was hot enough to blister unprotected skin.

Katie was making urgent noises, which emerged more like whimpers. He assumed she was giving more orders through clenched teeth.

"I'll get you out." He fumbled with the lever until it released. The seatback sprang forward, blocking the flames.

"H-h-how?"

He rolled the doggy-do bag into a tight cylinder. Leaning in, he shoved the makeshift plug into her free hand, and wrapped her stiffened fingers around it. "Stuff this in the opening. Make sure it's good and tight. Hurry. The can's melting." Sure enough, flames licked higher, searching for droplets of gasoline.

"I-I can't ... the fire ..." She was trembling all over.

He coughed, feeling smoke burn his throat. "I won't let the fire touch you." He thwacked the flames, banking on the leather to protect him. "Hurry. It's spreading."

Somehow, she tapped into an inner strength. After a brief struggle, she managed to plug the opening and yanked her hands away. "Done."

"Good work. Okay, follow me."

Her voice was barely a whisper. "I don't think I can m-move."

Sam wasted no time. Using his body to shield her, he reached through the fire to seize her under the arms. Ignoring the flames doing their damndest to eat through genuine leather, he hauled her forward. She was so tiny, he barely noticed the weight. Holding her around the middle, he made a one-handed exit from the vehicle, which was rapidly becoming an inferno. Once he landed, he flipped her into a fireman's lift and hightailed it.

A choked voice near his ear ordered, "Put me down, please. I prefer to walk."

He wasn't in any mood to reason with her. They had ten seconds, tops, before the container melted.

Crouching low, he covered ground in record time, headed for the dumpster. With luck, the reinforced metal would protect them from the explosion. They'd barely reached shelter when the gas can ignited with a roar that left his ears ringing. Seconds later, the parking lot vibrated from the blast.

Chapter 10: Explosion Aftermath

Behind the dumpster, Katie clung to Sam and drew in a shuddering breath of clean air. Her lungs rasped from the smoke she'd inhaled. Convulsed with tremors, she pressed her face into his throat and inhaled his comforting scent. She registered he'd draped something around her shoulders. His leather jacket.

Her legs wobbled. Specks floated across her vision. She would *not* disgrace herself by fainting in his arms. Despite her resolve, her knees buckled. Katie sagged against his body in a slow-motion slide.

Before she hit gravel, she felt powerful arms lift her off her feet. Soft hair tickled her cheek, a reminder that her head rested against Sam's naked chest. She had a faint memory of helping rip off his blackened shirt, which, being silk, had partially dissolved.

"You're safe, darlin'. I've got you."

Sam's voice, low and soothing, reminded her of bourbon and cream, all whipped together with a dollop of golden honey. Her eyelids drooped. How would he react if she snuggled in and purred? She blinked her way back to reality, and found a pair of golden eyes edged with the longest lashes she'd ever seen on a man staring back at her. His face was full of concern and, well, *kindness*.

"You need a doctor." His observation took her by surprise. Sam was more than a pretty face, surface charm, and great body. He was caring on top of brave, which was unspeakably sexy.

"I'm okay, really I am. The truck doors were open, so the smoke wasn't too bad." She masked her shocking arousal by giving orders. "Don't let anyone try to extinguish the flames. They might get hurt and sue you. Oh, and make sure someone calls 9-1-1. Also, you might want to clear the parking lot of other cars."

Crinkles appeared at the corners of his eyes. "There you go, giving orders. You must be feeling better."

She smiled to herself. It was nice to have someone worry about her for a change. "Thank you," she muttered. To her embarrassment, the words emerged as a croak. She cleared her throat. "I'm feeling much better."

A chorus of distant shouts indicated others had heard the explosion. Her imagination conjured up a host of curious goths, zombies, and vampires milling around the burning truck.

Every cell of her body buzzed with heightened awareness as she found herself plastered against a very warm, very sexy length of semi-clothed male. Unable to resist, she stroked him. Just a teeny-tiny bit. Brushing one nipple, as if by accident. For one insane second, her heart fluttered, until she came to her senses. Flushing with embarrassment, she pushed at him. "You may put me down."

The crinkles deepened. Dammit he'd sensed her reaction to his bare chest's proximity.

"Right now, please." She turned around as the shouts grew louder.

He obeyed with a promptness that was faintly insulting. Her feet landed with a crunch of gravel. The expanse of naked male beauty scrambled her brain. Levis riding low on lean hips, drew attention to his important parts. She bit back a whimper. What she could see of his body was beautiful, golden, and sculpted. She imagined the rest of Sam was even more glorious.

Stunned at her reaction, she blurted, "Sorry. I didn't mean to bite your head off. You risked your life to rescue me." With luck, he hadn't guessed her thoughts.

A tiny smile played around his mouth. Yeah, he'd guessed.

His grin widened. "More to the point, I sacrificed my leather jacket. And don't get me started on the silk shirt you ripped off my body."

Don't look there. Don't ...

She looked. By then, her entire face, neck, even her ears were burning. To disguise her discomfort, she spoke rapidly. "I'll replace your clothing, of course. I don't know how to thank you enough for everything."

"Between us, we'll figure it out."

She moistened her lips. "At the very least, you deserve an explanation."

"I was wondering if you'd come clean voluntarily or if I'd have to find other ways to coax the truth out of you," he said with a perfectly straight face.

Katie stiffened with shock. In mob jargon, *finding other ways* meant scary stuff would happen. Noting the heat in his eyes, she realized her mistake. He'd been hitting on her. Hey, it had been years since a man had dared hit on her, a major disadvantage of a possessive crime lord with a fixation.

She said, "The Allegrettis returned today to finish the job they started yesterday."

Concern deepened the creases on Sam's forehead. He remained silent for a long minute. "I guessed as much, but I appreciate your honesty." Over the shouts, which had grown louder, he said, "You can tell me everything later."

"I want to help you nail them."

Rooster's bellow drowned out Sam's reply. "Boss, where the fuck are you? Katie?"

Without looking away from her face, Sam yelled, "Over here. We're both fine."

She let go and peered around the dumpster. Rooster's boots stirred up puffs of dust as he raced toward them. A moment later, he wrapped Katie in a huge hug. "Thank God. Me and the guys thought the explosion killed you both while you were making out in the truck."

"We weren't making out." Sam looked at Katie and mouthed the word, "Yet."

A flare of heat branded her face.

Rooster's whisper penetrated her confusion. "Hon, I don't blame you for letting the boss do you, even in the back seat of a truck, but have you considered the consequences?"

Katie's brain froze. There hadn't been time to brief Rooster about zipping his lip about Luigi.

Sam rescued her. "What consequences? Nobody was *doing* anybody else in the truck. Katie was in trouble, I helped her, end of story."

"Trouble? Aw, shit. The explosion made me forget." Rooster grimaced. "Your granddaddy's in trouble."

Sam gave a gusty sigh. "What did he do this time? Piss off a zombie? Insult a vampire? Our new HR manager will have to handle it."

Rooster shook his head. "Hiram despises Deanna. Problem is, she's with him now, so you'd better haul ass to the *Voodoo Lounge*. Someone attacked him."

Katie let out a startled gasp. "Is he okay?"

But Sam didn't wait for the answer. He'd already taken off at a run. Over his shoulder, he hollered, "Keep everyone outside."

***

Forgetting everything else, Sam sprinted down *Kinki*'s main corridor. His granddaddy might be badly hurt or worse. After a moment, it dawned on him that Katie was close behind. He didn't reduce speed. Vandalism, truck fires, and now his granddaddy. Could this day possibly get any worse?

"Absolutely," a little voice inside his head assured him. *"If Granddaddy Hiram is hurt."*

The idea of anyone harming the old man made Sam stumble.

A commotion grew louder as he approached the *Voodoo Lounge*. A metallic clatter reverberated down the corridor and bounced off the walls. Sam slowed down and tilted his head to listen. The racket became more insistent, augmented by X-rated threats that were anatomically impossible, ending on a high note with, "Shit-ass, hyena-breath, rat-fuck, coward."

The iron band compressing Sam's chest loosened, allowing him to breathe again. If his granddaddy could cuss that fluently, he was okay.

Behind him, Katie's breathless voice echoed his thoughts. "Hiram must be in one piece. What a relief."

Sam pivoted to find her staring at him, her forehead furrowed with concern. White-faced and anxious, she chewed her lower lip. Damn, but she possessed the sexiest mouth he'd ever seen. He gave a curt nod.

More metallic jangling interrupted his mental turmoil. Granddaddy Hiram's voice, slightly muffled, hollered, "Get the hell away from me, woman. Be useful. Go find my grandson."

"Yeah. He's in tip-top shape, all right," Sam said.

"Who's he talking to?"

"Deanna Sweeney, our new HR Manager."

Granddaddy Hiram yelled louder, "Show me your ugly face, you gutless asshole. I'm gonna tear your arm off and beat you senseless with the soggy end." Unintelligible grumbling punctuated with inventive obscenities and multiple f-bombs followed the outburst.

"Enough cussing. There's ladies present."

"Sammy? About time. For the record, Deanna ain't no lady. I sent the bitch away."

"Don't talk that way. And Katie's here."

After a pause, Granddaddy Hiram lowered his voice. "Oops. Sorry."

Sam peered into the *Voodoo Lounge*. It was too dark to see anything. "Where are you?"

"Sammy? About time. Some asshat locked me inside a crypt."

In the abrupt silence, rapid footsteps clicked closer. A moment later, Sam found himself standing nose-to-nose with Deanna. She was a big-breasted, wide-hipped Amazon of a woman, all excellent qualities in his opinion. Granddaddy Hiram didn't view Deanna in the same favorable light, mainly because she'd curtailed his mischief on several occasions.

Deanna batted her baby blues at Sam. "I tried to help Hiram, but he's too distressed to listen." A little head shake dislodged the blonde hair so it swept over one cheek. Deanna's cushiony breast nudged his arm as she stepped closer. "Thank heavens you're here."

Behind him, Katie gave an audible snort.

Sam shifted away from Deanna. For reasons he preferred not to examine too closely, he didn't want Katie to think another woman turned him on.

"With the job fair going full tilt, I'm surprised to see you here, Deanna."

"Even HR managers take lunch breaks. I heard Hiram yelling, and here I am."

"Much appreciated." Sam shifted uncomfortably. His bare chest damn near sizzled under her examination.

"I adore the elderly." Deanna's voice was a touch breathier than usual. Her scrutiny meandered southward and settled in the vicinity of his dick, which, strangely enough, didn't react. Lucky for him, because Deanna was strictly off-limits. He wouldn't dream of hitting on State Senator Frank Martinelli's most recent mistress. He owed the politician too much to risk wrecking their friendship. To create a distraction, he made hasty introductions.

Deanna beamed a condescending smile at Katie. "Oh, my goodness. You're so tiny I didn't see you hiding behind Sam like a little mouse. Nice to meet you." Ignoring Katie's sudden inhalation, Deanna returned her attention to Sam. "Your grandfather's asking for you. If there's anything I can do, I'm happy to help."

"I've got it, thanks." Sam smiled to soften his words. "I'd rather you prepared Katie's employment contract."

"Of course." Deanna made no move to leave.

Shrugging, Sam strode into the dimly lit room. He checked over his shoulder to see if Katie was behind him, but Deanna had stepped into the doorway, blocking it.

Chapter 11: Rescuing Hiram

Recessed lighting cast deep shadows in the *Voodoo Lounge*. Katie fumed with frustration. Hiram needed her help, but a doorway crammed with buxom HR manager thwarted her efforts to follow Sam. The woman had shoulders rivaling a linebacker, and she wasn't yielding an inch.

While Katie waited for an opening to make her move, Deanna gazed after Sam the way some vegans eye a T-bone steak when they think no one's watching.

Katie tapped her on the shoulder, "Who would want to harm a helpless old man?"

Deanna turned. Her high-gloss lips twisted. "Helpless? Hah. I guess you don't know Hiram." Rummaging in her pocket, she came up with a pepperette. White teeth chomped into the sausage. "Atkins diet," she explained, chewing. "This is lunch."

A muffled voice emerged from the gloom. "It's about time you arrived, Sammy." A metallic clatter punctuated the complaint. "You gotta release me. I'd do it myself, but some asshole duct-taped my hands behind me."

"A pity whoever it was didn't duct-tape his mouth, too," Deanna, said, shifting a fraction of an inch. Katie ducked under an elbow, zipped past a remarkably lifelike live oak tree draped in trailing moss, and paused to catch her bearings in the gloom. As her eyes adjusted, she discerned a number of tombstones. On examining the area behind the remarkably realistic cemetery, she blew out a shocked breath. Inside a stone chamber containing a sarcophagus supported by two massive skulls, a hooded figure was kicking the metal bars barricading the entrance. She assumed the occupant was Hiram.

Katie turned her attention to Sam. He muttered a curse while fumbling with the padlock. More rattling filled the silence. His hands were too clumsy to insert the key.

"Shit. I must have the wrong key," he muttered.

He sounded so stressed, Katie headed straight for the crypt. "Hi, Hiram. Katie here. You keeping out of trouble?"

The hooded figure turned his head toward her. "Does a cat have climbin' gear?" Tufts of white beard escaped from the bottom of the hood.

While Sam labored with the lock, she distracted Hiram by chatting. Mindful of her brother's accusation of bossiness, she offered no advice. After watching Sam's unsuccessful tries at springing the lock, she changed her mind.

"You're too agitated." She extended one hand, palm up. "Let me help."

Sam dropped the key into her hand without a fuss. He must be more rattled than she'd thought. With smooth motions, she opened the padlock, removed the duct tape, then started on the hood. Conscious of Sam watching her every move, it seemed to take forever to untie the knot. Hiram stood still while she removed the hood and stroked damp white hair off his forehead. "Did anyone ever mention you're more charming and much handsomer than your grandson?" she asked.

"I get that all the time." Hiram grinned at her, revealing a mouthful of excellent choppers.

The sense of déja vu Katie had experienced on first meeting Hiram gripped her again. She wondered if his teeth were real, or if they floated in a glass of water overnight. As a mortician, she'd always fretted about losing a client's dentures.

"Are you sure you're in one piece?" Sam sounded worried. He ran his hands down Hiram's arms, as if to make sure.

"Not hurt, just royally pissed. While I was trussed up, I did some thinkin'. Wanna know what I'm gonna do when I catch the scumbag?"

Sam flicked a warning glance at Katie. "You do *not* want to hear this. Trust me."

"Anger release is vital." She gave Hiram an encouraging smile. "Go ahead."

"Don't say I didn't warn you." Sam shrugged and his lips twitched.

"First off, I'm gonna rip out that piece of excrement's entire puckered pink rectum." Hiram's grin broadened. "Then I'll sauté it in butter with garlic and a nice Chardonnay, tie a matching pink bow around the organ, and watch the fucker—sorry, coward—writhe in agony while eating his own asshole before dying."

Katie struggled to suppress a gale of laughter. When she was able to speak normally, she said. "Nice anger release, Hiram."

Sam draped an arm around Hiram's shoulders in a gesture that screamed protective. "Who did this to you?" His voice was so gentle, Katie's heart melted.

"Damned if I know. The sack of shit—oops, lady present—yanked the hood over my head. I can tell you the fuckhead—sorry—lowlife scum was 'bout as tall as you, and real strong. Before I knew it, I was all duct-taped and locked inside the crypt."

While Sam made soothing noises, Katie retrieved Hiram's glasses from the floor and settled them on his nose. "There you go. Good as new."

Sam took out his phone. "I'm taking no more chances with security."

Hiram clutched Sam's arm. "Who're you calling? Not the police, I hope. We don't want the press to learn of an attack on a senior citizen."

Sam patted Hiram's back. "It's okay. I'm calling State Senator Martinelli. He used to run a security agency on the side."

"Not a good idea," Katie interjected. Frank Martinelli's 'connected'." She knew this because Frank was Luigi's friend—not that she was predisposed to revealing this little secret.

"Common knowledge again?" Sam's assessing gaze held hers.

"Yup." Heat rose in her face.

"Strange how no one else knows."

She was pretty sure Sam hadn't finished grilling her, but Hiram's voice saved her from having to think of a plausible explanation.

"I don't trust that scum-bucket as far as I can throw him. It's time you called Nick."

Sam turned his attention to Hiram. "I tried Nick this morning. He couldn't or wouldn't help, didn't give a reason. Something's up with him."

"Why Martinelli?" Granddaddy Hiram asked.

"I know he can be bought and stays bought. If I offer enough, he won't mind waiting for payment until after the grand opening."

"And you know this how?" The words slipped out before Katie remembered she was keeping a low profile.

"I had a licensing issue with *Kinki*. Martinelli intervened with the New Jersey Liquor Commission. In exchange I made a donation big enough to fund his campaign twice over."

"In other words, you bribed a state senator," Katie stated.

"Bribe is such a strong word." Sam touched the screen of his smartphone while moving out of earshot to make the call.

Katie shoved her worry aside and told Hiram about the vandalism, the truck explosion, and Sam's heroic rescue.

As soon as Sam finished, Hiram pounced. "What did Martinelli say?"

"He promised to handle the situation with the utmost discretion. Until the vandals are caught, he'll install an undercover security detail to watch *Kinki* night and day." He nudged his granddaddy toward the door. "Time to get you home to put your feet up for a nice rest."

Hiram gave a loud snort. "In your dreams. I need a stiff drink after what that snot-eating, worm-headed sack of monkey shit did to me."

A flash of helpless desperation crossed Sam's face, revealing the depth of his distress.

Taking pity on him, Katie stepped in. "It's been a long morning, Hiram. You and I both need some rest."

Clearly concerned, Sam said to Katie, "I'm a selfish idiot. You almost died today, then you helped Granddaddy Hiram. Take the afternoon off. You deserve it."

Her relief faded when he added, "I know you're hiding something, Katie. Something big. I intend to learn the truth."

Chapter 12: Sam's Surprise Visit

All the way home, Katie watched her rear-view mirror. Although there was no sign of a tail, her life was spinning out of control. She'd never forgive herself if she was the reason behind the vandalism or the attack on Hiram.

Once home, she kicked off her shoes and moaned with relief. All she wanted was a hot shower, a bite to eat, and a few routine household chores to prove her life was back to normal. Josh was still at school, and she had three glorious hours all to herself before picking him up at The Annex.

Her thoughts drifted to Sam, the man who'd saved her life, the man who could have been plucked from a porno film, the man who would undoubtedly feature in her hottest sexual fantasies for nights to come.

She returned to earth with a thud when Luigi's voice echoed in her head. *"Fuhgeddaboudit, Katarina. You're mine."*

Bastard. Luigi would *not* control her thoughts. She'd fantasize about anyone she damn well pleased. And Sam pleased her. A lot.

As if sensing her distress, a marmalade cat materialized from the living room. Bluto twined around her ankles, meowing a greeting.

"How's my sweetest, handsomest fat-boy?" She scooped him up, staggering a little under his bulk, and tickled his tummy. "Are you gaining weight? Yes you are."

Warm and comforting, Bluto let his entire body go limp and cranked up the purr machine. He didn't give a damn about his weight and never wasted energy on worrying. Cats had the right attitude.

Lowering him, she headed upstairs to shower.

An hour later, she was still restless. Even a plate of Ma's special spaghetti failed to calm her anxiety. She thrust her damp hair behind her ears and hauled the vacuum cleaner from the broom closet. She'd stacked comics, toys, and three video games when the doorbell rang. Her first thought was that Luigi had escaped from prison, which told her how much he terrified her.

She shook her head. No one escaped maximum security. Right?

Her heart jack-hammered in her chest as she walked to the front door. Standing on tiptoe, she placed one eye to the peephole and immediately retreated. To make sure she wasn't hallucinating, she looked again.

The man outside was so tall, only the bottom part of his face showed. But there was no mistaking the chiseled jawline, the mouth that, incidentally, should come equipped with a warning label, the tanned neck disappearing into a silky shirt. Those could belong to only one person.

Too raw, too vulnerable, she wasn't ready to face Sam's questions. Not yet. Plus her sweats and an ancient button-up cardigan weren't exactly the height of sexy lounge-wear. Let him think she wasn't home.

Next thing she knew, the peephole went dark. He couldn't possibly see inside. She held her breath. If she so much as twitched, he'd know she was there.

"I know you're watching me." His voice was deep, and slow, and gentle.

Was he a mind-reader or what? She willed him to vanish.

"You're blocking the light."

She rolled her eyes. "Go away, Sam. It was a tough day."

"That's why I'm not leaving until I see your pretty face and make sure you're okay."

For one searing second, her world tilted. He sounded as if he truly cared. She almost unlocked the door. Then she remembered he could pour on the charm as easily as other men turned on a tap. The memory of Mango, or maybe it was Tango, coiled around him, all bouncy boobs and mobile hips, strengthened her resolve.

"I'm fine. Really. Go home to Hiram."

"He's asleep. I'm staying until you let me in. Contrary to what you might believe, I'm here to make sure you're okay after everything that happened today."

She gnawed her bottom lip. She could out-wait him.

Again, he showed remarkable mind-reading abilities. "No rush. I'll pass the time by entertaining your neighbors with a cowboy song or two."

She clamped her lips together.

"I should warn you I'm tone-deaf."

She didn't dignify his bluff with a response.

On the other side of the door, he cleared his throat and hummed in an off-key tenor. When he started singing, she barely recognized the opening bars of *Always on my Mind*.

Checkmate. A singing cowboy on her doorstep was bad enough, but a truly awful singer? Neighbors would call Ma. Family members would arrive. And what if Luigi had someone tail her? Sam would make an easy target.

Sighing, she opened the door.

In an instant, her foyer overflowed with bouncing dog and glorious man.

Sam looked like an honest-to-God movie star. Male sexual energy oozed from him. He'd changed into jeans that molded those long, lanky legs and other interesting parts. The black silk shirt, leather-and-silver belt, and boots she'd bet were lizard skin didn't hurt either. No wonder she felt dizzy with arousal.

He headed inside. Katie recovered and trotted after him.

"Sorry." Sam flashed that smile of his, the one that left her annoyingly breathless. "I brought Rex so he wouldn't wake my granddaddy."

Rex's tail swished in agreement. His eyes gleamed when Bluto rounded the corner. Tail erect, the cat marched over to the dog. Rex backed away until he cowered against Sam's legs.

"Now that's what I call an attack dog." Sam ruffled Rex's fur.

The cat stalked away with Rex at his heels.

Sam strode around Katie and into the living room. Her heart sank when he headed straight to one of the windows flanking the fireplace. There was a clear line of sight to *Paradise Gate*, which was built on an elevation three blocks away. Ma might notice a man in the window and come charging over.

He peered outside. "Nice place you have."

She darted a glance outside. So far, so good. "Let's sit." She indicated the sofa, which couldn't be seen from The Annex. Waiting until he sank into a corner, she perched at the opposite end. Desperate for Sam to leave, she adopted her most persuasive tone. "It's kind of you to worry, but as you can see, I'm great. Getting my housework done." She fought to keep her voice casual. "I need to get back at it."

"You appear jumpy."

She gritted her teeth. Clearly, he wasn't getting the message. "As I mentioned, I'm busy."

"After what happened, you should be relaxing. I'm here to offer a friendly shoulder to lean on."

Aw, he was being nice. Not fair. If she leaned on those broad shoulders, she might do something stupid. Like jump his bones.

She pointed a finger at him. "You're not fooling me for a second. You're here to grill me about the Allegrettis. I bet you're dying to know why I was in their truck."

His unrepentant grin caused her heart to kick. "Crossed my mind," he admitted.

It appeared the only way she'd get rid of him was to spill her guts. She sank into the cushions, striving to appear relaxed. "Fine. I'll tell you what I know." *At least, part of it.*

Sam examined her face for a very long beat before nodding. "Start at the beginning."

"Sure thing." His steady gaze made her want to squirm so she busied herself by tugging on a loose thread hanging from a button on her cardigan.

This was tricky ground. Her brother and Luigi were friends with the Allegretti brothers. As kids, the terrible four had spent many happy hours tormenting the neighborhood, like conducting a pretend cremation (on her, ha-ha, hence her fear of fire), or scaring the crap out of other kids by inviting them downstairs and showing off the latest corpses.

She settled on, "I've known the brothers since grade school."

"Let me guess. The Italian community again."

"Yep." The touch of skepticism in his voice compelled her to elaborate. "When I was growing up, there were kids' parties at the Italian Cultural Community Center. Ralphie and Enzo were always there." *Terrorizing the smaller kids.*

A subtle release of tension was evident in the way his expression lightened. "Sounds like fun. I bet you kept the other kids in line."

Grazie, Dio, Sam had bought her explanation. Hiding her background was harder than she'd imagined.

"Someone had to. So getting back to yesterday. I recognized Enzo and Ralphie, but not right away because of their makeup. They're bad news. I wondered if they'd vandalized your club. This morning, I was looking out the window and saw them again, so I went down to chat." She risked a glance.

He merely crossed one leg over another.

She wound the thread around one finger. "They'd stolen the truck and were sitting there arguing because Ralphie had crashed it." The thread was cutting off circulation, so she stopped winding and assessed his reaction to her story.

He folded his arms and stared back in silence. His eyes reflected astonishing intelligence.

She looked away. "Ralphie had never learned to drive a standard."

She stopped trying to stuff both hands into the baggy pockets when she realized her finger was attached to the button. She tried to break the damn thread. Tugging as unobtrusively as possible, she rattled on with the rest of her explanation, describing everything leading up to her sitting alone in a burning truck. Well, everything except that Luigi might be the mysterious client who'd ordered the damage.

One final tug and the thread snapped. The button shot away, but she pretended not to notice.

Sam stood, ambled over to the button and picked it up. "I believe this is yours." He pressed the button into her hand and sat again. "Why did you let those thugs escape yesterday when you believed they'd vandalized *Kinki*?"

Right. She'd missed that part. "To save your life. Remember when you went all macho on them? Well it pissed them off."

"And why should I care?"

"Everyone knows an Allegretti never goes anywhere unarmed. It's common knowledge. There have been incidents. Fatal ones."

After an eternity, Sam nodded. "Thank you. In that case, I owe you my life." He stayed silent for a few seconds, then proceeded to talk. "Okay, here's what we know. An important but unknown client hired the Allegretti brothers to vandalize *Kinki*. We have no idea why, except it was an important job." He'd summarized her nervous ramblings in two sentences.

"Exactly."

Except that the unknown client might or might not be Luigi, who might or might not have hired the brothers to put *Kinki* out of business, thwarting her last chance at independence, thus forcing her to marry him or flee. Even to Katie, the theory sounded far-fetched, so she kept her mouth closed.

She'd started to relax when she noticed Sam had moved closer, close enough to touch, his intent evident. "Thanks for explaining. Now, about that friendly shoulder to lean on …" Electricity crackled between them. He tugged gently on a damp curl and wound it around one finger. His hand brushed her cheek in a feather-light caress, leaving behind a shocking tingle that zapped right into her fun parts.

"What are you doing?" Mixed feelings of longing and trepidation caused her heart to thunder in her ears. She didn't have enough experience with men to handle a player like Sam.

He smiled as though he knew the effect he had on her. "I like your hair down and curling over your shoulders."

"I, uh, it's still wet," she muttered through a tight throat. Her heart thumped harder. A rabbit hypnotized by a snake probably felt the same. "It's unprofessional to wear it loose."

Luigi hated it when she wore her hair down. He claimed it was inappropriate for a mortician. Truth was, he wanted to prevent other men from noticing her. It occurred to Katie that with Luigi in prison, she was free to look as sexy as she pleased, even enjoy a round of hot, steamy sex if she chose to. And here she was—wet hair, ratty sweats, and a lumpy cardigan.

Sam leaned closer. A whiff of soap, cologne, and the seductive scent of pure, healthy male surged to her brain. He gave her a long look. "You're beautiful, you know."

Katie's toes curled in response to his slow smile. For the first time in a long time, a man's admiration didn't generate fear. She had no idea how a normal woman would respond, but was pretty sure hyperventilation wasn't the way to go.

Before her brain kicked in, words gushed from her mouth. "Your pupils are dilated." *God, kill me now.* "According to Cosmo, enlarged pupils indicate extreme sexual arousal. Are you flirting with me?" She got herself under control and pressed her lips together. Yeah, she needed practice in the flirtation department.

His smile broadened. "I must be slipping if you have to ask. But yeah, I was flirting."

So her babbling hadn't turned him off. She found herself snared by eyes that screamed amazing sex, something she'd yet to experience.

Forcing herself to ignore the butterflies in her stomach, she said, "You do it very well." One hundred percent certain he wanted to kiss her, she leaned forward.

The sound of a door slamming, followed by the thump of footsteps in the foyer broke the spell. Springing to her feet on shaky legs, Katie yelled, "Who's there?"

Bella's voice answered. "It's only us. I brought Josh home. You're early."

"Is he hurt?" Katie sprinted to the foyer. On seeing her child in one piece, scowling, and apparently none the worse for wear, she threw her arms around him. "What happened, baby?"

"Aw, Mom. I'm not hurt or anything." Josh squirmed out of her grip, so she looked at Bella for an answer.

"The school tried phoning your cell phone, then here. There was no answer, so they called The Annex."

"I got home early. They must have called when I was in the shower." Guilt hit Katie hard. Apparently, near-incineration followed by the attack on Hiram had affected her memory. She'd forgotten to check for messages.

She looked at Bella for answers. "What happened at school? Please don't tell me he got into trouble again."

"Yep. The school sent Josh home early for acting out. I picked him up and brought him here. Apparently he has tons of homework, so he should get started."

"I'll call the school after I talk to Josh."

Remembering Sam, she glanced over her shoulder in time to see him head back to the living room at warp speed.

Chapter 13: Sam Meets Josh

Unless Katie had taken in a younger brother or nephew or some such for an overnight or two—and Sam sincerely hoped she had—she apparently owned a son named Josh. Struggling to get his breathing under control, he scanned the living room for evidence of a child. Sure enough, video games and two action figures lay beside a stack of comic books on a side table. A wooden baseball bat stood in a corner. Pictures of a child at various ages of development studded one wall.

Yep. The evidence was there, but he'd been blind to everything but Katie.

The creamy yellow walls of her living room closed in on him. A cold sweat broke out on his forehead. Kids terrified him. In fact, he made a point of avoiding women who had children.

Shouldn't Katie have mentioned her kid? Most mothers talked about them all day long, obsessing over their accomplishments, bragging about their irresistible cuteness. Katie hadn't demonstrated any of those telltale symptoms. Hell, she hadn't uttered one word, not a whisper or hint about a son.

A smart man would leave, pronto.

Apparently, he wasn't smart at all, because he ambled into the kitchen to meet Katie's visitor. And possibly—he had a hard time wrapping his head around the notion—her son.

The kid caught Sam's attention first. The boy's resemblance to Katie was so strong, he had to be her offspring.

In one corner, Katie and a knockout blonde spoke to one another in low voices, no doubt discussing Josh's misbehavior. They were so engrossed in their conversation, they paid no attention to Rex dancing around the boy, backing him into a corner. The kid's eyes, wide with terror, silently begged him for help.

Blindsided by compassion, Sam grabbed Rex's collar. "Sit," he ordered, pushing hard on the dog's rump. Thankfully, Rex obeyed, and sat there panting. Forgetting for a moment how much he disliked children, Sam hunkered down. "This here's Rex. He looks big and scary at first, but he loves kids. Hold out your hand so he can sniff it. I won't let him hurt you."

The kid stared back, then looked at the dog. Ever so slowly, he extended his hand. Rex snuffled at it. A long, pink tongue swept over the fingers. The boy giggled and snatched his hand away. "It tickles."

Talking to kids wasn't as hard as Sam had feared. He made sure he had a good hold on Rex before saying, "I'm your mom's friend, Sam Jackson, but you can call me Sam."

"I'm Josh."

"Well, Josh, Rex likes you to scratch behind his ears and stroke his head. Watch." He demonstrated the dog's favorite head-scratch. "Want to try it?"

The kid did. Rex moaned in ecstasy. Josh grinned at Sam. "He likes it."

"Yep. I think he likes you too."

"I'm okay now. You can let go of Rex."

Maintaining a tight grip on Rex's collar, Sam got to his feet. "You sure? He might want to play."

The kid sucked in a lungful of air, blew it out. "I'm good with that."

"Okay, then." Sam released the collar, ready to step in if the kid freaked out. Rex shook his head, jingling his collar, then sprawled at the kid's feet. His tail thumped the floor, as if to say, *I know you're a kid so I'll be gentle.*

The kid scratched Rex's thick ruff of fur.

A woman's voice said, "Come here, Katie. Didn't you tell me Josh is terrified of dogs?"

Sam turned his head. He'd forgotten everything except the kid and the dog. For a moment, he'd even forgotten Katie.

He wasn't surprised when she introduced the boy as her son, Josh. The blonde woman turned out to be her sister, Bella.

Sam was pretty sure—make that hoped—the father was out of the picture.

Bella smiled, then busied herself, fixing coffee and goodies. Since it was Katie's kitchen, Sam had no doubt any snack would be chock-full of seeds, nuts, and fiber.

Josh, who had his arms around Rex's neck, buried his face in the thick fur so his voice came out muffled. "Mom's mad 'cause I got sent home from school early."

Katie stroked Josh's hair, brushing it out of his eyes. "Not mad, upset. You used to like school. Now, I don't know what to think. Last week, you hit other kids, talked out of turn. Today, you were rude to your teacher because she wanted to check your homework."

"I hate school. It's dumb." He glared at his mother. "I don't know why we can't find another house, somewhere far away from—"

Katie interrupted smoothly. "Josh, baby, we've discussed this over and over. We need to be close to Nonna Deluca so she can mind you after school while I'm at work."

"I hate the yukky stuff that happens there. Sometimes Uncle Rico talks about it."

"Sweetie, you know we can't move. Your nonna needs to know we're all nearby."

Sam noted an edge of desperation had crept into Katie's voice as she and her sister exchanged despairing glances across the room.

Josh jutted his chin and shoved his hands in his pockets. "That's dumb. Nonna's a grownup. She doesn't need us."

Sam ambled to the window, trying his damndest to stop listening. He didn't envy parents with children, especially unhappy ones. When her phone rang, Katie said to her sister, "Would you mind answering? It's probably the school. Tell them I'll call right back."

Bella answered the phone. After listening for a moment, her lips tightened. "Sure. She's right here." She handed the phone to Katie. "It's Luigi. He wants to talk to you."

Katie shook her head, causing her hair to fly around her face.

Sam slammed his brows together. "Who's Luigi?"

Katie ignored the question. "Hang up," she mouthed at Bella, motioning to the phone.

Bella held her hand over the mouthpiece. "You can't avoid him forever."

"Watch me. He damn near ruined my life."

Who the hell was Luigi? Josh's father? Blindsided by jealousy, Sam took the phone from Bella's hand. "She's unavailable," he snarled into the phone and ended the call.

Katie snatched her phone back and stuffed it in her pocket. "Don't ever do that again."

He faced her, hating her stricken expression. "I was trying to help. Would someone please tell me who Luigi is?"

As if Sam hadn't spoken, Katie stalked around him to confront her sister. "How did Luigi get my number?"

Bella shrugged.

Katie's voice rose. "Did you tell him?"

"No. Honest to God, I didn't."

Katie snapped at her sister in Italian. It sounded like an accusation.

A snuffle in the vicinity of his elbow made him glance down. Tears filled Josh's eyes.

Katie lowered her voice, saying, "Sweetie, your Aunt Bella and I need to talk in private. Go on into the living room with Mr. Jackson."

"His name's Sam."

"If it's okay with Sam, maybe Rex can go too."

Sam caught her apologetic glance. "Right." He forced his stiff mouth into a grin for Josh's sake. "Rex will show off his tricks."

Now what? It was one thing to speak to a kid with his mom and aunt in the same room. It was quite another to be alone with one. What, in God's name, would they *talk* about?

***

Sam parked himself at the opposite end of the sofa from Josh. He crossed one leg over the other. After a while, he switched legs. A pair of seagulls squabbled outside the window, emphasizing the silence. The kid watched the birds, probably wishing he was outside doing normal kid things.

But what? Throwing rocks? Eating live bugs?

Children scared the shit out of Sam for a good reason. What if he said or did something that screwed the kid up forever?

Like right now. He'd lied to Josh. Rex didn't know a single trick.

The silence between them lengthened. At least, it made eavesdropping easier. He strained his ears for an indication of Luigi's identity, but the sisters were speaking Italian.

He was thinking of joining the women, claiming the boy was thirsty, when Josh said in a tiny voice, "I answered the phone at Nonna Deluca's yesterday. I didn't recognize Luigi's voice because he was real friendly." He sniffled. "I told him Mom's phone numbers. She'll hate me."

Sam stopped eavesdropping and focused on Josh. "Your mom will never hate you. Parents love their kids, no matter what." Too bad his own daddy hadn't subscribed to that notion.

Josh's mouth quivered.

Sam damn near moved closer to console the kid, but stopped himself just in time. That kind of impulse would bite him in the ass, especially if Josh grew attached to him. He settled deeper into his corner.

Josh watched Rex, who was nose to floor, circling the room. "You said Rex would show me tricks."

At the sight of Rex's erratic movements, inspiration struck Sam. "He sure will. Rex is an expert tracker. See? He's tracking your cat."

"Bluto?" Josh bounced a little in his excitement. "No way."

"Watch." Infusing his voice with the phony enthusiasm exclusive to pet owners and parents of small children, Sam said, "Good dog, Rexy. Where's the pussy-cat?"

By then, Rex had reached the armchair. Ass up, head down, his tail sweeping wide arcs through the air, he gave an urgent whine. His nose twitched as he snuffled the dust ruffle.

"Good dog." Sam's voice dripped with encouragement. "Sniff, Rexie. Sniff."

"Hey, he's doing it. He's found Bluto."

A piercing yelp confirmed Josh's words. Rex edged away from the chair as the cat emerged in a low crouch, his belly grazing the carpet. Bluto's ears lay flat to his head, as if challenging the dog to come closer. Rex knew when to fold. He hurtled over to the sofa and clambered up to stand between Sam and Josh, trampling them in the process.

Sam was quick to seize the opportunity. "Lie down, Rex."

The dog circled a couple of times, his platter-sized paws barely missing some mighty important pieces of Sam's anatomy, and collapsed with a gusty sigh.

"Good dog."

Rex laid his massive head on Josh's lap and sneered at the cat, as if to say, "I dare you to come closer."

"Rex is a big baby," Sam explained.

Josh leaned over Rex and stroked the dog's head. "That's what Luigi calls me sometimes," he said in a tiny voice, "but only when Mom's not listening."

Sam wanted to pound a fist in this Luigi asshole's face. But Josh was waiting for a reaction, so he went for, "Aw, what does he know? I think you're brave."

Josh's hand froze on Rex's head. "Really?"

"Really." Sam dug deep for the right words. "Look at you, sitting there all calm with Rex's head on your knee. Lots of kids won't go near a big dog."

Josh resumed stroking. "I don't like Luigi." His voice strengthened, took on a defiant note. "I'm glad he's in prison."

So that was one of the secrets Katie was hiding.

A twinge of sympathy for Josh obliterated Sam's reluctance to step in. The kid needed a man's help, but damned if he knew what to say. His own old man hadn't been much of a role model in the advice department. Casting caution to the winds, Sam trusted that what came out his mouth wouldn't cause more damage.

"I'll tell you a secret, man to man, but you have to promise not to tell anyone, especially your mom and Aunt Bella."

Josh shot a long sideway glance at Sam. "I promise."

"Good. Because we're talking about serious stuff." Sam waited until he was sure Josh was paying attention. "My daddy was real mean to me."

"Really? Why."

"I don't know. I guess he was unhappy."

"But that wasn't your fault," Josh pointed out.

"Sometimes, it might have been," Sam admitted. "But mainly, I think my daddy felt like a big, fat failure. And whenever he felt bad, he took it out on someone weaker, in this case, me."

"Oh."

Sam relaxed. He didn't believe that pop psychology shit, but Josh's face brightened. After warning himself to mind his own business, he couldn't resist asking, "Who's Luigi?"

Josh resumed stroking Rex's fur. "We don't talk about him."

"Okay. But if you ever feel like blowing off steam, man-to-man, your mom knows how to reach me."

They sat quietly again. Sam checked the security situation at *Kinki* on his smartphone. All was well. The silence was companionable, broken occasionally by Josh's questions and Sam's answers. After several minutes, the two women entered the living room.

Josh jumped to his feet. "I'm sorry, Mom. I told him your phone number." His voice was so faint, Sam had to strain to hear him.

"It's okay, Josh," Katie said. "We figured that out."

"You mean you're not angry?" Josh asked in the same tiny voice.

Katie shook her head. Wordlessly, she held out her arms for a hug, and Josh flew into them. "Of course I'm not angry, baby. You thought you were doing the right thing." She kissed the top of her son's head. "I set up my laptop for you in the kitchen so you can work on the science assignment your teacher gave you. The deadline is tomorrow."

Josh plunked his ass on the sofa again. "I don't want to do a dumb assignment."

Katie sighed. "You need better marks. It's important."

A mutinous expression crossed Josh's face. "I don't care what that man thinks."

Sam was pretty sure Josh was talking about Luigi, not his teacher.

Katie flicked a nervous glance at Sam, confirming his suspicions, before she focused on Josh again. "It won't be so bad. I'll help. Science was one of my best subjects at school."

Sam knew how to take a hint. "Okay, I should let y'all get to work." He pushed to his feet and spoke to Josh. "Remember what I told you."

Josh flushed and blinked tears away. His next words were the last thing Sam expected. "I *want* to flunk school. Then the asshole might not want to see either of us again."

Sam pretended he didn't notice the pleading glance the kid flashed in his direction. Hell, no. This was a family matter, nothing to do with him.

Katie raised her voice. "Enough, Joshua. You're grounded until you apologize for your language."

"I don't care. Luigi *is* an asshole," Josh repeated. "He makes you cry all the time."

Bella blocked Sam's path to the door, preventing a fast getaway. "Do something," she hissed. "Josh needs a stricter hand. Apparently, he listens to you."

A bolt of pure terror shot through Sam. This was what happened when a man got himself embroiled in matters that didn't concern him. But Bella was right. Josh shouldn't get away with using cuss words to his mom. It was plain wrong.

Steeling himself, Sam entered the combat zone. When he reached Josh, he bent down, wanting to establish eye contact.

Josh focused his attention on Rex.

"Look at me, please." Sam waited until the kid obeyed before continuing. "Using cuss words to your mom isn't right." He paused, hunting for the right words. "Remember we talked about how people make themselves feel better by being mean?"

Josh nodded slowly.

"Well, when you feel bad inside and take it out on your mom by using a word you know she hates, it may feel real good for a few seconds. I get it. But the good feeling doesn't last. You disrespected someone who loves you. I bet you feel worse now than before."

One tear trickled down Josh's cheek.

Sam rose to his feet. "Don't you think you should apologize?"

Josh catapulted from the sofa and flew to Katie. He threw his arms around her. "I'm sorry, Mom, honest."

Katie said something inarticulate, her nose pink.

Sam waited until the fuss died away and said to Josh, "I want you to do your homework." Ignoring the kid's scowl, he dangled a carrot. "If your mom tells me you finished your homework without a fuss, I'll let you walk Rex next time I come over."

Josh brightened up. "Wow. Really?"

"That's bribery," Katie whispered, "and thanks." Her eyes were soft and liquid with emotion, and that was reward enough for Sam.

His pulse leaped in response, then drummed in his ears as the magnitude of his offer struck home. Damn, but life was spiraling out of control. For a man who never made commitments, when he blew it, he blew it big time. This commitment was to a *kid*, for chrissake. If he failed to follow through with Josh, he'd be exactly like his own daddy. But if he stuck to his promise, Josh would undoubtedly expect advice on how to cope with someone called Luigi. No one was less qualified in the counselling department than yours truly.

"I assume I'll see you bright and early tomorrow," Katie said, apparently unaware of his misgivings as she walked him to the door.

Sam forced a grin. "Yeah." With all his heart, he hoped Josh would forget his offer.

Although Luigi apparently resided in prison, he represented a complication Sam preferred to avoid, especially if he was Josh's daddy. He knew he should write Katie off as dating material. Somehow, he couldn't. Not yet.

But he could Google her.

Chapter 14: Escalating Worries

It was eight o'clock on day four of the job fair. Sam glugged his morning coffee while weaving through the crowd in *Kinki*'s main corridor. He was running late, but not from researching Katie's past as he'd planned. From the little he remembered after leaving her house yesterday afternoon, he'd headed straight to his favorite strip club, hoping to forget the commitment he'd made to a kid he barely knew. Her *son*, for chrissake. Possibly a criminal's son, too. Several shots of Jack Daniel's later, and he'd calmed down enough to focus on the dancers. None of the women was halfway appealing.

On reaching his office, he paused in the corridor to let his room-spins fade before facing Katie. He made good use of the time by dry-swallowing two extra-strength painkillers. In five minutes he'd be fully functioning, able to get a handle on his life, which was flying out of control.

Rallying, he sauntered inside, doing his damndest to adopt his customary swagger.

Katie was perched on the edge of a visitor's chair, jotting notes in her notebook. Today, there was no doubt in his mind she'd changed her appearance. The undertaker suit was gone. In its place, a floaty skirt swirled around her legs, and a matching blouse with contrasting jacket hugged her slender body. One of those stretchy things fastened her hair into a low pony tail.

Classy and utterly sexy at the same time.

He must have made a sound because she abandoned her notes and stared at him in a way that damn near made him forget his name. With calm, deliberate movements, which were an integral part of who she was, she closed her notebook and stuck the pen behind her ear.

"Good morning. Thanks for talking to Josh yesterday." She rewarded him with an uncertain smile, as if to offer thanks for not prying about Luigi.

For one brief moment, Sam got to see her vulnerability. He shelved his questions about Luigi. Taking care not to jiggle his head, he arranged himself in his chair and blinked to bring her into focus. "Hi yourself. You've got a real nice kid."

"Thanks." She examined him and frowned. "You're hung over again."

"A little tired, that's all." To distract her from his condition, he said, "You, on the other hand, look fantastic."

She smoothed silky fabric over what he figured were equally silky thighs. "The outfit's Bella's. She insisted I wear it." She hit him with a luminous smile.

Her scent slid through the air, teasing his senses, leaving him breathless. To hide his reaction, he asked about her evening. Because he was busy fantasizing about kissing her, he had a hard time focusing on her answer.

Which was a description of Josh's science assignment. Every single tiny detail.

He suffered in head-thumping silence while she expounded on the mysteries of wheels and levers, following up with a dissertation on how to make a simple machine with them. She was so delightfully earnest, he managed to grunt in agreement with everything she said. Finally, she stopped talking.

Drifting, he savored the silence until his brain kicked in. She'd asked him a question. A spurt of alarm caused him to lever his eyelids up to half-mast.

"Come again," he croaked.

Katie sighed and crossed one leg over the other, revealing sexy high-heeled sandals. "Sorry to disturb your nap, but which day works best for you?"

"For what?"

"You weren't listening to a word I said." She leaned in closer and studied his face, which he feared had a greenish tint. "You're *totally* hung over."

"Hell, no. Only a couple of beers to help me sleep."

Her nostrils flared, as if smelling his lie. "As I was saying, after you left yesterday, Josh and I had a long talk. Then he did an amazing job on his assignment. He'll probably get an 'A'." When Sam didn't react, her voice sharpened. "Don't tell me you've forgotten you promised Josh he could take Rex for a walk if he did his homework."

A jolt of adrenaline boosted Sam upright in the chair. "Of course I haven't forgotten. How 'bout Sunday?" he suggested, buying himself as much time as he dared. Sunday was four whole days away. By then, the kid might have forgotten his offer. Or accepted a play date. Or developed a positive attitude toward Luigi.

"Thanks. He'll be so excited. It was all he talked about last night." She rewarded him with a smile so brilliant it got his heart pumping faster.

"This dog walking thing is a one-time deal," Sam warned in a feeble attempt to get his life under control again. "Kids make me nervous."

"I don't believe it." She regarded him, sincerity written all over her face. "Whatever you said to Josh yesterday, he thinks you can slay dragons."

Sweat popped out on Sam's forehead, a sure sign it was time to extract himself, the same way he always did when someone got too close for comfort. Saying goodbye was something he excelled at. Sadly, he needed to stick around for his granddaddy's sake.

Unable to think of a better way to give her the hint, he switched on his computer. "Now, if you'll excuse me, I have bills to pay."

She ignored his deliberate brush-off. "Has anyone ever mentioned you have a tendency to develop cold feet?"

"You mean, besides you?"

She flushed, and he knew his barb had hit home, but her prying continued. "Who or what scared you so much you try to hide from real life?" she asked gently.

"My life suits me fine." He didn't want to examine her question too closely. In fact, he needed to change the subject. "Time for you to go plan me a kick-ass grand opening and let me finish the financials." He punctuated his words with rapid mouse clicks, peering desperately at a spreadsheet filling the screen.

After a beat, she took the hint and headed to her desk.

A half hour passed peacefully. Noting from time to time how Katie's glossy pony-tail swung over one shoulder to reveal the sweet curve of her neck, he paid some outstanding invoices. His dwindling bank balance was yet another area of his life that was out of control. Too bad the blackjack tables, so generous in the past, were now inaccessible. *Kinki*'s grand opening had better ease his money worries.

While he worked, Katie made back-to-back phone calls, all on his behalf, to caterers, newspapers, vendors of all sorts, band agents. He couldn't remember the last time anyone went out of their way to help him. After a while, he tuned her out. But each time she received an incoming call, he eavesdropped a few seconds in case this Luigi asshole had tracked her to *Kinki*. When the calls proved to be designers eager to discuss décor issues or suppliers negotiating equipment rentals or deals on toilet paper if ordered in bulk, he felt faintly foolish.

Jealousy was another unpleasant new wrinkle in his life.

Katie's cell phone chimed again. When she answered, her voice became guarded. After a brief silence, she turned her chair away and lowered her head, as if carving herself some privacy. "That's wonderful news." After a long pause, she muttered, "Of course, I'm happy." Another pause. "Yeah. Me too." She ended the call and bowed her head.

Somehow, Sam didn't think she was at all happy about the news. He gave up the pretense of working and rose from his chair. "That was Luigi, wasn't it?" He didn't wait for an a reply. "Do you want me to have a little chat with him."

She sucked in a breath. "Define 'little chat'."

He studied her face, which had drained of color. "Are you okay? "

"Answer my question."

Something was screwy. "Don't worry. All I plan to do is tell Luigi you want him to stop calling." Although he wanted to do more, a whole lot more, the bastard was in prison. Just as well Katie didn't know he knew.

He must have said the right thing, because color returned to her cheeks. "Leave it be. I'm handling it."

Sam was about to suggest a restraining order when his desk phone rang. He stalked over, still watching Katie as he answered, "Jackson."

The voice of the nightclub owner he'd met through one of Martinelli's fundraisers filled his ear. With mounting impatience, Sam listened to a diatribe about reduced profits of nightclubs in the area. When the guy paused for breath, Sam managed to interject, "I'm real busy, Vince. How can I help you?"

He listened in silence, his irritation mounting. As soon as an opening presented itself, Sam said, "Sorry, I have no intention of selling *Kinki*. Have a good day." As he disconnected, he remembered Katie had asked him if anyone wanted to buy his place.

When his phone chimed again, he placed the thought on hold. "Now what?" he barked, expecting to hear Vince's voice again.

"Samuel Jackson?" a woman's voice asked.

"Yes." Sam flicked a glance at Katie, hoping he hadn't handed out his number to a stripper last night.

"I'm calling on behalf of the municipal Department of Building Inspection. Due to a complaint, we've re-scheduled *Kinki*'s final inspection for noon today."

Sam shot out of his chair. "I'm afraid it's terrible timing for me, ma'am." He tightened his grip on the phone, scrambling to find the words to make it go away. "You sound like a nice lady. Isn't there something, anything you can do to help?"

"Impossible. The order came from the top. The complainant must be important. They've assigned Austin Mellow, our toughest inspector, to the case." There was a longish pause before the woman lowered her voice. "I shouldn't tell you this, but Austin knows *Kinki* used to be a fetish club. There's nothing he'd love more than to find a code violation to prevent your place from opening." A sigh travelled across the line. "I'm very sorry, Mr. Jackson. It has to be today at eleven o'clock."

Sam's gut twisted. He promised the woman two tickets to the grand opening for the warning before ending the call.

Katie was already on her feet. "Problems?"

"We have exactly two hours to clean up *Dracula's Lair* and prepare for a building inspection that'll shut us down if we fail to meet building code standards."

Chapter 15: Solutions

Tormented with guilt, Katie circled *Dracula's Lair*, crunching over rubble, while Sam fisted his hands on his hips and surveyed the mess without speaking. She was certain the anonymous informant was Luigi. Who else? And once the building inspector saw the damage, she'd be jobless. Her options were impossible. A return to the family business with its illegal activities was unthinkable, as was marriage to Luigi, while flight would break Ma's heart.

"We can't let a building inspection derail the grand opening," she said, as much for herself as for Sam. "We're both smart people. Let's think."

"It's my own goddamn fault," he muttered. "I thought we had another week before the inspection. I told the construction crew to put the finishing touches on *Mermaids* before fixing the damage to *Dracula's Lair*."

She gestured at the rubble. "The crew can shovel this mess and patch the walls immediately."

"And what about the hole in the middle of the floor? He can't miss it."

"Don't you dare quit. You're too close to the finish line. We'll hide it under a rug."

Sam looked like a man in desperate need of a drink. "That's an ancient trick. It'll never fool an inspector. And this one's chomping at the bit to shut me down."

"Cleanup first, then worry about a strategy."

He looked dubious but appeared to rally, picking up a shovel resting on a wheelbarrow. "I'll start moving rubble, you line up more help." He tossed her his phone. "Rooster's on speed-dial." He rolled up his sleeves and went to work.

She hit speed-dial and spilled the news to Rooster. Listening to the bouncer explain that some lightly-used display coffins had arrived, a solution presented itself.

Unable to hide her excitement, she said, "Round up all our workmen. Have them bring shovels, crow bars, wheelbarrows, and anything else they need to fix this place. Others can haul the coffins in here. And send someone to buy a deluxe makeup kit." She sighed as Rooster questioned her sanity. "I know exactly what I'm doing. Also, invite four or five people who can pull off a dramatic acting job. Oh, and bring plenty of tissues. I'll explain the rest later."

Ignoring Sam's quizzical expression, she hit speed-dial again. When Hiram answered, she summarized the situation and asked him to join them, ending with, "Bring Rex too and some Kanine Krunchies in a sealed baggie. Hurry."

Sam straightened and swiped a forearm across his forehead. "Granddaddy Hiram? Rex? Terrible idea. Mind explaining?"

He looked hot, mussed, and adorable. A smudge of dirt streaked one sculpted cheekbone, and a dribble of sweat disappeared down the neck of his silk shirt.

"It's a brilliant idea," she said, and began talking.

When she'd finished her explanation, she waited for Sam's reaction. He didn't answer immediately. At last, he said, "That idea is beyond genius. It's diabolical."

***

Fifteen minutes later, Katie found herself standing in the corridor outside *Dracula's Lair*, in awe at the speed and efficiency of the cleanup. If not for Sam's leadership skills, the room would still be a disaster. Under his guidance the men worked their butts off. Before long, with much bantering peppered with insults and profanity, the cleanup and repair were completed. Only the caskets were missing.

Sam loped to Katie's side, astonishing her with a damp and delicious bear hug. "I owe you. This was your idea."

The force of his animal magnetism hit her like a sledgehammer. Fortunately, Rooster's arrival saved her from doing something dumb like wrapping her legs around his waist. Four bejeweled women, all wearing false eyelashes, gobs of makeup, low-cut gowns, and six-inch stilettos accompanied him. Rex followed on their heels, tugging Hiram along.

Rooster announced, "Look who I found in *The Undead Zone*, rehearsing their act for the grand opening. *Queenz in Concert* in the flesh. These ladies are naturals for dramatic acting. Plus they have makeup." He displayed a cosmetic case the size of a suitcase.

Introductions revealed that the performers, namely Shannon Easy, Lotta Promises, Eileen D'Over, and Tess Tosterone, were either men in drag or transgenders.

Katie noted with amusement that Hiram stopped eying their chests in a big hurry.

With her team assembled, Katie launched into a description of the acting job.

When she stopped talking, applause filled the room. The excitement was exhilarating. So this was how a normal person experienced life—laughing, camaraderie, having fun. She made a mental note to do it more often.

In his enthusiasm, Sam wrapped his arms around Katie and hugged her. The scent of soap, sweat, and Sam enveloped her, sending her into a frenzy of lust.

Apparently unaware of the excitement building in her fun zone, he let go and addressed the group. "Y'all have instructions. I'm babysitting the building inspector, so I won't be here until the show begins."

Everyone nodded. Lotta gestured to the makeup kit. "We'll make Hiram look like the real deal."

Hiram glowed with satisfaction. "I love being the star performer." He stepped aside to let a worker roll the first of four caskets into *Dracula's Lair*. "Hot damn, this'll be better than my time in the rodeo ring."

Katie gave Hiram's arm a squeeze of encouragement. "Remember, no moving or talking. And keep the plastic baggie of Kanine Krunchies sealed until the last possible moment."

Hiram scrutinized a second casket trundling past. "Sweet. That one's mine. It's real shiny."

She nodded her approval. "Nice choice."

Sam addressed the workmen. "Place this coffin in the middle of the room. Make sure it hides the hole in the floor."

Eileen tossed her hair, sending her Cher wig's shiny dark locks swinging. "I hope the building inspector's a hottie. If he's cute enough, I might talk him into a date."

Lotta fluttered her hand. "Not if I get to him first."

"Dear Lord." Sam narrow-eyed each of the Queens. "Do not, I repeat *not*, come on to the building inspector. He's too straitlaced to handle it, and I need his signature on the dotted line before *Kinki* can open."

"Fine," Shannon said, pouting. "But you're a big meanie. The most prudish men in public are the ones who like being spanked in private."

"Hey, people." Katie clapped her hands to re-focus the cast's attention on the matter at hand. Once everyone stopped talking, she pumped her fist in the air and yelled the words she'd always dreamed of saying.

"Let's rock 'n' roll."

Over hand-clapping and laughter, the faint echo of high heels grew louder. A shout caused everyone to stop talking. All heads swiveled as Deanna bustled around the corner and zeroed in on Sam. The woman wore a low-cut red number, which, in Katie's opinion, was totally unsuitable for the office.

"Thank goodness I found you." Deanna twirled a strand of blonde hair, ignoring everyone except Sam. Her breasts heaved, demanding and receiving attention. "I overheard Rooster talking about the building inspection, so I've been trying to find you."

"Why?"

"There's been more vandalism."

***

Sam halted inside *Mermaids*. Knowing what to expect didn't stop him from feeling as though he'd been sucker-punched. Katie and Deanna would catch up soon enough. For now, he was alone with despair and his guilt.

With Martinelli's surveillance detail in place, he'd assumed it was safe to leave his granddaddy at home last night while he hit the town. Big mistake.

What the hell happened to the promised surveillance?

Water gushed from a ragged hole in the ceiling. Even if they closed the shutoff valve immediately, the dripping would continue for several hours. The good news—and it was a stretch to call it good news—was that the water was clean and had mostly landed in the oversized martini glass.

Sam groaned aloud. Who was he kidding? This was a disaster. Nothing would dry in time for the inspection. His dream was over before it began.

The click of footsteps gave him enough time to pull himself together before Katie and Deanna caught up with him. He hated the tension evident on Katie's face. She'd been amazing at *Dracula's Lair*. Too bad her brilliant scheme wouldn't save *Kinki*.

Keeping his voice neutral, he said, "What happened here, Deanna?"

Deanna flapped her hands. "Someone tore apart the HR powder room. The vandal must have cracked a pipe."

Sam raked his fingers through his hair. "I didn't install cameras in the washrooms."

Katie whirled on Sam. "This is a minor setback. We won't let it stop us." Her voice vibrated with determination.

She was magnificent, a born leader. He liked the way she said "we" as if they were a team. An unaccustomed warmth spread throughout his body. He refused to fold without a fight. Katie wasn't the only one who thought outside the box.

"You're right. I won't let the inspection close us," he said with growing confidence.

Katie reached out and gave his fingers a squeeze. "I knew you'd think of something. How can we help?"

Forcing himself to focus on priorities, he said, "Deanna, have a workman haul all the filing cabinets inside the powder room to hide the toilet and sink. Then fill the entire space with boxes, supplies, and binders. Make it tidy. If the inspector checks inside, all he'll see is storage space."

"Nice call." Katie nodded with approval as Deanna hustled away. "Very creative."

"Thank you. I try."

"You've thought of a way to handle the water damage in here, haven't you?" She waved her hand around *Mermaids*.

He refused to disappoint her, especially when her eyes glowed with trust. Concentrating on muscle relaxation, he sucked in a deep breath and let it out slowly. The idea, when it occurred to him, was so obvious, he should have thought of it sooner.

"There's a way to fool him, but it won't work unless you agree."

"I'll do whatever it takes."

He grasped both her hands in his, marveling at their softness, and waited a beat. "Have you ever dreamed of being a mermaid?"

Chapter 16: The Great Casket Caper

Sam steered Austin Mellow along the corridor. *Kinki*'s inspection was nearing completion. Only *Dracula's Lair* and *Mermaids* remained to pass muster. The building inspector was short, balding, and plain mean. So far, all the charm in the world hadn't thawed his attitude. The man's frustration with the lack of code violations so far was tangible. Mellow quivered with eagerness to close *Kinki* for good.

As they approached *Dracula's Lair*, Sam's pulse kicked up a notch. Taking a deep breath, he ushered Mellow inside saying, "*Dracula's Lair* is my favorite theme room. Note the clever use of coffins. Next week, dummy corpses will arrive. I'm told they'll be so realistic, they will fool even a mortician."

Inside the threshold, Mellow halted. "Shit," he squeaked. "That *is* a real corpse."

Hiding a grin, Sam followed him inside. A platform constructed over the hole supported a gleaming casket containing an occupant. Black tablecloths from *Inferno* concealed the platform and puddled on the floor.

Sam had to admit, Rooster made a convincing preacher as he delivered a knockout eulogy. A black vampire wig hid the scarlet topknot while a black wizard's robe concealed the rest of Rooster. Shannon Easy's large gold cross dangled around his neck. Sam guessed the clerical collar was fashioned from cardboard.

While Rooster droned on, Sam approached the guest of honor, getting up close and personal. He swallowed hard. Stretched out in the casket, arms crossed over his chest, Granddaddy Hiram looked pale, ghastly, and way too convincing for comfort. Beneath closed eyes, purplish shadows resembled faint bruises.

Rex snoozed peacefully.

Clustered around the casket, the four Queenz vocalized their grief. As soon as the newcomers entered, wails and sobs grew in intensity. Real tears streamed down their cheeks, leaving trails of mascara. They knew their method acting.

Rooster stopped in mid-eulogy and cleared his throat.

Rex immediately scrambled to his feet. His nose quivered as he sniffed the air. The dog's long, quavering howl made Sam shiver, even though he knew Rooster's cough was the signal for Granddaddy Hiram to crack open the Kanine Krunchie baggie.

Sam checked out Mellow's reaction and hid a satisfied grin. The man's eyes bugged out of his head.

White-knuckling his clipboard, Mellow made a shaky note before glaring at Sam. "May I ask what's going on here, Mr. Jackson?"

"Aw, tarnation." Sam whacked himself on the forehead. "In the excitement of a surprise inspection, I plumb forgot old Hiram's funeral was today."

Rooster gave them a disapproving frown and raised his voice to an evangelical pitch. "As I was saying before the interruption, Hiram lived a rich and full life. In all the years I knew him, he never missed a Rodeo Nite at *Kinki*. Words cannot express how much those little ponies will miss his discipline."

Mellow's breath grew audible. A pink tongue flicked out to moisten narrow lips. He whispered, "I heard about those Rodeo Nites where people pretended to be ponies and their handlers whipped the disobedient ones." Catching himself, he frowned and added, "Pure depravity, of course."

Sam nodded. "Disgusting. We're remodeling *Kinki* to eliminate all traces of corruption."

Shannon Easy wailed, "Poor Hiram, may his soul rest in peace, worked magic with his riding crop. What'll we do now that he's gone?"

"Outrageous," the inspector hissed. "Funerals in fetish clubs are surely illegal."

Sam smiled to himself. He'd been expecting the objection. "Well now, that's a common misconception, but home funerals are legal in New Jersey." He paused when Shannon's sobbing drowned him out. Lotta Promises joined in, causing him to raise his voice. "First of all, *Kinki* is no longer a fetish club, but when it was, Hiram considered it his home. He couldn't bear to leave, so I let him continue to live in his upstairs apartment."

Katie had recited every clause of the legislation to him. Come to think of it, she knew a hell of a lot about the ins-and-outs of funerals.

By then, all four Queenz were blubbering at a high decibel range. Sequins flashed. Rhinestones glittered. Augmented bosoms heaved. Tess Tosterone restrained a sobbing Eileen D'Over from throwing herself onto the corpse by wrapping a pair of muscular arms around her. When one hand landed on the swell of a surgically enhanced breast and cupped it, Sam noted Eileen's moans grew more insistent.

"Hiram taught me everything I know," Tess wailed, placing a riding crop in the coffin. "This is my favorite whip. I hope it will give Hiram pleasure wherever he's going."

"Outrageous." Mellow's gaze followed every move with avid interest.

From the corner of his eye, Sam caught Rex sniffing the air. He tensed in anticipation.

The dog exceeded expectations. Catapulting himself at the coffin while uttering a mournful howl, Rex's front paws scrabbled at the padding beside Hiram's chest.

Mellow backed away. "The damn beast wants to jump into the coffin."

Rex licked his chops with a large, pink tongue.

Blocked by two Queenz and a preacher, Sam could only watch as the dog gathered his powerful hindquarters in preparation for the leap. Eileen must have noticed too because she threw off Lotta's grip and flung herself onto the coffin.

Foiled, Rex settled back with a low whine. Strings of drool puddled the floor beside him.

"Shut the fuck up, all of you!" Rooster's bellow silenced everyone.

As if nothing had happened, he pasted on a pious expression and wrapped up the eulogy. "In conclusion, dear friends and pony-girls, Hiram would want us to remember the great moments we shared with him. The spankings, the humiliations, the whippings." He raised his arms in benediction. "Hiram may be gone, but his memory will live on in all of us forever. Amen."

"Amen," the mourners echoed. Tess leaned forward allowing the neckline of her dress to gape wider, displaying most of a fine rack that had obviously seen surgical intervention.

The inspector licked his lips while staring at her cleavage. He was breathing like a winded racehorse.

After a moment of silence, Rooster announced, "Party time."

"Where?" Mello asked, practically salivating.

Rooster flashed Sam a look of desperation. "My place. After we plant Hiram."

Unbelievable! Mellow was hoping for an invitation. Sam coughed discreetly. "We're nearing the end of our tour, Sir. Unless you have questions, I suggest we proceed to *Mermaids*, our flagship bar. If we're lucky, we may catch a preview of an act we call *Immortal Mermaids*."

Mellow' grin was pure, unrestrained lechery. "Lead the way."

Chapter 17: Memorable Aquatics

Approaching footsteps clattered a warning to Katie as she waited inside *Mermaids*. In response, her entire body, from the top of her scalp to the tips of her toes, jerked from the waves of tension surging through it. *Kinki*'s future hinged on her performance. She slid into the frigid water and shuddered. Her heart slammed against the sides of her chest with such force she feared an explosion.

Why, oh why, had she been dumb enough to agree to Sam's insane idea? Two summers as a wading pool lifeguard hardly qualified her as a synchronized swimmer. Desperation had made her agree to stripping down to her underwear and hopping into a giant martini glass filled with icy water, all to distract a building inspector from noticing code violations.

The thought of being next-to-naked in a glorified aquarium triggered a brief hyperventilation episode. She wrestled her emotions under control. A floating corpse wasn't the distraction Sam needed. Luckily, her secret indulgence was great underwear. Ever since her social life had evaporated, thanks to Luigi, seductive lingerie was all she had left to make her feel desirable as a woman. Today's choice was a red thong with matching push-up bra.

As the footsteps drew louder, she recognized Sam's voice describing *Mermaids*. Arranging stiff facial muscles into a smile so broad it surely exposed her gum line plus a couple of molars, she pushed away from the glass while executing an eggbeater kick.

Two figures entered the bar. The short guy with a bad comb-over must be the inspector. Mellow confirmed her guess by charging toward her semi-naked body, halting at the foot of the stage and staring at the vicinity of her boobs. At least he was oblivious of the ceiling damage, more-or-less concealed by black helium balloons.

Katie scanned Sam's face searching for a sign of the mock funeral's success.

He gave her a surreptitious thumbs-up. "Welcome to an *Immortal Mermaids* rehearsal."

Mellow's ragged breathing was audible in the empty bar. She feared he'd vault onto the stage and press his nose against the glass.

After a brief exchange with Mellow, Sam shouted, "My guest informs me he appreciates your aquatic skill."

Mellow waggled his fingers at her. "Please. Call me Austin. I'm a bona fide Atlantic City patron of the arts." Air whistled through his nostrils.

Katie trod water like crazy. "I'm Katarina." Crap. Mellow had one foot on the stairs.

Sam's next move took her by surprise. Using a combination of charm, flattery, and good-natured teasing, he diverted Mellow's charge for the stage and coaxed him over to one of the ringside tables for what he called a broader perspective of the artistic performance.

The force of Katie's relief caused her to sink. She promptly took in a lungful of water. Surfacing, she sputtered before regaining focus. The easiest way to begin, she reasoned, would be with an exaggerated backstroke.

Once her ears were immersed, their voices became a soothing background noise as she concentrated on her rusty backstroke.

A wolf whistle penetrating her peaceful world caused her to lose her Zen. Still swimming, she raised her head slightly in time to catch Austin's reaction.

"This act is much better than I expected." His voice quivered with excitement.

"I doubt *that*'s supposed to be part of the act."

Sam's booming voice alerted her to trouble. Blinking to clear her vision, she squeaked. One nipple had escaped its tiny push-up cup and aimed its puckered tip aloft.

"Hey, let's get closer."

Ears buzzing, Katie flipped over. Presenting her butt to the ceiling, she executed a duck dive. It wasn't a synchronized skill, but from the muffled cheering on the surface, it appeared Mellow wasn't a purist. Only then did she remember the thong.

Oh, God. Take me now.

She tucked everything, such as it was, back into place. After a while, her lungs threatened to explode. She popped to the surface.

Mellow was jogging toward her. Apparently, lack of skill coupled with insufficient boobage did nothing to deter him. It was a wonder the heat of his gaze didn't blister her skin.

Sam, whose trademark grin appeared a little ragged around the edges, captured Mellow's arm and whispered in his ear. She caught the words, "free tickets" and "topless" before submerging again.

When she surfaced, both men had resumed their seats. She splashed her way through her routine, executing a few wobbly leg-lifts interspersed with some crisscrosses that missed the mark. As a grand finale, she attempted a Vertical. It ended up being more of a Horizontal.

Applause and a prolonged wolf whistle rewarded her performance. Both men were on their feet. Based on Sam's grim expression, she guessed the inspector refused to depart.

Mellow said, "If this was a rehearsal, I can't wait to see the real thing."

"You're so sweet," she replied through clenched teeth. "Our opening act is much better. Three times better, to be exact, because there'll be three mermaids. And when we remove our clamshell tops during the grand finale—" She broke off in mock confusion. "Oh, dear. I hope I haven't spoiled the surprise."

Sam clapped a hand on Mellow's back. "I'm sure Mr. Mellow will keep our little secret."

"Yes." Mellow appeared to have difficulty squeezing out the word due to some heavy-duty breathing.

While the inspector ignored everything but her body, Sam gestured frantically at the ceiling before drawing his finger across his throat in a gesture of doom.

She glanced up. Her mouth went dry. Caught in a cross-draught from the industrial fan drying the place out, the black balloons floated wild and free, bobbing away from the gaping hole. Any second now, the motion would capture Austin's attention. If she didn't distract him, it would be game over.

Katie drew on inner reservoirs of determination. *Kinki* must pass the inspection, and she would do everything in her power to make it happen. To capture Mellow's attention, she blew him a kiss and waved.

In response, his nostrils flared. Sweat beaded his brow.

Channeling her inner Marilyn Monroe, Katie trotted out her breathiest voice. "Austin deserves a brief preview of our grand opening act." Fingering the front closure of her bra, she favored the inspector with her sultriest smile. "But only if everyone sits down like good boys."

Mellow appeared to be having difficulty speaking. And sitting. While staring at her chest, he gave a vigorous nod and eased down into the chair with obvious discomfort. His gaze was so heated, she expected him to self-combust.

"Sit," Mellow hissed at Sam.

Sam's eyebrows slammed together. "There's no way she can—"

This, from the man who spent his leisure moments in strip clubs? Before he blew it, she trilled, "Oh, Sam. I'm certain Austin's interest is purely artistic. A patron of the arts appreciates the skill and originality of the act, not the nudity."

She planned to stay underwater. Plus there wasn't a whole lot to see.

Mellow said, "If the act's as good as I think it'll be, I'll sign the inspection report today."

Sam didn't look the least bit happy. On the contrary, his expression was dialed to pissed. After a lengthy hesitation, he sat.

She backpedalled into the middle of the martini glass and submerged until water lapped around her mouth. Taking note of Sam's glacial expression, she unlatched her bra and slipped it off. Treading water like crazy, she twirled the garment overhead like a red flag.

Her strategy worked. There was a commotion in the audience as Mellow scrambled to his feet. "I gotta get closer," he said.

Sam's chair clattered as he, too, leaped to his feet, blocking Mellow. "We don't allow any audience member onto the stage during a performance. It's our policy."

Mellow gave him a sly glance. "I'm sure Katarina won't mind making one tiny exception."

"There are no exceptions." Sam's eyes were pure savagery, promising a world of hurt.

Katie's pulse scrambled. Sam was spoiling her plan. A quick glance told her the balloons were directly behind the men's heads. Another minute, and they'd be out of sight. Until then, it was up to her to capture Mellow's undivided attention.

She waggled her fingers and swam away.

The prospect of unfettered boob gave Mellow unexpected agility. He ducked under Sam's restraining arm and sprinted up the stairs to press his nose against the glass. At least he wasn't checking out the ceiling, she told herself, gazing around wildly for Sam.

She found him at the foot of the stairs, his phone held to his ear. Not that she wanted him to ogle her breasts in public, but small breasts were obviously of no interest to a man who received private lap dances from double-D stripper twins.

She glanced up. The balloons were bobbing along nicely.

Wrapping her arms around her chest, her bra clutched in a death grip, she kicked her feet, revolving ever-so-slowly. Mellow circled along beside her, undoubtedly hoping for a full frontal sighting. Sam took the stairs two at a time to position himself beside Mellow.

She ignored both men and focused on the balloons.

After an eternity, the balloons bumped against the far wall. Mission accomplished. She signaled Sam with a meaningful chin jerk, confident that Mellow wouldn't notice anything above her shoulders.

Sam gave a barely-perceptible nod.

Relief flooded Katie. The rest was up to Sam, and he'd better hurry or her muscles would cramp from the cold.

Sam tapped the inspector on the arm. "Mr. Mellow? We need to talk."

Katie's heart pumped a little harder. Sam had her back.

The horny little man didn't reply. His attention was riveted on her twirling body.

Katie shivered from the icy water. It wasn't easy producing a bright grin around chattering teeth.

Sam raised his voice. "Mr. Mellow. Your office called to remind you of your next appointment."

Mellow checked his watch and jumped as if he'd been stung by a wasp. "Crap, I mean goodness me. I had no idea it was so late." His forehead crumpled.

Sam said, "No problem. While you were admiring the act, I took the liberty of asking my HR manager to see you out. I hope you don't mind." He paused. "She's bringing two free tickets to the grand opening, which, of course, features *Immortal Mermaids*."

Crouched in the water, Katie shivered harder. She was approaching hypothermia when Deanna, with her red dress and exposed cleavage, made her grand entrance. Austin's eyes bugged out of his head. Never looking away from Deanna's boobs, he scribbled his signature on the inspection report and handed Sam his copy. Pocketing the tickets, he smiled happily and trotted off with Deanna.

Once Mellow disappeared, Katie struggled to untwist her sodden bra. Her fingers refused to work properly. The scrap of cloth remained defiantly knotted.

Sam's head and shoulders materialized above the rim. "I have a towel. First, I'll haul you out, no peeking, naturally. Then, you'll go into the ladies' room and get warm."

"L-look all you want," she said around chattering teeth, "but be quick or I'm an icicle."

He enveloped her shivering body in a gloriously cozy towel. His gaze seared her face. "What you did back there," he used a finger to dab a drip from the tip of her nose, "was one of the bravest, most unselfish things anyone has ever done for me. Once you're dressed, I have a surprise for you."

Her heart raced. Unless she was mistaken, his I-wanna-do-you expression promised pure, unadulterated, sensual pleasure.

Chapter 18: Revelations

Inferno's ladies' room was sumptuous enough for a reigning monarch. Surrounded in scented warmth, Katie sat at a sleek wood-and-glass vanity and admired the beveled-glass mirror.

It was decision time.

She closed her eyes to block out distractions. Sure, Luigi's phone call this morning with the news that his release was probable had thrust her into panic mode. She now saw his announcement for what it was—wishful thinking on his part. The same way he persisted in calling her his fiancée.

But the threat of his imminent freedom was a wakeup call. She deserved that orgasm, dammit, and she intended to go for it. Hey, she wasn't looking for commitment. All she wanted was truly excellent sex, and Sam was the perfect candidate, being the sexiest man she'd ever met, plus a highly experienced swordsman.

Shouldn't I worry about a broken heart?

Not worried. Nope. Not even a little bit. As a professional mortician, she was skilled at protecting her heart. Detachment was an essential quality, and she had it in spades.

Besides, this might be her last opportunity.

Arguing with herself, she opened her eyes and switched on the hairdryer. Bending at the waist, she dried her hair, letting the warmth smooth her emotions along with her hair. Several minutes later, she straightened, feeling clear-headed and confident. If everything went the way she intended, she would round out her day with the first orgasm of her life.

The pleasurable shiver vibrating through every cell of her body told her she'd made the right decision.

If Sam wanted answers, she wouldn't lie. She just might not tell him *everything*, like the part where Luigi insisted he was her fiancé. Or how any day now, he might be released. And especially not how she feared he might kill anyone who dated her.

Squelching the murmur of protest from her conscience, she tossed the fluffy towel into a hamper and dressed quickly. Stuffing her still-damp underwear into her purse, Katie made sure everything else was tucked in, zipped closed, and buttoned up. Winding her hair into a tight knot, she clipped it into place before glancing in the mirror.

Voilá Katie-the-Mortician.

She gave herself a mental head-thunk. It had been so long since she'd dared to look attractive, she'd almost forgotten how to find her sexy.

Removing the hair clip, she used her fingers to fluff the heavy waves framing her face. Slowly, deliberately, she undid her top button and examined the effect. Better, but not enough. On went Candi Coral lip gloss and a slick of blusher, then the big guns, a double layer of mascara and a spritz of complimentary *Florabotanica*.

On emerging from the ladies room, the sight of Sam in the waiting area caused her heart to pump a whole lot harder. He had a way of devouring a woman with his gaze, a way of tilting his head a fraction, as if absorbing her essence. Perfectly at ease, his long, lean, and most excellent frame unfolded from a dove-gray loveseat. His eyes gleamed with purpose. He strode toward her and handed her a steaming mug.

The sweet fragrance of chocolate and cinnamon filled her nostrils. "Thank you," she murmured. Lowering her lashes, she sipped her hot chocolate, feeling the weight of his scrutiny as he gave her a slow onceover. Oh, yeah. Good things were happening.

"You're gorgeous," he said, his voice low and husky. "You've changed something."

Heat circled her body, and it wasn't caused by the scalding drink. "Nope. Same old me."

Crap, she was terrible at flirting. To make conversation, she said, "Thank goodness Mellow's office called to check on him or I'd still be in the pool, floating face down."

"I lied. No one called."

"But I saw you talking on the phone."

A smile made his cheeks crease in the sexiest way. "Your teeth were chattering, so I called Deanna and asked her to escort Mellow out."

Sam's empathy was hard to ignore, but it would make leaving all the more difficult for her. "Oh. Well. Thanks again."

"It's time for your surprise. Let's blow this place for a couple of hours."

There it was again. Understanding. Kindness.

She tried the little distancing mind-trick she used as a coping strategy with the bereaved and assessed her feelings. Nope. Still liking him.

"Sounds great," she said. What's the surprise?"

"A ride on The Boardwalk. You need sunshine and fresh air to counteract the sleaze. And while we play hooky, you'll tell me those deep, dark secrets you're hiding." He settled his Stetson on the back of his head. "I'm particularly interested in Luigi."

And there was the buzz-kill.

***

Sitting side by side in one of Atlantic City's rolling chairs, they trundled along the Boardwalk. A canvas privacy partition separated them from the college student jogging along behind, propelling the vehicle.

Sam appeared so happy, so carefree, so *attentive*, Katie's hopes for a happy ending made a cautious re-appearance. It was difficult to sustain her sexy, she discovered, while acting as tour guide and simultaneously trying to scan the pedestrians for signs of danger such as a thug hefting a bazooka or maybe a pair of assassins waving hunting knives.

Dragging her attention back to Sam, she forced her shoulders to relax. "The Boardwalk is four miles long," she informed him.

Yeah, real sexy.

Their attendant swerved around a steel band hammering out *Everything's Gonna Be Alright*. She bounced against Sam. Her hands itched to reach for him, but she forced herself to straighten. Not knowing what else to do or say, she continued her spiel.

He shifted closer. They were arm-to-arm, shoulder-to shoulder. Electricity shot right to her important bits. A slight smile quirked his lips. Yeah, he knew.

Continuing her nervous chatter, she remained watchful for hitmen while pointing out landmarks. Sam was a great audience. He hadn't seen much of Atlantic City outside of casinos, bars, and strip joints, surprise, surprise. Every word she spoke appeared to fascinate him, even if he occasionally glanced at his smartphone. The first time it happened, he said, "Keep talking. I'm an accomplished multi-tasker. I can listen, enjoy a beautiful woman, and check in on my granddaddy at the same time."

Oh, boy. What other man took such tender care of an elderly relative?

If she dwelt on Sam's kind heart, she'd be in deep trouble. All she wanted was one fabulous orgasm. Surely, it wasn't too much to ask.

The attendant slowed to let a group of students cross in front of them. They looked carefree, untroubled by fear their date might be murdered. She'd forgotten what that kind of freedom felt like.

Once they sped up, she sensed Sam's impatience in his body posture. The interrogation was imminent. Before he could ask the opening question, she forced chirpiness back into her voice. "Enough about me. It's your turn. Tell me about yourself."

He replied readily enough. "Two dysfunctional parents, a lunatic granddaddy, and a bossy older brother. Big brother Nick was the perfect child, conscientious and responsible, always picking up the pieces, while I spent my time chasing girls, fooling around, and generally being a nuisance."

"So even then, you spelled trouble."

"Now that you mention it, yeah. It was my way of rebelling. Nothing I ever did was good enough for Eugene—that's my daddy, bless his heart, but damned if he deserves the title. He was always too busy to waste time with his family. If he ever attended a Thanksgiving dinner or a family birthday, I don't remember it. Ma told us he had an important job with late hours and frequent business trips, but I always wondered if there was more to it."

Sam's lips tightened and he turned his head, either because they were overtaking a pair of sexy showgirls in six-inch stilettos or if he was overcome with emotion.

She chose to go with door number two. "It must have been tough on your whole family. What about your mother?"

He turned toward her again, his face impassive. "Ma's a Southern belle. Divorce was a nasty word in her family. She coped with Eugene by hitting the social circuit hard and the juleps harder. Nick pretty much raised me while minding Granddaddy Hiram at the same time."

Katie's heart melted. Sensing deep hurt behind Sam's words, she changed the subject. "I noticed a computer science degree and a Harvard MBA hanging in your office. You did something right at university."

"Computers are fun, more like puzzle-solving than real work. Plus, my girlfriends did my assignments."

"Of course they did." She pictured cat-fights over who would write his essays.

He laughed, looking a tiny bit smug and, well, damn. Hot. Extremely hot.

"You're judging me, aren't you?" he asked.

"Little bit." Refusing to be sidetracked, she steered the conversation to his school years. "Since you didn't study or attend class, how did you spend your time?"

He started to answer, but stopped and sniffed the air. "Hold the thought. What do I smell?"

She inhaled the aroma of hot oil and deep-fried dough. "Funnel cakes. They're a seaside specialty."

"We need those."

"No we don't. There's a nice fruit stand up the way."

"I'm getting some." He motioned the attendant to stop, then hopped out to join the lineup at a food truck.

She frowned. Pop had suffered his fatal heart attack after scarfing down three funnel cakes. But why object? Sugar and fat would put Sam in the right mood, and she'd be long gone before death by funnel cake struck.

Two minutes later, he climbed inside balancing two paper-wrapped pastries. Rather than argue, she accepted the one he handed her. They started up again.

His mouth curved slightly as he sniffed the treat. "Grease, carbs, and sugar. My favorite food groups. Now where were we?" He took a bite.

"University days." She hoped she sounded casual.

He swallowed his mouthful. "Let's see. When I wasn't playing with computers, I mostly spent my days cutting classes and sleeping off hangovers. Too bad we didn't have funnel cakes at university. They'd have been an amazing hangover cure."

"And your nights?" she prompted. Unthinking, she took a bite of funnel cake. Damn, but it was delicious.

"I played bridge. I'm a good player, so people paid me to be their partner. Sometimes I hitched a ride to the nearest casino, and, oh yeah, I dated lots of women."

Of course he did.

They finished their funnel cakes, at least he did. She tucked the remains of hers into her purse for later. Funnel cake craving was a secret she'd take to the grave.

Katie licked the last of the sugar from her fingers. "I know you won enough money gambling to buy *Kinki*." She paused as they wheeled under an archway and past the ornate façade of the Trump Taj Mahal. "But is it true all the casinos in the region banned you from playing?"

He frowned, but didn't answer right away. "Granddaddy Hiram has a big mouth. I told him never to breathe a word of my card counting to anyone. Good job I love him."

"He's proud of you. He told me you put yourself through university by designing computer games."

Sam's face softened. "No kidding? I had no idea he remembered. Yeah, it's true. I loved the challenge, the creativity. Eugene, on the other hand, referred to my games as useless pieces of shit." He took a long breath. "Did you know my game, *Last Ghoul Standing*, was my inspiration for turning *Kinki* into a paranormal nightclub?"

This news surprised her so much, she stopped scanning the crowd for danger and stared at him. "How wonderful. With your imagination and technical skill, I'm surprised you didn't choose game software development as your career path."

Sam blew out a long breath. "You're beginning to sound like big brother Nick and Granddaddy Hiram."

Okay, so she'd hit a nerve. Nice going. She changed the subject. "Tell me about Hiram."

Sam's shoulders relaxed marginally. "My granddaddy used to ride the rodeos. A bull-riding accident damaged his brain's impulse control center. There's no filter between his thoughts and his actions. He moved into our place when, let's see, I was three, so he must have been around fifty, because he couldn't live alone."

"Hiram's not really your boss, is he?"

Sam's smile was a little naughty. "So you figured it out, did you? He cashed in all his retirement savings to invest in *Kinki*. That makes him my partner but most definitely not my boss. Until we turn a profit, he's my responsibility."

Her throat tightened as she remembered Sam's patience with the eccentric old man. "You try to hide your kindness," she murmured, "but it shows. You're a good man."

She knew he was moved because his face turned a shade darker under his tan. He ran one finger over her cheek. "Sugar."

A sizzle zapped through her body. "Pardon?"

"You're covered in sugar."

His face was so close she could see dark gold flecks dancing in his irises. Then he was staring at her mouth. Although the seduction had taken its time gaining momentum, it appeared to be underway. Feeling slightly dizzy, she dabbed her face with a napkin. "Gone?"

He smoothed a napkin over her cheek, "Careful or you'll remove the top layer of skin." His drawl was smokier than usual. "Let's get out and stretch our legs, shall we?"

"Here?"

She tried to hide her dismay. They were pulling up to one of Luigi's restaurants. Once they abandoned the rolling chair, anyone might recognize her.

"Sure. *Ristorante Katarina* looks good. It's got a great name."

Yeah. Over her objection, Luigi had named it after her. The last thing she wanted was to dine at a place where chefs, servers, and patrons might recognize her.

Before she could object, Sam stuck his head around the partition and asked the attendant to stop. The vehicle parked in front of her namesake. Her heart sank as Sam hopped out and pressed a few bills into the attendant's hand with a promise of more on their return. She had no choice but to follow.

"Let's go somewhere else." She walked at warp speed in the opposite direction.

He caught up with her. "Why? That restaurant looks great."

"Bad reviews. Something about cockroaches." She glanced over her shoulder to see if anyone was staring. Feeling all-too-recognizable, she squinted at him. "I forgot my sunglasses. Could I borrow your hat?"

"Sure thing." He placed his hat on her head. "It suits you."

"Thanks." She tilted the brim to hide her face and hurried on.

He strode easily beside her. "You're sprinting,"

She slowed to a brisk trot. "There's a great seafood shack near the beach. I have a craving for fish tacos."

Sam's inspection was unnerving. "You've been as jumpy as a caged squirrel all afternoon. Does it, by any chance, have anything to do with Luigi?"

She hurried on, pretending she hadn't heard his question.

***

Twenty minutes later, Katie found herself seated at a picnic table beside Sam while he polished off her last fish taco. Every other diner at *Tito's Fish Shack* had disappeared, taking with them her last hope of avoiding his questions. Although he'd maintained a relaxed banter during their meal, she sensed his impatience. His trip to the counter for more lemonade gave her a reprieve, which she put to good use, checking for lurking assassins under tables.

She was peering underneath the farthest picnic table when Sam's soft voice made her jump. "You lose something?"

She leaped to her feet and dusted her hands on her skirt, hoping her guilt didn't show. "My, my. Aren't you the quiet one? I was looking for my, uh, napkin. It blew over here." She hustled back to her seat.

He placed the drinks on the picnic table before picking a twig out of her hair and straightening the hat. Next, he sat directly across from her.

She adjusted the hat to sit low on her forehead, hopefully hiding her expression.

"It's time." He reached across the table to tilt the hat back again. "Tell me everything."

She chewed her bottom lip, deliberating about which facts to reveal.

Before she spoke, he jumped in. "Let me make this easier for you. I've already figured out you were a mortician, but there's plenty more you're hiding. I was an idiot not to do my due diligence before now, but I've been busy. I intend to Google you once we get back."

So he'd figured out her former career. Happily, he didn't appear put off. "My parents were first generation Italian-Americans. They owned and operated *Paradise Gate Funeral Haven and Crematorium*. Now my brother does. I'm the oldest of three, with one irresponsible brother and one beauty queen sister who ran away at age eighteen and only returned home recently. The youngest two were too much for my parents to handle on top of the business, so I made myself indispensable. I helped with chores, homework, cooking, you name it. I became a fixer, meddler, efficiency expert, and advice-giver."

She flicked a glance at Sam to gauge his reaction. And found herself snared by the sheer intensity of his unwavering scrutiny.

He shook his head. "Kinda like my brother, Nick. No wonder you're bossy. That kind of responsibility is tough. How was it at school?"

"Mostly, it sucked. The kids in elementary school called me 'Morticia' and begged to play in the embalming room because they wanted to see scary things. Stuff like that."

"No wonder you hate the name. And in high school?"

"Boys were afraid to date me because—" She broke off in confusion.

"What were they afraid of?"

"It's stupid." She took a long gulp of lemonade. She couldn't believe she'd almost told Sam the boys stayed away because Luigi terrified them. She forced a big, bright smile and told a partial truth. "Someone joked that if a boy was dumb enough to kiss me, he'd get an eternal 'stiffie.' It stuck. No one wanted to put it to the test."

"The boys were idiots."

They sat in silence. After a bit, Sam said, "Why did you become a mortician?"

"Family loyalty, mainly. Pop had a heart condition. We all knew he wouldn't last forever, so my brother and I both studied Mortuary Science."

"How does Luigi fit in?"

"It's a long story."

"We have all the time in the world."

Yeah, he looked as though he would wait all night if necessary.

"Fine," she said at last. "I guess it'll feel good to tell someone." She hesitated. "No it won't. You'll hate me."

"Nothing you say will make me think less of you." He leaned forward. "Tell me about Luigi."

"Luigi was—is—my brother's friend and in a strange way, his benefactor. It's complicated."

Children's laughter, shrieks from the Wild Mouse, and a seagull's plaintive cry filled the extended silence. Sam didn't press. He merely sipped his lemonade and waited.

A sense of inevitability washed over her as she chose her words carefully. "My brother Rico was nine, I was ten, and Luigi Guglione was thirteen when we first met. Luigi was the new kid in the neighborhood, an Italian immigrant. They put him in Rico's class. By high school, Luigi spoke fluent English and was in the correct grade. In spite of their age difference, he and Rico stayed friends. I think Luigi liked having a worshipper."

"Tell me one thing. Is Luigi Josh's father?"

Stick to the truth, she warned herself. "No. Josh's father was a student I met at university, my first love. He died in a car accident before I knew I was pregnant." He didn't need to know about the hit and run with Luigi being the prime suspect.

"What about Luigi?" Sam asked, as if sensing she was skirting the truth.

"Luigi is obsessed with me, and has been ever since I was fourteen. I never returned his feelings, but he insists we're destined to be together. Nothing I say or do seems to convince him otherwise. Ma and Bella call him my stalker." She didn't mention that Luigi now considered himself her fiancé, even if she didn't.

Sam drew her close. "What happened after Josh's father died?"

She leaned into his warmth. "While I was pregnant, Pop made monumentally bad financial decisions. Luigi saved the day by offering interest-free loans with an indefinite payment date. It was a huge amount. My father didn't ask about Luigi's money. He didn't want to know."

"Lenders usually want payback for a loan."

"It took a while for me to figure it out, but in return, Pop delivered no-questions-asked cremations. Death certificates were not a requirement." She fiddled with her drink in case she saw rejection in Sam's eyes. "Then Pop had his first heart attack and Luigi paid for his medical expenses. Although Josh was a toddler by then, Ma couldn't cope. I had to step in as funeral director. Three years later, Pop died of another heart attack after eating a stack of funnel cakes. For several years, I worked my butt off to repay the loans, but made only a dent in them. Then four months ago, I left *Paradise Gate* to start my own business." She paused to re-group, certain Sam would write her off as too much trouble.

"What happened four months ago?"

She drew in a deep breath. "Two things. I discovered Rico was still delivering his midnight specials to 'connected' clients, and Luigi became a lifetime resident in the East Jersey State Prison. In my mind, murder-one nullified the loans, so I was free to take Josh and move to an environment more suitable for child-rearing."

She risked a glance at Sam. He was frowning. She must have been out of her mind to tell him as much as she had. "I wouldn't blame you if you fired me."

His voice slid through her dark thoughts. "I'm not firing you." A gentle finger on her chin exerted pressure, forcing her to look up. Compassion softened his face. "I get it. Your family's entangled in questionable activities. It must be difficult."

He understood. To her horror, tears stung the back of her eyelids. She blinked them away and found herself babbling, "Thank you. Nearly everyone in town has heard of me. Nobody's willing to hire a former mortician to plan their parties." Plus they were afraid of Luigi.

Sam stood and circled the table, slipping in beside her, but she barely noticed he'd switched seats. "People don't understand it's a tiny step to go from organizing the final send-off for the dearly departed to planning a kick-ass event. I really need this job, Sam. If I fail, I can't return to *Paradise Gate* with Josh, and—"

"I think you're doing an amazing job."

It took a moment for his words to sink in. "You do?"

He nodded. "Because of you, we survived the building inspector. The mock funeral was pure brilliance, and your *Immortal Mermaids* act was beyond courageous."

"I'm glad I could help." Hopefully he didn't notice her scalding flush. And that he didn't recognize her desperation to make *Kinki* a success.

His eyes heated. "*Kinki* is a Goth nightclub. Goths embrace death. You understand death. It's a match made in heaven."

"Gee, thanks. I think."

"The dismal suits of yours are undertaker outfits."

"Mortician," she corrected. "But I'm not wearing one today."

Bella was right. Those suckers would be in the Goodwill donation bag by tonight.

"Excellent decision," he said. "But I can attest to the fact that those suits concealed the sexiest lingerie in the world." His voice was thick and gravelly.

The breeze blew her hair across her face, tickling her cheek. He twirled a strand around his finger before tucking it behind her ear. His warm fingers grazed her neck, and she found herself melting into a puddle of lust. A shiver of anticipation shot up her spine.

"Let's call it a secret vice."

His breathing quickened. "I prefer to call it a secret virtue." His hand lingered a moment longer before taking a detour. "You're way too buttoned-up for such a pretty day." He undid her blouse's second button, his fingers swift and sure.

"It's lucky all the customers are gone." She barely got the words out because she was having trouble breathing. The whole seduction thing was zipping along with no effort on her part. In fact, Sam gave every indication he was on board for the action. To reinforce her appeal, she said, "I hope you don't expect a relationship. This, whatever it is, it's just for fun, right?"

Her words caused him to frown and pull back. "Darlin'," he said, "you're chock full of surprises today."

A gust of warm wind tossed her hair before dipping down the open neck of her blouse to tease her breasts. A delicious sense of freedom rippled through her. She could do whatever she pleased with anyone she wanted, at least for the time being. It had been so long since a man had kissed her, she'd grown rusty.

No expectations, she warned herself. With Luigi's appeal pending, she wanted to experience normal while he was still behind bars. Was that too much to ask? She sucked in a deep breath hoping it would jump-start her courage.

"I have a confession to make," she whispered, snuggling closer.

"Oh?"

"Yeah. My underwear was still damp from swimming, so I'm not wearing any."

Her reward was Sam's sharp intake of breath.

Chapter 19: First Kiss

Katie commando? Sam damn near slid off the bench.

Before he could act on his insider knowledge, six customers toting hoagies, fish-burgers, drinks, and fries plunked down at the next table.

Sam eyed a wooden ramp leading to the beach. "Let's stretch our legs."

He led her along a path through the dunes, emerging onto the beach. Without talking, they removed their shoes. He stuffed them out of sight under the stairs and held out his hand. Together, they headed south toward the stones of a breakwater.

They walked without talking. It was enough that the sun and waves coaxed a tiny curve to her lips. Watching her splash through ripples, which foamed over the hardened sand, he felt a tingle of satisfaction at her rapt expression.

She smiled up at him. "Penny for your thoughts."

Her fresh floral scent made him ache for something he couldn't identify. If he'd ever wanted a woman so badly, he couldn't bring it to mind. He returned her smile. "I was thinking this feels right."

"I feel that way too." Her voice took on a teasing lilt. "I never thought I'd want to get wet again, yet here I am, up to my knees in cold water."

"You look carefree. It suits you."

The dimple made an appearance. She did a twirl and faced him, her face glowing. "This is amazing. Miles and miles of sand. I don't remember ever feeling so free."

"You're kidding, right?"

"Nope. I've lived near the ocean all my life. It's the first time I've walked on the beach with a man, only the two of us." She glanced over her shoulder, as if verifying they were alone before splashing through a wave.

Her sweet vulnerability stirred his protective instincts. He caught her hand and held it. "Then men in Atlantic City are blockheads."

The flash of pain disappeared so quickly he might have imagined it. But it had been real. She hadn't told him everything. Someone had hurt her badly. He suspected Luigi played a starring role in her secret, but he wouldn't push for answers. Overcome with an urge to pound the asshole's face to a pulp, he forced himself to walk quietly beside her. The rest of today was for Katie.

Once they reached the breakwater, he stopped walking and spun her around to face him. "You want to know what I think?" he asked.

She eyed him warily. "I don't know. Do I?"

"I hope so. In my opinion, a woman hasn't experienced life unless she's had a hot make-out session on the beach." He led her to the privacy of a rocky cranny.

In one swift motion, he removed the hat from her head, unslung her purse, and wedged both between boulders, saying, "You don't need these for what I have in mind."

He loved it that her eyes widened, displaying a heady mixture of curiosity and excitement. She stepped closer, then halted, a tiny frown furrowing her brow.

He fingered a curl blowing across her face. "Don't be nervous. I'll do all the heavy lifting."

She chewed her lower lip for several seconds in a most unflattering way before blurting, "There's more you should know about me."

Sam looped his arms around her waist. "I already know everything I need to know. You're beautiful, and smart, and sexy, and I want to kiss you." He couldn't resist nuzzling her neck and tugging her closer.

"You should hear about how ... oh, my."

He sucked one tender earlobe into his mouth and, praise be, she stopped talking. Her sexy little whimper fired his blood and made his breath hitch. When he started in on the sweet curve of her neck, her hands crept over his shoulders, whether from passion or to balance herself, he wasn't sure. His dick didn't care.

She angled her head, relaxing into him.

Holding himself on a tight leash, he captured her lips with infinite care. At first, the kiss was a gentle exploration. Pleased with her tiny hum of approval, he deepened the kiss, using his tongue on her, running it lightly across the seam of her lips.

With a soft sigh, she opened up, permitting entry. He tasted her heat and sweetness combined with a hit of cinnamon from the funnel cake. Her tongue danced against his, tentative at first, quickly becoming more assertive. Satisfied, he increased the pace, until she responded with a sweet, heady longing that caused the surrounding air to crackle.

Dimly aware of people talking on the other side of the breakwater, Sam tugged her blouse out of the waistband to explore the smooth, creamy skin underneath. But it wasn't enough. Wanting, needing more, he glided one hand up to cup her breast.

She looked into his face, her gorgeous eyes soft with passion and a touch of humor. "I hope all this heavy lifting isn't getting you down."

A startled bark of laughter slipped out. "I'm up to the challenge," he managed before her mouth fused to his.

She made the sexiest little murmur he'd ever heard. Taking it as encouragement, he slipped his hand under her skirt to stroke her thigh, and ... sweet baby Jesus. She'd told the gospel truth about going commando.

He slipped his fingers into the slick, damp warmth between her legs. When she arched into him, he damn near exploded.

Her stance widened, permitting easier access. He barely registered the sound of teenagers playing volleyball nearby until a burst of laughter restored his sanity.

Shaken, he extracted his hands from under her clothes. He, the man who *never* lost himself in a woman, had nearly taken her on a public beach. Katie had blown away his barriers, and that spelled danger.

"Why are we stopping?" she asked, her breathing choppy.

His chest heaved. "Not enough privacy."

"Oh, thank God." She slumped against him. "For a moment, I thought it was because of my, um, sexual appetite." Her pretty face flushed an adorable shade of pink.

He shook his head. In his sex-befuddled state, he must have misheard. "Say what?"

"Don't worry. Physical arousal doesn't signify emotional involvement. All I want is sex."

Yeah, his hearing worked fine. But that's what he wanted too, wasn't it? A good time without messy feelings. "You've got the right man."

But for some reason, he found himself wanting more. He didn't understand the attraction. For one thing, Katie was nothing like the women he normally went after or, to be precise, who went after him. She wasn't voluptuous, air-headed, or compliant. On the contrary, she was bossy, responsible to a fault, and connected with criminals. Most disturbing of all, she had a son.

Then again, she'd saved his club from certain closure. Sam couldn't think of another woman who would have gone the extra mile the way she had.

Katie spelled danger. Fortunately, there was a sure-fire way to get her out of his system. He needed to have sex with her. Lots of sex, the sooner, the better.

He dropped his voice to the husky growl that turned women on. "How be we go to your place and finish what we started?"

Her lengthy hesitation caused his smile to disappear.

"Sorry, but no," she said.

***

It chilled Katie to realize that she'd lost her detachment so easily. If Sam hadn't shown willpower, she'd have happily indulged in hot monkey sex right then and there, barely concealed by the breakwater from a beachful of volley-ball players, picnickers, and possibly a sniper with a long-range rifle. She'd tried to warn him about Luigi, but had let him silence her. The thought of his kiss had been too tempting.

Sam dusted off his hat by whacking it against his leg before cramming it onto his head. "What happened to friends with benefits?"

"I can't believe I nearly forgot Josh will be home from school soon." She marched away. His dismay would have been humorous if it hadn't mirrored her own disappointment. She bet it was the first time a woman had rejected him.

"Katie?"

His voice, thick and hoarse, stopped her in her tracks. She refused to turn around because if she did, his ready smile, his sun-kissed hair, the macho confidence that spelled pure testosterone would undermine her self-control.

When he spoke, his voice was closer. "I'm an idiot. Josh comes first. How about we have ourselves a real date?"

Heat shot through her body, but she shook her head. A real date might destroy her detachment permanently.

He pressed harder. "Get a sitter for Josh Saturday night. Come with me to the Martinelli fundraiser."

Her heart thudded so hard she feared it might break loose and pop through her chest wall. "Not a good idea."

"There might be more business in it for you. Eleanor—she's Frank's wife—throws all his fundraisers, and she's always on the lookout for talented event planners."

Damn, but Sam knew which buttons to push. She'd never met Eleanor, but her parties were the Holy Grail for event planners. Surely Luigi wouldn't object to her socializing with his friends. But no. Without detachment, a date with Sam was a recipe for heartbreak.

He pressed on, apparently undeterred by her silence. "Naturally, I'd give you a glowing recommendation."

God, she wanted to accept. Trouble was, she'd been dumb enough to think she could muzzle her emotions. Big mistake. During the kiss, she'd let her guard down.

From Sam's shadow, she knew he was within arm's length. He didn't touch her. "You'll meet all the movers and shakers in town. They're always looking for a good event planner."

A wave of yearning rushed through her. She hadn't attended a party since university.

By now, his breath was warm on her neck. "Martinelli may be corrupt, but he throws a mean party. The beautiful people beg for invitations to his fundraisers."

At the words *beautiful people*, Katie perked up. In a twisted way, the party could be her salvation. Sam wasn't a one-woman man. If she accepted, and oh, how she wanted to accept, he'd inevitably hit on someone else at the party, most likely several beautiful and glamorous someones, permitting her to regain her detachment. That way, she could have sex with him as planned, without emotional entanglement.

God, it was tempting. But she couldn't live with herself if something happened to Sam because of her. She had to come clean about Luigi, even if it meant missing out on a fabulous orgasm. And a party.

She turned to face him. "Before I give you an answer, I need to tell you something important." Her hair whipped in her face, tossed by the salty breeze. "I tried to tell you earlier, but—"

"I had other things on my mind." He removed his hat and placed it on her head, positioned it so it secured her hair while shading her face at the same time. "I'm listening now."

Her heart squeezed at the small gesture. She fell silent, unsure how to begin, grateful that he didn't push for answers. He simply waited.

"Fine," Katie said at last. "But once I'm finished, I imagine you'll want nothing more to do with me." She took a deep breath. "Remember I told you no one in town wanted to date me? It's because they didn't want to end up in a morgue."

"You never fail to surprise me. We should sit down for this." He led her to a chunk of driftwood, where they sat. "Go on."

She moistened her lips. "Joey—he was Josh's father—died in a hit and run accident. Everyone, including the cops, thought Luigi had him killed, but the cops couldn't prove it. Luigi claimed he was innocent." Refusing to look at Sam, she put a final nail in her romantic coffin. "To this day, most of Atlantic City believes Luigi murdered Joey. That's why I don't have much dating experience."

A lengthy silence caused her throat to close. Finally, Sam said, "It doesn't prove anything."

A spark of hope fluttered in her chest until she remembered Luigi's last phone call. "There's more."

"I was afraid you might say that."

She forced herself to look him square in the eyes. "Luigi keeps calling me from prison. He insists I marry him. Obsession and jealousy are a toxic combination. He says he's sick and tired of waiting for me to come to my senses. According to him, I'm his fiancée. Now that his mother's dead, there's no one to talk sense into him."

"What harm can Luigi do? He's in prison."

"Maybe not for long. His lawyer has launched an appeal, and Luigi claims the judge is in his pocket. Even if the appeal is rejected, he has a long reach and plenty of money. He'll go after any man who dares to date me. What's one more murder to a lifer?"

Sam enveloped her cold hands in his lovely warm ones. "Seems to me Luigi's not free yet and may never be, so let's not borrow trouble. It's a stretch to think he'll try to kill me for dating you. But for argument's sake, let's say he tries. I'll stay on my toes, plus I'm pretty good at taking care of myself." He stood and pulled her to her feet. "Be my date for the party."

Hadn't she hoped for this outcome? But the party had lost its appeal. She tugged her hands away and shook her head. "I don't want your death on my conscience."

"You're not responsible for Luigi's crimes. If it makes you feel better, I'll bring Rooster as my bodyguard."

She chewed her lip. "I don't know ..."

"I won't beg, Katie. You've explained the risks associated with dating you. I'm willing to take them. Here's how I see it. Either be my date for the party, and I'll show you the best time of your life, or we keep our relationship strictly professional. If you choose the professional route, I won't think any less of you, and I won't fire you."

Katie's heart raced. The orgasm she craved was still a possibility. All she had to do was be his date for the party.

She brushed sand off her skirt. "If Ma agrees to take Josh Saturday night, I'll be your date, but on one condition. For your own protection, it mustn't look like we're on a date."

Using one finger, he traced her lips. "For you, Katie, I can do a non-date."

Chapter 20: The Fundraiser Begins

Party noises increased as Sam and Katie, with Rooster clumping along between them, approached the Martinelli mansion. Sure, it wasn't a real date, and maybe a bodyguard was the smart way to go, but Sam didn't have to like it. Every cell in his body buzzed with equal amounts of lust and frustration. He itched to swap places in order to wrap his arm around his gorgeous non-date.

Sexy, tousled hair framed Katie's face. Stilettos designed purely to heat a man's blood raised her height by a good five inches. She smelled so delicious he had to suppress an urge to nuzzle the sweet, vulnerable spot at the base of her neck.

He eyed Rooster with resignation. The bouncer, who was humming *I'm a Slut* under his breath, smelled as though he'd bathed in Armani. In deference to this being a semi-formal event, he'd polished his industrial boots to a fine shine. The scarlet Mohawk stood erect in a neat row of spikes. Rooster's latex jumpsuit was studded with black and gold sequins. The suit had an attached hoodie, mesh side strips, and a zippered trap door in the rear (for reasons best left unspoken).

As they reached the double sweep of stairs, Sam remembered to check *Kinki*'s security. He'd installed cameras outside the club as an added precaution, but was taking no chances. Using his smartphone, he conducted a lightning-fast scan of his club and heaved a sigh of relief. Everything was quiet.

All excitement and animation, Katie peeked around Rooster's bulk at Sam as they started climbing. "If the Martinellis hire me for their next event, it'll put *Galas Unlimited* on the map." Her face glowed, presumably at the thought of multiple lucrative contracts.

If it had been anatomically possible, he would have kicked his own ass. He wanted Katie to desire him, not his business contacts.

Better still, he wanted her writhing with passion in his arms. And the only way that would happen was if no one tipped her off that he'd slept with many of the female guests. Yeah, he faced an uphill challenge.

Rooster rang the doorbell.

Katie held Sam's gaze while they waited. "So you'll make sure I meet the right people?"

He upped his smile's wattage. "I promised, didn't I? After tonight, you'll be Atlantic City's go-to event planner."

The front door swung open releasing a blast of noise that damn near bowled him over. Katie slipped inside followed by Rooster, leaving Sam no choice but to hustle after them. Halfway across the foyer, the bouncer stopped to flirt with a businessman in a pinstripe suit. Sam was more than happy to leave him to it.

Gusts of laughter punctuated the din of a rock band. Ears ringing, Sam led Katie through the crowded living room toward the terrace. Across the room, Rooster, who'd abandoned the businessman, no doubt because he was either taken or straight, gave him a thumbs-up and headed away. Hopefully he was hunting for hitmen, not a hookup.

As they inched through the throngs of party-goers, Sam contented himself with admiring Katie. A sexy red dress displayed more than a hint of cleavage. From there, the fabric clung to gentle curves before clinging to sensational hips to showcase almost every inch of her slim, perfect legs. He couldn't wait to discover if she wore anything but skin under the dress.

She gripped his arm, a sure sign of a memory lapse about their date status. "Isn't that Martinelli?" she whispered, pointing. "Behind the piano with a woman."

Sure enough, Martinelli was engaged in tight-lipped conversation with a blonde. The politician-smile was missing. Although Sam couldn't see the woman's face, she most definitely wasn't the senator's elegant wife. The woman gestured and shook her head, stepping away from the piano. Martinelli yanked her back and continued talking.

Katie's voice took on an excited edge. "Hey, it's Deanna, and they're fighting. There's no mistaking those brawny shoulders."

"Why don't women warm up to Deanna?"

Katie looked at him with a touch of pity. "You really have no idea, do you?"

Before she could enlighten him, Deanna bolted, elbowing her way to the front door. Martinelli waited until she'd disappeared before sauntering after her.

"I bet they're going somewhere more private," Katie said, echoing Sam's thoughts.

He nearly suggested they do the same thing, non-date rule be damned, when a furious shout caused the hairs on the back of his neck to prickle.

"There you are, you miserable, no-good, cowardly weasel."

Hoping against hope the screech wasn't directed at him, Sam turned around. Big mistake. A redhead with cantaloupe breasts and a furious frown arrowed his way. He might have slept with her. If so, the details were hazy. He grabbed Katie's arm. "Fresh air would be nice."

With a flip of her hair, Katie smiled sweetly. "Nope. This looks interesting."

By then, the redhead was on him. "Prick!" she yelled at the top of her lungs. "Asshole!"

"Hi, sugar," he said, stepping smartly out of reach.

"You've forgotten my name, haven't you?"

Yes. "Of course not. You're looking real good tonight."

Her frown deepened. "I guess you were too damn drunk to remember sleeping with me."

This did not look good. He took Katie's arm and tried hustling her toward the patio.

She shook him off and planted her feet. "Don't leave on my account. This encounter may work in your favor."

"I don't see how." Damn, but he needed a drink.

Next thing Sam knew, the redhead was drilling his chest with a pointy-nailed finger. "You miserable rat bastard. You promised to call me."

Something about the way her voice quavered got to him. Hell, he must have been so drunk he'd conveyed the impression he wanted commitment. She was right. He was an asshole. Always had been, always would be. Flicking a nervous glance at Katie, he focused his attention on the redhead in an effort to make things right.

"I'm truly sorry. I meant to call, but renovation problems at work sidetracked me."

The woman's face was set in stone. "Believe it or not, Sam, I don't give a damn. I've met a man who's worth ten of you." She turned to Katie. "As one woman to another, I'd like to offer free advice."

"Okay."

"Do not trust this man. He's a player. Once Sam gets what he wants, he'll be out of your life so fast, you'll think you imagined him."

"Good to know," Katie assured her. "But we're not dating. He's my boss."

Desperate to leave, Sam said, "Absolutely. She's one of my best employees. It was nice chatting with you."

He nudged Katie to get her moving before anything else happened. He had no idea what she was thinking. Hell, she was probably contemplating chopping his balls off.

They stepped outside onto the patio without another incident. Sam breathed a sigh of relief before remembering Luigi. He scanned the yard, but no one seemed remotely threatening.

Beside him, Katie chewed her lip and said nothing for a prolonged beat. He'd give a lot to know what she was thinking. At last, she shook off her tight-lipped expression and smiled at him. "This looks like something out of a fairy tale."

The constriction around Sam's chest diminished. He wasn't ready to lose her. Not yet. With minor tweaking, his seduction plan might still work. Acutely aware of her fragrance, he moved closer, not touching, but close enough to breathe in her scent.

Now that it appeared she didn't bear a grudge, he could appreciate the setting. The back yard was beautiful. Hundreds of twinkly lights sparkled in the chestnut trees. Dozens of white-clothed tables awaited evening diners. Each table glittered with candles, cut crystal glasses, and silverware.

Farther away, the swimming pool glowed like a jewel in the deepening dusk. A hazy recollection of a memorable skinny dip made his lips twitch before he sobered in a hurry. There would be no repeat performance tonight, leastwise not for him.

Katie's whisper drew his attention. "Remember, Frank Martinelli is Luigi's friend."

"How could I forget?" Sam said warily, wondering what was coming next.

"If the senator remembers me, please go along with whatever I say."

"Yes, ma'am," he said, thereby provoking a frown.

On their way to the pool, Sam flagged down a waiter carrying a silver tray laden with tall golden drinks. After passing one to Katie, he raised his in a toast. "To the most beautiful and talented woman at the party."

Managing the feat of appearing both skeptical and pleased at the same time, she raised the glass to those sexy lips. Other plans for that sensual mouth sprang to mind.

Her eyes sparkled. "This drink's amazing, like a fizzy fruit punch." Continuing to sip, she resumed walking, the stilettos making her steps shorter than usual.

Matching her pace, he sampled his drink. A citrus tang cut the sweetness of fresh peaches and mango. Delicious. Deceptive. Lethal. A drink to ensure romantic success.

His conscience kicked in. "Careful. You can't taste the booze, but there's three kinds of rum in the drink as well as orange liqueur, all topped off with champagne." He marveled at his own stupidity.

She took another gulp. "All I taste is fruit."

"They pack a wallop, so go easy. We both need our wits about us tonight."

They reached the pool area and stopped. She swayed as she drained her glass and held it out to him. "I'm still thirsty."

He steadied her with a hand on her elbow. "You grab a chair, I'll get you a soda."

"A soda? You're kidding, right?" She accepted a glass from a passing waiter. "These are harmless."

"We won't be eating right away, and—"

Martinelli's hearty voice interrupted her protest. "Sam, my man. I'm so glad you made it to our little soirée."

Although the politician was pushing fifty, his full head of dark hair, touched by a hint of gray at the temples, was artfully styled in a casual, youthful fashion.

Martinelli was arm-in-arm with his wife, Eleanor. Her welcoming smile had Sam grinning back with genuine affection. Since there was no sign of tension between the pair, he guessed she had no idea her husband was fooling around.

Sam greeted the couple and introduced Katie.

Martinelli examined her with a puzzled frown. A moment later, his face cleared. "Katarina?" His camera-worthy smile appeared. "I hardly recognized you." He whacked Sam on the back. "You've been holding out on me, you dog. I had no idea you were dating this dazzling creature."

Sam forced himself to smile back. "Not dating. My new event planner works so hard, she needed an evening off. I don't want her collapsing with exhaustion. It took some doing, but Katie finally agreed that a party with friends might relieve the stress."

Katie stuck out her hand. "Frank. How lovely to see you again."

Martinelli wrapped both paws around Katie's slender hand. "I'm flabbergasted, my dear. You're the last person I expected to see tonight."

"I know. Me too." Tilting her head, she flashed a confidential smile. "But Luigi is such a sweetheart. One mention of your fundraiser and he insists I attend, tells me I deserve to have a little fun in the company of friends he trusts. His number one priority is my happiness." She retrieved her hand and leaned a fraction of an inch closer to Martinelli. "Confidentially, he's a little over-protective about my happiness."

The smile vanished. Sam silently applauded Katie's quick thinking. Unless he was mistaken, she'd sent a subtle message that tattling on her would rile Luigi, while at the same time hinting about unpleasant consequences for anyone who hit on her.

Apparently unaware of any innuendos, Eleanor smiled at Katie. "It's true, my dear. Everyone needs a night off once in a while."

Katie returned her smile. "I'm glad I came. You have no idea how much Sam appreciates your husband's help."

"Frank is the most caring man I know. He tries to help small businesses succeed, claiming it boosts the local economy. But the real reason is he can't resist helping others."

Martinelli draped an arm around his wife. "All I did was whisper a few words to the right people in Alcoholic Beverage Control." He winked at Sam.

"Whatever you said, it did the trick," Sam replied obediently, making a deliberate effort to unclench his jaw. Sure, Martinelli had lit a fire under several bureaucratic asses to make the liquor license materialize, but it had cost him plenty.

Eleanor rested a slim hand on Katie's arm. "Let's leave the boys to their fun. We'll talk parties. I'm looking for ideas for our next fundraiser. After I pick your brain, I'll introduce you to Frank's colleagues and their better halves."

Over her shoulder, Katie mouthed, "Thank you," to Sam as Eleanor whisked her away.

A glow of satisfaction expanded in Sam's chest. Even if nothing happened between himself and Katie, she would meet important business contacts.

Beside him, Martinelli watched the two women, one blond, tall, and elegant, the other brunette, slim, and graceful, as they glided across the lawn. "You'd better watch your step with Katarina. She has powerful connections. Too bad. I'd sure like to get a piece of that."

Sam hated the way Martinelli's voice roughened, but he managed to force his words out evenly. "And you have a classy wife who thinks the sun shines out your ass, not to mention more women sniffing around than you know how to handle."

Martinelli chuckled. "For your information, the sun does shine out my ass, and I do know how to handle them." He sipped his martini while continuing to study Katie. "I love my wife. The rest mean nothing. But Katarina, though. She's special, you know what I mean?"

Oh, yeah. Sam knew. He shrugged. "Not my type."

Martinelli released a bark of laughter. "Liar. She's everyone's type."

Sam forced a grin to cover the quick surge of anger. The mere thought of someone else touching Katie's silky, intimate places made his skin crawl.

"We're business acquaintances, nothing more," he said.

Staring after her, Martinelli said, "Such a waste of a beautiful woman."

They continued contemplating the women in silence. After a moment, Sam stiffened. Three men joined the two women on the pool terrace. He swallowed a growl as one of them handed Katie a fresh drink and whispered in her ear. She rewarded the asshole with a smile. A goddamn ear-to-ear grin. A sucker punch to the gut would have hurt less. Damn, but he wanted to march over there and stake his claim.

Instead, he said, "It's good I caught you alone, Frank. I've been meaning to talk to you."

"Shoot."

"The morning after you agreed to establish surveillance, we had more damage at *Kinki*. Was there a problem?"

"Sorry. Didn't I tell you? Gosh, it must have slipped my mind. I left a message for my chief security honcho to assign a detail to *Kinki*. Turned out his wife was in labor and he didn't get my voicemail until the next day. Everything's in place now, so there shouldn't be any more slip-ups. They'll conduct 24-7 outdoor surveillance until you give the word to stop."

"Thanks. I knew I could rely on you." It crossed Sam's mind that Martinelli might have screwed him over for reasons of his own, but that didn't make any sense.

Martinelli waved at someone behind Sam and said, "Here comes Luciana, my head fundraiser. She has a huge crush on you. You've gotta make nice or she'll mope and drop the ball on me." A warning note entered his voice. "There are tens of thousands of fundraising dollars at stake here. Are you hearing me?"

Sam forced a smile he knew was a shadow of his normal grin. "Message received loud and clear." Make nice to Martinelli's head fundraiser, or he'd cancel *Kinki*'s security detail.

Chapter 21: Complications at the Fundraiser

Although prudence had forced Katie to switch to straight orange juice, a delightful warmth curled in her belly. She felt slightly tipsy. Two congressmen in black tie appeared fascinated by the view down the front of her dress. For some reason that struck her as hilarious. Her concern about gunmen disappeared. Hey, Rooster was guarding Sam, wasn't he?

With difficulty, she switched focus to Eleanor's conversation with the president of the biggest bank in town. True to her word, she was praising Katie as the hottest event planner in town, someone he should hire.

Too bad she might have to flee town to escape Luigi.

Once Eleanor wrapped it up and joined another circle of guests, Katie murmured an appreciative response to the banker. It struck her that Frank Martinelli was a lucky man. Not only was his wife beautiful, gracious, and wealthy—old-money wealthy—she was also happy to schmooze pompous assholes on behalf of a struggling event planner. What possessed him to hang out with the likes of Deanna, or Luigi for that matter?

While making small talk, Katie risked a surreptitious glance at the terrace. Sam was busy charming several women. Kisses flew, smiles broadened, cleavage flashed. Without the ever-present Stetson, his hair gleamed gold in the lamplight. He was knee-buckling hot, easily the sexiest man at the party.

He must have sensed her heated stare because in the midst of a cluster of adoring fans, he looked directly at her and raised his glass in a silent toast.

A flash of heat sped southward, causing very important body parts to quiver in anticipation. She wanted to snuggle in and nibble her way down that hard, delicious frame.

Her happy glow vanished when one of the women, a brunette wearing a prim navy dress better suited for a Sunday school teacher, captured Sam's attention by standing on tiptoe, flattening her most un-Sunday-school-teacherish boobs against his arm, and whispering something. His rich laughter rang out, clearly audible over the music.

When the woman turned her head, Katie sucked in a shocked breath. Sunday-School-Teacher's name was Luciana, and she was married to Luigi's partner, Vinnie Constantine. If Luciana learned Sam was her escort, she would blab to Luigi about his "fiancée" taking the dating plunge.

Katie recovered quickly. Vinnie outranked Luigi in the jealousy department, demanding that Luciana dress like a Sunday-school teacher so men would ignore her. Presumably Vinnie was out of town, perhaps whacking someone, and his wife was enjoying her freedom by hitting on Sam.

Happily, if Luciana ratted out Katie, she would also incriminate herself.

Consumed with an urge to annihilate Sam's female fan club, which had conveyed him onto the lawn, Katie stomped toward them.

Emerging from the darkness, Eleanor intercepted her headlong rush.

Sidetracked, Katie noted her hostess' worried expression, and asked. "Is everything okay?"

Eleanor's forehead puckered. "I hope this commotion doesn't turn into another skinny dip. I'd better find Frank and make sure he puts a halt to it."

"Is there anything I can do to help?"

"Don't get involved, trust me. It might get vulgar." Eleanor grimaced. "Last year's skinny dip was so raunchy, I'm told it was as scandalous as *Kinki*'s former fetish nights."

"How did you learn about those?"

"Oh, I've never actually attended one. But one evening, I was laying out a suit for Frank to wear and found an invitation. It was addressed to both of us so I read it. We were invited to a Rodeo Nite at *Kinki*. I asked him what I should wear. He told me I would likely hate *Kinki* and offered to check it out first. I was fine with that, otherwise I'd have had to skip my book club meeting. The next morning, he said I was smart to stay away. The activities he'd witnessed in the play rooms were so shocking, he'd left early and driven across town to catch a charity auction." She lowered her voice to a whisper. "There were *orgies*."

"How awful." Without doubt, Frank had been one blissful orgy participant.

"Frank disapproved of everything the club stood for and never returned. When he heard Sam was upgrading *Kinki* into an upscale nightclub, he vowed to do everything he could to help."

At the sound of excited squeals, Katie glanced around. By then, Sam had migrated to the pool area, along with a dozen eager camp followers. She said to Eleanor, "It looks like Sam needs help. You'd better go find your husband. I'll stay back."

With a nod, Eleanor sped toward the house.

Katie started moving. The golden boy's hair was deliciously tousled, and his skin glistened, as if he was experiencing the afterglow from a quickie. *Maybe he is*, a little voice in Katie's head whispered as she closed in on the action.

Women surrounded Sam. Luciana was stroking his ass. He tried to fend her off, but Katie could tell he wasn't putting any muscle into it. The slut switched her attention to undoing his shirt.

Two more woman joined the grope session. They reminded Katie of sharks engaged in a feeding frenzy. And Sam was their bucket of chum.

Blood rushed to her head, blurring her vision. If he wanted to escape, it wouldn't take a huge amount of effort. He'd undoubtedly slept with these women, or they wouldn't be bold enough to undress him in public. Oh, yeah, Sam was a player, through and through. A hound dog. A world of hurt awaited any woman dumb enough to fall for him.

Katie paused in mid-stride, struck by the awareness that jealous wasn't her friend. Without detachment, there would be no action for her, and hot, steamy action was her goal.

The realization prevented a headlong rush into battle. Gritting her teeth, she trotted over to the edge of the lawn, stepped over the paved edging, and slipped behind a tree in the deep shadows. Hidden, she leaned her head against the smooth bark, allowing deep, yogic breathing combined with visualization to calm herself down. This was a trick she'd used to achieve detachment before conducting a funeral, otherwise she tended to absorb the mourners' grief.

Before long, cool, gray tendrils of detachment crept around her heart. With grim determination, she smothered her jealousy.

Mostly.

Now that she'd mastered the whole detachment-without-jealousy thing, a fling with Sam was possible. Given his track record, the sex would be skilled beyond anything she could imagine. She deserved this orgasm. Nothing and no one would stop her.

A murmur of voices caught her attention. Although the conversation was mostly conducted in whispers, she recognized the Allegretti brothers' voices. Another person, more authoritative, appeared to be giving orders.

Although the evening was balmy, Katie shivered. She was alone in the darkness. How dumb could you get? She held her breath, afraid the slightest sound would give her away.

Listening intently, she caught the words "blackmail" and "kill the son-of-a-bitch," followed by an argument. Apparently, they reached an agreement, because the authoritative voice ordered, "Do it. There's no time to lose."

Louder now, one of the Allegrettis said, "Sure thing, Senator."

"Don't fuck up, or you're both dead."

She shuddered and shrank deeper into the bushes, barely noticing the scratch of twigs. A moment later, two figures materialized from the shadows. Once they disappeared, Frank Martinelli emerged and strode toward the house.

Her heart thumped hard. Frank had hired the Allegrettis to carry out a hit.

Thankful to escape undetected, she scanned the pool area for Sam. His fan club had reached the pool's edge, and there he was, surrounded by the women. His shirt was half-on, half off, but so far, he'd managed to keep his pants on.

Luciana was engaged in a one-handed fight with the zipper of her gown while struggling to undo Sam's zipper with the other. A woman yelled, "Skinny dip," and the rest repeated the chant. The two congressmen Katie had met earlier headed for the pool at top speed while loosening ties, buttons, and zippers. The banker was close on their heels. Loud splashes warned her she'd better hurry.

Okay, she had other plans for Sam tonight, and none of them involved a swimming pool.

***

The scent of chlorine stung Sam's nostrils. He didn't dare make a sudden move for fear of drawing attention to his plight. If Katie noticed what was happening, it would go poorly for him. Then again, how could she not?

No matter how you cut it, he was in deep shit. Ironically, for once he was innocent.

At previous fundraisers, he'd always been the first to strip down as a prelude to cannonballing, butt-naked, into the pool. Tonight, he had no desire to join a skinny dip, and the last thing he wanted was a crowd of half-naked women groping him.

Yeah, something was wrong, and the cause was Katie Deluca. For the last couple of days, he'd found himself enjoying her tart retorts to his suggestive comments. Night and day, he'd pictured her naked, those exotic eyes heavy-lidded with passion.

He managed to shrug off the women, including Martinelli's head fundraiser, a brunette called Lee or Lou or Lucy-something, whose appearance might be as innocent as a nun's, but who had the morals of a horny bunny. Things were looking up until a massive woman encased in red satin came from behind and slid a pair of meaty arms around his chest, rendering him immobile.

"Hey," he wheezed, struggling. "No fair." He wouldn't dream of hurting a woman, even one with arms a Sumo wrestler would envy.

Her voice squealed in his ear, "Okay girls, I've got him. Come and get it."

Lucy-something landed a hand in the vicinity of his dick.

With a Herculean effort, he swiveled his hips a millisecond before she hit pay dirt. He couldn't bring himself to be mean to a woman whose only crime was wanting a piece of Sammy—something he'd always welcomed in the past. Her actions would normally have sent him into a happy state of arousal.

Damn, but she was persistent. Releasing a long, ragged sigh, he peeled away her hand, which had slipped under his waistband and was zeroing in on his pride and joy.

Alarm shot up his spine when another volunteer shimmied out of her gown. Others in various stages of undress appeared united in a common goal—get Sammy naked.

He was contemplating a different approach when his spidey senses prickled. He scanned the area for danger. Someone marched across the darkened lawn, aimed in his direction. A real bad feeling gripped him.

Seconds later, Katie stopped in front of him, hands fisted on her hips. She was barefoot, shoes in hand. Her hair had loosened into a tumbling, sexy mess.

"I hope I'm not interrupting anything," she said in a saccharine tone, proving she had a major bug up her ass.

Sumo Wrestler, still holding him captive, assured Katie, "The more the merrier."

Simultaneously, he answered, "Good to see you." He smiled at Katie as if nothing unusual was happening. "The buffet's ready. You 'bout ready to grab a bite to eat?" Remembering it couldn't appear as if they were dating, he added, "It'll be a working dinner."

Although it was too dark to see her expression, he was pretty sure it was dialed to pissed. When she spoke, her voice was measured. "It might look strange if you visited the buffet table with a couple of women attached to your package."

This did not sound promising. "This is a huge misunderstanding."

Katie ignored him and addressed the women. "Nice job, ladies. Looks like you're on top of things."

Lucy-something surprised the hell out of him by staring at Katie and saying, "Holy shit. I never thought I'd find you here, Katarina. Make yourself useful and help with Sam."

"Thanks, but I'm here on business. I'm surprised to see you here without your husband."

"He had to go out of town." The woman's tone sounded defensive.

Sumo Wrestler said, "We all want a piece of Sammy. I hear there's lots to go around."

Katie nodded. "I bet Sammy is more than up for the challenge."

"He is now," Lucy-something confirmed, cupping Sam's crotch hard enough to make him wince. She nodded her approval. "Yowza!"

"That's a purely physiological reaction," he said, summoning a wide-eyed expression of innocence for Katie's benefit.

It was a wasted effort. She ignored him and whipped out her phone, capturing the Hallmark moment with her camera. "Call this insurance."

She flashed a shark-like grin at Lucy-something. "I'd keep my mouth shut if I were you."

The woman let go in a big hurry and nodded. "Understood."

Sam was too grateful for the release to care about the reason. "I was explaining to these persuasive ladies how I have pressing business priorities, so I won't be skinny dipping tonight."

Another woman tossed her bra aside with a flourish. Her breasts sprang aloft with a quiver, as though eager to greet him. "We're aiming to change Sammy's mind," she said. A moment later, her thong followed.

Don't look there, moron.

The visual impact of her Brazilian resurrected a hazy memory. Yeah, he'd slept with her.

Katie's glare signaled her understanding.

Ever so slowly, she placed her shoes on a bench and stepped closer to the group. "Very persuasive tactics, ladies." Her voice was calm, friendly. She turned to Lucy-something, who struggled to remove her dress. "Need some help?"

"I'm good."

"Oops." Katie's sudden lurch wouldn't have fooled a child. She pretended to catch herself by pressing both hands against Lucy-something's ass.

There was a scream and a splash. In a few seconds, her head appeared, streaming water.

Katie peered into the pool. "I'm *so* sorry. I slipped."

"Bitch."

"You did that on purpose," he whispered.

"You're welcome. Luciana's connected. I may have saved your life."

Another hip-swing took out two more groupies. After a few seconds, they surfaced, laughing and sputtering.

"Were they connected too?"

"Who knows? You can't be too careful when it comes to assassins."

On the far side of the pool, two congressmen stripped and jumped in. Sam listened in admiration as Katie addressed the women. "Ladies, those guys are congressmen. Better still, they're rich, they're naked, and they want a good time. Go for it."

They shucked their clothes and went for it.

Katie retrieved her shoes. Swinging them on one finger, she faced Sam, her expression a mixture of defiance and determination. "That was the least sensible thing I've ever done, and I loved every minute of it. Ready to leave?"

His heart gave a leap of hope. Perhaps he still stood a chance. Tugging her to his side, he nudged her into motion. "Nice work."

She shrugged off his arm and stumbled. "Not dating, remember?"

He replaced his arm. "We're getting out of here. Everyone's too drunk to remember details." As he half-carried, half-supported her, he looked into her face. "You were jealous. Admit it."

She shook her head. "Nope. To be jealous, you must have feelings for the other person."

A ridiculous sense of disappointment gripped him. Which was a huge problem, seeing as how her unpossessive nature should make him a very happy man.

She trailed her fingers over his bare chest, leaving a trail of sparks. "Hey, I have an idea." Her words slurred slightly. "Josh is at a sleepover. Let's go to my place and see what happens." Her hand inched lower to stroke his abs.

His arousal was instantaneous. "There is a God," he breathed. "I thought you'd changed your mind."

"Don't worry. I know how you feel about commitment. I assure you this will be just sex, no strings attached—exactly the way you like it." Her hand slipped under his waistband, heading south.

All the air left his lungs. Gently, but firmly, he removed her fingers. After two tries at an answer, he muttered, "Perfect."

As he hustled her away, he heard her say, "In case I forget, remind me to tell you something later."

Chapter 22: Sophistication? Not!

Katie and Sam entered her kitchen. He looked relaxed, too relaxed, as if he did this every night of his life. She gave herself a mental head-thunk. He *did* do this every night.

Out of the corner of her eye, she watched him make nice to Bluto. As those large, capable hands stroked the soft fur, she suppressed a tiny whimper of anticipation. Bluto, slut that he was, rolled onto his back in feline euphoria, and offered a furry chest. From the high-decibel purring, Katie assumed Sam had acquired another fan. A little shiver of anticipation ran down her spine as she visualized the application of those same magic fingers to her own chest and, well, everything.

She tried to calm herself by keeping busy—closing curtains, re-folding a perfectly aligned dishtowel, and removing two glasses from the cupboard. Her entire body quivered with anxiety coupled with impatience as she contemplated what lay ahead—a night of slow, sensual lovemaking delivered by a man who understood a woman's body.

Her sexual experience was sadly limited. But, hey, no problem. Loosened up by three rum punches, faking carnal sophistication would be a snap. For the first time and possibly the last (if Luigi was released), she intended to explore the mystery of why everyone found sex an intoxicating pastime. If Sam lived up to a fraction of his reputation as a player, she'd soon have the answer.

Her good parts contracted in anticipation.

Buying time to coax her sexual persona out of hiding, she reached into the fridge for the Prosecco she'd chilled. The cork's soft pop demonstrated advanced sophistication. She'd poured the first glass when a pair of very large, very warm hands gripped her hips from behind. Heat slashed through her. Releasing a squeak, she whirled around to face Sam. Bubbly wine shot from the bottle, blasting him mid-chest.

Her hearted pounded harder. Wet silk molded his torso's every ridge, every muscle, and he owned more than his fair share. It was ridiculous how hot he looked. Doing her best not to drool, she tried to speak. On the third try, her voice cooperated. "You startled me. A warning would be nice, something like, oh, I don't know, a bell around your neck, or..." Damn, her brain had gone into hiding.

One corner of his mouth quirked upward as he took the dripping bottle from her shaking hand and set it on the table. "No harm done."

Oh, God, kill me now.

She tore a handful of paper towels from the dispenser and dabbed his chest. "I'll dry you off so the wine won't leave a stain."

"Easy there, Katie." His silky voice slid over her frayed nerves as smooth as poured cream. The sight of him unbuttoning his shirt was mesmerizing.

"It'll be fine, I promise," he assured her.

Was he talking about his shirt or something else?

As he exposed more tanned skin and lovely chest hair, she kept wiping his torso, all the time chattering like an idiot. "Of course it'll be fine. Why wouldn't it be fine?" She dabbed faster. "White wine shouldn't stain a black shirt, but it's silk, and silk is temperamental."

Please, someone, anyone, shut me up!

He reached out with one hand and pried the paper towels from her grip. Using the other hand, he placed his forefinger over her lips. "I don't give a damn about my shirt." He removed his finger, leaving behind a pleasant tingling.

She tried to control her breathing while he undid his remaining buttons. In no time at all, she found herself nose-to-sternum with a sleek, muscled chest sprinkled with enough hair to make the landscape interesting.

She sucked in a deep breath. Big mistake. He smelled as delicious as he looked. Her good parts agreed. A droplet of wine slowly gathered on the tip of his left nipple. Unable to resist, Katie leaned forward and licked it off with a flick of her tongue. Hah. Surely, that demonstrated top-notch sexual sophistication. Tilting her head to examine his face, she noted his eyes had darkened, hopefully with passion.

"I, uh, thought wine would be nice before we, um ..." Unable to finish the sentence, she thunked her forehead against his chest.

"Look at me, Katie." He tipped her chin using one finger. "Please?"

She did. And melted.

"We don't need wine," he said. "I want you to remember everything."

At his kindness and understanding, her breath caught in her throat. "Oh ..." Since the ability to speak had deserted her, she draped his shirt over a chair to dry.

"There's no need to be nervous." Using one of his magic fingers, he traced the shell of her ear, sending a shiver down her spine. "I'll take good care of you."

"I'm not nervous. Nope. Not at all." Funny how her bones had melted.

She backed away. He followed until she found herself sandwiched between the counter and the delicious golden body she itched to stroke. And lick. And nibble—a tiny bit.

Okay, so she was experiencing physical arousal. Emotions played no part in her turmoil. Nope. She was nicely detached.

Sam's blinding smile left Katie so dizzy she barely noticed when he snagged a lock of her hair and wound it around his finger.

"Let's get rid of your dress."

The smile in his voice made her toes curl and her heart bounce around in her chest.

"Um, okay. Why not?"

While he watched, his eyes heavy-lidded and sexy, she stretched behind her back and hunted for the zipper. Duh. She'd forgotten that a narrow fabric fold, held in place by a zillion microscopic hooks, concealed the sucker. No wonder it had been price reduced, even for a consignment store.

"Let me help."

"I'm good." She contorted her body while groping around, hoping the sweat beading her upper lip wasn't visible. "These tiny fasteners are tricky."

"I have excellent fine motor skills. Turn around and relax."

"I *am* relaxed, dammit."

Heat broiled her face as she presented her stiffened back to him. While his fingers dealt with the hooks, she worked on achieving a higher level of detachment, not to mention sophistication. She was almost there when he said, "I love that you're nervous." His voice had roughened to a husky growl. "It makes what we're about to do extra special."

She twisted her neck to assess whether or not he was mocking her, and found herself staring at his mouth. Her breath hitched in her chest. "I might disappoint you."

His fingers stilled. "Why on earth would you think that?"

"I may not have the skill you expect in a date."

After a long pause, he said, "Excuse me?" The two soft words reverberated in the quiet kitchen.

She chewed her lip, then said, "I've only done it twice, well two and a half times to be precise, and it didn't work out so well." She clamped her mouth shut. Luckily she'd caught herself before divulging her partner's jackrabbit ejaculation.

"Josh's father?" Sam remained utterly still.

Afraid to turn around, she nodded. "Uh-huh. I was too young to realize it wasn't normal. I thought it was my fault. There's no need to worry, though. I'm sure I can satisfy your needs. I'm a self-trained expert on sexual gratification."

Warm breath stirred her hair. "Self-trained?"

Had she said something wrong? "Yes. I'm a voracious reader. I've read tons of how-to books on sexual intercourse, everything from *The Joy of Sex*, to *Kama Sutra*." She hoped her sincerity would reassure him.

"Katie—"

"I also studied the *Fifty Shades Trilogy* and other erotic novels. I have a subscription to *Cosmo*, too. There's a huge amount of educational help available, so I'm certain I'm competent." Was it her imagination, or did his fingers fumble?

"That's commendable and, uh, extremely proactive of you," he said in a choked voice. "But right now, I'm as far from worried as a man can get."

Cool air brushed her skin as he drew the zipper down. Blood pounded in her ears. Without turning around, she slipped out of her dress, letting it slither to the floor. Large, warm hands slid onto her hips and spun her around to face him.

"Look at you. Perfect."

Her nervousness disappeared. The underlying hoarseness in his voice encouraged her to step closer. A heartbeat later, she threw one arm around his neck to hold him in place, while her other hand got busy exploring, pressing her against cold granite. His throaty growl and instantaneous reaction were more satisfying than anything the books described.

A pang of guilt sank sharp little teeth into her libido. Before things heated up, Sam deserved to know what she'd overheard at the fundraiser.

"Sam?"

His fingers glided over her skin to find her bra fastening. "Patience, Katie. These things are tricky." A moment later, the garment joined her dress, leaving her wearing only a garter belt, thong, stockings, and stilettos.

The sudden hunger in his eyes made her feel sexy, desirable, powerful. His mouth trailed a scalding path from her neck, along her collarbone, and circled the swell of one breast, as if acquainting itself with every inch. A delicious decadence took over as she savored the sensations.

Oh, yes, please.

She gave it one last try. "We should talk," she gasped.

He didn't look up from what he was doing. "Talk is highly over-rated."

She yielded with a soft sigh. "Totally," she whispered, arching her back.

***

Sam wanted Katie so damn much, his heart tried to pound clean out of his chest. Pressing her perfect body against the kitchen counter, he put his many years of expertise to good use. Swirling his tongue around one pink nipple, he sucked the pointed tip gently, and ever so thoroughly. A throaty moan rewarded his efforts. He slipped one arm under her shoulder, the other beneath her thighs, and swept her off the ground.

"Upstairs. We need a comfy spot for *Kama Sutra*'s more advanced positions." He whipped up several stairs, and Katie's arms tightened around his neck.

"Sam?"

"Don't worry." He reduced speed marginally, uncomfortably aware of his hard-on straining the zipper of his pants. "I won't let you fall."

"I know. Only, you're kidding, right? About applying *Kama Sutra* immediately? The book advises couples to start slow, working their way up to the more complicated postures."

"I don't mind skipping a few steps," he assured her, too turned-on to chat. "I'll teach you what you need to know. I'm thinking we'll kick things off with the good old Rocking Horse before tackling The Nirvana—I find women enjoy that one—then there's—"

"We should start with something more straightforward. I suggest a classic or two from *The Joy of Sex.*"

Her voice penetrated his excitement. He stopped on the landing and examined her troubled face. He was an asshole, so immersed in his own gratification he'd forgotten her inexperience.

He nodded. "A graduated approach? Great idea."

She released a breath she must have been holding. "Excellent."

He hid a grin. She was adorable. In spite of being all soft and quivering and nearly naked in his arms, Katie managed to sound bossy. Only her quickened breathing indicated she might be nervous. Or aroused. He intended to address both conditions.

Gathering her slim body closer, he sped up the remaining stairs.

Chapter 23: First Lovemaking

On reaching the upper level, Sam's lips twitched with amusement at Katie's terse instructions. "Turn left. Farther. At the end of the hall."

With his arms full of naked, quivering woman, he was only too happy to obey. Nudging the door open, he entered her bedroom. Bluto tried to squeeze past, meowing. Sam used his toe to nudge the cat backward, then elbowed the door shut carefully to avoid decapitating the animal.

Gently, almost reverently, he lowered Katie to the floor, sweeping the bed covers aside. A bedside lamp provided dim lighting. Acutely aware of the anxiety she was trying so hard to hide, he fished out a condom from his pocket, unwrapped it, and placed it on the bedside table.

Stuffing the wrapper into his pocket, he turned to find she'd already stepped out of her thong and kicked it aside. With an athletic lunge that took him by surprise, she landed on the bed where, holy shit, she propped her naked body on one elbow. She looked infinitely, outrageously erotic. All the blood left his brain and shot to his dick.

She thrust her breasts out. "I'm ready. Do me."

He found himself at a sudden loss for words. A naked woman barking out an order to "do" her was another first.

"Did I say something wrong?" Her voice wavered. "*Cosmo* claims explicit sex talk turns men on."

His brain kicked into action again. Katie was scared silly, yet here she was, faking sophistication, trying to please him. He pressed a kiss on her forehead. "Looking at you turns me on. You take my breath away, and that's a fact."

She lay perfectly still. The low lighting caressed her body. Up close and personal, she was all dainty curves, enticing shadows, and gentle swells. Sam's breath caught in his throat and he grew so hard it was painful. "You left your garter belt and stockings on."

She nodded. "I heard men find them sexy."

Adorable.

"Your books got it right." He stripped off the rest of his clothes and sank onto the bed. Trailing his hands slowly across her satin shoulders and down her arms, he inhaled her sweet fragrance. Tenderness engulfed him. Clasping both her hands in his, he made his voice strong and reassuring. "We'll go as slow as you want. I aim to make it memorable for you."

Her lips parted, and her breathing quickened. "I'm sure you will. Let's do it."

He stifled a bark of laughter. "Still giving orders?"

"It's not like I do this every day. The tension's killing me."

"Come here." He nudged her onto her back. While cupping one delicate breast, he lowered his head and used his tongue to trace a path to that soft, kissable mouth and brushed his lips across hers. At her sharp intake of breath, he nibbled her bottom lip, drawing its fullness slowly into his mouth. She tasted of Prosecco, all winey and delicious. A strangled moan encouraged him to give her lip a deeper pull before releasing it.

Her eyes sprang open and a tiny frown furrowed her brow. "Is everything okay? Am I doing it wrong?"

"Christ, you're beautiful." He ran his finger down her cheek. "I've been dying to do this all week. Working beside you was torture."

"You said talking was highly over-rated."

Right. All she wanted from him was a masterly roll in the sack. He tamped down the sharp little claws of hurt. A long-term relationship was the last thing on his mind, too.

Leaning in, he covered her mouth with his, forcing himself to take it slow when all he wanted to do was feast on her. As soon as she responded, he deepened the kiss, parting her lips with his tongue.

Tentative at first, then getting the hang of it nicely, her tongue met his, joined, twined, in a slow, slick dance, until he was more aroused than he could remember. He placed her hand on his throbbing erection. "See what you do to me?" he whispered.

She snatched her hand away. "Oh, my."

"I know," he said proudly. "I'm more aroused than I can remember. But I promise I won't hurt you."

She jack-knifed into a sitting position. "It's not that."

"Then what?"

"Let's move to a chair."

Her no-nonsense tone stopped him cold. He raised himself on one elbow and tried to gauge her expression. "You haven't changed your mind, have you?"

"Of course not." She was breathing as hard as he was while staring in the direction of his hard-on. "But I'm afraid you're really, *really* turned on. *The Joy of Sex* clearly states that a sitting position delays ejaculation for over-excited males."

Typical Katie. She'd obviously invested a lot of thought, not to mention research, on the topic. Stifling a rueful laugh, he cupped her face in both hands. "No one has ever complained."

"Yeah, that's what Josh's father said too, but he lied. He had problems with his, uh, staying power. It was over so fast, I barely realized it had happened."

Sam's heart squeezed. So *that* explained the two and a half times of unsatisfactory sex. Josh's dad had been one inconsiderate dude. Katie deserved only the best.

No doubt taking his silence as an admission of guilt, she rushed on, "Maybe you don't have a problem, but let's not take any chances." She glanced at a chintz chair sitting in shadowed elegance beside the window.

Sam figured sex with Katie would be memorable, whether sitting, standing, or hanging upside down from the ceiling. Since she was using him as a sex toy, no strings attached, he'd make damned sure he gave his peak performance. She would remember tonight long after he'd disappeared from her life.

He raised himself on one elbow, looked at her glowing face, and his heart melted a little. "A sitting position's a terrific idea."

Their eyes met and held for a long beat.

Katie wasn't sure Sam's agreement pleased her or not. She'd done her due diligence on the implementation. The woman must straddle the man. Vaulting into the saddle wasn't exactly her idea of sophistication.

"Are you re-thinking the chair?" he asked, his low voice echoing her thoughts with eerie precision.

She shivered as his breath, warm against her ear, stirred her hair. "Nope," she lied. "We should get into a sitting position in case you, uh, by accident ..." She stopped, unable to complete the sentence tactfully.

He cupped her cheeks, his hands warm and gentle on her skin. "It's time to stop thinking and enjoy the ride. I'll help when the time comes, but that'll be later. For now, I want to get you in the mood." When she protested, he shushed her, saying, "It'll be okay. A mandatory warm-up is part of my code."

She frowned. "You have a code of conduct governing the delivery of sexual favors?"

The corners of Sam's mouth kicked up a notch. "That's one of the reasons I'm so popular. Satisfaction guaranteed."

"All right. Proceed," she whispered, figuring he had so much experience he could probably coax a climax out of a rock.

"First, I want to do a couple of things to relax you." His mouth moved from her cheek to her neck, and worked some magic there. Shivers of pleasure trickled along her spine. Who knew the neck was an erogenous zone? Her heart thumped harder.

"I feel pretty loose already," she said in an effort to hurry things along. To illustrate her looseness, she made an expansive gesture.

Big mistake. Her hand brushed his main action zone.

Unable to resist, she wrapped her fist around his length, testing, squeezing. It was a tantalizing handful—warm, velvety, and rock-solid-hard. Her reward was a responsive twitch and a rough growl.

He strained against her hand. "Oh yeah. Don't be shy."

Pleasure unfurled inside her belly, circled a couple of times, and arrowed to her important bits. On a surge of feminine power, she gripped him more firmly, glorying in his heat, his strength, his hardness. And it was all for her.

At his sharp intake of breath, anxiety clouded her sexual excitement. What if he climaxed too fast? She snatched her hand away, knowing all too well what to expect. Determined to experience her first man-made climax if it killed her, she pushed into a sitting position. "You're obviously more than ready. What are we waiting for? It's time for the chair."

Strong hands pressed her into the mattress. "Not yet. We have all night."

"You might not last that long."

"I will. Promise." A gentle kiss tickled one corner of her mouth, then the other. "Tonight is for you, so relax and enjoy."

Everything inside her softened in the face of his empathy. More than anything, she wanted to experience what others took for granted—guilt-free, joyous sex. She wrapped her arms around his body, knowing she'd chosen the right man to grant her wish.

Her mind emptied as he trailed kisses over her chest. When he lingered on her breasts, she bit her lower lip to suppress a moan. At last, she couldn't help herself. "Oh, God. I never dreamed, Ahhhhh ..."

He raised his head. "Shhhh. Let yourself go."

Feeling his clever hands head south, igniting a fire everywhere they touched, she arched into him with a shiver of pleasure. A dull ache expanded somewhere deep in her belly.

"Oh, Sam. Please." She wasn't sure what it was she wanted, but she sensed it lay within reach.

"Christ, you're beautiful," he said, parting her folds gently. "Spread your legs for me."

Katie obeyed, glorying in the hoarseness of his voice. "Soon?" Unable to keep still, she shifted restlessly.

"I'm here for you. Let it happen."

His fingers glided across her most intimate folds, spreading moisture, teasing. The sensation was so fierce, so exquisite, she nearly catapulted from the bed.

He slipped one finger inside. "Oh, God, you're so hot, so tight."

The pressure built. "It's ... I'm ..." She gasped, unable to keep her hips from rocking.

He shifted, and his mouth was on her. First low on her stomach, and then, he was *there*.

At the hot suction of his mouth, she let out a strangled cry.

He raised his head, his pupils dilated with desire. *For her.* And for the first time in her life, everything felt right. This must be how normal felt.

"Let go, Katie. You deserve this."

His tongue stroked, generating a bolt of electricity that felt so delicious, she arched against his mouth, digging her fingers into his shoulders. Nothing in the books came close to describing the delicious ache building inside. Pressure gathered, coalesced into a rush of heat. On a triumphant moan, she thrust herself against his mouth and let go. Her body convulsed as an exquisite orgasmic rush consumed her. Arching her back, she cried, "Sam."

He held her until the aftershocks subsided, then nibbled his way up her body. In a post-orgasmic haze, she faced him, her languid movement intended to provide better access to anything he wanted. When he got to her mouth, she sensed his smile.

"Did it feel as good as the books claim?" he asked.

Recovering her power of speech, she croaked, "I had no idea ..."

"I'll take that as a yes. I aim to please." He wrapped his arms around her. "I hope you realize we're only beginning."

Emerging from her post-coital fog, she sprang upright. "I can't believe how selfish I am, taking advantage of your amazing staying power. According to *Cosmo*, this sort of situation is excruciating for the man."

A slight smile curved his lips. "Nothing you can't fix."

"Oh?" A shiver of anticipation rippled through her body. He was gloriously hard and, oh, God, so big. All because of her. "I see what you mean. I'll do my best."

"Fair enough."

Imitating his technique, Katie straddled his thighs. Using the pads of her fingers, she explored his chest, glorying in how his nipples responded to her feather-light stroke. A man's nipples were seemingly as sensitive as a woman's.

Bending, she touched her lips to his chest, unable to resist a taste. When his breathing quickened, she raised her head. "Is this okay?"

"Christ, yes."

She worked her way south, making sure to take her time. On reaching his belly, she raised her head to examine his face. "I can't believe I'm ready again. Is this normal?"

"Oh, yeah." Although ready to shatter from the sweet torture, Sam forced himself to lie immobile. Her hands slid across his lower belly, where they hesitated. Sensing her indecision, he reached behind and gripped her ass in a gesture of encouragement. "It's okay to touch me. I don't think we'll need the chair."

She responded with a hum of approval, settling lower against him, until her moisture slicked his thighs. Already aroused beyond belief, he worried about exploding before her clever little hands reached his dick. Feeling her fingers encircle him, he released a rough groan.

She stopped what she was doing. "Oh, my God. Am I hurting you? Those damn books didn't explain it right."

"Better than okay," he managed. If he shut her down, it was unlikely her inner sex goddess would ever surface again. "You're doing it exactly right."

"You'll tell me if I make a mistake, won't you?" A rhythmic hand movement accompanied her words.

Unable to speak, he nodded.

"I told you I'm a fast learner."

Every cell of his being strained toward a rip-roaring climax. Struggling to curb his body's natural reaction, he said in a strangled voice, "There's a lot to be said for book learning."

In response, she upped the tempo, proving she was, indeed, a quick study.

If he didn't stop her, it would be game over for him. Before the unthinkable happened, he rolled her onto her back, claiming top position to suckle her breasts. His other hand took a detour to her inner thigh, where each slow caress approached her folds and withdrew, never quite touching, never quite satisfying. Finally, he reached the sensitive nub. She was wet and ready. He used her moisture to stroke her into a frenzy of need.

"Oh, please." Katie strained for release. I need to ... I want ...."

He looked down at her with unaccustomed tenderness at such a moment. "This time, we'll go together." He slid the condom on. "Ready?"

"Yes. Oh, yes." She gripped his hips. "Teach me."

He eased inside and paused, giving her time to adjust to his size. "God, that feels good. So hot and tight." She raised her hips, forcing him deeper.

He drove into her with everything he had, losing himself in her silky heat.

With a soft moan, Katie met his urgent thrusts, wrapping her legs around his waist in a frenzy of need. "More," she demanded, drawing him closer as the tension built once again. He obliged by placing his hands under her hips and tilting her to achieve a better angle.

Straining for release she rocked her hips against his to deepen the penetration. Then she stopped thinking altogether and gave herself over to the heat gathering low in her belly.

Sam drove deep, again and again, slamming hard and fast into Katie's yielding body. Glory be, she was so hot and tight.

Crying out her astonishment, Katie dug her fingers into Sam's butt, holding him in place. Her muscles contracted as her world exploded around her in a blockbuster climax.

Incapable of stopping himself even if he tried, Sam noted that Katie was most definitely having the time of her life, before he, too, exploded.

He'd barely experienced his last glorious spasm when the doorbell chimed.

Chapter 24: Untimely Interruption

Sam's heartbeat was still thundering in his ears when the doorbell rang a second time. His first thought was, *Shit!*

His second was, *Luigi.*

Kissing his post-sex euphoria goodbye, he released Katie's warm, silky body and swung his legs to the floor. "I'll answer the door." He pulled on his pants. "Wait here. I'll be right back." There was no point scaring her if he was wrong.

Katie sprang upright. "No. I'll get it. Josh might be hurt. Or sick. Oh, God, I never should have let him stay at a sleepover. At the very least, I should have phoned." All mama lion defending her cub, Katie catapulted out of bed. "Where's my robe?" She opened the closet door and seized a short cover-up.

Searching for a weapon, anything, Sam glanced into the closet. Spiky-heeled shoes caught his attention and he grabbed one. As an afterthought, he threw a filmy black garment over his arm. As weapons, they weren't great, but better than nothing.

Belting her robe, Katie darted past him, headed for the door.

Adrenaline pumping, he moved faster than he had in years, pinning the door closed with his shoulder in a protective move. "Wait. What if it's someone Luigi sent?"

She stopped pummeling his arm. "Oh, my God. You're right. If it was Josh, his friend's parents would have called. What if Luigi knows about us?"

The doorbell rang again, this time accompanied by a loud hammering. There was no time for argument. Sam was halfway down the stairs, stiletto in hand, filmy thing over one arm, with Katie hard on his heels, when a voice bellowed, "Open up, Boss. I know you're in there."

Sam slowed his descent. "Rooster."

She slipped past on the staircase. "I'll let him in."

Once inside, the bouncer took one look at Sam, another at Katie, and grinned. "Nice to see you two lovebirds managed to hook up. Great taste in shoes there, Boss." Rooster batted his eyes and made a dramatic air-kiss. "For a moment, I thought you were coming out of the closet."

"Hey, the shoe has a heel like an icepick and I planned to use the filmy thing to toss over—never mind. Can't whatever it is wait until morning?"

"Nope. I'm taking a personal day tomorrow."

"The hell you are. You're on the front desk. You agreed to the schedule last week."

Rooster thwacked his forehead with the heel of his hand. "Fuck. I forgot. Have a heart, Boss. I hooked up with a hot congressman and he's outside, waiting for me. You have no idea what he's hiding beneath those pinstripes."

"And I never want to find out. Sleep or no sleep, you'll haul ass into *Kinki* bright and early tomorrow. I need someone I trust on the desk." There were times Sam hated being the boss, and this was one of them. "Now, sit. This won't take long."

Ignoring Rooster's grumbling, Sam buttoned his shirt while Katie handled the preliminaries such as drinks, snacks, and cat introductions. Once they'd seated themselves around the kitchen table, Bluto leaped onto Sam's knee and curled into a soft, warm weight.

Katie jumped right in. "You both need to hear what I learned, so I'll go first."

Sam didn't like the sound of that. "You have news? Why didn't you mention it sooner?"

She gave him an odd look. "Duh! Busy."

"Good point."

She nodded and started describing the meeting between Martinelli and the Allegrettis. Sam listened with growing unease. When she finished, his mouth was too dry to speak. He latched onto his beer and took a healthy slug. The abrupt movement disturbed Bluto, who cracked his eyes into reproachful slits before drifting off again.

Rooster filled the silence. "Holy shit."

Sam plunked his beer onto the table, causing Bluto to flee. "Holy shit is right, Katie. Martinelli's entering the next US senator race, but only as a stepping stone for the White House. That kind of ambition makes a man dangerous." All things considered, he thought he kept his voice remarkably calm.

"Stop yelling. They hadn't a clue I was there."

"Right, Because if they had, you'd be dead." Sam knew he'd raised his voice again, but it appeared the volume control wasn't working. "You overheard Martinelli and two thugs negotiating a hit."

"I did," Katie said. "And I'll learn who the target is next time Frank visits *Kinki*."

Sam shook his head. "Martinelli's too dangerous."

"Is that a fact?" She jutted her chin at him in a way Sam recognized as trouble.

Ice-cold terror made his skin crawl. Instead of yelling at her, which every fiber of his being craved to do, he stood and placed both hands on her shoulders. "If you listen to nothing else I say, please listen to this. Keep your distance from Martinelli. What would Josh do if something happened to you?" The words, *What would I do?* hovered on his lips. Thankfully, he retained enough self-control to swallow them. Instead, he said, "I'll figure out something else."

To his relief, Rooster supported him. "Sam's right, hon. Leave it alone."

"Fine," she said. "Frank's off-limits. But if the voting public learns he fooled around in *Kinki*'s play rooms during its fetish days, I doubt they'll be impressed."

Sam's beer went down the wrong way. Between sputters, he said, "Who told you about the play rooms?" He sat down again.

"Eleanor." Katie gave his back a hearty thump that damn near dislodged a lung. "Not in so many words, of course. I doubt she meant to let it slip, but you'd managed to stress her out."

"Holy shit, Boss. What did you do? It's gotta be bad."

Sam thought hard and came up dry. "Not a damn thing."

Katie looked amused. "Eleanor saw you as the instigator of another skinny dip at her classy fundraiser."

"That's not only unfair, but unwarranted. At least this time. And how does it tie in with Martinelli fooling around in *Kinki*?"

"Eleanor didn't want me to see what went on at a skinny dip. I think she was trying to protect you. She was so flustered she compared last year's skinny dip to an orgy at *Kinki* during its fetish days."

He listened in mounting disbelief as Katie described Eleanor's revelations, ending with the orgies. Once she wrapped it up, he said, "You're full of surprises."

"I try." Katie's mouth twitched. "I bet Frank was a frequent flyer at those orgies."

Rooster nodded. "You're right. He was a regular. If memory serves, he particularly enjoyed being spanked."

Now that was a picture that burned itself into a man's brain. "Is there anything else you want to tell me?" Sam hoped like hell Katie would say no.

"Now that you mention it, yeah. I should warn you about Luciana. To refresh your memory, she was the Sunday school teacher lookalike attached to your package."

Sam winced. She must be referring to Martinelli's head fundraiser. "I didn't lead her on. Promise." He gave Katie his best knock-em-dead grin, hoping she wouldn't hate him. "I'm not remotely interested in her."

She frowned in return. "Good. Because she's Vinnie's wife, and Vinnie used to be Luigi's second-in-command."

Sam stopped smiling. "Again, not interested."

"Even if you were, the photo I took will keep us both safe."

"How so?"

"Vinnie's the most jealous man in the world, worse than Luigi. He never lets Luciana go near a party without him, but she let it slip he's out of town."

Sam processed what she'd said and raised his glass in admiration. "The photo is insurance. Brilliant."

Pink stained her cheekbones. "Simple common sense," she said, adorably flustered.

Rooster broke in. "Are we finished here? Let me tell you what I learned so's I can leave."

Sam said, "Aside from discovering the glories of your congressman during quickies in the bushes, which by the way, we do *not* want to hear about, what did you learn?"

Rooster turned beet-red. "How the hell did you … Never mind. I snooped. I stalked. I eavesdropped. I listened to discussions about *Kinki*'s former owners." For Katie's benefit, he added, "They're both in prison indefinitely for murder, improper disposal of human remains, assault with a deadly weapon, and more. Sam's brother and sister-in-law took them down."

Katie took a dainty sip of water before saying to Sam, "The owners sold you their fetish club at a ridiculously low price, right?"

"Right." In case she got the wrong idea about his interest in fetish clubs, Sam added, "But you may have noticed I'm renovating it into an upscale Goth nightclub."

"You must have spent hours and hours inside *Kinki* before you bought it."

Sam saw where she was headed and hastened to reassure her. "Not as many as you might think. I saw right away it would be an excellent investment. And FYI, I didn't set foot in any of the play rooms."

"Excuse me, children." Rooster rapped on the table. "I overheard a snippet of conversation between Martinelli and Deanna. I didn't dare get too close, but I gather it had something to do with *Kinki*. Martinelli was pissed off with her for some reason."

Sam and Katie exchanged a glance. "What do you think it could be?" he asked.

"No idea. It could be anything."

Rooster got to his feet. "Gotta run. There's a horny congressman waiting to pleasure me, so I'll leave you with this final piece of information." Ever the drama queen, he paused before saying, "Oliver Hathaway, one of *Kinki*'s former owners, is housed in the New Jersey State Prison." He made a speedy exit.

Katie turned to Sam. "That's the same prison Luigi's in. Could they have met one another?"

"Possibly, but I don't see how it matters."

"Me neither. But I don't like coincidences."

Sam took a closer look at her face and wrapped his arms around her. "Hey, pretty lady. How're you feeling?" He nuzzled her neck. "You okay?"

To his surprise, she stiffened and strong-armed his chest to put some space between them. *Not* the response he expected.

***

Right away, Katie knew she'd hurt Sam's feelings. She hadn't meant to push him away, but her move had been instinctive. She had to say something to make things right.

Try the truth. Right. She could do that. "You deserve an explanation."

"Did I do or say something wrong?"

"No, it's not that."

"Then what?"

"I didn't know how to react. Nobody ever asked me how I was feeling. Not after a tough funeral when my chest felt so tight I thought it might explode, not after Pop died and I was left to manage *Paradise Gate* by myself, not even after my boyfriend died, leaving me pregnant and scared."

"You're one very special woman. Brave, smart, sexy too." He stroked one finger down her cheek, leaving a trail of sparks. "So how is this a problem?"

Her breath hitched in her chest. At that moment, she knew she was in trouble. Somewhere along the way, perhaps between orgasms, she'd misplaced her detachment. She genuinely *liked* the man behind the sexy exterior, the man who concealed his huge heart behind a mask of a philanderer.

This was dangerous territory. She couldn't let herself get too attached.

As she considered wriggling away, he worked his thumb gently along her spine. A small electric charge shot into places Katie had hoped would remain neutral. She didn't have to look at Sam to know his cheeks had creased into a broad smile. It would be suicide to yield to the feelings washing through her.

She dug deep to find the strength to say, "We need to talk."

"You sure you wouldn't rather talk later?"

Katie looked at him and felt a clutch in her heart. She had to end things tonight. Break it off. Immediately. Before she got hurt. He'd find another woman in no time. It was what he did, who he was.

By then, his fingers were working their magic along her shoulder blades. Trying to ignore her body's enthusiastic response to his caress, she said, "I need a break."

He slid one hand around her body to palm a breast. "Of course you do. After everything we did, you must be feeling real tender down there. I know a trick that'll—"

"No, I was thinking more along the lines of … oh, my."

His fingers traced her nipple. The sensation was so fierce, she didn't want him to stop. In order to delay the orgasm she felt coming, she peeled his hand away. He resumed stroking, and she wanted to lose herself in pleasure. Her thighs loosened in anticipation.

Bad thighs.

She forced herself to put some distance between them. It was one of the hardest things she'd ever done. "Let me finish, Sam. It's important. Where was I?"

For a long beat, he said nothing, standing there looking unbearably sexy and unless she was mistaken, slightly wary. He finally said, "Needing a break."

"Right." This came out as a gasp because he was using one finger to trace a pattern on her arm. One glance at his face, and she melted. He oozed sensuality, and her body verified that the man was an excellent teacher. All she needed was a brief time-out to regain her detachment.

Quickly, before she changed her mind, she said, "It's time you left."

***

Sam figured he'd heard wrong. Or misinterpreted. He was the one who did the leaving, not the other way around. With Katie, he'd already decided to make an exception to his rule and spend the entire night. Hell, he'd stashed a collapsible toothbrush in his pocket. This was the closest he'd come to commitment, and she was booting him out? There must be a mistake.

He found his voice. "Say what?"

"I need my space. This is just sex, remember?"

Her words felt like a body blow. His dates must have felt like this when he'd asked them to leave. He forced a grin. "Absolutely. Friends with benefits." He kept it casual, as if he didn't feel as though a grenade had exploded in his gut. "I was about to head out anyway. How 'bout we plan more 'just sex' later today?"

"Sorry. Josh and I have a family dinner tonight."

"Invite me." Sam flinched. Had he really said that?

"Nope." Katie patted his hand. "You'd hate it. Trust me."

He had a hard time wrapping his head around the fact that his feelings for Katie were unlike anything he'd felt for the other woman he'd dated. None of them had made him want more. He wasn't sure what it was about Katie, or what he wanted, exactly, but one thing was certain. He longed for more than he thought possible.

He stood there and wanted to convince her to let him stay. Instead, he said, "No problem. I'll get dressed and out of your hair."

Chapter 25: Work Complications

After Sam's departure, sleep eluded Katie. Sometimes God punished by delivering exactly what you requested—in this case, really, truly excellent sex. She tried pressing her face into the pillow to erase memories of their time together. Big mistake. With each inhalation, Sam's lingering scent filled her nostrils. She threw the pillow across the room, telling herself to get a grip. It was just sex, nothing more, made memorable only by his considerable skill.

As soon as dawn brightened the sky, she hauled herself out of bed. Sunday was her day off, and Josh would be at his friend's house until late morning. But the grand opening was getting closer and deadlines loomed. Going to work would be a useful distraction. By the time Sam rolled in, if he did, she'd be home and playing with her son.

Traffic was light, the commute speedy. She parked, and entered *Kinki*. Behind the desk, Rooster looked greenish. It must have been a memorable night. Moving on autopilot, she reached her office. The door stood ajar.

She peeked inside. Her world narrowed until all it contained was Sam seated behind his desk. Her girl parts gave an enthusiastic throb of recognition.

His hair was all cute and rumpled, her favorite bedroom look, which was where they would still be if she hadn't been dumb enough to kick him out. He leaned down and smiled at something hidden behind the desk's modesty panel.

Katie let out a soundless sigh. How sweet. Sam had brought Rex with him to let Hiram sleep late.

Thankfully she'd worn decent sandals and one of Bella's cute sundresses. Not that she'd dressed to impress in case Sam showed up. No way.

Rex came up from behind and licked her feet, triggering an involuntary squeak.

Sam's brilliant grin flashed, warming her from the inside out. "Hey, pretty lady," he said softly.

Her knees and other parts liquefied in tandem. Consumed by a haze of lust, she stayed silent in case her voice emerged as another squeak. She'd taken two steps when a blonde head emerged from the desk well, followed by the rest of Deanna. Bright, searing pain made Katie gasp. She'd walked in on a blow-job. No wonder Sam was smiling.

She took in Deanna's mussed hair, her flushed cheekbones, the boobage straining to burst from a low-slung neckline. The Atkins diet hadn't made a noticeable difference.

Apparently unaware of another presence, Deanna offered Sam a sultry smile. "Mission accomplished." Her voice sounded huskier than usual as she deposited a handful of papers on Sam's desk. No doubt they'd served as a kneeling pad.

At Katie's involuntary gasp, Deanna looked up. "Katie. I didn't hear you come in." She stuffed the loose papers into a file folder.

Heart pounding, Katie drew on her years of practice at hiding emotion and unclenched her jaw. "Obviously."

She made sure her voice was neutral when she addressed Sam. "I didn't expect anyone to be here on Sunday morning, least of all you, especially after—" She snapped her mouth shut before she made an idiot of herself.

Sam looked anything but contrite. "I couldn't sleep, so I came in to catch up on my paperwork." He examined her face with the same quiet intensity he no doubt reserved for the casino. "You're upset."

"What? Upset? Me? Nope."

Flopped beside Sam's desk, Rex raised his head and whined.

Sam flashed her a knowing grin. "Even Rex knows you're lying."

She shot her nose into the air and drew herself to her full height. "How you spend your Sunday morning is none of my business."

Deanna tucked a strand of hair behind her ear. "Time to go." She dumped the files into a briefcase, and headed for the door. Over her shoulder, she said, "Thanks for everything you did this morning, Sam. You have no idea how much you helped." She sashayed out the door.

Sam unfolded, revealing six-plus feet of gorgeous male animal. Katie snuck a peek at his crotch and blew out a sigh of relief. Nice bulge, but that was his normal package. There was no obvious erection, and his fly was fully zipped.

"You're checking me out," he said.

"Am not." She edged toward the door.

He blocked her retreat. "You thought Deanna was pleasuring me under the desk."

Her face warmed. "You must admit, it looked bad."

"Is that an apology?" He closed in on her.

"It's all you'll get." She shoved at his chest, more to touch him than to push him away. "Move. I have work to do."

"No rush." He dragged her against him. "Don't you want to know why Deanna paid our office a visit?"

"Nope." She found her hands gliding up his arms. So much for detachment.

He massaged her spine with slow deliberation. "What with the explosion, vandalism, and inspection, she was behind schedule with the hiring. But after last night's party, she felt queasy and needed to be close to a toilet—she called it a rest room. The HR powder room is still out of commission, so she borrowed this office, end of story." He nuzzled Katie's neck.

"Oh." She leaned in, filling her nostrils with the scent of woodsy cologne, soap, and sexy man. "Why was she under your desk?"

"She dropped a résumé on the floor. Papers drifted under the desk. She was picking them up." His voice deepened. "Lordy, but you smell delicious."

Katie tried to conquer thoughts of desk sex. She leaned back and tilted her head to improve ease of access. "I'm certain I locked the office door when I left yesterday."

His breath stirred her hair. "As HR Manager, Deanna has a master key."

He slid his hand down Katie's side, and her important bits gave a mighty throb. With a slight posture adjustment, one boob found its way into his palm, surprise, surprise.

A delicious shiver shot down her spine. "Let me guess. You helped because she was vulnerable and needy. You're that kind of guy. It's all good." Feeling pretty vulnerable and needy herself, Katie pressed her body against his hard, lean frame. Her hips did an involuntary wiggle.

When he spoke again, she noticed his voice had grown husky. "If you don't stop that, I'll need a long, cold shower."

"Not many bosses would go that extra mile." She delivered one last hip rock for good measure. "Stopping now."

"Hah. You were jealous." A smile accompanied his words. "Are you sure this thing between us isn't more than 'just sex'?"

Is that how Sam saw it? A tremor of hope ran down her spine. She quelled it immediately. Sam wasn't a permanent relationship kind of guy. "In your dreams. Let me go. I have work to do." She extricated herself, which was harder than she liked. "There's the menu for the grand opening, and we need to discuss your idea for a background video during the ceremony, and I need to write your speech, and—" Her heart stuttered when Sam's finger landed on her lips, silencing her nervous chatter.

"I'll do the video and write my own speech, you work on the menu." His breath was hot against her cheek. "But as my brother says, it's important to finish what you start. So in the interest of following his advice, I'll be pestering you again once we're away from the office."

Something in his voice made her believe he saw right through her insistence that what they had was "just sex."

***

An hour later, Sam was ready to call it quits. He'd completed a grand total of nothing. Zero. Zilch. He checked his security cameras for the tenth time before casting a scowl at the crux of his problem. Katie looked delectable, all concentration and intensity.

He wanted to smooth out the tiny frown furrowing her brow as she tapped the keyboard. His fingers itched to investigate silky territory barely concealed by the flimsy sundress, which was, in his opinion, a vast improvement over her mortician attire.

On the verge of making his move, he hesitated, unsure of her reaction. For as long as he could remember, his charm worked miracles on women, that is, until last night. He had a hard time believing Katie had kicked him out of her house then compounded the snub by refusing to invite him to dinner tonight.

Yeah, he'd misread her signals. And he'd sure as hell underestimated his own reaction.

She scribbled something in the ever-present notebook. His belly quivered. Even the damn notebook was cute. He was in deep shit.

A man might think she was ignoring him, except every now and again, he caught her flicking a glance in his direction. To test the waters, he grabbed the phone and dialed a random number, disconnecting before it rang. She stopped typing. He spoke to the dial tone, sensing her effort to hear every word. Good sign.

With the receiver held close to his ear, he tilted his chair while pretending to engage in breezy banter. Glancing sideways, he noted she was flipping pages and chewing a pencil. He kept a straight face and continued conversing, extending a dinner invitation for tonight, accepting a refusal, and disconnecting after a promise to be in touch soon.

He'd set the scene. It was time for the action.

He faked a disappointed frown at Katie. "That's my third rejection today."

Katie cleared her throat. "Too bad you can't find a date."

"You didn't think I was calling another woman, did you? Hell, no. That was my brother, Nick. He and his wife have plans for tonight, and Granddaddy Hiram has Bingo."

"That's only two."

He made damn sure he smiled. "You're the third. It's not too late for you to invite me for dinner to ease the pain. I can't remember the last time I enjoyed a home-cooked meal." His face ached with the effort of holding a jaunty grin in place.

After an extended pause, she shook her head. "Bad idea. Taking you to a family dinner would send Ma the wrong message. She's anxious to see me married."

She'd blown him off again. He should be happy but he wasn't. Sensing it was the wrong time to make another pass, he refrained from suggesting they head out for brunch. Instead, he got to work, acutely aware that she was tidying her desk. Hell, she was leaving.

When his phone rang, he answered. Katie stopped stacking papers and tilted her head. Just a touch.

The cute real estate agent he'd met in a bar last week answered his greeting. Lowering his voice to a confidential murmur, he pretended not to notice when Katie nearly fell out of her chair trying to hear what he had to say. According to the agent, someone wanted to buy *Kinki*. The offer didn't interest him. He booked an appointment anyway, to remind Katie that other women wanted a piece of Sammy. He'd cancel later.

As soon as he disconnected, the phone rang again. This time, it was Rooster at the front desk. When Sam understood what was happening, his mood improved. "I'll be right down."

He stood and told Katie. "Front desk. Martinelli arrived while I was on the phone, and so did my corpses. Rush order, special delivery on a Sunday."

"Your what?" Katie's voice was faint.

"Dummy corpses," he elaborated. "I had them custom-made. They're on their way to *Dracula's Lair*."

Katie raised one eyebrow. "Sunday morning's an odd time for Frank to pay a visit, especially after his party. I bet he's here to see Deanna."

"He could be checking up on his surveillance detail, but I doubt it. Let's find him." Sam punched some buttons on his phone. After paging through several screens, he said, "Houston, we have lift-off. Martinelli and Deanna are in *Dracula's Lair*. Let's take a little walk and check out those corpses."

Rex scrambled to his feet at the word *walk*.

Katie's lips twitched. "Wow. There's an offer I don't hear often."

"Please don't grill Martinelli," Sam reminded her. "We don't want to spook him."

"Don't worry. I'll be low key. I don't want Frank reporting on me to Luigi."

***

Out of the corner of her eye, Katie caught Sam's intense expression in her peripheral vision as they headed for *Dracula's Lair*. His solid warmth beside her had her heart jack-hammering in her chest.

Perhaps sensing her reaction, he turned his head. "You sure you don't want to invite me to dinner?"

"Couldn't be more sure." That would *so* not be the path to detachment.

They stopped outside the open door of *Dracula's Lair*. It was the first time she'd seen the room since its restoration. The hole in the floor was gone and all the coffins resided in their correct location. Frank and Deanna were huddled together in the rear corner, their voices low and urgent. The senator, perfectly groomed in a dove-gray business suit, appeared to be chewing her out, and she was far from happy about it.

When Rex trotted in, Deanna glanced up and stared. A millisecond later, she waggled her fingers with a welcoming smile.

Her recovery was so abrupt, Katie at first thought she'd imagined the dispute. The sheen of tears on Deanna's cheeks told her otherwise.

A lovers' quarrel?

"Hi again. Gotta run, work to do." Deanna moved past them at a good clip considering the four-inch stilettos she wore. "Nice corpses. See you later." With a bright nod in their general direction, she whizzed out the door and disappeared.

Frank's expression was tuned to pleased surprise. "My, my. Fancy finding both of you here, and on a Sunday." His famous smile bathed them in its glory.

Not knowing what to say, Katie merely nodded. She admired the way Sam smoothed over the awkwardness by greeting Frank with a cheery, "Good morning, Senator. Nice to see you again so soon. What brings you here?"

"I was on my way to church and took a little detour to check out your club, make sure the security surveillance detail is in position. Deanna assures me there's been no more damage."

Sam nodded. "So far, so good."

Hoping her smile didn't look phony, Katie she gushed, "You look wonderful this morning, Frank, even after hosting a magnificent function that must have lasted until dawn. I had the best time ever. Is your charming wife here with you? I'd love to thank her in person for her kindness." Katie wondered what Eleanor saw in her husband.

"She was a little under the weather this morning. I told her it was okay to stay in bed. I'm sure the good Lord understands the effect of too many rum punches."

"Of course." Katie knew for a fact that Eleanor had consumed nothing but water at the party. Mindful of remaining low-key, she carefully made no mention of seeing the Allegrettis at the fundraiser or of overhearing Frank contracting out a hit.

Frank strolled over to one of the coffins and propped up its inhabitant, laughing at the rope of plastic intestines spilling from a gaping stomach wound. "This guy looks exactly like my mamma's great-uncle."

Sam stuck to Frank's side. "It's all about ambiance. We went for the rotted-out appearance. Look at how his complexion is a weird greyish-pink with discolorations."

"Very effective." Katie bit the inside of her cheek to stop herself from blurting out the true facts, that reputable funeral parlors took great pains with makeup and hair styling to make the deceased look as lifelike as possible, not recently exhumed.

Frank fingered the coffin lining. "These caskets feel nice and comfy."

This time Katie couldn't help herself. "Oh, they are. The most expensive ones are fully padded. Relatives take comfort in knowing their loved one rest comfortably." She faltered when she realized both men were staring at her. "Just sayin'."

Frank grinned, eying her with too much interest for her liking. "You're the expert, Katarina. Let's have Sam test-drive one. It'll be fun." He hefted the corpse and draped it over another coffin, letting the arms flop over the sides. "Sam, my man, climb in."

"I don't think so."

"Aw, come on. Don't you want to know how it feels?"

Sam's face paled under his tan. "I hate enclosed spaces. It's a thing."

"Surely you don't want the beautiful Katarina to think you're a coward." The senator's smile broadened. "Pretend it's a soft, comfy bed. I dare you." He winked at Katie

Katie tensed, prepared to do battle. A glance at Sam's face told her he was aware of her burning desire to jump to his defense. His eye roll and tiny head shake warned her to keep quiet. Her heart melted when she realized he was protecting her.

Sam gripped the side of the coffin. Crap. He was taking the dare, all to convince Frank there was nothing was going on between them.

She tried to give him an easy out. "Are you sure? You wanted to review the final budget figures, and I have to leave soon to pick up Josh from his sleepover."

Sam produced a weak smile. "This'll only take a couple of seconds. What doesn't kill you makes you stronger, right?" He nodded at Frank. "Here goes."

Doing her best to look unconcerned, she examined another corpse while Sam pulled off his boots and made a big production of climbing inside and lying down. Once he stretched out, he said, "Very nice. Cozy, but an inch or so too short for me."

Rex whined as Frank reached for the lid. Sam attempted to raise himself on his elbows, but Frank pinned him with one hand while lowering the lid with the other. "Give it a proper try." He let go and the lid dropped into place with a thump. "Sorry. My hand slipped."

Katie didn't try to hide her anger. "You closed it on purpose." She fumbled with the lid.

Frank placed one hand over hers, stilling her fingers, and leaning over to whisper in her ear. "Perceptive as well as beautiful. If you're real nice, I can kick your career into high gear." He gave her hand a final brief squeeze and let go. "Say the word, babe, and I'll take care of our incarcerated friend."

Was it possible he'd issued a veiled proposition coupled with a bribe and an offer to kill Luigi? It struck her that a contracted hit on Luigi might already be out there.

Frank released her hand and rapped the casket once. In his normal voice, he said, "Tell Sam I hope he can take a joke. Look, I'd better run or I'll be late for church. I'll call you soon—about our next fundraiser, of course." He strode from the room.

She wanted to find soap and water to wash her hands. Senator Martinelli was a dangerous, two-timing slime ball, possibly a murderer, disguised as a God-fearing, happily married churchgoer. Katie's heart went out to Eleanor.

Muffled shouts from the coffin reminded her of Sam's plight. The lid was heavy, but she managed.

His eyes were wild and unfocussed. Sweat dribbled down his face, soaking into his silky shirt. His chest heaved with the force of his breathing as he scrambled to hoist himself out of the casket. "I couldn't push the lid," he said between gritted teeth. "I don't believe the bastard locked me inside."

"It's heavy. Although it's a common misconception, caskets don't lock spontaneously," she assured him. "In order to lock one, the funeral director uses a special wrench to unscrew a bolt in the end of the casket, inserts a casket key into the hole, and turns it."

Convulsive shivers wracked Sam's body. She recognized the exact moment he registered her presence because he pulled himself together. It must have taken all his strength, but he crossed his arms to hide the tremors. "You must think I'm a coward."

"Far from it. You faced your biggest fear to distract Frank from his suspicions about us."

"You caught that, huh? I'm claustrophobic."

At the slight hitch in his voice, her throat slammed shut with sympathy. "Yeah, I caught that, too."

He massaged the bridge of his nose with thumb and forefinger. "I wasn't always afraid."

He was obviously trying to control his emotions. For her benefit. The lump in her throat expanded. "No need to explain."

"My father locked me in our toy trunk as a punishment for some shit I pulled." He cleared his throat, as if aware of his unsteady voice. "I was only eight years old, but the bastard forgot about me and disappeared. Good job Nick heard me yelling, or I'd have been there overnight."

He was trying to make it sound like it was no big deal. Her pulse raced in sympathy for that terrified little boy.

Wanting to make it all better, she threw her arms around his neck and kissed him. It began as a comforting kiss, but soon morphed into something else. His lips applied the exact right amount of pressure as his tongue tangled with hers. She rocked her hips against him. He deepened the kiss until she was ready to do him on the floor of *Dracula's Lair*. Feeling her legs quiver, she decided caution was overrated, and kissed him, giving it everything she had.

Screw detachment.

Several minutes passed in a haze of sensuality before he drew back, his chest heaving. His eyes glowed with passion and something else, causing her breath to catch. So he felt it too. She shivered as he ran his hands down her spine.

With obvious reluctance, he backed away, saying, "As much as I want to continue what we've started, this isn't the time or place. You're having dinner with your family tonight so why not invite me? Afterwards, we'll pick up where we left off."

Trying to draw air into her lungs, all she could do was to shake her head.

As tempted as she was, inviting Sam to dinner with her family would be a huge mistake. First of all, the invitation would imply she had feelings for Sam (so not true). Plus Ma would pressure Sam to marry her, and her brother would engage him in a pissing contest. But worst of all, Josh might get too attached to a man he'd never see again once they left town.

Sam's voice interrupted her thoughts. "Haven't you forgotten something? Today is Sunday. It slipped my mind earlier, but we already agreed Josh could walk Rex tonight. You have to invite me to dinner. I made your son a promise."

She deserved the Worst-Mother-in-the-World award because she'd totally forgotten.

Chapter 26: The Facedown

At five o'clock on the dot, Sam arrived at The Annex, all spruced up, smelling good, and toting a bottle of Chianti.

Before he could ring the bell, Josh answered the door. On catching sight of Rex, the kid threw his arms around the dog. Bouncing with excitement, he engaged Sam in a mile-a-minute discussion of an after-dinner dog walk. He didn't run out of steam until a rounder, whiter-haired version of Katie barreled in, enthusiastic about having, as she put it, such a handsome young man join them for dinner.

Sam handed over the wine, introduced himself, and added some flattering words that made her blush. Once she'd identified herself as Katie's mother, established his marital status (single), and his relationship with her daughter (he stuck with boss), she hugged him before returning to the kitchen. He could damn near hear the chime of wedding bells in Signora Deluca's imagination.

Katie took her time sauntering into the hallway, accompanied by a man Sam assumed was her brother, Rico. After introductions, Sam went all-out in the charm department. It was a wasted effort. Rico appeared unimpressed, and Katie's thunderous look promised a world of hurt for forcing the dinner invitation.

After a long and, at least for Sam, uncomfortable silence, Katie said, "I have to help in the kitchen. I'm counting on you to entertain one another until the dinner is ready." She disappeared, leaving Sam alone with Rico, who was best buddies with Luigi. Great. He probably figured Sam was encroaching on his friend's claim on Katie.

"Let's go downstairs for a few minutes." Rico said with a smirk.

It didn't take Sam long to realize Rico was messing with his head. *Downstairs* meant the business end of *Paradise Gate*. A sole client occupied a padded gurney in the middle of the preparation room. Pine air freshener failed to mask the bite of formaldehyde. Doing some heavy-duty mouth breathing, he made damn sure to hide his discomfort.

"What do you think?" Rico asked, his smirk broadening.

Yeah, definitely entering the machismo dance. Steeling himself, Sam ambled closer to the gurney. Pretending the corpse was one of the dummies in *Dracula's Lair*, he pushed aside a metal tray containing surgical instruments and managed to check out the body, or to be precise, half-body, without puking.

The deceased's top half was immaculate in a formal jacket, arms folded across his torso, white hair brushed away from a high forehead. His dark-framed glasses reflected the florescent lighting, lending a macabre note of animation to the elderly face.

The man's bottom half was conspicuous by its absence.

For God's sake, don't show any sign of weakness. "Kinda short, isn't he?" Sam drawled.

Rico raised one eyebrow. "Car bombs are unpredictable. This one vaporized Signore Romano from the hips down, but left his top half pretty much intact—if you don't look too closely."

Sam didn't intend to look at all. "This sort of thing happen often?"

"Often enough. Romanos have enemies, Delucas get business."

"I assume y'all are fixin' to have a closed casket." Sam hoped he's kept the horror out of his voice.

Rico gave a shark-like smile. "Nope. The Romanos don't take no for an answer, so I promised the family we'd make him look natural."

"Surely you could have talked them into being sensible."

"I don't know shit about the client side. That was Katie's job."

"Not anymore," Sam said. "She works for me."

Rico gave Sam a hard look. "She thinks she's too good to be a mortician now that she's found a fancy job cozying up to a *bartender*." He spat out the last word.

"Night club owner," Sam said evenly.

Rico's brows slammed together. "What?"

Trying to forget the fact that Rico interacted with criminals, Sam said. "I'm a nightclub owner, meaning I manage bartenders, chefs, and everyone else in a very large, very upscale nightclub."

"Is that a fact? How be you tell me how to fix up Signore Romano for an open casket viewing?"

Adrenaline pumped through Sam's body in giant spurts. He recognized a full-scale pissing contest when he saw one. After pretending to examine the body, he drilled Rico with a cold stare. "I'll do better than that. I'll fix Signore Romano myself, on one condition."

Rico fingered a scalpel lying on the metal tray, making a clinking sound. "I never did care for conditions."

Hoping Rico, like most bullies, was also a coward, Sam grinned, adding a little extra toothiness and a macho strut for good measure. "Make that two conditions, but who's counting?"

"Who the hell do you think you are?"

"Someone who cares about your sister." Ignoring the scalpel's clink, Sam scowled and took one step closer until he was nose-to-nose with Rico. "Condition number one, stop talking to Luigi. Your sister gets upset, which means I get upset." He took another step forward, enough to force Rico to shuffle backwards. "Condition number two, get out of my face. I don't like it, and I guarantee you won't enjoy my cranky side."

They exchanged glares. Rico caved first. "Katie told you about Luigi?"

"Yeah." Sam did his damndest to act as though everything was normal. He made a show of turning his back on Rico to study the corpse. His heart thundered in his chest as he imagined the scalpel slicing into his flesh.

"Fine," Rico said with a final metallic clink as he dropped the scalpel. "What's your idea? It'd better be good."

Sam blew out a soundless sigh. "You got the pants and shoes?"

Rico slipped a pair of dark pants from a hanger, and draped them onto the gurney where the pelvis and two legs should have been. He placed a pair of shiny black shoes at the end.

"Toss me those newspapers," Sam ordered, pointing to a stack on another rolling trolley in the corner. He guessed even morticians took breaks to read the newspaper.

Again, Rico obeyed, wheeling the contraption over to the gurney.

Sam peeled off some sheets. Paper rustled as he crumpled and stuffed the wad into the left pant leg, shoving it up to the general pelvis area.

"You've gotta be kidding," Rico said. "*This* is your brainwave?"

Sam channeled his inner badass. "Got any better ideas?" He continued working. Rip. Crumple. Stuff. After a while, he stepped back to admire his handiwork. The legs looked better than he'd hoped.

"Not bad, I guess," Rico admitted. "As long as no one touches him, it'll pass inspection."

"It's your job to discourage touching." Sam gave the pants a final tweak. "Now for the shoes. Got any duct tape?"

As he worked, Sam imagined Katie dealing with the terrible realities of prettying up death. And all because of family loyalty and a willingness to do whatever it took to help, no matter the cost to herself. He had no desire to cause more trouble for the family. It was time to end the pissing contest.

He pulled out his phone. "Gotta check up on my club." He sensed Rico watching as he scanned every room in *Kinki*.

Sure enough, Rico asked, "What are you doing?"

Yeah, he was thawing. "Long distance surveillance I installed in *Kinki*. Watch," Sam said, demonstrating how it worked and pocketing the phone.

"Cool," Rico said. "Got anything else by way of security?"

"Frank Martinelli set up outside surveillance. His detail keeps an eye on the exterior perimeter, night and day."

"State Senator Martinelli?"

"One and the same."

"Hey, he's a friend of *Paradise Gate* too," Rico volunteered.

Sam could read Rico's mind. *He's gotta be connected if he's buddies with Martinelli.*

"No kidding." Keeping his tone noncommittal while attaching Romano's left shoe, Sam said, "A mortuary must be a tough business to run. Katie mentioned your family experienced financial difficulties."

"We struggled for a while, but we're okay now."

"Because you wrote off Luigi's loans?

Rico smiled. "Hell, no. That would be a dangerous game. He forgave the loans, said he didn't need payment because we were going to be family. I haven't had the nerve to tell Katie yet." Rico jabbed a thumb at a large photograph on the wall above the embalming table. "That's Luigi. The day before the cops hauled him in, he insisted we hang it somewhere Katie would see him every day. She wasn't happy about it."

Sam studied the portrait with loathing. The bastard was movie star handsome, with his artfully messed hair and open-necked black shirt revealing chest hair and part of a tattoo. There was something chilling about him. It was the eyes. They were the eyes of a rattlesnake. Or a killer.

"Yeah, he looks dangerous," Sam said. "Everyone's better off with Luigi in lockup."

Rico grinned. "Exactly. If he gets out on appeal, he'll be pissed with me. Word of our special services has spread. Other well-connected members of society want us to handle tragic and sudden deaths discretely, if you get my meaning."

Sam got the meaning. Only too well. He nodded and re-focused his attention on positioning both legs. "Signore Romano looks normal to me. What do you think?"

Rico examined Sam's handiwork. "Hey, you're a natural."

"Thanks." Sam was grateful Rico couldn't see his face as he folded the remaining newspapers. It gave him a chance to process what he'd learned. What better way to dispose of enemies than by cremating them, all without the benefit of death certificates?

For the first time, Sam understood Katie's urgency. If *Kinki*'s grand opening wasn't successful, she had nowhere to turn. No one would want to hire her, but she and Josh couldn't return to *Paradise Gate* as long as Rico rubbed shoulders with criminals.

He gave Rico a man-to-man backslap. "Can I give you some advice?"

"I guess not."

"Stop delivering those free funerals before the cops find out. And they will, guaranteed. If you go down, so does *Paradise Gate* and your entire family with it. If they subpoena Katie to testify, she'll have to tell the truth. It would damn near kill her. And FYI, no woman in her right mind wants to hook up with a man who's already in bed with murderers." Sam fixed Rico with a level look. "Think about it."

Katie's voice interrupted Rico's reply. "Dinner's ready."

Chapter 27: Deluca Dinner

Sam dislodged the nose nudging his knee, but he was too late. Drool soaked into his pants, reminding him of his dumb-ass promise to Josh.

The table groaned under its load—platters of prosciutto-stuffed veal called *saltimbocca di vitello*, eggplant in red gravy with melted cheese, fettuccini Alfredo, and more. After one unfortunate food alarm incident, Rex was quiet for the rest of the meal. Too quiet. Josh must be slipping him scraps. Not wanting to draw attention to himself and the after-dinner walk, Sam ignored an entire slice of veal disappearing under the table.

He looked across the table at Katie. She shifted the platter of veal out of Josh's reach and glanced at Sam with a knowing smile. It appeared forgiveness for forcing the dinner invitation was in the air.

Signora Deluca's sharp elbow interrupted his contemplation of what lay under Katie's pretty sun-dress. "*Mangia*. Eat. You're too skinny."

Bella said to Sam, " Ma says that to anyone under 300 pounds."

"It's true. Look at the boy. He's skin and bones."

"Signora Deluca," Sam said, "This is, without a doubt, the best meal I've eaten since leaving Texas." He speared another slice of veal.

A brilliant smile illuminated the woman's face, transforming her into a beauty. "*Grazie*. Have more *Melanzane alla Parmigiana*." She heaped more eggplant on his plate. "I like you, Sam Jackson. I don't know what happened downstairs, but you must have impressed my son."

"We got along fine, didn't we?" Sam grinned at Rico. "In fact, we got along so well, I want to invite Rico, Bella, and you, too, Signora Deluca, to *Kinki*'s grand opening. Feel free to bring a date or a friend. I'll see y'all get VIP tickets allowing you to come inside early."

Their enthusiastic acceptance signified approval.

Signora Deluca said something to Katie in Italian.

Katie flicked him a glance. "You're embarrassing me, Ma," she muttered. "He's my boss, nothing more."

"It's time you settled down. You're not getting any younger."

"Ma, cut it out. I mean it. If you don't stop—"

But Signora Deluca had fixed her attention on Sam. "What are your intentions regarding my daughter?"

Sam froze, his fork halfway to his mouth. Truth be told, his feelings were all over the map. He settled on an abridged version of the truth. "Uh, we haven't discussed it." He cast a pleading glance at Katie.

She rescued him by saying, "Get off his case, Ma. He's my boss, nothing more." Katie shot him a brilliant smile.

Her words should have reassured him. Instead, they left him feeling hollow.

Every head at the table swung in Sam's direction. In pure desperation, he turned to Josh. "You up for walking Rex now, before it gets dark?"

Josh's fine features lit up. "I was afraid you'd changed your mind."

Sam forced a sickly grin. "Never." He glanced at Katie. "Are you ready?"

Katie shot out of her seat. "Absolutely. We'll have dessert later."

On the way out of the dining room, Josh lowered his voice so only Sam could hear. "You've gotta help me with something, but I don't want Mom to know, okay?"

There was no escaping without looking like a total ass-wipe. Sam nodded his agreement, knowing he was making a huge mistake. What if he screwed up the kid for life?

Once Josh disappeared around the corner with Rex, Katie stepped closer and cupped Sam's face with both palms. He held his breath as she caressed his cheek and said, "Josh wants to talk to you, man-to-man, about a problem he's having at school," she murmured. "I'm sorry to dump this on you, but he doesn't have a father, and Rico, well, you've met Rico. You're the only person I trust."

Katie trusted him with her son. Other than feeling squeamish, Sam didn't exactly know how to react. He tried to imagine how she must feel under the burden of providing a stable environment for Josh while caught between Luigi's threats, Rico's questionable business dealings, and the stress of ensuring *Kinki*'s success.

He disguised a shaky breath as a cough. "Sure thing. You can count on me to do everything possible to help Josh."

He only hoped he wouldn't break the kid.

***

Fixing a wary eye on Josh, who'd sprinted after Rex across hard-packed sand, Sam was acutely aware of Katie's hand nestled inside his. His worries about Luigi's vindictive nature and long reach returned. She'd obviously forgotten they were sitting ducks on an open beach where bodies could disappear without a trace. He wasn't about to remind her.

As surreptitiously as possible, he inspected their surroundings. All clear.

Katie squeezed his hand. "Don't look so worried, Sam. It'll be fine."

"Easy for you to say." He kicked a pile of cold seaweed with his bare feet. "It's a simple matter to screw up a kid. I should know. Look how I turned out."

"I think you turned out great. Follow your instincts."

Yeah. If he followed his instincts, he'd be fleeing the scene. "I'm the least qualified person on the planet to dole out advice to a child."

"Not true, Sam. You're the perfect person to talk to Josh. You understand firsthand how indifference wounds a child. People's feelings matter to you. Have faith in yourself. You'll never mess up the way your father did."

"I'll say the wrong thing. Either that, or I'll say the right thing, and Josh will think he can depend on me."

Yeah, he had an uncanny knack of saying the wrong thing. Like now.

After a long pause, she said, "Don't worry. I'll make sure Josh understands we're leaving town after the grand opening. I'm investigating jobs in Alaska. Luigi won't think of looking for us there. He knows how much I hate the cold."

Shock held Sam immobile. "That's the first time you've mentioned leaving town."

"Two for the price of one. Escape Luigi, remove myself from your life."

To cover his surprise, Sam let out a bark of laughter that held no trace of amusement. He was living the dream—dating a sexy woman, no strings attached, and an expiry date in sight. So why did it feel more like a punishment than a gift?

Hand in hand they walked past a family playing Frisbee in the lengthening shadows. He fought the image of strolling through a field of Texas bluebonnets, a laughing Katie by his side, a little girl with dark, curly hair clutching his other hand, and Josh laughing at Rex's silly antics. Nice picture, but not one with his nametag on it.

Ahead, Josh and Rex splashed through the water. The kid showed no sign of wanting to have a heart-to-heart. Not that Sam was complaining. With Rex to distract him, Josh might forget he wanted to discuss a problem.

Sam scanned the beach again and found no sign of a threat. Only ripples from the incoming tide, glimmering pink and gold and purple, reflecting the setting sun.

Sam hoped his relief didn't show. "I think Josh has changed his mind about talking."

"He's having the time of his life. Every boy needs a dog. Look at them."

Sam squinted into the sun in time to see Rex charge into the surf and grab a hunk of driftwood thicker than a man's arm. Turning, the dog headed for shore and shook himself without releasing the branch.

"Hey, Sam." Josh waved at them. "Look at Rex's new toy."

Katie dropped Sam's hand and gave him a meaningful look. "Why don't you go talk to him now?" She gave him a gentle shove.

Sam's heart lodged in his throat. "Are you sure you want me to do this? It might be better coming from you. You're his mother."

"He needs a man." She gave him another shove, this one not so gentle. "I'll stay here."

Rex's bark and Josh's squeals of mirth reminded Sam that every child deserved a life where laughter came easily. If he ignored Josh's plea, he would have a hard time living with himself. With a single nod, he trudged forward.

Digging out a dog treat, he gave one sharp whistle.

Rex did an about-face. Dragging the branch behind him, he raced over, releasing the branch only long enough to snatch his Kanine Krunchie from the air before chomping on the log again. Josh followed, dragging his feet with obvious reluctance. From his scowl, Sam figured the kid was reconsidering the notion of spilling his guts.

When Josh reached him, Sam took a stab at conversation. "Been doing your homework like a good boy?"

The dumb question earned him an eye-roll and a grunt.

Son of a bitch. Sam had no idea how to relate to a nine-year old. He glanced over his shoulder at Katie, and she gave him a thumbs-up. Not knowing what else to do, Sam clicked his tongue at Rex and walked faster.

With a toss of his head, Rex crunched the branch and danced along beside him. When Josh caught up, Sam tried again. "You got any summer plans? You know, like, uh, camp, or swimming, or playing with frogs." He shut up. What the hell did kids do during the summer anyway, besides get into trouble?

"Nope."

After a minute or two, Sam couldn't take it any longer. He shortened his stride until he and Josh were in step. "Okay, Josh. You wanted to talk to me. I'm listening."

"I've changed my mind."

"See, your mom's depending on me to get to the bottom of this, so start talking or we go home."

"I'll run away from home."

The news shouldn't have surprised Sam, but it did. He had the presence of mind to say, "Bad idea. Right, Rex?"

The drenched canine executed a classic wet-dog shake.

"See, Rex agrees." Sam wished he'd brought a towel.

"I don't care. My life sucks."

Sam stopped beside a beach bench and sat. "Let's get comfy." Turning a blind eye to the resentment steaming off the kid, he waited until Josh parked himself.

For openers, Sam said, "I ran away from home when I was eight."

Josh stopped fidgeting. "Why?"

"My daddy yelled at me all the time." He refrained from mentioning the slaps that accompanied the tirades.

"What happened?"

"My brother found me and brought me home."

Josh scuffed his bare feet through the sand. "I don't have a brother. Or a father either."

Sam recognized his mistake. He moistened his lips. "Maybe I can help with whatever's bothering you. But you have to talk."

The silence lengthened. Sam knew enough not to break it. He tensed, certain the kid was about to cough up whatever was troubling him.

When Josh spoke, his voice was so low, Sam had to strain to hear him over the waves. "Every month, my class has Career Day. A mom or dad comes to the classroom and talks about their career. It's my turn, but I don't have a dad and everyone knows Mom used to be a mortician who drained and pickled dead bodies. I want to stay home."

"Have you told your mom?"

"Yeah. She said I couldn't stay home."

"Sounds about right." Sam knew where the kid was headed, and he pumped up his pitch for Katie's attendance. "It could be a real interesting talk. Some kids might want to be morticians when they grow up. Your mom knows lots of cool facts about the undertaking business."

"Yeah, right." Josh gnawed his lip for a few seconds before blurting, "Could you talk?"

Sam's gullet went so dry it made a clicking noise when he swallowed. He cleared his throat and croaked, "Your teacher wouldn't approve."

Josh's forehead puckered. "I figured you'd understand, but you don't." He darted away, heading down the beach.

Sam moved fast to block the kid's escape. He gripped Josh's shoulders, feeling the fragile bones beneath his fingers. "Listen. I bought a bar with gambling winnings. A teacher doesn't want the class to hear anything like that."

"Mom said you put yourself through university by designing computer games. You could talk about that." A tear spilled down Josh's cheek.

The single tear damn near broke Sam's heart. Shocked out of his self-absorption, he realized he'd been willing, no, *eager*, to pretend the kid's problems didn't exist. Exactly the way his own daddy had. He would *not* let history repeat itself. Heart flip-flopping in his chest, he cleared his throat. "I might be able to do it."

Josh flung his arms around Sam's neck and held on tight. "Thanks," he whispered. "I knew you'd understand. Besides, you have four whole days to practice."

Sam's gut heaved. "Four days?"

"Yeah. Let's tell Mom."

***

By the time Katie managed to pry Sam loose from her family, the moon sailed through a sky sprinkled with stars and feathered with wispy clouds. A silvery glow lit the pathway she used as a shortcut home. Ahead, Rex crashed through bushes in pursuit of Josh.

With Sam's arm clamping her to his side, they walked in silence, mainly because she was incapable of speech. God, he smelt good, but that was no excuse. What the hell was she doing? Instead of hanging onto her detachment, she'd let him sneak past her defenses. She shot a glance at her son, yet another worry. Josh had a serious case of hero-worship for a man who would soon leave their lives.

"Penny for your thoughts," Sam said.

I have it bad for you.

Katie blew a strand of hair from her face. "You don't need to walk us home. I've memorized every stone, bump, and root on the pathway."

His arm tightened. "It must be Josh's bedtime. I was hoping you'd invite me in for a nightcap. You may recall I mentioned the value of finishing what we start."

She and her girl parts thought alike. "Really? You can think about sex after a Deluca family dinner?"

He gave a low laugh. "I think about sex whenever I'm near you." He pressed a kiss onto the top of her head. Her happy zone went all tingly.

It was hard to argue with a tingly happy zone, but she stayed strong. "I'm flattered, I think. But shouldn't you have lost interest in me by now?"

"Probably. But for some strange reason, I haven't. Perhaps because you smell so good." He nuzzled her neck, raising goose bumps. "Plus you're the bravest woman I know."

She stopped walking. "You must be confusing me with someone else."

He sniffed deeply, tickling her ear. "Nope. I'd never confuse you with another woman. Your scent is unmistakable. Sweet and sexy at the same time."

She hoped her cheeks didn't glow in the dark. "That's not what I meant."

"Katie, sweetheart." He placed both hands on her shoulders, turning her to face him. "Tonight opened my eyes to the challenges you've faced all your life, especially with your brother and the business. You're the bravest woman I know."

She looked away. No way would she let him see the spark of hope he'd ignited. "But I'm a coward. Luigi terrifies me."

"Look at me, Katie. Please." Once she obeyed, he said, "Luigi scares you silly, yet you're bending over backwards to give Josh a better life."

Her throat was so clogged with emotion, she merely shook her head.

He must have taken it as denial, because he continued, "You befriended my granddaddy, and he's not for the faint of heart."

She laughed softly. "Hiram's a character. He's easy to love."

"Okay, you won't get serious about anyone because of Luigi, I understand, but ..."

Electricity sparked between them, its intensity catching her off-guard.

"But what?" she whispered, her pulse picking up speed.

He cupped her face. She leaned into him, holding her breath, waiting for his answer.

An answer that didn't happen because a yellow taxi peeled up and screeched to a halt beside them. The window rolled down and a head of white hair poked out. "Hey, Sammy," Hiram yelled.

Katie had a sinking feeling she and Sam had lost a pivotal moment.

***

The interruption startled Sam into silence.

His granddaddy hopped out and waved a fist at him. "Here you are, you greedy, overstuffed, heartless dawg." He hastened to add, "Not you, Katie, I'm talking about Sam."

The driver stuck his head out. "Good luck, suckers," he said and zoomed off.

Sam prayed for patience. "What's up?"

"You went out and left me a lousy salad to eat, that's what's up. Your note said you were having dinner with Katie's family. They're Italian. I bet dinner was Italian. You know I love Italian. If you'd told me, I would have ditched Bingo for Italian food. Another stunt like that, and I'll make you sorry. Very sorry."

"I already am. Look on the bright side. It was an Italian salad."

"I don't eat rabbit food." Granddaddy Hiram jutted his chin.

Sam slid a despairing look at Katie. "You said he was easy to love. Settle him down. Please?"

"This one's all yours."

Sam blew out a hard-done-by sigh and addressed his granddaddy. "Okay, spit it out. What's wrong?"

Hiram gave a derisive snort. "Pasta deficiency is what's wrong, but that's not all. I need to talk to you. Now. Alone. It's real important." He placed a hand on Katie's arm. "Sorry, but I have to steal Sam."

Both embarrassed and resigned, Sam turned to Katie with a sigh of regret. "This isn't what I had in mind to round out our evening, but once my granddaddy makes up his mind, he never changes it. For everyone's sake, I'd better get him home."

Katie stood in the moonlight looking sweet and sexy and all-around adorable. She flung her arms around Granddaddy Hiram and kissed his cheek. "Don't you worry about stealing Sam, hear? I should get Josh to bed anyway."

Frustration made Sam's toes curl. For a man who didn't do commitment, a weird urge to pull Katie close was overpowering. Fortunately, or possibly unfortunately, the interruption had happened before he'd gone and said something stupid. He sent his granddaddy to the truck to wait, explaining that a gentleman always walked his date home. When he and Katie reached the front door, they found Josh and Rex occupying the doorstep.

"You said you liked *Doctor Who*," Josh reminded him, scrambling to his feet. "It's on tonight."

Katie came to the rescue. "Sam has to go home. His granddaddy needs him."

Feeling he should say more, Sam said, "I'm real sorry, Josh. It would have been fun." Noticing the disappointment etched on Josh's face, a pang of guilt caused him to say, "Another time. I promise."

To his surprise he meant it.

"Cool," Josh said, grinning at him.

Katie, who'd unlocked the door, told Josh, "Go get ready for bed and don't forget to brush your teeth. Then we'll talk about *Doctor Who*."

"Okay. Bye, Sam." Josh dropped his voice so only Sam could hear it. "Don't forget to tell Mom about Career Day." He disappeared into the house.

Sam waited until the sound of running feet faded before reaching for Katie. The kiss he gave her was slow, and deep, and thorough.

***

Once on the road, Sam lent Granddaddy Hiram his phone to call in a take-out order for a foot-long Italian hoagie, immediate pickup. With luck, food would keep the old guy quiet. It did. They drove the rest of the way in blessed silence.

On reaching their apartment, Rex bounded inside. His tail thumped from side to side, knocking newspapers off the cocktail table. Granddaddy Hiram stomped in last, slamming the door, a sure sign of irritation, impatience, or both.

Sam said, "Okay, I'll bite. What's important enough to interrupt my date with Katie?"

"I need every cent of my money," his granddaddy said in an aggrieved tone. "Now."

The demand blindsided Sam. He flopped onto the recliner, hoping he'd heard wrong. "Come again."

His granddaddy stayed standing. "You deaf, boy? I need my money. I'm fixin' to return to Texas."

Sam fought the panic gnawing his innards. "Since when?"

"I've been romancing a couple of lovely ladies I met in *Golden Sunset Manor* where I lived before moving north. All online, of course. They can't get enough of me."

Sam blinked in horror. "You've been using my computer for sexting?"

"How do you think I pass the time of day? Video chat software's real handy."

Sam couldn't shake the vision lodged in his brain. "Don't jump into something you might regret." Christ, he was beginning to sound like a father, a *real* father. He didn't want to examine the thought too closely.

"You promised I'd more than double my investment. I want my money."

Sam's chest tightened, becoming downright painful. His granddaddy had no idea how broke they were. "You'll get it, but it takes time. Our money's tied up until after the grand opening. Why don't you sit and we'll discuss it." He flexed his shoulders to ease the rigidity of his muscles.

Granddaddy Hiram stayed standing. "What's to discuss? The grand opening's next weekend, and that's too late." He jutted his beard at Sam, looking more than ever like a mutinous old billy goat. "I have to sign now or the opening in *Golden Sunset Manor* will disappear."

Tasting the bitterness of desperation, Sam said, "I wish I could help, but I can't. Even if the grand opening's a smash hit, there won't be liquid cash right away."

Granddaddy Hiram waved his arm to encompass the entire apartment in his gesture. "Look around. This place sucks. I spend most of my days alone in a dump above a bar." He heaved a heart-rending sigh. "I want to return to San Antonio."

"Tell you what." Sam laced his voice with artificial brightness. "I'll book an appointment with a real estate agent to sell *Kinki* right after the grand opening. You'll be in the retirement home of your choice before you know it."

With a typical mood switch, his granddaddy grinned. "Okay. There's a decent turnover in retirement homes." He grinned, apparently unaware of the turmoil he'd caused. "I'm gonna celebrate with the last slice of cheesecake."

Sam marveled at how he'd dodged the bullet. For now. "You just ate."

"A hoagie only goes so far. My food box is full, but my dessert box is still empty." He stomped to the kitchen with Rex at his heels.

Grateful for a moment's solitude, Sam slumped into his chair.

Over the clink of cutlery, Granddaddy Hiram hollered, "Your daddy called."

Sam sat bolt upright. "What did he want?"

"Nick and Gracie are hosting a barbecue for him next Sunday. We're invited."

Sam considered banging his head against the wall. "I'm not going. Sure as shit, Eugene wants something."

The fridge door closed, dishes clattered. Granddaddy Hiram walked into the living room with the cheesecake, and sat. "He insists you come."

Sam gave a sarcastic bark of laughter. "Yeah. We're so close."

"I think he wants a reconciliation."

Sam squelched the spark of hope flickering in his chest. Once upon a time, he might have hungered for Eugene's love, but he'd toughened up, smartened up. "Not happening."

"He's my son, and I want to see him. You have to drive me."

Sam merely grunted. He had to get the hell away before he exploded. Ignoring his granddaddy's startled expression, he strode out the apartment, headed for a strip joint called *Happy Hustler Bar & Grill*. The food was cheap, the drinks plentiful, and the girls easy.

Life was closing in on him with alarming speed. On top of being a target for hitmen, and that was bad enough, now his granddaddy wanted his money back, and Eugene was sailing into town to remind him he'd never amount to a pinch of coon shit. But those weren't close to being main problems, hell, no. What truly scared the shit out of him was one sexy, five-foot-nothing dynamo.

Overnight, his feelings for Katie had taken a dangerous turn, but today, today he'd done something so dumb, so stupid, even he was appalled. Today, he'd promised her son he'd be a stand-in dad at Career Day.

Yeah, he was in big trouble.

Chapter 28: Sexy Game

The next morning, Sam had showered and shaved by the ungodly hour of eight o'clock. Given the absence of his normal Monday hangover, the aroma of frying bacon wafting into his bedroom should make his mouth water. Today, not so much. A mental re-assessment of yesterday's events, especially his promise to Josh, caused his stomach to cramp.

In the past, a trip to *The Happy Hustler* was better than a happy-pill. But not last night. In spite of the strippers' best efforts, his thoughts had drifted to Katie and Josh. After one drink he'd returned home early, conducted a walkaround, and crawled into bed.

That was plain *wrong*.

Tucking a fresh shirt into a clean pair of jeans, he padded to the window. Casting a glance outside, he zeroed in on Katie's car entering the parking lot. She'd dropped Josh off at The Annex to catch the school bus, and was headed for their office. The pain in his gut ratcheted up a notch. Apparently he wasn't close to getting her out of his system.

"Clearly, you're in deep doo-doo, Sammy."

San whirled around. "Don't you ever knock?"

"I did. Three times." His granddaddy took a huge bite out of a bacon-and-egg sandwich.

"Sorry. Which doo-doo might you be referring to?"

The old man's face split in a broad grin. "Hell, boy. It's obvious. You've lost interest in all women except our sexy little event planner."

"You're imagining things." Sam knew his voice sounded strained.

"You came home before ten o'clock last night. Don't try to deny it. I always check the clock when I get up to pee. The light was on in your bedroom." Granddaddy Hiram waved the sandwich under Sam's nose.

Sam's gut complained at the smell. "I was tired so I came home early."

"Don't go handin' me a steamin' pile of bullshit. I saw how you looked at Katie, and I can't say's how I blame you. She's on the ball, loyal, and real pretty." He jabbed Sam in the chest. "You're in love."

"Bullshit." Sam forced a laugh. "Sure, I like her. She's sexy as hell, but what we have is lust, not love."

"It's love. And she returns the feeling. Best you grow a pair and pop the question before she slips through your fingers. I want to see some great-grandchildren before I croak."

"Not happening." Sam raked his fingers through his hair, not giving a good rat's ass that he'd spent ten minutes in front of the bathroom mirror styling it to look as though he hadn't.

"When it's right, it's right. As soon as I met your grandmother, God rest her soul, I knew she was the only woman for me."

The ache in Sam's stomach spread to his chest, making speech difficult. "All Katie wants is a good time. And that's dandy, seeing as how it's all I have to offer."

"Hah. I bet you can't last one day without having your hands all over her."

"Shows how much you know. I'll treat her like my goddamn sister all day."

"Twenty bucks says you can't do it."

***

The bet with Granddaddy Hiram weighed heavily on Sam's mind as he sauntered into his office. He stopped dead at the sight. His pulse pounded in an alarming way before he got his legs moving again.

Behind her desk, Katie looked adorable, all focused and businesslike in a button-down, white blouse, gold stud earrings, and a pearl necklace. She'd wedged the phone between her ear and shoulder and was scribbling in her notebook. He flung himself into the visitors' chair opposite her, waiting for her to finish. A fantasy of coaxing her out of the prim outfit flashed through his head—until he remembered his bet.

Like a goddamn sister, he reminded himself.

Katie flashed him a brief smile while conducting her phone conversation, something about a press release. After more negotiation, she ended the call and turned the full glory of her bright, trusting smile on him.

He forgot to breathe. Yeah, the sister thing wasn't working. He stood and yielded to the impulse to nuzzle the sweet, vulnerable spot at the nape of her neck. The scent of soap, s

hampoo, and fragrant female set his heart racing. "Hey, pretty lady," he said softly.

All flustered and soft-eyed, she smiled at him. "Hey, yourself. I assume everything's okay with Hiram."

"Sure. Why not?" He forced himself to put some distance between them. That way, he might be less tempted to grab that curvy little body.

"He wanted to talk to you," she prompted.

Sam's brain clicked into gear. "Right. He's keen to move into a retirement home." He wouldn't burden Katie with the knowledge that the only way it could happen was if the grand opening was a success.

"That would be lovely for him."

Her eyes were warm and inviting, reminding Sam of the richest dark chocolate. If he wasn't careful, he could lose himself in her sweetness. "Yeah. He's lonely, needs more friends." Sam continued his retreat until his chair cracked the back of his legs. He dropped into it, glad of the support.

"Is there a problem?"

"My brother's holding a family barbecue this Sunday. Timing couldn't be worse. That's only six days before the grand opening. My granddaddy insists on going so I have to drive him."

She raised one delicate eyebrow. "It must be important to Hiram."

"My father's in town and wants me there. It's a command performance. Eugene, bless his heart, never does anything without a reason."

"You needn't go alone. I could go with you as your cheering section."

A variety of emotions clutched at his heart. Gratitude and hope topped the list. After a prolonged silence during which he came close to refusing, he said, "I must warn you, I've never told Eugene how his neglect and abuse affected me, probably still does. On Sunday, I intend to speak my mind for the first time. I'll try to be civil, but it won't be pretty."

"All the more reason you'll need support."

His throat tightened, making speech difficult. Until now, every woman he'd dated wanted a piece of Sammy. Only Katie offered support and encouragement, no strings attached. Which grasped Sam's heart and twisted.

"Okay. Thanks," he said.

"Then it's settled. I'm your date for the Sunday barbecue."

Placing her pencil on the desk, she rose and swayed toward the door. Her stretchy little black skirt, decidedly unbusinesslike, molded the sweet curves of her ass. High heels made her legs look ridiculously sexy. She locked the door and walked toward him.

He hardened immediately. He felt like one of Pavlov's dogs.

"Refresh my memory," she said, standing before him, fiddling with her top button. "Where were we last night before Hiram arrived?"

He remembered only too well where they were, also what they were doing. Feeling his self-control slipping, he said, "Are you sure this is a good idea?" Shit. He couldn't believe his dumb-assed remark.

"Oh, I think you'll find it's a terrific idea. Better make sure the camera is turned off." She undid her top button.

Glory Hallelujah.

Never looking away, he fumbled with his smartphone and did what she asked. With all his heart, he hoped Luigi hadn't managed to plant a voice-activated bug in his office seeing as how he wasn't about to break the mood to check.

She continued unbuttoning her blouse. "After you left, I had time on my hands, so I conducted extensive research on sexy games. Slutty Secretary sounded like fun."

All the spit dried clean out of his mouth. She'd zeroed in on his favorite fantasy.

The blouse landed on her desk. Today's bra was white and sheer, revealing her soft curves. He moistened his lips at the sight of rosy nipples thrusting through delicate fabric. He'd never seen anything so erotic in his life.

"Would you like me to take dictation, Mr. Jackson?" She discarded the wisp of a bra as she stood before him, naked from the waist up. "Let me get my notebook and pen."

Remembering the bet, he stopped her with an abrupt gesture. "Katie—"

She straightened her glasses, which appeared to have steamed up. "You look extremely tense. If you have no dictation, I'll help you relax before your next meeting."

Staring at her breasts, he made one last heroic effort. "I don't want to hurt you."

"You won't. I'm extremely flexible." Her lips curved. "You can thank yoga."

He gripped the arms of his chair to restrain himself from leaping at her as she stood before him wearing only a tiny skirt and ridiculously sexy shoes. "That's not what I meant."

"I know. You meant you don't do commitment." She didn't wait for his comment. "I'm good with that."

"You shouldn't be good with it. What I mean is … I don't know what I mean." He took a long breath and tried again. "This thing we have together, it can't go anywhere. You deserve better."

"Ah, Sam. Don't you realize? You're the best there is."

He felt his heart give. "You know nothing about me."

"I know all I need to know. In spite of the bad boy image you hide behind, you can't disguise your thoughtfulness and sensitivity."

Everything inside Sam warmed. "Where did that come from?"

Her next words rendered him speechless. "You treat everyone with courtesy and compassion. You rescued a dog as big as a pony from the pound, you give a difficult old man a loving home, and although kids terrify you, you're amazing with Josh. I could go on." She kicked off her shoes. "Or should I continue my relaxation treatment?"

It occurred to Sam he needed Katie in his life. Needed her to melt the ice surrounding his heart. Ungluing his tongue, he said, "Relaxation treatment, please."

She leaned in. "In that case," she said in a stern tone, "no more talking."

"Yes ma'am." He removed her glasses and placed them on the desk. Then he cupped her breasts. The feel of her skin, so soft and warm and silky made his breath hitch. He circled the nipples with his thumbs. She shuddered, made a low, sexy hum in her throat, and straddled his chair, offering.

He obliged, circling one perfect nipple with his tongue, before drawing it gently into his mouth and sucking hard enough to elicit a whimper. She believed he was the best, so he would deliver nothing but the best. He shifted his mouth to her other breast and continued the process until he thought he must explode. She saved him by pushing away.

"What's wrong?" he said.

"I'm violating the dress code," she explained. "My skirt is unsuitable for the office. Please don't fire me, Sir. I'll take it off." A quick tug and a wriggle got rid of her skirt, revealing equally sheer, equally revealing panties. God, she was beautiful. He held his breath as she slipped her thumbs under the elastic, and shimmied out of her last wisp of clothing.

As she stood before him, gloriously, unashamedly naked, he sucked in an audible breath. No other woman had ever made him feel this way— terrified and confused, protective and aroused—all at the same time.

She looked at him with a mysterious smile. "You're much too tense, Mr. Jackson. Perhaps you'd relax if you wore fewer clothes."

He smiled. "Works for me." In a matter of seconds, he lost all his clothes. Reaching for her, he delighted in how she melted into his arms with a soft sigh.

***

Feeling more than a little naughty, Katie shivered and clutched Sam's arms before her legs gave out. Her plan to etch herself in his memory was well underway. His erection pressed against her stomach with shocking familiarity. She whispered, "As the boss, you must inform your secretary of your requirements."

"This area is unsuitable for what I have in mind. There's a better place." His breathing was rapid, as if he'd been running.

She let him grasp her hand and lead her to the alcove. But instead of taking her in his arms as she expected, he took a folded sheet from a filing cabinet, shook it out, and spread it over the couch.

"You keep a *bed sheet* in the office?" It came out more tartly than she intended.

He straightened, flashing a grin. "I use a sheet to protect the couch from massage oil."

"Oh," she said, remembering. "Of course … Pizza Girl."

His smile widened. "Aw, that's sweet. You're jealous."

"Merely curious." Before she said something needy, she hastened to add, "Please lie down, and I'll start the treatment."

"Yes, ma'am." He obeyed, and in a surprise move, tugged her on top of him.

"Hey, not fair," she said, laughing, while doing her best to ignore her fun zone, which throbbed with enthusiasm. "Did you know kissing relieves stress by creating a sense of connectedness, which releases endorphins, the chemicals that counteract stress?"

"Excellent. Because I'm feeling real stressed. You'd better get to work."

Before she chickened out, she pressed a light kiss onto each of his eyelids. Encouraged by the way his breathing roughened, she dragged her lips ever-so-slowly to one ear, which she took into her mouth, nibbling and sucking gently. From there, she worked her way down one side of his corded neck, across the tender indentation below his Adam's apple, where she lingered a few seconds to glory in the rapid pulse beat, and up his neck again to the other ear.

When she drew away, a low sound escaped him. "Kiss me," he murmured.

Katie put everything she had into the kiss, all her pent-up longing, all the molten feelings she'd tried to suppress. She withheld nothing, letting him know, without words, how she felt. She used her tongue, her teeth, and her nails as she nibbled, and sucked, and thrust, clutching him close, then closer still, and it still wasn't enough.

She kissed her way down his torso, pausing to lick, then suck his nipples. Sensing his tension as he lay motionless, Katie shifted lower, then lower still, until she reached ground zero.

"That feels so goddamn good."

To her satisfaction, his voice was husky as she encircled him with her mouth.

She proceeded to do her damndest to drive him ever-so-slowly out of his mind. On sensing he'd reached the brink, she dragged her lips away and kissed her way up the taut belly.

"What's wrong? Why are you stopping?" Sam's voice was laced with equal parts of concern, desire, and frustration. Those molten eyes revealed his passion.

Dazed and breathless, she raised her head. She wanted him inside her, melded with her. Yet she needed to hear him beg. It would be a start.

"Did that relax you?" She tried to sound innocent.

"Not by a long shot."

"Oh dear. What should we do about it?"

"This." In the blink of an eye, he clasped her body tight to his, and flipped their positions, pinning her to the couch. He licked one breast, sending sparks shooting into important places, then raised his head, leaving her throbbing.

"Open for me, baby. Don't make me beg." His voice was laced with honey and thick with desire.

"Do you have a condom?"

"Shit. No."

He looked so distressed, she hid her smile. "A slutty secretary is always prepared." She slipped out from under him. Conscious of his heated gaze on her naked body, she padded into the office, retrieved the condoms from her purse, and returned to the sofa.

"This was an ambush," he accused, laughing as he unwrapped one and rolled it on.

Katie's heart executed an excited somersault in her chest. "Little bit."

"Well-organized as well as slutty. I like that."

She opened up. His hot length slid into her, and she rocked against him, the exquisite sensation dragging a moan from her lips. She wanted him so much, it scared her.

"Ah, Katie—"

He took her where she wanted to go. Several times.

And as she tumbled into love with Sam, she forgot the threat of Luigi's release and let herself dream.

***

An hour later, Katie made a heroic effort to get herself under control. Slowly, she disengaged from Sam, taking her time, doing her best to act carefree.

This whole episode had been a huge mistake. What had begun as a lark to prove that all she wanted was great sex had morphed into out-and-out lovemaking. At least, on her part. But along the way, she'd sensed a change in Sam, too. She almost believed he wanted more than merely a good time. She'd never felt so thoroughly and utterly possessed. If she didn't know better, she'd swear he cared for her.

She scooted to the other end of the couch and sat, taking care to cover herself with one corner of the sheet.

He propped himself on one elbow and regarded her. "Seriously? Isn't a little late for modesty?" He tugged the sheet away. "I love looking at you, Katie. You are beautiful, every gorgeous inch of you."

She made a grab for the sheet. "Hey, we're at work."

He laughed and held the sheet out of reach. "That's why Slutty Secretary is so much fun."

So she'd been wrong thinking he felt something more for her. All he wanted was the rush. She laughed to cover her embarrassment. "I aim to please the boss."

He sat, moving closer until their hips connected. He folded one of her hands in both of his. "Katie—"

"It was fun, wasn't it?" she chirped. "We're good together. Next time, I'll find another game. There's Naughty Librarian, or you might enjoy Bachelor Party." She tried to extricate her hand. "It's getting late, Sam. I really must get dressed."

"Katie, we need to talk."

From his expression, she gathered it wouldn't be a happy talk. Her heart flip-flopped in her chest, and she stopped struggling to free her hand, letting it lie like a limp fish in his grip. "If you tell me you didn't have fun, I won't believe you."

"I had a wonderful time. Better than I should have." A muscle in his jaw flickered.

"But ...?" she prompted, resisting the urge to cover herself again with the sheet. She'd been so certain he would tell her he loved her. Obviously, she'd misread the signals.

"But I don't do commitment." He stroked a finger down her cheek. The tender gesture contradicted his words. "Love only leads to trouble, and I refuse to hurt anyone."

"Love should heal, make you stronger. Who hurt you so badly?"

"What makes you think anyone hurt me?"

A wave of tenderness swamped her. "Never mind. I get it, Sam. I went into this with my eyes open. I'm not looking for love, simply great sex." She stretched her smile wider. "You're sticking to your end of the bargain beautifully. When our time together is over, I'll leave with a grateful heart, no regrets."

"Katie," he said softly. "If I did do commitment, I'd pick you."

"Super." The damndest thing was, she believed him.

He frowned. "Don't sound so excited. My ego's taking a shit-kicking."

"I could make it up to you tonight."

This time, she did not imagine the flicker of apprehension that crossed his face before he said, "Sorry, I already have plans. It's a business thing. I probably won't see you until tomorrow because I have meetings this afternoon."

Katie swallowed the lump lodged in her throat. "No problem. I've been thinking we should take this more slowly. I need to spend more time with Josh."

"Sounds good to me." But he didn't look happy.

That made two of them. At least she had the Sunday barbecue to dream about. A date with Sam to meet his family was enough. Yes it was.

They got dressed in silence.

***

Sam remained slumped in his chair after Katie pressed a hasty kiss to his forehead and hurried out to meet with the classic rock band's agent. He tried to ignore the choking sensation that clogged his throat as the office walls closed in on him. He had to escape, to flee, to run as fast and as far as possible from his responsibilities.

Eugene had him pegged. He was an irresponsible screw-up.

No wonder he always hurt the women who got too close. Yet he'd let Katie slip under his guard and find a spot in his heart. He told himself his strange, scalding need for her was merely lust, something familiarity would eradicate.

Luckily, all she wanted from him was sex. That he could deliver, hopefully after their date for the barbecue. But no matter how hard he might try to make a relationship between them work, he knew he would break her heart. It's what he did. That is, unless Luigi killed him first.

It was time to get serious about selling *Kinki* and extricating himself before it was too late. After the sale went through, he would re-pay his granddaddy and see him settled, then he would cut out. Another city, preferably out of state would be good. Another country, even better.

Footloose and fancy-free would feel good again, Sam assured himself. Real good. So why did something he knew was right feel so wrong?

He tried to ignore the strange, hollow sensation he felt at the thought of life without Katie. In time, he would grow accustomed to the notion. In the meantime, dating other women was the smart way to go.

He picked up the phone to call the cute real estate agent to re-schedule an evening appointment. She'd seemed interested in more than business.

Chapter 29: Finding Trouble

The rest of the long and challenging day dragged on for Katie. After working straight through, she stood, stretching her arms to work the knots out of her muscles. Eight o'clock, but so what? Bella had taken Josh to a movie to let her work late. Sam must have left during her meeting with the agent, and he didn't return. A couple of neck rolls later, she was able to shake off the feeling that he was avoiding her. Meetings ate up a lot of his time, and he'd mentioned some sort of business event this evening. If that's what it was.

She didn't feel like going home to an empty house. After locking up, she wandered down the hall and tried Sam's apartment in case he'd returned. No one answered. Shaking her head in an attempt to erase her suspicion that he was with another woman, she headed downstairs for *O-Positive Café*, Hiram's favorite hangout at *Kinki*.

Not that she was looking for Sam. Nope. But in case he was inside, she entered the restaurant with a confident hip-swing. Ignoring the café's blood-red décor, which creeped her out, she scanned the room. The staff had left for the day, but one lone customer's white hair stood out like a beacon in a sea of gore. Hiram sat at the counter, a plate heaped with pastries in front of him. He was devouring a lemon Danish.

But no Sam. She had it bad. Feeling foolish, she released a long breath.

Hiram glanced up. On seeing her, he crammed the remains of the Danish into his mouth, chewed hard and swallowed, then chomped into a cinnamon bun the size of his head.

She slung her purse behind the bar and handed him a napkin. "Nice dinner. Nourishing. Don't you realize vitamins and minerals are the building blocks of—" She broke off at the sound of bickering in the corridor. The voices sounded familiar.

Hiram swiped the napkin over his beard. "Anything wrong?"

The argument grew louder.

She made a shushing motion and tilted her head to hear better. "Oh crap. It's the Allegrettis. Behind the bar. Quick. We'd better hope Sam's watching on his smartphone." She grabbed Hiram's hand and hauled.

For a geriatric, he put up a fight worthy of a trapped wolverine.

Seeing no choice, she freed his arm so he could snag the cinnamon bun plus a buttermilk donut. Then they both hunkered down behind the counter.

Once hidden, he whispered, "There were more goodies on the plate."

Before she could answer, two men stumbled inside.

Sensing Hiram's temper was about to explode, she made a frantic motion for silence. "Shhhhhh. These'll have to do. If this is who I think it is, they have guns."

For once, Hiram obeyed. She should mention guns more often.

One of the men said, "Holy shit. Looks like someone threw a bucket of blood in here."

"Fuckin' A." The sound of a belch was startlingly loud in the silence. "This place looks like a slaughterhouse."

Katie eased her head up to see Ralphie and Enzo. They were sharing a mickey.

Ralphie's voice came closer. "Looky here. A good Samaritan left goodies behind. I love butter tarts." After a few seconds, he mumbled, "Hey, these things are fantastic."

"Bugger," Hiram whispered. "That stinking sack of monkey shit 's eating my butter tarts—uh, 'scuse my language."

Katie clutched Hiram's hand and gave it a squeeze to convey the urgency of staying silent. He settled back with a sigh.

Enzo's voice boomed out, "How can you think of your fuckin' stomach right now? We were supposed to trash *Kinki* again, but that didn't happen, and we're already late for our meeting with the boss."

"Did you hear that?" Hiram's whisper vibrated with outrage. "These assholes are behind the vandalism."

"Shhhhh," Katie breathed, clutching Hiram's arm.

Oblivious of their presence, Ralphie said, "Fine. Let's get outta here. We'll stop on the way and pick up a coupla cheesesteaks."

"Fuck, no. There's no time. It was your dumbass idea to sneak in the back door and hide in the fuckin' coffins till the coast was clear. We shoulda waited outside until everyone left for the day, then picked the lock."

"Who knew we'd fall asleep?"

Enzo's voice dropped to a low growl. "If we're late, the boss will fuckin' kill us. This was your fault, so you can explain why things ain't happening as quick as he wants."

Ralphie's nervous giggle rang out. "Good job I've got the gift of the gab. And a big, honkin' gun if things go wrong. Let's scram."

Katie chewed her lip, praying they would leave. Immediately would be good.

"In a minute," Enzo said. A stool grated on the floor as he sat. "Donut first."

"I'd rather have a cheesesteak," Ralphie whined.

Feeling Hiram quivering with outrage, Katie tightened her grip on his arm while the brothers gobbled donuts. At last, the pair pushed away. Still arguing, they left.

"Wait here." Katie's heart thumped in her ears as she tiptoed to the door in time to see the brothers taking the wrong turn, away from the exit. She returned and said, "They went the wrong way. We'll dash upstairs and phone Sam before they figure out where the parking lot is."

"'Scuse me, little lady." Hiram pushed past Katie and took off at a brisk pace.

Amazed at his speed, she followed. Although she tried to keep up, the high heels put her at a disadvantage. She got a bad feeling when he zipped past the stairs.

"Where are you going? Your apartment's upstairs. I'll cook dinner."

Hiram sped up. "Screw healthy eating. I'm jonesing for cheesesteak, so I'm going with those guys."

She took off her shoes and sprinted. "No. You can't do this."

"Watch me." Hiram moved faster and out the door. His laughter floated back from the parking lot.

When she reached the door, he'd already reached the lone pickup parked near the door. To her horror, he hopped into the back seat and disappeared.

Familiar squabbling grew in volume. The Allegrettis had realized their mistake and were retracing their steps. They couldn't see her yet, but it was too late to retrieve her purse. Unable to leave Hiram alone, Katie slipped outside and raced to the truck, flinging herself inside seconds before the brothers emerged from *Kinki*.

Chapter 30: Stowaway Caper

Why, oh why, Katie wondered as they crouched beneath a smelly blanket in the back seat of the Allegrettis' truck, hadn't she gone home and waited for Josh and Bella to arrive?

"Goddamn blanket smells like puke," Hiram muttered.

She fought her gag reflex as they waited, motionless. Her best option was to sneak Hiram away if the brothers stopped for cheesesteaks.

Beside her, Hiram squirmed like an eel. If they were to escape in one piece, she had to keep him calm. As much as she hated to call Sam, who was probably on a hot date, it was all she had.

She reached for her purse, and a knot formed in her stomach. She remembered she'd left her purse, which contained her phone, behind the counter.

Footsteps crunched and the Allegrettis climbed in. Doors slammed, the engine roared to life, and they rocketed off.

Hiram whispered, "I hope they stop for cheesesteak. I want one with fried onions and real Provolone, not that Cheez Whiz shit."

"Forget your stomach," she pleaded, hearing a note of desperation creep into her voice.

Enzo yelled over the noise of a faulty muffler, "Look at the fucking time. We've got ten minutes. Vinnie's gonna be pissed if we're late. You know how he gets. Guido the Gimp's never been the same since the boss shot off his foot."

At the name Vinnie, she tensed. Vinnie Constantine was Luigi's right hand man.

There was a long pause before Ralphie said, "Fine. We'll eat later."

"Shit," Hiram hissed, followed by a muffled, "Sorry."

With a squeal of tires, the pickup skidded around a corner and made more sudden twists and turns.

Hiram whispered in Katie's ear, "This asshole's driving's gonna kill us."

Fortunately, the blanket and the truck's racket smothered the complaint. "Shhhhh. These people have guns. And if they hear you, that's what'll kill us, not the driving."

Her words must have sunk in. Hiram stayed silent. Until now, she'd suspected Sam had exaggerated his grandfather's impulse control problems. But tonight, under pressure, the full extent of Hiram's brain injury was evident. Her respect for Sam grew as she remembered how gently he handled Hiram's eccentricities, applying a combination of humor and genuine caring.

The Allegrettis grew silent, no doubt dreading the impending confrontation with Vinnie. Five minutes later, they turned onto a rutted track. The truck slid to a standstill, engine idling. There was a metallic rattle and the squeak of gate hinges, and they resumed a slow crawl until rolling to a stop. Ralphie killed the engine.

Enzo's voice, shockingly loud, filled the truck. "Make sure you got your piece handy, Ralphie."

"In my pocket. Let's do it."

The brothers piled out and crunched away over gravel.

She turned to Hiram and whispered, "I want you to stay quiet and hidden until I give the signal. Okay?"

She sensed his nod.

She pushed the blanket aside and peeked outside before dropping back. Enzo and Ralphie were half-way across a deserted yard surrounded by heaps of dirt, rubble, and equipment, all enclosed by a ten-foot fence. A crane towered over a partial structure consisting of rebar and metal beams. She couldn't see Vinnie.

On top of a neighboring building, a neon sign advertising the Inlet Convention Center caught her attention. "It's a construction site," she whispered to Hiram. "We're near the inlet."

"Hot dang. That means we're close to the Inlet Cheesesteak Palace."

As she shushed Hiram, a figure, presumably Vinnie, emerged slowly from the shadows to join the brothers. He was shorter than the Allegrettis. More and more certain she was looking at Vinnie Constantine, she sank out of sight.

Hiram nudged her. "What's happening?"

"The brothers are talking to Vinnie. It's too dark to see much and I can't hear anything." Staying low, she rolled down her window.

Out of the night, a voice roared, "Assholes." No trouble hearing Vinnie now. For a little man, he had a huge voice. A torrent of rapid-fire Italian followed the outburst.

"What did he say?" Hiram asked.

"Nothing I care to repeat."

Hiram struggled upright. "They're too busy to notice if we sneak out."

Katie managed to grip his shoulders. It took all her strength to press him down before he got them both killed. "We're parked under a street light. They'll see us. Please remember I have a child who relies on his mom being in one piece."

Hiram subsided with a grumble.

Moments later, the same harsh voice yelled, "I'm paying you two dickless butt-wipes to soften up the owner so's he begs me to take *Kinki* off his hands, and you're telling me you didn't trash the place again?"

"Fuckers." Hiram's voice vibrated with outrage.

Katie was too engrossed in the unfolding drama to shush him. Ever so slowly, she raised her head in time to catch two indistinct forms backing away from the third.

Ralphie's voice wavered. "Take it easy, Vinnie. We ran out of time. There were too many people around. We'll go back tonight and finish the job." All three figures moved into a circle of light cast by a floodlight.

Katie didn't blame them for not confessing they'd fallen asleep in a coffin. She flopped down and fumbled for Hiram's hand. "This is bad. Real bad."

Hiram snuggled closer and squeezed her hand. "Do you recognize Vinnie?"

She fought to speak around the flannel lining her mouth. "Yeah. It's Vinnie Constantine. He's one of New Jersey's biggest criminals."

It was obvious to Katie that Luigi had heard about her contract at *Kinki* and ordered Vinnie to sabotage the place.

"Whooo-eeee. He don't look very big to me."

Hiram had that right. Vinnie barely reached Luigi's shoulders. She said, "Word is Vinnie's responsible for dozens of murders and disappearances. But he's smart. Never leaves a trail."

Outside, the shouting escalated. Ralphie yelled, "Hey, why are you pointing that thing at us?" Pure terror filled his voice.

"Ralphie's gift of the gab ain't working." Hiram fumbled for the door handle. "Here's our chance."

Katie linked her arm with his to restrain him. "No. They'll kill us."

He broke free and wriggled away. "I'm outta here, and if you're smart—"

The crack of one shot followed by two more in rapid succession stopped Hiram's break for freedom. "Shit. What was that?"

"A double-tap after Vinnie was down," Katie explained, hanging onto Hiram's jacket to hold him in place. "Someone meant business."

She glanced out the window. Enzo and Ralphie crouched over a motionless form. After several minutes of discussion, each grabbed a foot and dragged Vinnie toward the truck.

"Hide." Katie grabbed the blanket, and threw it over their heads. "Not a sound," she warned. Hiram's cold hand gripped hers and tightened. The idea of thugs terrifying an old man infuriated her.

Hiram's whisper filled the truck. "If those sons-a-bitches so much as lay a finger on you, little lady, I'll skin them alive with a cheese grater and use a sharpie to draw pictures on any patch that's intact."

So, not terrified. Swallowing a nervous giggle, she addressed her champion in a takes-no-crap kind of voice, the one that worked on her brother. "Stay. Hidden."

"But it smells like puke."

"Please?"

Hiram's long-suffering sigh as he draped the blanket over himself was eerily similar to his grandson's.

As they crouched together beneath the blanket, scraping sounds drew closer and stopped. Footsteps crunched. Enzo's voice outside the window made them both jump. "Let's wrap him good and tight in this tarp and tie it shut."

After much grunting and rustling, a meaty thump rocked the entire truck.

She gripped Hiram's hand tighter, picturing the brothers dumping Vinnie's corpse in the truck bed. A moment later, the Allegrettis climbed in. After fumbling with keys, they shot into the night, stopping only for the gate.

They drove in silence for several minutes. Katie assumed the brothers were in shock. When Enzo spoke, his voice quavered. "Thanks, man. You saved my life."

Ralphie said, "The fucker was gonna kill us. What else could I do?"

The truck rocketed through a turn, throwing Katie on top of Hiram.

Enzo yelled, "Slow the fuck down."

"Can't. We gotta get rid of the corpse. If Vinnie's gang fingers us, we're dead." Ralphie tromped on the gas. The truck rumbled along for several minutes, turned two more corners, and screeched to an abrupt halt.

"Here?" Enzo's voice cracked. "You've gotta be kidding. We shoulda left the bastard at the construction site."

"If we'da done that, we might as well have left a signed confession."

"Holy shit, Ralphie. You're not just another pretty face."

Both men exited the truck.

Katie held her breath as the brothers' footsteps crunched past them. Thumping indicated they were offloading a heavy object. Like Vinnie.

"Can you unlock the door?" Enzo asked.

Ralphie said, "No sweat. I hope *Kinki*'s owner's still out."

Katie's heart somersaulted at Hiram's hoarse whisper. "Hey, the bastards brought us home. Door-to-door service. Remind me to thank them."

A wheezing grunt drowned Hiram out. Enzo's voice sharpened. "Support the shoulders."

"Bastard's not as light as he looks." A sound reminiscent of a melon hitting concrete made Katie shudder.

"Aw, shit," Ralphie muttered.

After more thuds and groans, Enzo said, "This ain't working. We gotta load him onto the dolly over there. Thoughtful of someone to leave it out."

Accompanied by grumbles, curses, and grunts, the loading process commenced. Katie's imagination provided a vivid picture of a corpse strapped to the dolly.

"They're gonna find the stiff, you know," Enzo said. "It'll stink."

"Yeah, but the cops'll think Jackson iced the bastard."

Hiram's breath intake was clearly audible. If Katie hadn't been clutching his arm, he'd have sprung from the truck. "They want to implicate my Sammy. I'm gonna—"

Katie refused to let go. "Calm down, Hiram," she whispered, desperately trying to find the words to reach him. "If they kill us, imagine how bad Sam will feel."

Hiram stopped struggling. He pushed the blanket aside to stare. "Sammy would be devastated if he lost you. I've never seen him so taken with a woman."

She tried to absorb Hiram's words, barely registering the squeak of wheels.

His voice jolted her to reality. "They're heading up the loading ramp." He paused. "Ralphie's picking the lock. Hey it's open and they're wheeling Vinnie inside."

"Where'll we stash the stiff?" Ralphie asked.

Good question. Katie tensed, waiting for Enzo's reply. The door closed on the answer.

Hiram scanned the parking lot and hopped out. "Sammy's truck ain't back yet so he's still out. How about that? He don't have to know we were gone."

"Wait." She sprinted after him and blocked his path. "We have to call Sam and tell him everything. It may save his reputation, his club, even his life."

"Shi—I mean shoot. You're right. Let's phone from inside."

"We should wait here until they leave," she replied. When he hesitated, she added, "They have guns, remember? Plus Sam might return and we need to warn him."

"The *Golden Grill Diner*'s on the next block. We can ask to use the phone, and it has a view of *Kinki*, so we can see them leave." He hit her with his irresistible grin. "I hear a cheeseburger and fries calling our names. My treat."

Chapter 31: Post-Stowaway Reactions

Once Katie wrapped up her confession, Sam unclenched his jaw long enough to take a slug of his drink. Thank God he'd had the foresight to pour himself a double. Tilting his recliner, he rubbed his temple to ease the pressure. His brain rebelled, refusing to picture what might have happened to the two stowaways. Taking care to downplay his horror in case he set Granddaddy Hiram off by losing it, he said, "It appears y'all had an exciting evening." A muscle in his cheek jumped like a living creature.

Granddaddy Hiram kept quiet, as if shocked at hearing the foolhardy risks they'd taken.

Katie filled the silence by chirping, "Look on the bright side. We both survived. Better still, the Allegrettis have no clue we witnessed the whole thing."

Sam mulled over the story in paralyzed silence, let it sink in how close they'd come to dying. Realization struck him a sledgehammer blow. The story was so off-the-wall, they had to be pranking him, bless their hearts. Somehow, some way, the pair had cottoned on to the fact that his evening event was a date disguised as a business meeting. The stowaway story was to teach him a lesson. It had worked.

He flashed a broad grin to show he could take a joke. "Okay, I get it. Y'all are messing with my head, right?"

In response, Katie wrinkled her forehead in a fair imitation of annoyance. For a moment, he got distracted by the way a loose strand of ebony hair curled onto her neck. She pushed it behind her ear with a simple, feminine gesture, tempting him to gather her in his arms.

The twinge of longing fled when she spoke with brisk precision. "I wouldn't kid about witnessing a murder."

Not the reaction he'd expected. He downed the rest of his drink. The alcohol burned its way to his stomach. "Please tell me this is a joke." He shot a pleading glance at his granddaddy.

Granddaddy Hiram shook his head. "Clean out your ears, boy. You heard the little lady. The Allegrettis wanted cheesesteaks. I wanted cheesesteak, too, so I hid in their truck. Katie went along to keep me out of trouble. We solved the vandalism mystery and witnessed a murder. The corpse is stashed inside *Kinki*. End of story."

"I need another drink." Sam muttered.

Aware of Rex at his heels, he stalked into the kitchen, pulled down the bottle, and poured another double. If their story was true, and he was beginning to believe it was, they were lucky to be alive. Granddaddy Hiram's brain injury had endangered his own safety, Katie's too.

As the thought of losing two of the most important people in his life sank in, he started to shake. Guilt, already simmering, bubbled harder. If he'd stayed home instead of yielding to his dumb-assed craving for freedom, he could have taken his granddaddy for cheesesteak. Hell, Katie could have joined them, and the three of them would have enjoyed a fun evening together. He fought a sudden yearning for something undefinable and unsettling.

In the meantime, drowning his sorrows wasn't the way to go. He dumped the contents of his glass into the sink and opened a can of Mountain Dew.

An inquisitive nose nuzzled his fingers. With a twinge of sadness, he ruffled Rex's ears. "Don't worry, boy. Before I leave, I'll find a good home for you too."

With a smile locked firmly into position, he sauntered into the living room to see his granddaddy had dragged his chair closer to Katie. They were deep in conversation, as if they truly cared for one another. The word *family* took up tenancy in Sam's head. Katie. Josh. Himself. Rex. Bluto. A couple more kids. Laughter. Granddaddy Hiram for visits.

He snapped out of it. Commitment, marriage, and family weren't for him.

Rex trotted over and flopped at his granddaddy's feet.

Katie stared directly at Sam and her eyes softened. "Come join us." She patted the cushion beside her.

Dear God, she was gorgeous. If he didn't know better, he might think he meant something to her. Something important. To cover his sudden loss of speech, he knocked back his drink before sitting. Her scent—vanilla and coconut soap and a fragrance that was pure Katie—teased his nostrils, Remorse seized him. Today's stunt—dating another woman when he knew damn well the sexiest, sweetest woman he could ever hope to meet was waiting for him—beat all his other dimwitted feats, hands down.

Granddaddy Hiram shot Sam a knowing grin. "Looks like you've recovered from the shock of our news."

Sam ignored him. "Assuming there is a corpse, we have to find it."

"Of course there's a corpse," Granddaddy Hiram interjected. "We both saw it."

"Did anyone check Vinnie's pulse after the shooting?"

Katie and Granddaddy Hiram stared at one another. "No," Katie answered.

"So Vinnie could still be alive." Overriding their protests, Sam continued, "When you got back here, what did you do?"

"What do you think, boy?" Granddaddy Hiram asked. "Hell, we confronted two thugs with huge guns and a small corpse."

Sam hid a grin.

Katie's face went all earnest. "We were worried the Allegrettis would find us if we followed them inside, so we went to the *Golden Grill Diner*. I couldn't call earlier because I'd left my purse behind." Her gaze raked his face. "I hope I didn't interrupt anything important."

She couldn't possibly know he'd spent three hours over dinner with a hot real estate agent. Never letting his smile slip, Sam said, "I was glad you called. My meeting was real boring." True enough. Due to lack of interest in his date, sexy as she was, he'd been contemplating cutting out when Katie called.

"The music sure was loud." Her tone sharpened. "It must have been challenging to hold an important discussion with your, ah, business colleague while competing with a violin serenade."

He told himself Katie might suspect, but she didn't know for sure. The urge to throw his arms around her was overpowering, but he was pretty sure it would piss her off. He went for her hand instead, but she snatched it away. He settled on, "Observant as well as beautiful."

She narrow-eyed him. "Bite me."

He feigned ignorance. "I plan to. Later. But we digress. Since you didn't stick around, you can't be sure Vinnie's inside. He could have regained consciousness and walked off." Sam was grasping at straws and he knew it.

Katie frowned. "Highly unlikely."

"I should call the cops."

After a long pause, Katie said in a small voice, "There's more."

"Aw, no. Tell me you're kidding."

"I should have mentioned it sooner, but Vinnie Constantine is—was— Luigi's right hand man. Either Luigi heard I'm working for you and asked Vinnie to trash your place, or Vinnie was out to undercut Luigi while he's in prison. Either way, if their gang hears of my involvement—and they will if you call the police—there's no telling what they'll do to *Kinki*," she paused, "or to Hiram and me for being accomplices in Vinnie's murder. At least, that's how they'll see it."

Sam gulped his Mountain Dew, wishing it were straight Jack Daniels. "Okay. No cops. I can't let anything bad happen to either of you." Shocking himself, he moved over, wrapped his arms around Katie, and kissed her long and slow, relieved that she kissed him back. He drew away reluctantly. "Tell you what. I'm searching every inch of *Kinki*, then we'll decide what to do."

"I'm coming with you," she said.

Granddaddy Hiram jumped out of his chair. "Me too. We'll take Rex as our cadaver dog. He'll sniff out the corpse."

Two hours later, they called it quits. Dead or alive, Vinnie wasn't there.

As they headed back, Sam said, "Without a body, there's no proof of a murder."

"Where's Rex?" Katie asked.

Granddaddy Hiram shrugged. "He's not much of a cadaver dog. He took off long ago. I'm heading back to the apartment."

Sam pulled Katie aside, and gripped her arms. "I don't think you should be alone tonight." Next thing he knew, his mouth bypassed his brain. "Spend the night here. My granddaddy's a real sound sleeper."

Well, hell. This did not mean he was in love. He was merely being considerate. He held his breath, waiting for a response to the question he'd never once asked a woman.

She didn't answer. Which was okay, seeing as how he was having second thoughts.

"Katie?"

She didn't move, just looked at him with those eyes. "You keep forgetting I have a son. Bella took Josh to a movie tonight, special treat, something involving pandas. They'll be home any minute now. I'll ask her to stay the night with me, keep me company. We can both sleep in my bed, the way we did as kids."

"Granddaddy Hiram and I will follow you to make sure you get home safely."

Chapter 32: Josh's School

After three incredibly busy days, during which Sam barely saw Katie except for a few stolen moments, he climbed the steps of Seaview Heights Elementary School. He'd made Josh a promise and intended to keep it. He didn't know what he was going to say to the kids, but whatever it was, hopefully, he wouldn't make things worse for Josh.

He pressed the bell beside the front door. A receptionist answered and he explained who he was. Apparently, he passed muster because she buzzed him in.

On entering, the odor of musty books and glue undercut by the tang of industrial-strength cleanser hit him. He inhaled deeply, and memories rushed in. As a kid, he'd viewed school as a refuge from his daddy.

He signed in at the office, picked up his visitor's lanyard, and got directions to Josh's classroom.

The drone of childish voices reading in unison warned him that morning classes had started. As if sensing his presence, a small figure emerged from a classroom at the end of the corridor and raced toward him.

"You came," Josh's voice echoed down the empty hallway.

Guilt coursed through Sam's body. "'Course I did, buddy. Didn't I say I would?" Hopefully he made it sound as though the notion of crapping out had never crossed his mind.

"The receptionist called, so the teacher sent me to find you." Josh grabbed Sam's hand and tugged. "Hurry. Class has started."

Sam enfolded the small hand in his, shocking himself with his protective gesture. As soon as they reached the classroom, Josh yanked his hand away and scampered to his desk. Sam was good with that. No self-respecting nine-year-old would be caught dead holding his father's hand or, in this case, stand-in father.

Sam entered the classroom cautiously. The woman stopped writing on the dry erase board, removed her glasses, and batted her eyelashes. "You must be Sam Jackson. Welcome to the grade four Career Day. I'm Miss Johansson, but please call me Lois." Sam swore she thrust her breasts at him. "Class, say hi to Mr. Jackson, Josh's stand-in dad for today."

Several voices piped, "Hi, Mr. Jackson."

Sam cleared his throat in preparation for the career speech. "I'm a friend of Josh and his mom, and I'm here to tell you a little bit about a former career. But first, I have a question for you." He paused. "Have any of you heard of a video game called *Last Ghoul Standing*?"

"I love that game," one kid called from the back of the class.

Sam grinned. "I invented and built that game."

"Shut the front door," a poster child for grunge exclaimed.

"Charlie," Miss Johansson chided. "Watch your language."

Sam smiled to himself. He had them where he wanted. "It's the gospel truth. The royalties from *Last Ghoul Standing* put me through university."

For the next fifteen minutes, Sam spoke from the heart, revealing more than he'd ever intended. He described the hours he'd wasted as a university freshman playing online games instead of attending class. He described how as a sophomore, he'd signed up for software development classes to raise his grades. That way, instead of wasting his time playing someone else's games, he'd developed his own. His most challenging game, *Last Ghoul Standing*, incorporated everything he enjoyed most—action, adventure, horror, the supernatural, a complex puzzle, shootings, killings, zombies, the works.

The rest was history. Royalties from the sale of *Last Ghoul* funded the remainder of his studies. The class didn't need to know they also funded his lazy lifestyle for several years after graduating with a Harvard MBA.

For the next half hour, he answered questions, discussed creativity, and generally encouraged the kids to follow their dreams.

When the bell rang, Josh dashed over to Sam and flung his arms around his waist in a little-boy bear hug. Sam had no choice but to hug back, wrapping his arms around the skinny form and awkwardly patting his shoulder. The kid smelled of clean clothes, shampoo, and a hint of bubble-gum. Sam didn't have experience when it came to kids, but even he realized Josh had a taken a morning bath.

Shit. If he'd known a Career Day presentation was such a big deal it warranted a morning bath, he'd never have agreed.

"You were the best pretend-dad ever," Josh whispered.

Frozen with dread, Sam barely saw Josh join the group of boys heading outside, all elbowing one another and laughing.

Yeah, big mistake. If he could, he'd whack himself over the head with a two-by-four for encouraging Josh to believe this pretend-dad might be a permanent fixture in his life. Worse, he'd accepted Katie's offer of support at the Jackson family barbecue on Sunday.

He started to sweat. One thing was crystal clear. Immediately after the grand opening, he was selling *Kinki*, moving his granddaddy back to San Antonio, and leaving Atlantic City for good.

In the meantime, he would avoid Katie as much as possible. It wouldn't be easy, but he needed to cool things down between them. And if that didn't work, no doubt the family barbecue would do the trick nicely.

He turned on his heel and headed off to a late meeting at his bank.

Chapter 33: Barbecue Begins

Sam spent the next two days avoiding Katie by working his ass off. By the time late Sunday afternoon rolled around, every cell in his body buzzed with equal parts horniness and dread. The thought of an entire evening with Katie triggered the former condition, while his upcoming confrontation with his father caused the second. He had a sinking feeling that a face-off with Eugene at a family barbecue was one huge mistake, as was this date with Katie. Sure as shit, tonight's festivities would drive her away forever.

The thought of losing her twisted his gut in an odd way, so he focused on the bright side. Tonight would relieve him of the unpleasant task of dumping her.

When the time came to head out, Granddaddy Hiram hoisted himself into the back seat instead of riding shotgun. Rex hopped in beside him. The next stop was Katie's place. She answered the door immediately, as if she'd been waiting. Waves of longing rippled through Sam. A red clip fastened her hair into a ponytail that swept over one shoulder of her silky red-and-white blouse. Loose tendrils escaped to curl around her cheeks. He wanted to wrap his arms around her, stroke the silky skin, but knew that if he indulged himself, he'd be lost.

Hoping Katie hadn't noticed his hunger, he helped her climb into the passenger seat. Tormented by her fragrance, coconut shampoo, body lotion, and something else, a scent that was pure aphrodisiac, he pointed his truck in the right direction and tromped on the accelerator.

Upon their arrival at Nick and Grace's faux Victorian house, Rex and Granddaddy Hiram scooted ahead. Murphy, Grace's schnauzer, greeted them with excited yips, and trotted after Rex. Sam let Katie take the lead, following her down a narrow pathway toward the back yard.

His heart drummed in his chest, drowning out her words of encouragement. Hugged by white capris, her perfect ass flexed with every step she took. Hypnotized, he noted there was no panty line. To distract himself, he focused on her strappy little sandals. Bad idea. A silver ring encircled one of her red-polished toes. The ridiculously sexy sight alleviated neither his desire nor his guilt over exploiting her generous spirit.

Now that they'd arrived, Sam discovered that confronting his father seemed a whole lot less appealing. He was contemplating sneaking away before Eugene noticed his arrival when Katie slipped her hand into his.

Demonstrating that spooky ability to read his thoughts, she said, "It'll be okay, Sam. It'll only be possible for you to have a healthy relationship with your father if you clear the air first."

"I don't want a healthy relationship with Eugene. I prefer it when our mutual dislike seethes and bubbles beneath the surface, boiling over occasionally."

"You don't mean that."

"It's served me well for thirty-two years."

But he let her pull him into the back yard where happy hour was in full swing.

***

Remorse nibbled at Katie's conscience when she thought of how she'd left Josh at home with Bella. Again. Surely a good parent, especially one whose work gobbled up every waking moment, would have cancelled a date to spend time with her son. Not that Josh minded. He was too excited about ordering in pizza and watching some movies with his aunt to even notice his mother was gone.

Tucking her guilt away, Katie sucked in a deep breath and prepared to meet Sam's family. She'd offered him support, and support was what she intended to deliver, whether he liked it or not.

She hated to see the lines of tension bracketing his mouth as he scanned the yard. His reluctance to join the laughing group clustered around a table set up as an outdoor bar was palpable. She'd accumulated tons of experience in conflict resolution while organizing funerals, and it looked as though she'd use all of it tonight.

Forcing herself to relax and appreciate the beauty of the evening, she took in the view. The Jersey Shore, a long arc of twinkling lights, edged the dark ocean as far as the eye could see. Garden lighting cast an intimate glow over the small gathering on the patio. The smell of smoke from a charcoal grill filled the air with the promise of summer. On the lawn, a table with seven place settings promised al fresco dining.

She leaned closer to Sam, conveying her wordless support.

As they stood there, shoulder to shoulder, one very fine man wearing a black shirt, light pants, and loafers, strode across the lawn to greet them. He pumped Sam's hand with an exchange of insults. This must be Sam's older brother, Nick. Katie liked him immediately. What woman wouldn't appreciate those gorgeous gray eyes? Nick grinned at Katie, causing her to add an irresistible smile to his list of assets.

"Hi. I'm Nick, the good-looking brother. You must be Katie. Welcome to the Jackson family barbecue. Let me fix you both a drink." Nick poured two drinks from a tall pitcher and handed one to Katie, the other to Sam. "White sangria."

Sam sniffed his drink, frowned, and shook his head. "Got anything stronger?"

"You sure about that?" Nick asked. "You'll want your wits about you tonight, especially around our daddy."

Demonstrating her support, Katie ignored Sam's scowl. "I agree. Please listen to Nick."

Nick grinned at Katie. "Brave as well as beautiful. I do believe my little brother may have met his match. Come with me and I'll introduce you."

They made their way across the patio toward two women, who were laughing at something Hiram had said. The curvy, dark-haired beauty turned out to be Nick's wife, Grace, and the woman with fluffy white curls, psychedelic caftan, and love beads was Grace's Auntie Beth.

While Katie responded to the greetings, she kept a close watch on Sam. With a sinking feeling, she noted his expression was grim.

At last, he asked, "Where's Eugene?"

Grace's eyes clouded with concern. "Your father's not here yet. I'm sure he'll arrive soon."

"Seriously? Some things never change," Sam muttered. "I should have known better than to think Eugene and I might have a chance to clear the air tonight."

Grace said, "If it matters, I think clearing the air is a wonderful idea."

"Me too," Katie said.

Granddaddy Hiram interjected, "Hell, my son's always late. I hope y'all aren't holding dinner on account of Eugene. I skipped lunch today to make room for the big, honkin' steak I'm planning to devour tonight. You know how I get real cranky when I'm hungry."

Nick grabbed the tongs and a dangerous-looking knife, saying, "Yeah, we know how you get, and it's not pretty. Dad promised he'd be here for dinner, so I'll go do mysterious and manly things to my meat." He gave Grace a huge, smacking kiss before heading into the smoke.

"Be careful, hon," Grace called after Nick. "We don't want any damage. I'm partial to your meat." Her contagious laugh rang out.

Katie took an immediate liking to her hostess.

Hiram said, "Nick needs my help or he'll burn the steaks." He hurried away accompanied by Rex.

"Hey, don't feed Rex anything," Sam yelled after them. "You know what spicy food does to his digestion."

They must have reached the food because Rex responded with a loud bark that morphed into his food alarm.

"I'm going to stretch my legs," Sam announced. "Anyone want anything?"

There were no takers.

Katie examined him with suspicion. "I hope you're not sneaking away to hide before your father arrives."

His guilty expression would have been comical if she hadn't sensed the deep hurt underlying his desire to flee.

He wrinkled his forehead. "You promised to support me tonight."

Her palms grew damp, but she steeled herself to stay strong. "Believe it or not, this is what support looks like. You need to stay and find out why Eugene wants to talk to you."

"In that case, I need another Sangria. Maybe five."

Sam stomped off in the direction of the bar. As soon as he'd disappeared, Katie found herself pressed against Beth's cushiony body, enveloped in a hug and a cloud of Shalimar.

"Holy shit," Beth said upon releasing her. "This time, Sam picked himself a winner. You have guts."

Katie voiced her misgivings. "I hope I didn't overstep. Eugene wants to speak to his son. There's no way that'll happen if Sam avoids him all evening."

She squirmed under Grace's scrutiny. Had she grown another head, or what?

At last, Grace said, "Wow. We all expected a doormat. From everything I've heard, you're the first of Sam's dates to stand up to him. Bravo."

Katie's gut twisted. "I was trying to help."

"It was a compliment. For what it's worth, I think you did the right thing."

In the distance, Nick yelled, "Gracie. Help."

Grace rolled her eyes at Katie. "Uh-oh. I'd better go rescue our dinner." She headed toward the billowing smoke.

In a confidential tone, Beth said to Katie, "I bet Sam hasn't mentioned this, but you're also the first woman he's ever introduced to his family."

"Ladies. I hope you're not discussin' my deep, dark secrets."

Katie jumped at the sound of the smoky drawl behind her. Apparently Sam had decided to stick around. "Of course not," she lied, infusing her words with conviction while making a mental note to learn more of Sam's secrets from Beth.

"You're a such a spoilsport, Sammy." Regret tinged Beth's voice. "We were just getting started."

Sam gave an easy laugh. "Two can play at that game." He turned to Katie. "Don't let Beth's fluffy white curls and angelic expression deceive you. She'll lead you astray in a heartbeat. Let's see, she enjoys smoking Acapulco Gold with her Canasta Crones—"

"Hey, that was for poor Millie's arthritis. As hostess, I had to be polite and join in."

Without missing a beat, Sam continued, "Then there were Beth's 'special' brownies—"

"Desperate times, desperate measures."

"But my favorite is the time Beth was Grace's getaway driver."

"What did you do? Rob a bank?" Katie couldn't imagine either woman committing a crime.

Beth laughed. "Worse. We went undercover to find a stolen dog in *Kinki* during its fetish club days. But my all-time best was teaching Murphy to poop on my nasty neighbor's lawn. That dog is one quick study. Remind me to tell you about it later." She flashed a mischievous grin.

The three were laughing when a rich southern voice cut in. "Mind if I join y'all?"

Katie eyed the handsome middle-aged man, hoping her curiosity wasn't obvious. Sam was the image of his father, at least, he would be in twenty-five years. An attractive hint of silver threaded Eugene's dark blond hair, and his face bore a few more lines than his son's. It was spooky how both men possessed the same rangy build, killer grin, and sexy tiger eyes.

Without visible hesitation, Beth said, "Hey, Eugene. It's about time you got here. I was just saying I'd better go help Grace serve dinner." She bustled away, leaving Katie alone with the two men.

***

In case Katie tried to leave him alone with his father, Sam slipped a hand around her waist. She'd said she would support him, but all she'd done so far was talk him into staying until Eugene decided to grace the party with his presence.

He let his lip curl, just enough to show how he felt. "You decided to join us at last."

Katie defused the uncomfortable moment by sticking her hand out with a friendly smile. "Katie Deluca. I'm surprised Sam never mentioned his resemblance to you, Mr. Jackson."

Eugene beamed. "Please, call me Eugene. And yes, I'm told we're very much alike."

Whenever people compared him to Eugene, Sam wanted to puke. He willed his voice to remain steady. "Only in appearance. Deep down, where it counts, we're nothing alike. I figured you were giving this party a miss, same as always."

Beside him, he heard Katie's deep inhalation. Thankfully, she remained silent.

On the surface, Eugene appeared unruffled, but from the rigid set of his shoulders, Sam knew he'd scored a direct hit.

Undeterred, Eugene said, "Seems we got off on the wrong foot tonight, Sam. I apologize for my tardiness. I underestimated the traffic. I was visiting an old friend in Cape May, at least he used to be a friend. Guess I screwed up that friendship beyond repair, too."

Katie jumped in. "Traffic is terrible this spring. They're re-paving the Garden State Parkway."

Sam's glare deepened. She'd cut off the remark hovering on his tongue about how Eugene's famous "traffic miscalculations" had ruined every one of birthdays until he got old enough to not give a shit.

As if sensing he'd dodged a bullet, Eugene addressed Sam directly. "You're a lucky man. Katie's a young woman a man would be proud to bring home to meet the family."

Sam looked at Eugene for a long moment. A lifetime of swallowing his father's criticism boiled, bubbled over. "As opposed to the only other date of mine you met?"

"She was a stripper."

"She was a social worker. The reason she danced was to pay for her daddy's cancer treatments."

Eugene's face paled. "I had no idea. You didn't say anything."

A red haze clouded Sam's vision. "You were too busy getting drunk. And when did we ever sit down and have a heart-to-heart? I'll tell you when. Never."

"Sam?" Katie tugged his sleeve.

Undeterred, he continued, "What were you doing in a strip joint?"

"It was a stag for your cousin, Braden. You were invited too."

Right. He'd declined, then ended up in the same strip club, go figure. Braden was a royal pain in the ass, with his advice on the perils of a loose lifestyle. But Sam had started venting, and he wasn't done. Not by a long shot. Drawing on righteous anger, he loaded the Howitzer of accusations, took aim at Eugene, fired. "At least I'm single and free to date anyone I want. Unlike certain married men I know."

"Sam." Katie's shocked voice penetrated his anger.

"It's okay," Eugene said. "I was a terrible husband and a worse father. I wish I could undo the things I did. Unfortunately, I can't."

Sam didn't give a shit about Eugene's wretched stab at an apology. "Too little, too late. Don't expect forgiveness for all those years of neglect, condescension, and abuse."

Katie turned to Eugene. "It's the stress of the grand opening only a week away."

Eugene latched onto the opening, saying to Sam, "Speaking of the grand opening, I've heard good things about what you've done with *Kinki*. I'm a financial planner myself, so if there's anything I can help with—"

"You don't trust me. I should have known."

Eugene looked baffled. "That's not what I said."

"It's what you implied. Nothing I did was good enough for you." Mindful of Katie, he tried to remain calm. In a more reasonable tone, he said, "I know to the penny how much I've spent so far, what I intend to spend, and the amount in my bank account." Which was dwindling on a daily basis, but that was his little secret.

"I didn't mean to insult you. From what I've heard, your nightclub is extraordinary. I hope you've included me on your guest list."

Before he could deny it, Katie chimed in. "Absolutely. The whole family's invited, including Braden and his wife. Hiram gave me the names and addresses."

Sam leveled his gaze at Katie. "Say what?"

"They're your family, Sam. It's the right thing to do."

"She's right," Eugene said. "It'll be a privilege to join you and celebrate your success."

He'd endured enough of Eugene's bullshit. He was about to open his mouth and ask the real reason he'd graced the Jersey Shore with his presence, but Rex's food alarm cut off his words.

Seconds later, the dog thundered toward them, a string of sausages trailing from his jaws. Murphy scooted along beside him, springing into the air, trying to nab a bite. Behind them, Granddaddy Hiram puffed along bellowing, "Stop. Thief."

Rex dropped the sausages and chowed down as fast as he could, gagging a little as he gulped some whole.

Granddaddy Hiram skidded to a halt and hugged Eugene. "Hi, Son, good to see you." Catching sight of Rex licking his chops, he added, "Aw, shit."

"You can say that again." Sam glared at his granddaddy. "What kind were they?"

"Spicy Italian with black pepper and garlic. Rex snatched them before I noticed."

"How many?"

His granddaddy turned all shifty-eyed. "Uh … I wasn't counting."

Sam fished several waste bags from his pocket with a grim smile and held them out. "Don't say I didn't warn you."

"Forget it," Granddaddy Hiram said in an aggrieved tone.

Rex belched. Then he farted, circled twice, and assumed the position. Back hunched, tail pumping, the dog emptied his bowels. That done, he offered the transfixed audience a wide doggie grin, made a couple of backward scratches in the grass, and repeated the process.

Twice.

Into the awestruck silence, Nick's voice hollered, "Dinner's ready. Come and get it."

Chapter 34: Jackson Family Revelations

Granddaddy Hiram tried to make a fast getaway.

Sam whipped out one hand and gripped his granddaddy's arm. "Oh, no you don't. You forgot to watch Rex. You're cleaning it up." He handed the bags to his granddaddy.

"Ow. My arthritis," Granddaddy Hiram whined. "I can't crouch."

Sam knew he couldn't leave his granddaddy alone to face the mountain of dog shit. "Fine, I'll stick around and help, but you owe me."

Eugene extended one arm to Katie with a smug smile. "Looks like Sam and my daddy will be occupied for a while. Please allow me the honor of escorting you to the table."

Sam tuned his expression to do-whatever-the-hell-you-want.

In his usual slimy way, Eugene sealed the deal by slathering on some guilt inducement. "Surely, you won't reject a lonely man."

Katie hesitated, then placed her hand on Eugene's arm. "Of course not." Over her shoulder, she mouthed, "Sorry," to Sam as she walked away with Eugene, leaving him behind to deal with the dog shit, his granddaddy, and Rex.

Granddaddy Hiram was surprisingly cooperative, a sure sign of guilt. With two of them on poop duty, the task was accomplished quickly. After banishing Rex to the fenced-in dog run, Sam and his granddaddy cleaned themselves up and set out across the lawn to join the others.

A wave of laughter floated on the calm evening air, triggering a resurgence of anger. Everyone had started without them. Drawing closer, Sam eyed the seating arrangement. Nick sat at one end of the table facing Grace at the other. Noting Eugene had seated himself beside Katie, he scowled. That left Beth and two empty seats on the opposite side.

Nick waved them over, yelling, "Hurry before the good stuff disappears. Katie made sure we saved you guys the best steaks."

They took the two empty seats. Sam reached for the wine, then changed his mind and switched to water.

Katie aimed a sympathetic smile at him. At least he hoped it was sympathetic. She mouthed the word, "Sorry," again, causing his throat to close.

Before she spotted his vulnerability, he concentrated on loading his plate with steak and some green stuff. Childhood memories of his daddy's betrayals bounced around his head like ping-pong balls, picking up speed with each revolution, their power to hurt undiminished.

Katie surprised him by saying, "Hiram, would you mind switching seats with me? I'd like to sit beside Sam."

The transfer was executed without incident, and Katie settled in beside Sam. Under the table, she squeezed his hand, while asking Beth a question.

Family conversation resumed. During the meal, Katie described every aspect of *Kinki*, emphasizing Sam's innovative ideas, until even Eugene looked impressed.

And just like that, Sam knew how much he wanted, no, *needed*, Katie beside him for a long, long time.

He was pondering his terrifying epiphany when he caught her staring at him, as if memorizing his face. Her wistful expression crashed him back to reality. Yeah, she recognized what he'd forgotten—the improbability of a happy ending.

Nick's booming voice penetrated his semi-catatonic state. "Earth to Samuel. If you're still alive, come in, please."

Sam emerged from his daze. "Yeah?"

Nick said, "About time. It's hard to compete with a beautiful woman for a brother's attention."

Determined to live in the moment, Sam gave a genuine smile. "A beautiful woman is one of life's gifts. You, on the other hand, not so much."

"I'm wounded, deeply wounded." Nick's lips twitched, a telltale sign he was having fun.

"Sure you are. Remind me why I should listen to you."

"I'm feeding you a perfect steak, medium rare, the way you like it."

Sam heaved a theatrical sigh. "It's a little charred, but okay, you have my undivided attention."

"Good. I have an announcement." Nick's face creased in a broad grin.

Sam recollected his brother's refusal to take on the security job for *Kinki*. "Does your big news have anything to do with you refusing new clients?"

"It does." Ignoring the murmurs, Nick raised his voice. "I've sold my company because I'm leaving the security business. Gracie and I are returning to Texas. We've bought a ranch in the Hill Country, not far from San Antonio. I plan to operate it as both a working and dude ranch. Gracie will run her pet spa in one of the outbuildings."

"And I'm going with them," Beth interjected, her voice quivering with excitement.

"Y'all are leaving the Jersey Shore?" Sam asked. In spite of his disappointment, he made a speedy recovery for their sake. "Good for you. Plenty of space and fresh air, less dangerous job."

"Exactly. It's a great place to start a family. There are several properties for sale in the area. You should think of joining us."

"Great idea," Granddaddy Hiram said. "You've decided to sell *Kinki* after the grand opening, and I'm moving back into *Golden Sunset Manor*." He lowered his voice to a stage whisper. "Those Texas gals get amorous during a country walk, if you get my drift."

Sam shuddered. But damned if moving south didn't make sense. A new life in Texas Hill Country sounded appealing. He pictured a white house in a small town, Katie and Josh by his side, a baby.

Katie's sharp elbow jab caught Sam's attention. He caught a flash of surprise and hurt on her pretty face before she asked, "When did you plan to tell me about the sale?"

Yeah, he could see why she'd think he'd shut her out. Remorse twisted his gut. "I should have mentioned it sooner, but I only decided last night. I wanted to tell you once we were alone."

Beth bounced in her seat, every part of her body jiggling. "Isn't it wonderful? I'll be Nick and Gracie's live-in babysitter."

"That was our news, Beth," Nick said. "You promised Gracie you wouldn't blab."

"Oops. Sorry." Beth looked far from sorry.

"It's okay, Auntie Beth," Grace reassured her. "You're excited."

Sam's brain circuits scrambled to process the information. Searching for clues, he studied a madly-grinning Nick, then Grace, seated opposite her husband. Her face glowed with an inner beauty. He choked out a question to Katie. "Are they sayin' what I think they are?"

"I believe so, yes."

Emotion gripped Sam with such force, he couldn't breathe. A baby. A miniature human. A little girl with Nick's steadfast nature, Gracie's big blue eyes, and of course, Uncle Sammy's photographic memory. How cool was that? He stood slowly.

"Are you okay?" Katie whispered, her eyes wide with concern.

Warmth shot through his body at the knowledge that she cared. He smiled at her and nodded. Finding his voice, he bellowed over the outburst of excited chatter. "You guys are growing a new addition to the Jackson family?"

Grace nodded. "In six months."

Sam couldn't stop grinning. He leaped around Katie and Beth to stand behind his brother. "Up," he ordered.

Nick twisted his head to eye him warily. "Why?"

"Don't be a pussy. A baby announcement calls for the circle jump."

Nick had invented a celebration game he called "circle jump" as consolation for their daddy's absence during every childhood triumph. Eugene would damn well witness it today.

Nick leaped to his feet. "You asked for it, baby brother. But the winner's gonna be a real man, not a candy-ass punk like you."

They crouched, facing one another. Sam did the countdown. When he reached one, the two men charged with ear-piercing whoops. Seeing as how a bear hug was a requirement, they fused together, jumping in a tight circle, hollering at the tops of their lungs.

Murphy, never a dog to ignore fun times, shot out from under the table, yapping his encouragement. Saliva sprayed as he tried to gnaw their shoes. Settling for clamping both front legs around Sam's calf, the dog balanced on his hind feet and went for it. Sam shook his leg to dislodge the dog.

Murphy clung like a limpet.

Between gasps of mirth, Nick said, "You're slowing down. You ready to beg for mercy?"

Sam tuned Nick out, a skill he'd honed over the years, and jumped faster. Round and round they went.

Between gusts of laughter, Nick was breathing hard. "You appear to have … puff … experienced a little accident."

Sam glanced down and froze on the spot. A damp stain disfigured his best wool-and-silk-blend dress pants. He released Nick in a big hurry and tried to pry Murphy loose.

With a moan of ecstasy, the damn dog tightened his grip.

Nick patted Sam's arm. "Shouldn't be much longer. I think Murphy's getting to the best part."

"Sweet lord a' mercy," Sam yelled, casting an accusing glare at his brother. "I hope that's drool."

"I win. You let go first."

"Make yourself useful. Pull him off. I don't want to hurt him."

Snorts of laughter erupted from the three women, Katie included, who stood nearby. They were splitting a gut at the sight of Murphy humping his goddamn leg. Shit.

Gracie grabbed a slice of steak from Nick's plate and used it to coax Murphy away. "I'm so sorry," she said while Murphy trotted off with the meat. Her grin spoiled her apology. Between snorts of laughter, she explained, "He's been fixed, so the wet spot's only saliva. It means he likes you."

Sam forgave Gracie for laughing being as how she was an expectant mother. Mindful of the baby, he gave her a gentle hug along with a kiss on both cheeks. "You and Nick will be great parents. Congratulations."

Amidst the hooting and cheering and back-slapping, Sam noticed Katie's wistful expression. For one fleeting moment, he imagined the exhilaration coupled with tenderness he'd feel if they were married, with a baby on the way. As if sensing his thoughts, she came and stood beside him. He almost believed his fantasy could happen, that they could leave Luigi behind and settle down together somewhere far away.

The sound of a knife clinking against a glass caused every head to turn and stare at Eugene. Trust his daddy to steal the limelight. Why was he not surprised?

Eugene placed the knife on the table. "Y'all may all be wondering why I wanted this little get-together. What I'm about to say may come as a shock, especially to my sons. You'd best get seated."

Everyone sat in a big hurry.

Eugene remained standing, shifting from foot to foot, looking as if his tightie-whities were lined with thorns. Finally he said, "There's no easy way to say this, so I'll come right out with it. I owe y'all an apology." He paused, took a very long breath.

Sam itched to shake his father for milking the moment.

Eugene's next words came out as a strangled croak. "I'm a gambling addict."

Sam's water glass stalled half-way to his mouth.

"That explains a lot," Granddaddy Hiram muttered.

"Is that why Mom isn't with you?" Nick asked.

Eugene cleared his throat and avoided eye contact. "I guess y'all would find out sooner or later, so I might as well come clean. Your mother has left me, and I don't blame her. She insisted I go into recovery, or there wasn't a hope in hell she'd let me inside our house again. Part of my twelve-step program is to make amends, so that's what I'm doing. Making amends for the way I treated my sons." He looked at Sam. "Especially you, Samuel."

Sam clunked down his glass, barely noticing that the water spilled out. A glance at Nick told him his brother felt the same jolt of shock.

Since Nick appeared disinclined to talk, Sam said through clenched teeth, "All those years, you lied to us. Night after night, we thought you were working." He paused, willing his voice not to break. "Hell, Mom lied too. Whenever you missed a soccer game or school play, or Thanksgiving and our birthdays, she told us you were working."

Eugene flashed him a pleading glance. "Your mama tried to protect you."

But Sam wasn't finished, not by a long shot. "You weren't working, were you? You were gambling, drinking, and screwing around. Mom had to have known."

Instead of denying it, Eugene said, "Your mama was the only child of very rich, very straitlaced parents. One whiff of scandal, and by scandal, I mean divorce, they would've disinherited her faster than a hot knife through butter." He gave a weak grin, probably trying to lighten the moment.

Nick looked at Sam. "Grandma and Grandpa Cunningham were horrible, remember? We dreaded their visits."

But Sam refused to be distracted. "So Mom sacrificed her sons for an inheritance. She should have taken us and run."

"Don't blame your mother. She was in denial. She'd talked herself into believing a fantasy that made it possible to hang onto both her marriage and her parents, at least until they died." He paused. "My gambling and drinking damn near destroyed the family. But I want to make things right."

"Never gonna happen. Nothing you say or do will ever compensate for a fraction of the damage you did. We lived in chaos. Do you realize—"

Nick's calm voice interrupted Sam's tirade. "Hold on, Sam. I know you were more deeply affected, but let our daddy say his piece."

"Thank you, Nicholas. You've always been dependable. As I was sayin', there's no excuse for what I did. I'm ashamed to say I was relieved when you took charge of your younger brother, then my own daddy after his rodeo accident. It made it easier for me to stay away."

Looking stricken, Granddaddy Hiram said nothing.

Sam's stomach tightened. But he'd be damned if he'd let his father see how much his words hurt. He took a stab at keeping his voice neutral. "If Nick was the dependable son, I guess I was the trouble maker."

Shit. His voice had wavered. Shame, guilt, and anguish, emotions that felt eerily familiar whenever in Eugene's presence, jumped out to bite him in the ass. Somehow, being around his father managed to reduce him to the helpless, scared little boy of his childhood.

It still hurt like hell.

Pain flickered across Eugene's face. "It was my fault, not yours, Sam. I ignored you, let you run wild, and then, when you found trouble, I punished you. Please find it in your heart to forgive a weak, stupid man."

Screw that. As far as Sam was concerned, Eugene could shove his plea for absolution where the sun never shone. He had no intention of letting the bastard off the hook.

"Did you know that whenever the garage door opened, I used to run and hide in the attic, or cried under the covers when I was supposed to be asleep?" He kept his tone light, conversational. "Thank God you didn't come home often. According to you, I couldn't do anything right. Worst part is, I believed it."

For a moment, Eugene looked his true age. "I never knew you felt that way."

"I didn't want you to see how close you came to destroying me. I thought you hated me.

Eugene looked around at all the shocked faces. "Can we do this somewhere private?"

"Nope. I came here to speak my mind, and that's what I intend to do. Remember the time Mom left you in charge for five days while she took an art workshop? I woke up the first morning with a stomach pain but you wouldn't let me stay home. The school had to call an ambulance, then the hospital couldn't reach you, so they sliced out my appendix without parental consent. I spent four days in the goddamn hospital without a single visit." He fixed Eugene with a glare. "Not one single fucking visit."

Eugene turned white. "I'd forgotten about that. I must have been off on a bender."

"I figured I'd pissed you off again." Sam threw out the question that had plagued him all his life. "Why did you pick on me? What was wrong with me?"

Under the table, Katie laid her hand on his. Welcoming her silent comfort, Sam relaxed his clenched fist and let her hand slip into his, a lifeline in a chaos of emotion.

When Eugene spoke, his voice was rusty. "The brutal truth is you reminded me of myself. Every time I looked at you, I saw everything I'd thrown away."

Sam figured he must have heard wrong. "Say what?"

"You looked like my mini-me, you walked with that same swagger, talked like me, intonation and all. You inherited the same photographic memory, the same affinity for games of chance. You were so full of mischief and charm, so damn smart it actually hurt. I was afraid you would throw it all away, the same way I did."

Eugene fell silent, as if overcome with emotion. But that wasn't possible. His father didn't do emotion, leastwise not unless it was anger.

It was the moment Sam had dreamed of, but now he wanted to be anywhere else, like hunting down corpses inside *Kinki*, or shoveling more of Rex's shit, or on the beach ducking an assassin's bullets, pretty much anywhere but here, listening to his father humiliate himself in front of the family.

He must have telegraphed his thoughts to Katie, seeing as how she tightened her grip, forcing him to stay seated. He reached across for her wine glass and chugged its contents.

As if oblivious of Sam's turmoil, which was Eugene's standard behavior, he picked up where he left off, his voice steady and strong. "There I was, in the process of pissing my life away, and there you were, Sam, a bright, shiny future ahead of you—but only if you didn't screw it up."

"Give me a break," Sam muttered.

"I didn't want you to turn out like me, so I tried to straighten you out the best I could. I fucked up. If I could change what I did, I would."

Sam stood slowly. It was too much to process, too difficult to believe. Disoriented, he strode away without saying a word.

A moment later, he returned and towered over Eugene. "Was that supposed to be an apology?"

"Yes. Couldn't you tell?"

"I wasn't sure."

"So as there's no misunderstanding, I was a lousy father. I offer my humble apology. I've been an asshole, and I'm trying to change. I want to connect with you, and I haven't a clue how to go about it, seeing as how I never tried when you were a kid."

Eugene sounded contrite. God knows, that was another first. Sam's chest tightened. "You were an asshole."

"Still am."

"Fucked if I forgive you."

"No need, Son. I love you anyway."

"Shit. You never played fair."

This time when Sam stalked away, he made sure he didn't look back.

Chapter 35: Sam's Reaction

Sam pounded along the moonlit beach, stumbling across loose dunes and splashing through incoming surf. The air was surprisingly warm, thick with the salty smell of the ocean. A wave surged over his feet, soaking him to the ankles, before receding with a sucking sound. He lurched forward, too furious with Eugene, too confused over the half-assed apology, to notice the aching cold.

At first he thought the cry floating on the breeze belonged to a seagull. Behind him, the call, louder now, pierced his turmoil. It was no seagull. He pivoted slowly to face the figure closing in fast. For a wisp of a woman, Katie knew how to run.

She halted a few feet away, curling her bare toes into the cold sand. It seemed to Sam she was assessing him, gnawing her bottom lip as if considering the best approach to take when addressing someone seething with toxic emotions.

He took pity on her, breaking the tension with, "Where did you learn to run like that?"

"High school. Sprinting's a great stress reliever. Plus, who knows? One of these days I might have to run for my life."

Her words startled him into examining their surroundings. It was too dark to determine if anyone crouched behind a dune with a sniper's rifle and night-vision scope. He seriously doubted it. Otherwise he'd be dead. Satisfied of their safety, if only temporarily, he regarded her with remorse. "Christ, Katie. I'm a self-absorbed asshole. I can't believe I forgot about Luigi."

"Your father's news wiped everything else from your brain."

His desire to embrace her, to lose himself in her warmth and generosity, was shocking. But if he touched her he'd lose it, and he couldn't imagine anything more of a turn-off for a woman than a man bawling his heart out on her shoulder. He shoved his hands in his pockets.

"All this time, I believed Eugene was a workaholic."

She stepped closer. "Which explains your aversion to a normal nine-to-five job."

"That's the least of it. Ever since I can remember, I thought I couldn't do anything right. Eugene made me believe I was useless. Unreliable. A failure." He damn near choked on the last word because Eugene had been right. He'd blown all his money. Granddaddy Hiram's too. They were teetering on the edge of bankruptcy.

Katie reached out and simply stroked Sam's cheek, her touch calming him. "No wonder commitment terrifies you. It makes perfect sense. I've done extensive reading about how underlying fears sabotage our relationships."

"Of course you have. Okay, I'll bite. How does feeling like a failure make me commitment-challenged?"

"Easy. No one can reject you if you reject them first."

Her words dried the spit clean out of his mouth. Trying to hide the fact that she'd hit the bullseye, he asked, "Is that what you think I've been doing? Pushing women away? And let's not forget taking the easy way out."

"I didn't say that. You did. What do you think?"

"I think you sound like a shrink, answering a question with a question."

He risked a glance at her. She merely compressed her lips. Damned if Katie wasn't one of those rare women who understood the power of silence. It was obvious she was prepared to stand there for hours, if necessary, until he answered her question.

"Give me a moment."

"Take your time."

Recognizing the very real need to examine his memories, his emotions, and yeah, his goddamn *feelings* in order to free himself, plus seeing no other alternative, he mulled over the past in light of his new findings. While she dabbled her toes in the water, he took his time, remembering the string of women he'd walked away from, the dozens of dead-end jobs he'd abandoned. It was an ugly track record.

At last she returned to his side and broke the silence. "Any insights?"

"Yeah, and they're not pretty. Every single day, I walked away before anyone learned I was trouble and dumped me. After I let my daddy convince me games software development was a useless talent, I took the easy jobs in case I blew the difficult ones. My trademark became quick turnovers with jobs, quick turnovers with women. I convinced myself that if I walked out, I couldn't fail." He started walking.

In a flash she was at his side and jogging to keep pace. "Except now. Think about it. You're not taking the easy way out this time." She gave a little grimace. "At least, not yet."

He slowed marginally and thought about his recent effort to make *Kinki* a success. He also considered the unexpected richness of his relationship with his granddaddy now that they shared living quarters. His relationship with Eugene was precarious, but at least he was here, wasn't he? And last, but far least, he reflected on the woman keeping pace at his side.

He hadn't dumped her, at least, not yet.

His flicker of optimism was faint but it was there. Every fiber of his being wanted to believe he could do the right thing rather than the easy thing.

"True," he agreed. "There's nothing and no one in my life right now that doesn't challenge me in more ways than I imagined possible."

"And here I thought I was easy," she quipped, slipping her hand into his. "Some might say slutty."

A surprised laugh slipped past the tightness in his chest. Katie was special. In the face of his resistance, she was forcing him to see things clearly. That was unconditional support. He stopped walking and summoned the courage to face her. The moon shed enough light to illuminate her face.

The emotions shining in her eyes humbled him and simultaneously scared him shitless. Her determination. Her hope. And, unless he'd misread the signals, her love.

Confirming his fears, Katie said, "I love you, Sam. I didn't mean to. I was certain I could avoid falling in love." Her mouth twisted. "Guess that didn't go according to plan."

Fighting his panic, he shook his head. "Don't say that. I have nothing to offer." Instead of wrapping his arms around her, the way every molecule in his body screamed at him to do, he backed away.

"You have plenty to offer." She followed him as he retreated another step. "You're the kindest man I know. And you're loyal. You try to hide it, but you'd do anything for Hiram, Nick and Grace too. Then there's courage. You risked your life to save me from a burning truck. And don't get me started on Josh. I know kids terrify you, yet you give him the support he needs."

He didn't say anything, simply regarded her for a long moment. He knew damn well what she wanted. She wanted him to say it too. Part of him wanted to, but a bigger part, the part that had always kept him safe, refused. Instead, he placed her hand against his lips, kissed the palm gently, and let go. "As you said, we're good together. I don't know what I'd have done tonight without your support."

"Are you being deliberately obtuse? We're better than good together. You feel it too. I know you do."

The damndest thing was, he did. And it scared him shitless. But no matter how hard he tried, the words refused to come.

"Still not talking?" she asked. "Fine. I'm willing to give it—give us—my best shot. And, as you know, my best shot is pretty damn impressive." Her sigh was the saddest sound he'd ever heard. "Anything you'd like to add?"

"Katie …" He wanted her so badly, he could scarcely think. But time after time, when he tried to squeeze those three little words around the constriction in his throat, he failed dismally.

"It's okay," she said at last. "I shouldn't have dumped it on you out of the blue like this. It's too much for you to swallow, especially on top of Eugene's apology."

She walked away, shoulders stiff, head erect. Sam knew if he didn't grow a pair and tell her how he felt, he'd regret it for the rest of his life.

"Wait!" Hunger and hope pounded in his veins.

If anything, she sped up.

Damned if he'd let her get away. In ten seconds, he was beside her, then in front of her blocking her escape. Katie twisted her head away, but not fast enough.

Tears shimmered on her cheeks. "I'm fine," she muttered.

"Neither of us is fine." He gripped her shoulders firmly to make sure she didn't escape. "I want to tell you …" He opened his mouth, but nothing happened. He tried again. The words stayed lodged in his throat.

She shook her head. "You can't say it, can you?" Her words contained a world of hurt.

"I'm doing my best. Please, Katie, give me a little time to get used to the notion."

"How much time do you think you'll need? A day? A week? A year?"

"I don't know how to love. Hell, I don't know what love feels like." Fighting to keep the desperation from his voice, he tried again. "All I know is when I'm with you, I feel different."

She expelled a sigh that spoke of exasperation, frustration, and pain. "Different how?"

"I care for you," he said cautiously. "I want you in my life."

"The same way a dog lover wants a labradoodle in his life?"

"No. You're important to me. That counts for something doesn't it?" Shit. He was blowing it. Afraid she might escape, he wrapped his arms around her waist and pulled her in.

Katie stopped struggling. In fact, she was so still, he feared she might have stopped breathing until she whispered, "It's okay, Sam. It counts for plenty."

He shook his head in disbelief. "I don't know what's wrong with me."

She slid her arms around his neck and gave him a watery smile. "Old habits die hard. Something tells me you won't be able to move on until you're able to forgive your father and, more importantly, yourself."

"Forgive Eugene? Forget it. He doesn't deserve my forgiveness."

"That's not for me to say. But you'd be doing it for yourself, not Eugene. Forgiveness wouldn't condone what happened to you or make it okay. It's about freeing yourself from the resentment consuming you every time you think of him or even hear his name. As long as you feel the way you do, you'll remain stuck."

"Right now, it's hard for me to wrap my head around the notion of forgiveness. But I'll give it some thought. Promise."

"That's all I ask. For now."

Fortunately, she dropped the subject and let him tilt her head for a kiss. And what a kiss it was. The kind of kiss that made him lightheaded, not to mention plenty hot. The kind of kiss that inevitably led to other things— except for the fact that she placed both hands on his chest and pushed him away.

"It's getting late. I have to get back for Josh, and you need to take Hiram home."

"I'm not losing this opportunity to be alone with you. Not again." He stripped off his shirt and spread it over the sand. "If you're good with it, I want to make love to you. Here. Now."

She was more than good.

And while he showed her how he felt, even if he couldn't say the words, they both forgot that someone might be lurking in the darkness, waiting to end their happiness.

Chapter 36: Katie Confides

The next day, Katie called for girl-support in the form of a pity luncheon with her sister. Really, she was too busy to take a break, so busy she'd made arrangements for Josh to stay with Ma and Bella at The Annex until after the grand opening, but she needed to spill her guts about Sam to an empathetic listener.

Lunch turned out to be a brilliant idea because she also needed to eat. Who knew Bella would be the soul of patience? She listened to a description of Sam's inability to say those three little words. She handed over a tissue when needed, which wasn't often, all things considered. Above all, she insisted they share a dessert called Death by Chocolate.

Katie ate the lion's share of the dessert without a single twinge of guilt. Hey, romantic issues called for chocolate, didn't they?

Once they'd finished, Bella said, "Sam's an idiot. I know exactly what you need to bring him to his knees. I mean that in the best possible way."

Katie put her napkin beside her plate and stood. "I knew you'd help."

A short time later, they were inside *Knotty Girl Fashions,* Atlantic City's go-to store for sexy evening wear. Based on the displays and half-naked mannequins, Katie gathered the place stocked everything from latex jump suits and leather bustiers, to his 'n' her lubes and sex toys.

With Bella leading the way, they squeezed past a cluster of twenty-somethings giggling over a display of outrageously sexy lingerie, slipped around the glass-encased counter full of expensive-looking costume jewelry, and entered an entire section devoted to evening-wear.

"May I help you foxy ladies?" a husky voice behind them asked. "We have a brand new shipment of gorgeous wet-look outfits, and look at these exquisite peek-a-boo gowns." The saleswoman exuded a familiar perfume.

"These are exactly what I had in mind," Bella said, stroking the fabric.

"I adore the way you think," the woman said.

"Never," Katie said simultaneously, fingering a slinky backless number with a non-existent front. "I can't wear these." She faced the statuesque saleswoman and did a double-take. "Tess? You work here?"

"Oh, my God. Katie." Tess Tosterone squealed, wrapping muscular arms around her and squeezing. "I own *Knotty Girl.*"

After exclamations of surprise, Katie made the introductions.

With a little hair-toss, Tess said to Bella, "The last time I saw your sister, she was directing a cast of drag queens on how to scare off a building inspector by conducting a fake funeral."

Bella laughed. "Impossible. Not Katie."

"She was amazing," Tess stated, ignoring Katie's frantic hand signals. "*Queenz in Concert* dubbed it The Great Casket Caper."

Bella's eyes widened. "Who are you, and what have you done with my perfect sister?"

Duh. This could be embarrassing. To allay Bella's suspicions, Katie gave an abbreviated and highly sanitized summary of the incident, minimizing her role. "I didn't do much," she concluded. "The Queenz and Hiram did everything. About the dress—"

Tess didn't take the hint. "We may have been good, honey, but you were amazing. I heard your topless swimming act sealed the deal."

"Seriously?" Bella exclaimed, then lowered her voice. "My sister, woman of unexpected talents. Please tell all."

"I think we're going to be great friends," Tess said, and described Katie's aquatic extravaganza.

In the silence following Tess' story, Katie waited with resignation for Bella's reaction. As sisters, they had never been particularly close. These revelation would deepen the wedge between them.

Bella threw her arms around Katie for the second time in one day. "My God, Katie, I love it. You were always too responsible and trustworthy for words, but you have a deep, dark, illicit streak. Who'd have thought?"

Katie hugged her sister, feeling as though she and Bella had turned some sort of corner. They were a unit. A family. Feeling more optimistic, she flipped through the hangers on the racks. "Let's find me a dress. Accessories too, and of course, perfect shoes."

"Oh, yeah." Bella smoothed her hand over a gown. "Something so irresistible, Sam will pop the question."

"Men are obtuse." Tess' sympathy was tangible. "If Sam's dumb enough to make you unhappy, he deserves agonizing torture. I'm guessing you want a gown for *Kinki*'s grand opening. Something that will have him on his knees. In more ways than one."

"These dresses are beyond my price range," Katie confessed.

"Not to worry, hon." Tess disappeared. After a moment, she returned with a sparkling confection over her arm. A red satin bustier and matching panties—more like high-cut briefs—formed the base for a glittering handkerchief skirt consisting of nothing more than dozens of crimson-and-gold beadwork strands stitched onto a waistband.

A wave of longing washed over Katie. The dress was exactly what she wanted—a power dress that would convince Sam he loved her. At last, she said, "It's beautiful, but I can't afford something like this."

Tess smiled. "Someone returned it, claimed the beadwork lacerated her ass every time she sat down. She got a total refund, but I can't re-sell it. I had it dry-cleaned and kept it because I couldn't bear to get rid of it. I think it'll fit you perfectly."

"I'll stay standing all night." Katie accepted the hanger and entered the changing room.

"Try these shoes," Tess called, holding out a pair of strappy gold stilettos. "They're last season's, so they're on sale."

After several difficult minutes due to the bustier's snug fit, Katie emerged, taking shallow breaths.

Bella did an ego flattering double-take. "Holy shit. I didn't realize you owned so much boobage."

"It's an illusion." Katie gasped for air.

"You look gorgeous, hon," Tess assured her.

"Strut your stuff," Bella ordered. "Work it."

While Bella cued her on catwalk moves, Katie threw her shoulders back, thrust her hips forward, and started moving. Customers applauded as she swept past. She circled the dress department, then swept through lingerie and sex toys, loving every minute of it.

By the time she finished, Katie was slightly breathless, partly because the bustier compressed her lungs, but mostly because she felt empowered to face Sam.

"I'll take everything," she informed Tess.

Bella threw her arms around Katie. "You have definitely found your sexy. That color makes you look like an exotic princess. On the day of the grand opening, I'll fix your hair and help with your makeup."

Tess examined Bella from head to toe. "You know your stuff. If you're ever looking for a job, I'd love to hire you." She handed Bella a card.

Bella examined the card and stared at Tess. "Are you serious?"

"My top salesperson is on maternity leave, and I need someone for the next few months. You have the class and style I'm looking for, plus you're Katie's sister."

Bella flicked Katie a glance. "I'm babysitting a very special little boy this week. How about Monday?"

"Deal. It's temporary, mind, but you'll love it." They shook hands.

After Tess hugged them both, Bella looped an arm around Katie's waist. "It's mani-pedi time. My treat. What's the most luxurious salon in Atlantic City?"

"I'd love to, but I can't. There's a meeting with a caterer, then I have to deal with the HR manager over a couple of recent hires, and I want to take Josh for dinner because I won't see much of him for a few days, and—"

"I get it. You're busy."

Yeah, that plus she'd already spent too much time in public, especially in a store called *Knotty Girl Fashions*. If Luigi heard, he'd be royally pissed.

Chapter 37: More Trouble in *Kinki*

Two days after the barbecue that shook Sam's life, he stood on the sidewalk outside the largest bank in Atlantic City and marveled at his nerve. Scores of pedestrians jostled past, but he barely noticed due to the waves of relief that engulfed him. His accomplishment was either an act of sheer brilliance or total lunacy. With an empty bank account and no investments to speak of other than a nightclub that hadn't generated one cent of profit yet, he'd secured bridge financing to tide him over until the proceeds from *Kinki*'s grand opening rolled in.

He'd created a financial buffer.

A gambler knew better than to quit when he was on a roll. Now that he'd accomplished one near-impossible task, it was time to tackle another—telling Katie this whole friends-with-benefits thing didn't work for him. He wanted more. A whole lot more.

He could do it. Forgiving Eugene didn't factor into it.

Before he crapped out, he sent Katie a text message. *Need to talk. Our office, thirty minutes.*

She replied immediately, an excellent sign. *OK, see u then.*

They reached the office at the same time. Katie entered first, notepad in hand and slightly breathless, as if she'd been running. She halted so suddenly he plowed into her. Which normally would have been fun, except for one tiny detail.

Their office was a disaster.

All notion of a romantic heart-to-heart disappeared. Every book from the bookshelves lay scattered on the floor, spines broken, pages creased. The contents of both desks formed a crazy jumble of pencils, notepads, staplers, and assorted papers. All the filing drawers were open, the contents dumped.

Color drained slowly from Katie's face. "The files. Destroyed. Why? How?"

Gripped by fury, he struggled to keep his voice even. "Someone was looking for something. Or trying to scare me off. Or hates my guts." Luigi flashed to mind.

"Maybe Ralphie and Enzo returned," she ventured.

"Not likely. I tightened security. But it could have been an inside job. Looks like someone's trying to force me to cancel the grand opening."

Katie twisted her hands together. "They're doing a fine job of it. I can't finish preparations without those files. I knew I should have scanned everything and stored them on The Cloud, but I've been so busy." Her voice trailed away.

"It's not your fault." Sam dropped to his knees and gathered papers. "I'll gather, you sort. We'll restore those files."

She nodded, and they got started, stacking papers on one side of the conference table and file folders on the other. He positioned two chairs. Sitting side by side, they scrutinized the papers and slowly recreated the files. The entire time they worked, Sam's mind churned as he rehearsed all the things he wanted to say to her.

Hopefully, once he got the L-bomb out of the way, the rest would be easy.

An hour passed, mostly in silence except for an occasional question. At last, she stuffed the last paper into a file folder and stretched, thrusting her breasts out.

The motion caught his dick's attention. "I think that does it." He made sure he addressed her face instead of parts south. "I, um, have a couple of things I want to tell you."

"I'm listening."

Sam took a moment to think through the points he'd rehearsed. The words never made it out his dumbass mouth. Hell, no. What popped out instead was, "You and I, we make a real good team."

Nice approach, jackass.

"*That's* what you wanted to tell me? Are you serious?" She examined his face as if searching for clues. Her frown indicated she wasn't happy with what she found. "Yeah, you are. Well, here's the thing. You're paying through the nose for this particular team member's event planning skills. Hiram was very generous with my compensation. Consequently, I try my best to accommodate your wishes—and I'm not referring to bedroom activities. Consider those a gift."

"Well, hell. That's not what I meant, and you know it." She merely quirked an eyebrow, so he blundered on. "I meant, um, on a personal level, we're real good together." He snapped his mouth shut. He had no clue why the right words refused to come.

"Are you finished?"

"No. There's more." He rushed on in case she walked away. "I, uh, was hoping we could pick up where we left off." No sooner had the words left his mouth, Sam knew this wouldn't end well for him.

Her face whitened. "Where we left off," she repeated, as if testing the words. "I assume you mean in the bedroom gymnastics department."

"No, that's absolutely not what—"

Katie continued as if he wasn't talking. "Good. Because I have too much self-respect for that." She sat and re-hung a file folder with shaking hands, frowning as though her life depended on its proper alignment.

Pain arrowed through Sam. "You can't mean it."

"But I do."

Panic tightened his chest. He'd blown it. There was still time to fix it, but he couldn't get the words out. Intellectually, he knew Katie could make him happier than he'd ever been, and vice versa. But based on his appalling performance, it appeared his heart refused to believe it. Deep down where it counted, a worm of doubt whispered he'd never be good enough for her.

If it was anatomically possible, he would kick himself in the ass. Those therapists he'd visited on and off (mainly off) weren't kidding. The longest distance in the world was, indeed, the twelve inches between head and heart.

As he contemplated a different approach, the clump of running feet distracted him.

Rooster skidded into the office. His face was bright red, he was panting, and sweat beaded his brow. Between gasps, he said, "Trouble. Follow me."

***

Katie's mind was chaotic as she followed Rooster and Sam. Before the interruption, she'd needed every speck of willpower she possessed to pretend she was indifferent to Sam. Her face burned as she remembered how he'd assumed they would simply continue as before—in the bedroom—as if she hadn't told him she loved him. He'd as good as flung her love in her face.

It was probably for the best. Although Luigi hadn't shown his hand yet, Katie sensed he was waiting until the timing was right. It was impossible to avoid Sam during work hours, but she'd make sure nothing romantic happened between them. Until she left town with Josh, it would be employer/employee relationship, nothing more.

At least, that's what she told herself as she made her way toward whatever problem Rooster had discovered. It was easier to be pissed-off than heartbroken.

On entering the *Voodoo Lounge*, the first thing she noticed was the naked woman. She was hard to miss because, well, she was naked, not to mention strapped on top of a stone sarcophagus. Moving closer, Katie realized the woman wasn't moving. Her eyes were closed, her complexion chalky under heavy Goth makeup, and a rubber ball gag filled her mouth, held in place by leather straps.

Rooster said, "I tried to revive her, but it didn't work. Maybe she's dead."

Sam fumbled for the blonde's nearest wrist, which was pinned under a heavy leather strap. "Aw, crap," he muttered, "I can't find a goddamn pulse."

Katie took a harder look at the woman's face and did a double-take. "*O Dio mio*. It's Deanna."

Rooster scrutinized the inert body. "You're right. Those boobs are unmistakable."

Without being asked, Sam stripped off his jacket and draped the supple leather over Deanna's body, covering all the important bits. "I need something to cover her face too. There's no pulse, so she must be dead."

"Let me try." Katie moved closer and pressed her fingers to Deanna's neck. The pulse was faint but detectable. "She's alive, but not for long unless we get that thing out of her mouth. To give Deanna a fighting chance, she worked on the gag's fastening. The sucker was more complicated than it looked. She tugged harder, but the leather resisted her efforts.

"Let me." Sam's fingers moved with remarkable speed. The gag fell away like magic.

Katie muttered, "You're remarkably knowledgeable about fetish equipment."

"I have a gift for mechanical gadgets."

After one beat followed by another, shuddering breaths shook Deanna's body.

Relief tipped Katie over the edge. "According to what I recall from reading about bondage during my research, Deanna was wearing a ball-gag.*" Shut up, shut up, shut up.* "There are also bit gags, cleave gags, butterfly gags, and more. For some, gags have connotations of punishment and control, and thus serves as a form of humiliation." Aware of Sam and Rooster watching her in astonishment, she couldn't stop talking. "If a person is sexually aroused by a gag, it's considered fetish paraphernalia, but I wouldn't know. Hey, I'm not really into BDSM, unless it was with the right person, and I don't see that happening, and—"

Mercifully, Sam interrupted her monologue, saving her from self-destruction by placing his finger over her mouth. "Shhhh. Don't. It'll be okay, Katie, it will."

Rooster stooped to pick up a whip. "I always suspected Deanna's Miss-Goody-Two-Shoes act was phony." He snapped the whip. "She's into hard-core kink. Impressive."

"Hey, the poor woman's unconscious," Sam chastised him.

Rooster slapped the whip against his thigh and winced. "This could be used in a BDSM movie. We could call it *When Bondage Goes Bad*."

Sam ignored him. "It doesn't look like equipment malfunction to me. Deanna didn't truss herself to the sarcophagus."

Katie licked her lips, which were suddenly dry. "You're right. Someone else was with her. I wonder when it happened, and why the other person left her here like this."

"Hey, she's regaining consciousness," Rooster said.

Deanna moaned, stared directly at Sam and mumbled, "… so … sorry for …" The words died away as she lapsed into unconsciousness again.

"Why is she apologizing?" Katie wanted to shake the information out of Deanna.

"No idea. I'm calling the hospital." Sam pulled out his phone and dialed.

The ambulance arrived within minutes, and paramedics carried Deanna away. Sam surprised the hell out of Katie, slipping his arms around her and drawing her close. Before she could duck away, which of course she would have done if she'd had her wits about her, he kissed her silly. It was the kiss of the century, no, the millennium. If she didn't know better, she'd have said he was communicating his love for her. Her head spun, her heart battered her rib cage, and her fun parts buzzed with excitement.

He placed his hands on her shoulders. "I have to go to the hospital to make sure Deanna gets everything she needs." He paused, gave her a searching look. "Are we okay?"

Her pulse kicked in again, and she nodded. "I can wait a little longer."

Sam pressed a gentle kiss on the tip of Katie's nose. "I may be an idiot, but I'm not giving up on us. That's a promise."

Chapter 38: Katie Receives a Message

Katie spent the next two days engaged in a cyclone of activity. She saw Sam only in passing, and twice for a whole fifteen minutes by grabbing coffee over hasty debriefings.

Night was well and truly underway when she staggered in her front door and slammed it shut behind her. She kicked off her shoes. The purse landed beside them with a dull thud. All she wanted to do was crawl into bed, and tonight she could do just that. Until after the grand opening, Ma and Bella were taking care of Josh. For the next few nights, there would be no homework requiring her help, no school lunches to fix, no bedtime negotiations, no shower-time battle.

She should be consumed with relief and gratitude, and of course she was. But the silence left her feeling lonely and longing for her son's chatter.

There was no point in turning on a light. The full moon filtering through the window generated more than enough to satisfy her needs. She made her way into the kitchen and rummaged in the fridge. Grabbing a bottled water, she re-hashed the last two days, starting with the trashed office and Deanna's equipment malfunction, and continuing on a downhill trajectory. Who knew sound systems were impossibly temperamental or that head chefs pitched hissy fits on an hourly basis? Sam had taken on the HR management role in Deanna's absence, supervising the small army of support staff, dealing with employee complaints, smoothing ruffled feathers (which he excelled at), while at the same time tripling his efforts on the security front, barely catching any sleep at all.

Thankfully, doctors believed Deanna would make a full recovery with minimal, if any, brain damage. The bruising on her neck indicated either rough sex or attempted murder. So far, she'd refused to talk.

Headed for the living room, Katie stopped to listen. The whisper of sound she'd heard was surely outside. She remembered locking all the doors. Reassured, she took a swig of water then halted at a soft creak.

Someone was moving inside the house. A trickle of fear ran through her, receding only when she remembered Bella had said she'd drop over to pick up Josh's soccer shoes. Yeah, she must be upstairs.

Another muted sound, definitely not upstairs, caused the water to make a quick exit from her nostrils. Sputtering, she whirled to run, but didn't get far. A strong hand shot out to grip her arm, damn near dislocating her shoulder in the process.

Even in the dark, she could tell the invader was tall, bulky, and very, very strong. Driven by panic, she whacked the bottle onto her assailant's head. The plastic bounced off his skull, and fell to the floor, spilling its contents. Using her free hand, she tried to claw his face. A sharp twist of her arm left her gasping in agony.

"Nice try, Katarina. Next time, use a glass bottle."

He knew her name. Somehow, that terrified her more than his brutality. Panicking in earnest, she tried to break away. In response, his grip tightened until she had to bite her lip to prevent a scream from escaping.

"Be a good girl and nothing bad will happen. Don't make me hurt you."

She stopped resisting and nodded. The grip loosened and she let him haul her into the living room. Her chance would come. Maybe.

"Much better. Please take a seat," he said, all fake geniality.

Katie collapsed onto the sofa and massaged her throbbing shoulder, trying to look meek while maintaining high alert.

"You should change your locks," he said in a conversational tone. "A child could open them."

She peered at the featureless figure, and her skin crawled. Her guest wore a dark balaclava. "Who are you?" she demanded.

"A messenger. Let's just say we have a mutual friend."

Luigi.

"Why are you here?" she asked.

"I informed our friend about everything I witnessed on the beach Sunday evening. To say he was unhappy was like calling a force-five hurricane a stiff breeze. He wants me to give you a message."

Adrenaline surged. So did fear. She let out a shaky breath. "I don't know what you're talking about."

"Babe, I used night vision binoculars. It was real interesting what you two were doing. Innovative and touching at the same time."

Katie attempted to speak, but the words stuck in her throat. She tried again, and this time her voice worked. "What's Luigi's message?"

"He wants you should dump your asshole boss."

A chill gripped her with such force she had trouble drawing a breath. She moistened her lips. "And if I don't?"

Moonlight bounced off a flash of teeth in the balaclava's mouth hole. "Then Jackson will experience a very tragic accident."

Incapable of speech, she absorbed the horror of his threat. Her freedom, such as it was, had ended. To save Sam's life, she had to leave town with Josh, and right away.

As if reading her mind, the sinister figure continued in an amused tone, "Tut-tut, Katarina. If I were you, I wouldn't do anything foolish like leaving town with your son. If you did, guess what'll happen next."

"I'll bite. What?"

"No more Sam Jackson. No more mother, sister, and brother. And after those regrettable deaths, Luigi will track you to the ends of the earth. When he finds you, and I guarantee he will, you can kiss your handsome little son goodbye, too."

The intruder's amused chuckle raised goosebumps all over her body. Whoever he was, Luigi's buddy was a coldblooded killer.

She clenched her jaws together to keep her teeth from chattering. Once she collected herself, she said, "Please tell Luigi I apologize for my actions. I'll do what he asks."

"He told me you were quick on the uptake. By the way, he wanted me to tell you something else."

Unable to speak, she nodded numbly.

Another flash of teeth made an appearance. "His appeal is going better than expected. You can expect to see him sooner rather than later, so be ready to get married right away. Pack something nice for your honeymoon. After the wedding, you'll both be leaving town quickly." He walked away, but when he reached the door, he stopped and added, "Oh, yeah, and bring your son if you wish. Congratulations, Katarina."

She sat motionless in her cozy living room until she was certain he'd left before dissolving in a sobbing heap on the sofa.

Chapter 39: The Breakup

Overnight, Katie reached a decision. She would break up with Sam immediately, but wouldn't let Luigi force her to resign until she'd ensured everything was in place for the grand opening. It wasn't much, but it was the best she could do. Tonight was time enough to hand in her resignation. She looked up in time to see Sam hurry past the door of *Inferno*. She dropped her clipboard on a table and dashed to the door. "Sam. Stop," she called.

He skidded to a halt and made an about-face. "Katie." His blinding smile left her gasping for breath. "We're in the home stretch."

Katie swallowed the lump in her throat. Clearly, he had no premonition she was about to stomp on his heart. But at least she could make sure he lived to see the grand opening and start a new life without her. It was enough. It would have to be.

"We need to talk," she said more sharply than she'd intended. A night of non-stop crying had left her feeling as though someone had punched a hole in her chest and ripped out her heart.

His smile dimmed. "Sure thing. I always have time for the sexiest woman I know."

She blinked back the tears burning her eyelids. Sam mustn't see her cry. If he didn't buy what she was about to say, he was a dead man. Swallowing the wail that wanted to escape, she tried to think happy thoughts.

Puppies. Angels. Kittens.

"Let's talk in here." Without giving him an opening to disagree, she addressed the staff. "Take a break, guys. Be back again at three thirty to finish up, then go home and get a good night's sleep. Tomorrow's the big day."

By the time everyone left, he'd arranged two chairs in a corner. They seated themselves without talking.

He stared at her, his expression unreadable. "This is bad news, isn't it?"

She clasped her hands tightly in her lap. "I'm afraid so. I didn't get much sleep last night, thinking about the best way to tell you. There's no good way, so I'll simply say it. I'm breaking up with you."

"Ah." He looked at her for a long moment, his eyes bleak. "I was afraid of that. It's because I couldn't say those three magic words back, isn't it?"

"Apparently you still can't say you love me, but that isn't the main reason."

The lines of pain furrowing his face mirrored how she felt, but he couldn't know she was hurting too. He must believe he disgusted her. Drawing on strength she didn't know she possessed, she said, "I read about the disease of addiction."

His face contorted. "Don't. Please don't go there."

Her nails dug into her palms. She couldn't, *wouldn't* stop until he believed she was serious. Sucking in a deep breath, she hit him with a double-whammy. "At best, you're the adult child of an addict, which would explain your inability to establish solid relationships. At worst, there's a genetic component to addiction, and you've inherited it."

"You're kidding, right? You can't possibly blame me for my father's faults."

It took iron resolve to get her emotions under control so she wouldn't sob. "Look at it from my perspective, Sam. By all accounts, you're exactly like Eugene with your gambling, booze, and women. It's in your hard-wiring. With Josh to think about, I can't risk that you've inherited the same cravings as your father."

Her heart skipped a beat when he pried her hands apart and grasped them, as if afraid she might bolt. "You're breaking up with me because of Luigi. Admit it. The bastard got to you somehow."

Sam didn't know about last night's visit, *couldn't* know. She shook her head in denial. "No. It's not like that at all." Gritting her teeth against the pain ripping through her chest, she said, "I think it best that we part ways now, before anyone gets hurt." She freed a hand to stroke his cheek, as if that could lessen his pain.

He jerked away from her touch. "That ship has already sailed, darlin'. I can't believe you're willing toss everything away—the chemistry, the flash and heat, hell, even the laughter and liking between us simply because of Eugene."

She ignored the huskiness of his voice. "Given the circumstances, it's best that I don't attend the grand opening. But I assure you, I will work as late as necessary to finalize preparations.

His short, low laugh sounded more like a sob. "Hell, Katie. I would expect nothing less from you."

Chapter 40: The Kidnapping

During her final hours at *Kinki*, Katie tried not to think about her bleak future. She welcomed the non-stop emergencies, chores, and temper-tantrums. Even Rooster had a meltdown and needed comforting. Finally, she'd finished everything she could do to support the grand opening. Sam would have to handle tomorrow alone.

A chilling numbness filled her as she closed her drawer for the last time and pushed away from her desk. Her head throbbed and her eyes were scratchy from the tears she'd shed. She realized with surprise it was pushing ten o'clock and everyone had left for the day. She had no idea where Sam had gone, or when he'd disappeared, nor did she want to know. His absence was a relief, or so she told herself.

Emotionally drained from the strain of hiding her heartbreak and terror, she was too keyed-up to go home to an empty house. Socializing was out of the question. But she had one teeny-tiny detail to complete before leaving for good.

She had a corpse to find.

All week long, serious doubts about Vinnie scrambling to his feet and walking away had plagued her. By her calculations, his decaying body should have begun to stink. She had to find him before the stench became gag-worthy.

Hoping Sam was right, that Vinnie was alive and raising hell somewhere, she locked the office door for the last time and started her search.

For twenty uneventful minutes, Katie poked into every nook and cranny, sniffing the air for a few seconds before moving on. Everything smelled of cleaning product, fresh wood, and drying paint. She ventured into an intersecting corridor, and her footsteps faltered. She sniffed suspiciously. The sweetish odor of putrefaction hung in the air. She continued walking, telling herself it wasn't necessarily Vinnie. Hey, it could be a rotting sandwich. Or a dead rat.

The smell increased.

Yeah, it was a dead rat, all right—but not the furry kind.

Nearing *Dracula's Lair*, a rustling accompanied by steady cursing grew audible. She tip-toed closer and peeked inside. Her heart jackhammered in her chest at the sight of someone bent over, trying to haul an occupant from one of the coffins. The intruder straightened, and she recognized the white hair and beard.

Once her voice started working again, she croaked, "Hiram."

"Shit-on-a-stick," Hiram hollered, waving a can of air freshener and giving a prolonged blast. He lowered his hand. "Jesus, Katie. Don't sneak up on a man. I damn near drowned you in *Pine Breeze*." He shook the can. "This shit's supposed to help you to breathe happy, but it's useless. I should've gone for *Linens 'n' Leathers*."

"I doubt it would be an improvement." She eyed the dummy, which was draped over one side of the coffin, its arm trailing on the floor. "You're supposed to be at the Seniors' Center. Why are you here?"

"Bingo was cancelled. Then I remembered Vinnie and went searching. Bastard's beneath the dummy corpse." He grabbed the dummy's arm and tugged again. "You?"

"Didn't feel like going home. Rico's at an overnight conference in Philadelphia, Bella's away for the night too, and Ma took Josh on a school overnighter. They'll all be back in time for the grand opening." There was no point in telling Hiram she'd dumped Sam, and after tonight, they'd never see one another again.

"Huh. You think *this*'ll be more fun?" Hiram gave another yank. The dummy landed on the floor with a soft thud. Immediately, an unspeakable stench filled the room.

Katie clapped a hand over her nose and mouth, stifling a gag. The odor, dense, vile, and shockingly sweet coated her skin and settled into her hair and clothes.

Hiram backtracked a step. "Whoo-eee. My sense of smell ain't great, but that stink's a bitch." He aimed the can inside the coffin. A jet splatted on the plastic-wrapped occupant.

"That won't help. I'm calling Sam."

"Don't. He'll feel duty-bound to call the cops."

"It's his nightclub. He needs to know." She'd turned away to grab her phone when a hand grasped her upper arm. "Cut it out, Hiram," she said, scrolling through her contacts. "I'm calling him."

The hand on her arm tightened. "Fuhgeddaboudit, babe."

Stifling a scream she whipped her head around and found herself nose-to-nose with Ralphie. Beside him, Enzo pointed a large handgun at Hiram. With a shiver, she noted both men wore disposable plastic gloves.

"I'll take the phone," Enzo said.

"Sure thing." Katie forced a weak smile while handing over the phone.

Hiram said, "I bet you're here for Vinnie."

Katie bit her lip, but remained silent, hoping they were too drunk or too stupid to understand the implications of Hiram's statement.

Ralphie examined Hiram's face with a puzzled frown. "You remind me of someone."

Simultaneously, Enzo said, "Hey, how'd the old guy know why we're here?"

This would be a great time to duct tape Hiram's mouth shut. Katie grasped at the only straw she could think of. "We named this dummy Vinnie, after Luigi's buddy. The others are Salvatore, named after a guy I went to school with, Betty-Sue's over there in the pink dress, and—"

Hiram interrupted her recitation. "You guys whacked Vinnie and brought him here. We were hiding in your truck the whole time." He glared at the pair. "You're in big trouble."

"Do tell," Enzo said.

Before Hiram compounded the damage, she jumped in. "We're on your side, guys. We know it was an accident. We want to help you with Vinnie."

"How?"

She had to buy some time. Sooner or later, Sam would return and help them. "Moving a corpse is tricky, especially one that's been deceased as long as Vinnie. You need to understand what to expect." Launching into a lecture on decomposition, she described the process by which organic substances—like Vinnie—were broken down into much simpler forms of matter, and how gases accumulate inside the body. She finished with, "Vinnie's in an intermediate stage of decomp. It's important to be cautious when handling him."

Enzo looked as though he wanted to toss his cookies. "The coffin's too heavy, even for four of us to lift, and I ain't touching him."

"Me neither," Ralphie added, "but these two will, seein' as how Katie's the expert with stiffs and the old one's a royal pain in the ass." He peered into the coffin and backed away in a hurry. "Good thing we brought plenty of plastic sheeting. It'll hold Vinnie together and seal in his juices while they lift him."

Hiram scowled. "I ain't going near that thing." He jutted his beard in Vinnie's direction.

"We'll be happy to help," Katie said, and gave Hiram a quelling glare. Praise be, he subsided with a muted grumble.

Ralphie waved his gun at Hiram. "Can I shoot this one?"

Enzo gave Ralphie the stink-eye. "If you kill the old guy, you'll have to help Katie move Vinnie."

"Hell, no."

"Okay, then. They move the stiff now, you get to kill them later."

Ralphie chuckled. "Works for me. This gives new meaning to 'wet work', don't it? Haw-haw-haw."

Katie refused to panic. She placed a hand on Hiram's arm for a warning squeeze, and said, "We can tip the coffin to dislodge Vinnie, but we'll never manage to carry him by ourselves. He may be small, but they don't call a corpse 'dead weight' for nothing."

"Not a problem, babe. Wrap him in plastic sheeting, tie him good and tight, and strap him to a dolly. Our truck's at the loading dock."

"Can I kill them once Vinnie's on board?" Ralphie asked.

"Better not," Katie interjected quickly. "Luigi won't like it."

"Luigi'll never find out. Besides, when he hears we whacked Vinnie, he'll promote us."

"For killing his second-in-command?" she asked.

"Hell, Vinnie wanted to look legit by buying a string of clubs at a rock-bottom price. That's why he hired us to trash the place—to convince Jackson to sell at a low price."

In a way, Katie was relieved. Luigi had nothing to do with sabotaging *Kinki*. Vinnie had tried to double-cross his boss by taking over his turf while he was in prison.

She tried another approach. "Fine. But if you kill us, you'll have to unload Vinnie yourselves at the other end."

"She has a point," Enzo said. "Here's what we do. First, one of us moves Katie's car so no one will look for her here. At the other end, they get to unload Vinnie, then we'll kill them too."

***

Enzo drove Katie's car to a side street while the others waited nearby, engine idling. Ralphie sat behind the wheel holding a gun on the two captives, who were squeezed into the passenger seat. Vinnie reclined in the truck bed, concealed under a tarp and wedged in by a toolbox. Once Enzo climbed into the truck's rear seat, Ralphie put his gun away, and they sped off into the night.

One thing crowded out all Katie's other worries. She and Hiram would die tonight. Nothing she did or said would prevent it. She'd never be able to make things right with Sam. Worst of all, her son would grow up an orphan.

Beside her, Hiram muttered something involving brainless, inbred scum.

"I told you this was a mistake," Enzo lamented from the back seat. "What are we gonna do with three corpses?"

"Good job we came prepared," Ralphie answered. "We're regular Boy Scouts."

"What do you mean?" Katie asked.

"Never you mind," Ralphie said.

Hiram said, "He's talking about his big-ass toolbox."

"Yeah, Mr. Know-it-All. Besides screwdrivers and such, we have a hack-saw, six knives of different sizes, and a couple of hammers."

Katie's stomach heaved. She refused to think of what they planned to do with those tools. If she panicked, they were finished. "You could let us go," she said, without much hope. "You and I have known one another for years. We won't say anything, and there's no proof you were inside *Kinki* tonight. You boys were real careful to wear gloves. Nice move, by the way."

"Thanks." Ralphie bared his uneven teeth in a broad grin. "It was my idea. I hate to kill you, babe, but we can't leave any loose ends." He tromped on the gas.

"Easy, there," Enzo hollered. "We don't want Vinnie flying out."

After several minutes of uneventful driving, Katie tried again. "You can't chop us up. Three bodies? Give me a break. You've watched *CSI*, so you know it would be way too messy, leave too many clues. They'd find you within hours. And where would you put the pieces? Besides, Ralphie hates blood."

Enzo whacked the back of Ralphie's head. "Fuck. She's right. Blood makes you puke. I ain't chopping them up all by myself. So now what?"

Ralphie glanced at Enzo in the mirror. "How 'bout we whack 'em over the head and dump 'em into the ocean off a pier?"

"Every pier big enough to carry a truck is lit up like a Christmas tree, asshole."

Ralphie furrowed his brow. "Then we'll shoot 'em."

Katie said, "You'd still have to get rid of our bodies, and that's not so easy. They'll find us and trace the bullets to the gun that you use. Plus there'll be blood."

Never taking his eyes off the road, Ralphie grinned. "I know the perfect place. Sure as shit we won't leave no clues where we're headed." Wheels squealed as he turned at the next set of lights.

As casually as possible over the sound of her heart jack-hammering in her chest, Katie asked, "Where are we going?"

"Somewhere you're gonna feel right at home."

Chapter 41: Luigi Arrives

For the rest of the day, Sam held his anguish at bay by keeping himself busy with a million and one tasks, one of which was locating a buyer for *Kinki*. This evening's final meeting had landed his ass in the middle of a traffic jam on the Garden State Parkway, but at least the buyer was ready to sign on the dotted line, pending the results of tomorrow's grand opening.

Now, while sitting in his truck in the middle of a pileup, with nothing better to do than obsess about the breakup, Sam finally got it. Something was off. There wasn't a mean bone in Katie's body. She would never in a million years throw Eugene's addiction in his face, leastwise not without a compelling reason. He'd been right all along when he'd told her the only thing that made sense was that Luigi had threatened her or her family. She'd tossed him a smelly red herring to make him back off, and it had worked. Almost.

Sam tightened his hands on the wheel as traffic inched past the blockage, an eighteen-wheeler lying on its side. He needed to find Katie and learn the truth. They could develop a solution together. Once past the accident, he floored it. Four hours late and cursing, he wheeled into *Kinki*'s large, empty parking lot and switched off the engine.

Katie's car was gone.

Ticking silence filled the cab. Fighting a deep, visceral sadness, he rested his forehead against the steering wheel.

He wanted to howl, bellow, drown his loss in Jack Daniels, throw down a couple of grand in the nearest casino, anything to relieve the pressure in his chest. Instead, he got a grip on himself. It was time to face life head on.

He disembarked, intending to touch base with his granddaddy before heading over to The Annex to find Katie. He was nearing *Kinki*'s entrance when he found himself grabbed from behind and sent flying through the air.

After landing hard on one shoulder, he swore and rolled, using momentum to regain his feet and face his assailant. The lights he'd installed as an additional security feature shone directly on the asshole's face. Flat, black eyes he recognized dominated the impassive features.

Luigi had found him.

Remembering to protect his neck during a head-butt, he tilted his chin down a fraction, clenched his teeth, and tensed his neck muscles. Banking on the element of surprise, he lunged forward using his entire body weight, going for Luigi's face.

A scream of pain rewarded his efforts. He smiled grimly, dancing backward, out of reach, and assessed his handiwork. Blood dripped from a cut slicing across those sculpted cheekbones. Gratifying, but not as debilitating as a nose-crunch.

"Tsk, tsk. That's a nasty cut," he drawled. "Best you get stitched up or it'll leave a scar."

"*Testa di cazzo!*" Luigi's snarl promised a world of pain.

Anticipating immediate retaliation, Sam assumed a fighting stance.

Luigi merely pulled a gun from his pocket and aimed it at the center of Sam's chest. "I heard about you and Katarina." His voice was low and raspy. "I was planning to shoot you on sight, but I've changed my mind."

Sam eyed the gun, which looked as big as a cannon. "Works for me."

Luigi's smile flashed, shark-like, then vanished. "Good to hear. Because I know a better way to kill you. Best part? Katarina will watch you writhe in agony while begging for death. Too bad she's not here, but you and I together, my friend, will find her."

Secretly, Sam wanted to fall to his knees and beg for mercy, at least for Katie if not himself. But he knew better than to show fear. Channeling his inner James Bond, he bared his lips in a smile. "Luigi, you are, indeed, a prince among men. Now I understand why Katie feels the way she does about you."

Big mistake. Luigi's lips tightened into a grim line. His breath whistled like a winded racehorse. Quick as a snake, he backhanded Sam across the face. "Toss your phone into the bushes and pull out your keys, asshole. You're driving. Don't do anything dumb."

He obeyed without argument, mainly because of the gun. Also, his entire face throbbed like one giant toothache. Even his hair hurt.

Given the murderous scowl darkening Luigi's face, it occurred to Sam he'd be unable to help Katie if Luigi killed him now. Better to suck it up and become Luigi's newest yes-man.

***

Sam pulled into Friday night traffic. He hid his satisfaction when Luigi fished out a white handkerchief and pressed it against his cheek to sop up a trickle of blood.

"Where are we headed?" He tried his damndest to ignore Luigi's murderous expression coupled with the gun in his hand.

A muscle in Luigi's jaw twitched. He ignored the question while texting with his free hand. Once finished, he said, "Katarina's house. Stick to the speed limit because I'll kill any cop who stops us." He emphasized his words by jabbing the muzzle into Sam's ribs.

Sam cursed at the sharp pain and swerved into the wrong lane, narrowly missing an oncoming truck. After regaining control, he used one finger to push the gun away. "Do that again, and we both might die." So much for being a yes-man.

Luigi grunted, but the metallic pressure of the muzzle lightened.

They passed through several traffic lights without incident. To take his mind off his predicament, Sam said, "I'm guessing your appeal came through." He hoped his voice projected polite interest instead of the rage pulsing through his body.

"I was released on—what the fuck did they call it? Oh, yeah, *personal recognizance* pending my appeal. Assholes wanted me to wear a tracking bracelet, but that didn't happen." Luigi stretched his lips in a wolfish grin. "You'd be surprised who and what money can buy. Someone should do something about corruption, yes?"

Sam held his peace for a beat, but after a moment couldn't resist asking, "Why did the court think your appeal had merit?"

"A technicality. One of the cops handling my case fucked up."

Luigi had as good as admitted his guilt.

After a few minutes of driving, Sam asked, "What's your plan with Katie?"

Luigi gave him an assessing look followed by a shrug, as if judging him a non-threat. "You sure you want to know?"

"Yeah."

"Katarina and Josh get exactly five minutes to pack. You drive us to a tiny and very private airport where Katarina watches me kill you so painfully, she'll never dare look at another man as long as she lives. You and your truck disappear without a trace, while me and my happy little family leave the country in a small jet. When we reach our destination, a preacher marries us, and we live happily ever after."

Sam had nothing to say to that. Conscious of the gun, he drove the rest of the way in silence and braked in front of Katie's darkened house. "Her car's not here. I bet she's out on the town."

"She'd better not be. I sent her a text saying I was on my way over." Luigi gestured with the gun. "Out."

After determining no one was home, they piled back in. Luigi said, "Drive to The Annex."

Sam drove without comment, parking around back while contemplating ways to overpower Luigi, each more painful than the last. Movement at the *Paradise Gate* loading area caught his eye. His stomach cramped when he realized he was looking at Katie, Granddaddy Hiram and the Allegretti brothers.

"Out," Luigi ordered again.

Mindful of the gun, Sam preceded him to the area beside the service entrance. Hugging the shadows, they stood in silence.

Under his breath, Luigi muttered something in Italian, ending with, "What the fuck?"

For the first time, Sam agreed with Luigi. Granddaddy Hiram and Katie were trying, without much success, to stow a heavy yet strangely floppy bundle onto a trolley. One of the Allegretti brothers waved his arms, obviously giving directions.

Granddaddy Hiram's curses floated on the night air. He shut up abruptly when one of the brothers waved a gun at Katie. After a lengthy struggle and some help from Enzo, they managed to load the bundle. Both brothers were bickering. The only word Sam caught was, "Vinnie."

Son of a bitch. The brothers had returned to *Kinki* for Vinnie. Unless he missed his guess, they planned to cremate him. Bye-bye evidence. Hiram and Katie must have blundered onto the scheme. It all made a weird kind of sense, including the canvas dropcloth spread over the ground, presumably to capture leakage.

Luigi whispered, "Move." A gun-jab emphasized the order.

Loathing his yes-man role, Sam did exactly what he was told. Together they stepped out of the shadows and approached the foursome. Katie was the first notice them. She grabbed his granddaddy's arm, no doubt to shut him up.

Granddaddy Hiram stared directly at Sam and grinned. "Sammy. About time. These two dickheads kidnapped us from the club. Tell your buddy behind you to stop pickin' his nose and shoot them with that big-ass gun he's carrying."

Both Allegrettis swung around. One of them said, "What the fuck—"

"Well, well, well, if it ain't the Allegretti boys." Luigi twisted Sam's arm behind his back sending pain shooting from shoulder to fingertips, while pointing his gun at Granddaddy Hiram. "Who the hell is the old asshole?"

There was a beat of silence.

Sweat beaded Sam's brow, and not only from the pain. His granddaddy would react poorly to being called an old asshole.

"Who you callin' an old asshole, shithead?" Granddaddy Hiram snarled. "Why I—"

"Easy there," Sam yelled. "If Luigi shoots, he might miss you and hit Katie by mistake."

Both Luigi and Granddaddy Hiram apparently got the message. His granddaddy snapped his mouth shut and contented himself with glaring in Luigi's direction. Luigi reacted by jabbing his gun into Sam's bruised ribs again, causing a bright burst of pain to blossom, presumably as inducement to advance.

Sam swallowed a curse and stepped forward.

Ralphie waved his weapon. "Lookee here. It's *Kinki*'s asshole owner. Who's his buddy? I can't see his face."

Luigi prodded Sam again, using him as a human shield, saying, "Take it easy, boys. You don't wanna wreck my first hour of freedom."

As they stepped into a circle of light, Ralphie croaked, "Luigi? Holy shit!"

Another gun materialized, this one in Enzo's hand. "Perfect. Martinelli hired us to—"

Ralphie whirled on his brother. "Would ya like a megaphone, asshole?"

Sensing the Allegrettis posed a more immediate danger than Luigi, Sam halted beside the dropcloth. Luigi remained behind him, refusing to step into the open.

"What was that about Martinelli?" Luigi's voice was butter-smooth.

Granddaddy Hiram, bless his heart, jumped right in with the answer. "He's talking about the contract Martinelli took out on you seein' as how he doesn't enjoy being blackmailed. Katie overheard these two assholes seal the deal at a fancy fundraiser."

Behind Sam, Luigi said, "Is this the truth, Katarina?" Hurt and disbelief vibrated in his voice.

Taking advantage of his enemy's momentary lapse, Sam jabbed an elbow into Luigi's unprotected solar plexus, which was softer than it appeared. A quick whirl, and his knee connected with the bastard's crotch.

A roar of pain rewarded his efforts.

"Shoot!" one of the Allegrettis yelled.

Sam dropped to the ground and lay prone, protecting his head with his hands. His ears rang with the sound of rapid-fire gunshots. All around him, flying lead, screams, and warm liquid filled the air. He grimaced when he realized the liquid was blood, and the weight pinning him to the ground was two hundred pounds of very dead crime lord.

When the shooting stopped, Sam didn't move a muscle.

"Holy shit," someone said into the silence. "This looks like a fuckin' massacre. I'm gonna puke."

"Good thing they landed on the cloth," another commented

Granddaddy Hiram yelled, "I'm goin' over there and kissing my Sammy goodbye." His voice cracked. "Then I'm gonna make both you assholes sorry you ever saw the light of day."

"Hiram. Come back," Katie shouted over the sound of shuffling footsteps.

"Stop," Enzo yelled.

"Ah, leave them be. They ain't going far."

Two sets of footsteps approached, then stopped. Gentle hands stroked his hair.

"You can't be dead, Sammy. Don't leave me," Granddaddy Hiram wailed.

"Oh, Sam," Katie whispered. "This was all my fault."

Sam cracked one eyelid. Silhouetted against an overhead light, Katie and his granddaddy leaned over him. He opened both eyes and blinked to show them he was very much alive. Swallowing the lump in his throat, he murmured, "I'm not hurt. Go back." He resumed his corpse imitation.

"He's okay, Hiram," Katie whispered urgently. "Let's go."

An Allegretti yelled at them. There was a scuffle, protests, then a muffled conversation. Sam couldn't make out what anyone was saying, but didn't dare so much as twitch in case the brothers discovered he wasn't dead.

Sam was on the verge of desperation when Katie's voice announced, "You can't cremate all five of us. It would take too long. You'd still be at it tomorrow afternoon." She enunciated every word so clearly, Sam figured it was for his benefit.

"Now what? Any bright ideas?" Enzo's voice held a trace of panic as he drew nearer.

Ralphie's voice floated across the quiet parking lot. "We roast Vinnie, Katie, and Old Grumpy here."

Sam wanted to mash his fist into Ralphie's face. He restrained himself by remembering the Allegrettis had guns and weren't afraid to use them.

"What about this pair?" Enzo asked, nudging Sam none too gently with his toe.

"Wrap 'em up real tight, and when we're done here, we'll dump 'em."

"Remember what Katie said about bullets. They'll be evidence," Enzo said. "Plus you hate blood, and I ain't digging no bullets outta no corpses."

"We'll get rid of the bodies so's no one finds them."

"How?"

There was silence for a moment. Presumably they were mulling over their dilemma.

"Got it," Enzo said, his voice brightening. "We steal a boat, weigh the bodies down, and toss 'em overboard."

"You're a genius, Enzo."

"I am. You deal with Vinnie. I'll get another tarp and haul this pair into the truck."

Chapter 42: The Great Escape

After five minutes, Sam freed himself from the tarpaulin encasing his body. Sucking in lungfuls of sweet, fresh air, he discovered he was in the truck bed, lying on top of something yielding, yet lumpy. Controlling his gag reflex, he rolled off Luigi's corpse.

Hunkered down, he watched his granddaddy wheel Vinnie through the delivery entrance of *Paradise Gate*. Katie followed, then the Allegrettis, one of them pointing a gun, while the other lugged a massive toolbox. The heavy metal door started its slow descent.

Grabbing a tire iron from the truck, Sam sprinted across the intervening distance. With mere inches to spare, he threw himself under the door and rolled inside.

The loading area was spacious, dimly lit, and mercifully devoid of Allegrettis. If he hoped to rescue Katie and Granddaddy Hiram before something terrible happened, he had little time.

The layout of *Paradise Gate* was etched in his memory. Loading area, display room, five slumber areas, a chapel, and front lobby on this level, crematorium and preparation room downstairs. Katie, Hiram, and Vinnie were most likely downstairs. The elevator was off-limits, but there were stairs off the lobby.

Hearing voices, Sam slipped into the display room and closed the door behind him. It made a clicking sound. He tested the handle and groaned aloud. Without a key, he was stuck. While he jiggled the handle, the sound of bickering grew louder. He slipped behind the closest casket, which happened to occupy a trolley in the center of the room.

Straining to hear, Sam made out the words, "... shouldn't kill them yet ... *Mumble* ... load Vinnie into a coffin ... *Mumble* ... how to operate the fuckin' oven ..."

In seconds, the door would open. The Allegrettis couldn't miss him, soaked with blood and crouching behind a center-stage casket.

The brothers' voices grew louder. "I vote we do the old fart first. He's a nut case," one of them said.

"Nah," the other answered, "Vinnie first. His stink's making me gag."

"I wonder how long it'll take to cremate all three."

"Dunno. Katie can tell us before we whack her. At least the joint ain't open for business until morning."

Knowing he had no choice if he wanted to stop them, Sam gritted his teeth and climbed into the display casket. Thank God he'd had the foresight to steal the tire iron. He positioned the tool strategically to create the tiniest sliver of space before silently lowering the lid.

Darkness pressed against his eyeballs making him crazy, so he folded his arms across his chest and tried his damndest to think happy thoughts. Nothing came. He tried counting backwards from 1,000, but quit when he reached 987.

What were the Allegrettis doing?

The itch, when it came, started on the left side of his head. Recognizing it as a stress reaction, he ignored it. As if pissed off, the prickling crawled across his scalp and down his neck, an army of ants engulfing his body in fire. Before long, every inch of skin throbbed with a constant, relentless agony. There was no sound from the room. Knowing he wouldn't last much longer, he visualized scraping his nails over the skin.

After several more minutes, he'd had enough. Raising the lid an inch, he sucked in a deep breath of air.

A rough voice, surprisingly close, growled, "Hey, I can't hardly see my fuckin' hand in front of my face. All I have for light is my phone. Hit the switch."

"Shit. I can't find it."

It appeared the thick carpet had muffled the brothers' footsteps,

Sam let go in a big hurry. The force of the lid banging shut dislodged the tire iron. It popped out and landed on his head. He forced himself to remain motionless. With luck, the dribble of moisture trickling down his temple and soaking into the nice, satin pillow was sweat, not blood. At least the itch had disappeared.

"Hey, did you hear that?" one of them asked.

"Hear what?"

"I thought I heard a noise."

"I bet it's a ghost. There's probably thousands of ghosts here seein' as how so many stiffs have passed through."

"Shut up, asshole."

Sam damn near jumped out of his skin when a voice blasted in his ear, "Let's grab a coffin for Vinnie. He deserves that much. This one looks good. I'll check it out."

To Sam's horror, the coffin lid opened. A light shone on his face. He squeezed his eyes shut and stopped breathing, holding himself as rigid as an iron bar.

"Fuck me." The lid slammed shut before Sam could re-position the tire iron. "This thing's occupied. The stiff's covered in blood."

Sam's casket shook under a heavy weight landing on it with a metallic clatter.

"Hey, take it easy, Enzo. You scratched the lid."

"It won't matter where this guy's going."

"Pick another coffin and make sure it's empty this time. I'll get a trolley from the hallway. We'll take it downstairs to the furnace for Vinnie's big send-off."

"Katie'd better tell us how to work the oven before we whack her."

"She will. Locking 'em in the preparation room will soften her up. No bullets, mind. We'll strangle them, maybe break their necks so there won't be any blood. We'll do 'em real quick, before they know what's happening."

"That's a nice touch, Enzo. Thoughtful."

"It's gonna be a long night. I need a drink first."

"Great idea, I brought booze."

"Hey, me too. Let's go somewhere comfy. I'm kinda partial to the Tranquility Room."

"You're a fuckin' genius. Babbo Lou rested there during his visitation. Drinks first, business later."

Sam waited five minutes. Once he was sure they were gone, he pushed on the lid. Nothing. By then, sweat streamed off his body. He pushed harder. Still nothing.

This was it. He would go slowly mad inside a coffin, while two criminals got shit-faced before killing Katie and his granddaddy.

Then he remembered the thump of something heavy being placed on the coffin. The toolbox. His energy renewed, he pushed again. Desperation lent strength to his arms. The toolbox shifted, making a scraping sound. He was taking up weight-lifting once this was over. Gathering his strength, he gave another thrust that damn near blew out an artery. This time, the lid lifted, toppling the toolbox to the floor with a muffled thud.

With silent thanks for the plush carpeting, he climbed out, collecting the toolbox and tire iron before tip-toeing out the door.

***

By the time they reached the preparation room, Katie had formulated an escape strategy born of desperation. After the Allegrettis slammed the door shut she listened for the padlock. Once it clicked, it took her mere minutes to find an embalming scalpel and slice through the ropes binding Hiram, another five minutes for him to return the favor, and another twenty to dye his hair and dab on his makeup. When she'd finished, she barely recognized him.

A clash of metal on metal in the hallway outside the room caused her heart to somersault into her throat. Glancing at Hiram, she nodded. They wouldn't go down without a fight. Her heart ached at the thought that if she died tonight at the hands of thugs, her son would be an orphan. Galvanized by the thought, she jumped to her feet with renewed energy and faced the door, scalpel in one hand, operating scissors in the other.

Hiram opened a plastic container of formaldehyde and yelled, "If you pricks know what's good for you, you'll stay outside."

A muffled voice said, "It's me, Sam. Stand back."

Katie's terror over imminent cremation vanished. They high-fived one another and backed away. Hiram disappeared into the linen closet, no doubt to surprise Sam.

After several minutes of hammering, the door flew open. Sam burst inside, a tire iron in one hand, the toolbox in the other. He was so blood-caked, Katie barely recognized him.

"Sam, you need a doctor." She tried to keep the quaver out of her voice as she touched his cheek, then his temple. She noted he leaned into her touch.

"Don't worry. It's mostly Luigi's blood."

Her bones liquefied with the relief she felt. "Thank God. You took so long, we thought the Allegrettis had killed you, for real this time." She had the presence of mind to grab the protective gown and pants Rico had hung on a hook and handed them to Sam. "Here. You'll feel better if you clean yourself up and put these on. There's the sink."

"Thanks." Sam scanned the room as he stripped to his boxers and kicked his blood-caked clothing aside. "Where's Granddaddy Hiram?"

"Getting ready." She nodded at the closed door of the linen closet. "In there."

"Thank God he's safe too."

While Sam cleaned up, they filled one another in on the highlights. As they talked, Katie stared at his body, memorizing every inch of sculpted muscle. She ached for Sam, not physically, although that was a definite yes, but at a deeper, more primitive level.

When he slipped on the protective wear, she hid a sigh of regret.

Fastening the gown, he said, "You may not believe this, but I hid in a coffin to escape the Allegrettis."

That shocked her out of her misery. "But you have claustrophobia. That's the most courageous thing I've ever heard."

"Trust me, if there had been another choice, I'd have jumped on it."

Although Sam minimized his heroism, she realized he'd done the thing he feared most to save their lives—at least, Hiram's life. There was no doubt in her mind she was merely collateral salvage. After destroying his love and trust the way she had, she was lucky he was civil to her. In the meantime, there were other priorities, like escaping alive so she could tell her son how much she loved him.

"We'd better get out of here before they return," Sam said. "I'll get my granddaddy."

"I think he has a surprise for you."

On cue, Hiram opened the door and stepped into the room. He'd wrapped a white sheet around his body, toga-style, and draped the end over one shoulder. His waxy complexion gleamed under the preparation room lights. "Hi, Sammy. Look. I'm a changed man. I look twenty years younger."

Katie eyed her handiwork with pride. With the white beard shaved, chalky makeup, and his hair and eyebrows dyed black, Hiram did, indeed look like a different man.

Sam's face creased in concern and he turned as white as Hiram. He recovered quickly and gripped his grandfather by the elbows. "What happened? How about you tell me what's going on?" His love for the old man showed in his protective posture, his gentle voice.

"I'm gonna scare the shit out of those two goons." Hiram bounced on his toes. "It was Katie's idea, so she gets to explain."

Sam held Katie's gaze for a long beat. "Something tells me I'm not going to like this."

She suspected he was right. To fortify herself, she took a deep breath. "We needed a plan in case you didn't get here in time."

Sam folded his arms. "I'm listening."

"Okay, so right from the start, Hiram looked familiar, but I couldn't place where we'd met. Today I figured it out. A couple of years ago, I embalmed Lou 'The Hammer' Allegretti. He was Enzo and Ralphie's grandfather, their *babbo*. Hiram looks remarkably like Babbo Lou. Same bushy eyebrows, heavy glasses, and commanding nose." She took care not to call it 'bulbous' in case she hurt Hiram's feelings. "But the white hair and beard had me fooled. It was Hiram's incredible smile that jogged my memory."

"Katie says Babbo Lou and I have the same great teeth, only his were fake and mine are real." Hiram clicked his teeth together several times. "I'm gonna pretend to be Babbo Lou's ghost. By the time I'm done, they'll both need a change of tightie whities."

"Holy shit," Sam muttered. "Tell me I haven't fallen down the rabbit hole."

Hiram rattled on, "This place is great. There's makeup and all the cosmetic shit they use on the stiffs, uh ..." He cast a guilty glance at Katie. "I mean, the deceased. So Katie had me shave. Next, she dyed my hair and eyebrows and made me up to look spooky, and taught me how to speak Italian. Listen. *Buona sera*."

"Excellent accent," Katie said.

"This is insane. I won't let you do it." Sam picked up the tire iron and selected a hammer from the toolbox. "By now, the Allegrettis are drunk. They think I'm dead, so I'll surprise them as soon as they open the door."

Hiram ignored Sam. "Listen to me, boy. They have guns. This way's better."

Sam's mouth opened, most likely to argue, but before the protest reached his lips, metal clinked and the door crashed open. Ralphie and Enzo stood inside the room, guns extended.

From the liquor fumes wafting inside, she assumed they were dead drunk.

The incomprehension written on their faces as they entered the preparation room might have been comical if Enzo hadn't waved his gun under Sam's nose, and yelled, "What the fuck? We killed you."

Hiram stepped out from behind Sam. "*Ciao, ragazzi*, hello, boys." His broad grin displayed all his teeth for maximum effect. "*Che piacere rivederla.* It's good to see you again."

His Italian was perfect. Katie couldn't remember the last time she'd felt so proud of anyone.

Color drained from the thugs' faces. Ralphie's mouth dropped open and a thread of saliva dribbled onto his shirt. He let loose a howl that rattled the instruments on a metal tray.

"Babbo Lou," Enzo whispered. "You're dead. We cremated you." The gun shook as he pointed it at Hiram.

Katie's stomach plummeted, but Sam covered the distance in a low crouch. His kick was lightning-fast. Enzo's shot lodged in a leather recliner instead of Hiram's chest.

Ralphie fell to his knees, whimpering, "*Santa merda.*" The gun dropped from his limp fingers and skittered under a trolley.

Sam dove, rolled, and came up grasping the weapon in both hands. In another lithe move, he sprang to his feet, the gun pointed at the middle of Enzo's chest.

Hiram jumped up and down. "Go for the balls, Sammy. The balls. Shoot the asshole's pea-sized balls off, that is, if he has any."

Sam said, "Enzo, my man. Count your lucky stars my granddaddy isn't the one holding the gun. Now listen carefully. I want you to use two fingers to place your gun on the floor, then your phone. Ralphie, your phone too. Slide everything to me."

"One of you has my phone," Katie said. "And car keys. Add them to the pile."

She tensed, ready to use the scalpel if either of them tried any funny stuff. Lucky for them they obeyed.

Holding Ralphie's gun on the Allegrettis, Sam picked up Enzo's gun and stuck it in his belt, then shoved everything else except a phone into his pockets. "Time to call the police."

"No police," she said.

A muscle in Sam's jaw bunched. "Tell me you're kidding. They killed Vinnie, kidnapped and planned to kill you and my granddaddy, executed a hit on Luigi, thought they'd killed me, and you say I shouldn't call the cops?" His voice, which had grown louder with every point, ended on an incredulous note.

Yeah, Sam was royally pissed, but she wouldn't let him throw everything away. Not when they were so close to the finish line.

She went for humor. "Nicely put. You're obviously not just another pretty face."

In response, his eyebrows slammed together and he flipped open the phone using one hand. Okay, not amused.

To her relief, Hiram supported her. "You got your stupid hat on today, boy? The grand opening's tomorrow. If the cops learn these two varmints stashed Vinnie inside *Kinki* for over a week, they'll close the club until they finish fartin' around with the crime scene."

"Holy flaming hell." Sam made an obvious effort to rein in his temper. "Don't you get it? These two moronic pieces of shit deserve everything that's coming to them."

Enzo's eyes shot sparks of hatred at Sam. "You're gonna regret calling us 'moronic pieces of shit.' *Capisce*?"

"Shut up." Sam looked as if he wanted to follow Hiram's urging to shoot Enzo in the family jewels.

Katie gave Sam her tolerate-no-crap look. He might be willing to throw away everything he'd worked for by calling in the police, but she wouldn't let him. It was her job to ensure a successful grand opening. Choosing her words for maximum impact, she spoke softly. "You once told me Hiram had invested his entire retirement fund in *Kinki*. That means if you go down, he does too. Can you live with that?"

"That's hitting below the belt." Sam gave her an long, distraught look that wrenched her soul.

"It's reality," she whispered. On watching Sam's shoulders slump, she figured she'd burned her last bridge with him. But at least he snapped the phone shut.

The silence hummed with tension before his expression softened, and he put the phone away.

"You won't shoot us, will you?" Ralphie's voice took on a note of desperation.

Katie held her breath as the silence lengthened. At last Sam said, "Nope. Out of the goodness of my heart, I'm turning you two jackasses loose."

"You're letting us go?" Enzo asked.

"You're letting them go?" Granddaddy Hiram echoed his words.

Katie was too shocked to comment.

Ralphie reacted to the news by collapsing into the recliner. "*Grazie a Dio.*"

Sam's smile was chilling. "Don't get too happy, boys. You have some new chores."

Worried that Sam may have taken a hard blow to his head, Katie tugged his sleeve. "What are you doing, Sam," she whispered.

It was as if she hadn't spoken. Sam pinned the thugs with an icy stare. "First, you guys will load Vinnie onto your truck to keep Luigi company. Then, you'll leave these premises and dispose of their bodies." He shrugged. "Or not. Your choice."

Ralphie and Enzo traded glances. "Sure thing."

"See, I don't give a hairy rat's ass what you do after you leave. Those corpses are your problem, not mine. The main thing is you'll never show your ugly faces near any of us again."

This must be part of Sam's strategy, Katie thought wildly, but damned if she could figure out what it might be. She tugged his arm. "What are you doing?"

He continued pointing the gun at the Allegrettis. "By the time we do a thorough cleanup, there'll be no evidence left. Vinnie was plastic-wrapped, so all we need to do is swab down *Kinki* and dispose of the used casket. There'll be no clues here either. Luigi died on a tarpaulin, all nice and neat, and we'll cremate my blood-spattered clothing along with anything else that might raise eyebrows."

Katie finally caught on to Sam's strategy. It was sheer genius, placing the responsibility for the murders where it belonged, on the Allegrettis. The iron band compressing her chest released. "In that case, shouldn't we also cremate the coffin you occupied?"

"Absolutely." The warmth in Sam's eyes when he looked at her made her feel better.

"But there's one more thing you should pay attention to," he continued, waving the gun at the Allegrettis, who had the sense to look apprehensive. "Don't even think of coming after us later to tie up some loose ends by killing us."

Ralphie and Enzo imitated bobblehead dolls.

Sam's face creased in a vicious grin. "Wise decision, ladies. Because if any one of us dies under suspicious circumstances, my lawyer, who, I warn you, is a ball-buster, will hold a notarized document describing everything that went down leading up to and including tonight's events. This same document will identify the perps, namely you boys. So get lost, dump the bodies, and live your miserable lives."

Never taking his gaze off the Allegrettis, he spoke to Katie. "If you don't mind keeping my granddaddy company, I'll accompany the brothers outside to make sure they leave."

***

Half an hour later, Sam watched the truck's tail lights disappear as the Allegrettis peeled out of the laneway and, hopefully, out of their lives. He pulled out one of their phones and used it to dial the police. When he finished the call, he walked back inside and joined Katie and Granddaddy Hiram. Both phones would join his bloody clothes in the coffin.

Katie was at the rear of the loading area swabbing the floor with a mop. His granddaddy saw him first and toddled over, gripping an empty bottle of bleach. "Hey, Sammy. We've cleaned up everything. You were gone so damn long, we were beginning to worry."

Katie turned. It seemed her dark eyes lingered on him, or maybe it was his imagination. "Are they gone?" She left the mop and rushed over.

"Yeah. But they won't get far." She looked so sweet and anxious Sam wanted to wrap his arms around her, but this wasn't the time or the place.

"How can you be so sure?"

He held her gaze for a long beat. "After they left, I called in an anonymous tip to the police, complete with license plate number and names. We're in the clear."

She sagged a little, as if she'd been holding herself together. He went to steady her, but she pulled away and started chatting a mile a minute.

"It was Hiram's idea to bleach away the bloodstains on the floor. Thank goodness the display room carpet is white, so no one will notice some patches. Next, we brought the bloodstained coffin downstairs and threw your clothes into it. I was waiting to see if there was anything else that needed to go in before I load it into the cremator and program the burner to operate all night. Did you know everything is automated? All I need to do is—"

Sam pressed a finger gently over her lips. "Shhhh. It's all good. Before you push the start button, I'll dump their phones in the coffin as well, then drive you home."

Katie checked the wall-clock. "Goodness, it's three a.m. Time flies when you're having fun. No need to drive me anywhere. I'll sleep at The Annex so I'll be here when Ma returns bright and early with Josh. For a while, I thought he'd be an orphan."

She was drained and trying hard not to show it. "Good idea. You look exhausted. Granddaddy Hiram and I will head over to *Kinki*, and I'll toss the guns into the Intercostal on the way. He'll go straight to bed. Rooster will help me make sure *Dracula's Lair* is fresh and clean."

With visible effort, Katie pulled herself together. "I guess everything caught up with me all at once. Getting kidnapped and watching a man die in a hail of bullets takes a lot out of a woman."

She was acting funny, but Sam put her skittishness down to stress. "We need to talk, but not now. I'll find your car and drop it off. Go get some sleep. Tomorrow will be a long day."

Chapter 43: Grand Opening Begins

Katie's reunion with Josh was joyous, stupendous, life-affirming. Okay, so her sobbing alarmed him at first, but she assured him they were tears of joy because she was happy to see him (no lie there). His favorite brunch, pancakes with sausage, scrambled eggs, and a gallon of maple syrup sealed the deal. He was so busy eating, he barely noticed when she promised that after tonight, she wouldn't need to work such long hours.

She wouldn't be working at all unless she found another job.

Focusing on the positive, she told herself life would return to normal after the grand opening. Better than normal. With Luigi dead, there would be no more hit men or threats, and she didn't need to move to Alaska. It was all good, that is if you ignored the fact that Sam was leaving their lives for good. There was no coming back from the words she'd thrown in his face. Even so, at some point before dawn, he'd gone out of his way to deliver her car and slip the keys through the mail slot.

Once Josh had departed with a friend for yet another sleepover, Katie, with Bella's help, prepared herself for the grand opening. Three hours later, dressed, waxed, and plucked, she sped to *Kinki* for her final evening of work before her contract terminated. She was confident she looked fabulous—sensual, hot, desirable. Hey, if her sexy outfit from *Knotty Girl Fashions* convinced Sam to forgive her, that was an added bonus.

The lineup outside *Kinki* was five-deep, stretching from the new parking garage all the way to the front door. Slipping around back, she jumped the line by using the delivery entrance.

Once inside, she took a moment to calm herself. When she felt more grounded, she slipped on a mask and leather arm bands, her tribute to *Kinki*'s former fetish club incarnation. Looping the dainty chain of her gold mesh purse over her shoulder, she clutched her notebook and dashed along the corridor as fast as four-inch stilettos permitted. Dozens of last-minute chores demanded her attention, and that was perfect. Keeping busy was an excellent way to avoid Sam. Evasion, she assured herself, was prudence, not cowardice.

She reached the lobby and halted. Men shouldering television cameras, some trailing cables, followed reporters with microphones, all intent on reaching their destination. Bartenders, servers, cocktail waitresses, musicians, and other staff, all wearing costumes, milled around like ants as they hurried to their final briefings before the doors opened.

Off to one side, she caught sight of Rico and Bella standing together examining the crowd, the lobby, the employees. They both appeared to be vibrating with excitement.

Rico must have seen her too, because he waved her over, shouting, "Holy shit, this place is sheer genius. Zombies, vampires, even mummies."

Rico's next move took her by surprise. He opened his arms and said, "I want to give both my beautiful sisters a hug."

Katie and Bella exchanged an astonished glance before all three fused together. It felt, somehow, *right*. As if they'd crossed a barrier she hadn't even realized existed.

When they broke apart, Rico beckoned her closer and whispered, "Tell Sam I'm taking his advice. As of today, the free funerals stop before I'm in too deep." Katie was still reeling with shock when he did it again. "Hang on to him Sis. That man is so in love with you, even I noticed."

Not any more, she thought. She'd killed any love Sam might have felt for her.

"Yowza," Bella whispered, staring at someone over Katie's shoulder.

Katie turned her head to see who'd captured her sister's interest. Her breath hitched at the sight of six-plus feet of lithe, hard perfection jogging toward her. She'd lingered too long. No way was she ready to deal with Sam and the breakup now.

"Sorry, gotta go, stuff to do," she muttered, and took flight as fast as her stilettos permitted, which wasn't saying much.

"Katie."

His voice, surprisingly close, stopped her in her tracks. Knowing she couldn't outrun him, she turned to face the music. And promptly lost her train of thought.

Except for a small strip of adhesive on his forehead and a black eye, barely noticeable under a layer of concealer, Sam was more drop-dead, movie-star gorgeous than usual. He'd mentioned he'd be black tie, but she hadn't anticipated the impact. A perfectly tailored black tux molded his rangy frame. He wore the blindingly white shirt and black bow tie with the same easy grace as he did his cowboy garb. His lazy smile was far too sexy for his own good—or hers, for that matter.

"You look beautiful." His voice was a little husky and a whole lot sexy.

She locked her knees to stop herself from melting onto the floor. "Hey, Sam. You look great too, then again you pretty much always do." She clamped her mouth shut before she babbled something she would regret.

His gaze landed on her face. "You've been avoiding me. We need to talk."

"Right. But the grand opening starts in exactly …" she rummaged in her tiny purse for her phone and checked it, "forty-four minutes and fifteen seconds. I have a dozen chores on my to-do list." She displayed her notebook, more as a shield than anything else.

"Fine. We'll talk later. Look, you're busy, but could you squeeze in one more task?"

"Certainly." Avoiding eye contact, she straightened her mask and waited, pen poised.

"I need you to find those DVDs I prepared, the ones of *Kinki* in its glory days as a fetish club. They're in my desk, top drawer, right hand side. The audio-visual guy needs them. I'd do it, but Eugene phoned a minute ago to say he's almost here. Somehow, he talked Mom into a reconciliation. I should go greet them."

The news shocked her into smiling up at him. "That's wonderful. Of course you should go. They must be bursting with pride over your accomplishments."

"Time will tell." He handed her his desk key.

She stuffed it down the front of her bustier and made a show of jotting the task in her notebook. "Anything else?" she asked, still writing.

"Yeah. We need to talk."

Katie snuck a glance at his face. From the jut of his jaw, she knew he wouldn't stop hounding her until she agreed. There was probably some legalese about closing out her contract, also payment upon completion of her assignment.

She hit him with what she hoped was a serene expression. "Let's meet in *Mermaids* after the ceremony. With this dress, I need a stand-up bar." And she walked away, aware of the beaded strands swaying around her legs.

Five minutes later, Katie stood behind Sam's antique desk and opened it. Sure enough, lying inside were three DVDs. She placed them on top of the desk and continued to search the other drawers for more. Finding nothing, she was about to leave when she remembered the file drawer.

She gripped the handle and tugged. When it resisted her efforts, she yanked harder, but the vandalism must have damaged the drawer. She moved to get a better angle and heaved. The drawer flew open, hitting the floor with a crash. Files tumbled out and papers scattered across the floor. Inside the desk, she noted one of the slides was twisted. No wonder the drawer had jammed. Sam would need to have it repaired.

After gathering files and papers and stacking them, she straightened the drawer in case it tripped someone. If it hadn't been on the floor in front of her, she wouldn't have noticed a false backing with three inches of space behind it. She peered inside, and a tingle of anticipation gripped her. She'd found a secret compartment, and unless she was mistaken, there was something wedged inside.

The space was narrow, and it didn't help that adrenaline made her shake. She inserted her hand. Fingers connected with a thin, flat object. Slowly, carefully, she twisted it loose.

Her excitement blinked out. Another DVD. During the cleanup, Sam had taken his files and stuffed them, willy-nilly, into the drawer. It must have fallen from a folder and dropped into the hidden compartment.

Making a mental note to give the disc to Sam in case it contained confidential data, she placed it in her purse alongside the others. After untangling a few beaded strands and straightening her mask, she hurried downstairs. If nothing else, she'd make sure Sam had the kick-ass grand opening he so desperately needed.

***

As Sam paced the length of *Inferno*, his mind wasn't on the opening ceremony, not by a long shot. Last night, Katie was too emotionally drained to see straight. Tonight, he intended to make things right between them. He'd rehearsed everything he wanted to say. All he had to do was squeeze the words out. Maybe she'd settle for a new house and moving in with him.

His train of thought scrambled when she hurried through the door, all flushed and sweet and adorable. A wave of tenderness blindsided him. Somehow, she'd managed not only to pierce his armor, but blast it away, leaving him feeling naked, raw, and needy.

Without so much as a glance in Sam's direction, Katie handed the DVDs to the deejay. Her sparkly skirt swung around those gorgeous legs. Every time she took a step, the beads parted to reveal more than they concealed. From the deejay's avid expression, he'd noticed too.

She bestowed a bright smile on the little bastard as Mellencamp's voice belted out *Hurts So Good*. They were doing a test run. Images of *Kinki* rolled onto the large screen behind the stage. Before long, happy fetishists lashed one another with whips and riding crops. He'd burned the DVDs himself from old footage kicking around. This scene, he knew, was exactly five minutes and thirty-five seconds long. He glanced at the time. Fifteen minutes before liftoff.

Across the room, Katie spoke to the deejay, making the asshole smile. Sam was no longer willing to wait until after the opening ceremony to spill his guts. His rapidly revised plan was to take her aside before the doors opened.

He sauntered over to where she and the little weasel stood. Before he could whisk her away, a cloud of perfume alerted him to more company. Tess Tosterone, dressed as a vampire in a Cher wig and slinky black dress, air-kissed Katie before bestowing a huge hug on him.

"I'm stealing Katie. She needs a last-minute touch-up." Tess batted thick, black eyelashes at Sam. "Not to worry, hon, I'm referring to her makeup." She drew Katie away.

Uneasiness gripped Sam on noting Katie didn't protest and didn't look back at him, not once. In spite of the fact that Luigi could never torment her again, it seemed she couldn't make a fast enough getaway.

To distract himself, he scanned the room, and found more distraction than he needed. Unless he was hallucinating, Rex's head had popped up. Sure, it disappeared, but the same thing happened again. And again. He strode across the room.

Platters of finger-food lined bar. His apprehension mounted when he caught Rex straining toward sausage rolls with the single-mindedness of a lion stalking its prey. His granddaddy's eyes bulged with the effort of hauling on the leash.

Rex shook his head and pointed his muzzle in the air, nostrils quivering.

"Quiet!" Sam hollered, ignoring the shocked expressions around him.

His don't–mess-with-me voice defused the food alarm. Rex subsided with a grumble, his attention fixed on sausage rolls.

Sam turned to Granddaddy Hiram, who looked dapper in a rented tux. The black hair and eyebrows really did subtract a couple of decades from his age.

"I told you not to bring Rex tonight."

"Did you?" his granddaddy said, the picture of innocence. "Must be my hearing."

Sam opened his mouth to have Rex removed when Katie materialized beside him. He lost his train of thought. Maybe she'd be open to exchanging a kiss for good luck.

Her voice, all crisp and businesslike, told him not to push his luck. "The lineup's so long they opened the doors early. I told the camera crew to start filming and to keep rolling until one of us gives the signal. And whatever you do, be careful what you say. They have directional mikes that'll catch the sound of a fly's footsteps at fifty yards." With that, she hustled away.

Before he could make a fool of himself and follow her like a lovesick puppy, several hundred guests started pouring into *Immortals*. It looked as though everyone on the invitation list had accepted. Some would be relegated to standing room only, others would have to wait in the lobby or other areas to watch the opening ceremony on closed circuit TV.

By tomorrow, he'd either be filthy rich or a pauper.

Aware of cameras capturing his every move, Sam shook hands, thumped backs, kissed cheeks, and generally schmoozed until his face felt frozen into a permanent grin.

"Sam, mind if we talk for a minute?"

Sam stopped smiling. That voice could belong to only one person. He was on the verge of snubbing Eugene, but for some reason changed his mind. Instead of moving away, he strode toward his father, who was weaving his way through the crowd.

"You came," Sam said, by way of greeting. "Where's Mom?"

"Somewhere near the door with your cousin, Braden. I needed to see you alone."

"I don't have much time. We're starting soon."

"I'll be brief." Eugene cleared his throat a couple of times and shifted from one foot to another. At last, he said, "I don't have enough years left on this planet to make up for the harm I did to you, but I want to try. If you'll let me." His eyes pleaded for forgiveness.

Sam opened his mouth to refuse, but nothing came out. His lifelong hostility toward his father had faded. No, not faded. Disappeared. Apparently, nearly being killed did strange things to a man, things that messed with his head or, more accurately, cleared his head. Bottom line? Life was too short and too precious to stumble through it in a fog of resentment.

Remembering Katie's words about forgiveness, he looked his father in the eye. "How about we work on mending our fences together."

Eugene's eyes were suspiciously bright. "I love you, Son. I want to make up for all those years that we lost."

Sam's eyes stung. "Me, too, Dad."

Eugene opened his arms. Sam hesitated, then stepped into them, and they hugged one another for dear life. It didn't last long, but that hug melted the hard, cold knot that had occupied Sam's chest for so long, he'd taken its presence for granted.

After they broke apart, Sam said in a choked voice, "I'll catch up with you and Mom later."

"Count on it." Eugene's voice was equally choked.

Chapter 44: The Opening Ceremony

Sam waited for *Inferno*'s doors to close before stepping onto the stage. An eruption of applause caught him off-guard. He smiled and waved for silence, searching the crowd until he found the one face he wanted. For one wild moment he imagined he saw longing in Katie's sweet, haunted eyes, that is until she caught him watching. Her expression switched from yearning to indifference.

He wanted to invite her onstage to share the moment, but she looked away. He took that to mean, "Get lost."

Images flickered on the screen behind him, and the crowd settled down. Springsteen's rendition of *The Ties That Bind* started up, an accompaniment to a spicy BDSM clip from one of *Kinki*'s former Rodeo Nites. He made a few preliminary remarks before launching into his speech, a run-down of *Kinki*'s fetish club history and its new incarnation as a Goth nightclub. He was so focused, he barely noticed the music had changed.

Soon, the snickering began.

He hadn't said anything funny. A bad feeling crawled along his spine, but he soldiered on, describing highlights of the evening ahead. By the time he got to the *Immortal Mermaids* act, pretty much everyone was busting a gut and pointing. He cast a covert glance at his fly to see if it was open. It wasn't, but the pointing and whispering continued. He came close to panicking until he realized they were staring at the screen behind him.

He turned and squinted. Shadowy people were conducting some sort of ritual. He stepped back for a better look, and all the cells in his body went on high alert.

Holy flaming hell. Everyone onscreen was naked.

He gripped the microphone and yelled at the deejay, "Turn it off."

The little shit ignored the order, his gaze glued to the screen.

"What are they doing?" someone shouted. The voice sounded like Mellow's.

"Daisy chaining," replied another.

"Jeez. I always wondered how that worked."

"Close your filthy eyes," a woman's voice screeched.

Sam looked closer and froze. Everyone onscreen was engaged in oral sex. They alternated face-up and face-down positions, forming a circle of bodies.

"Turn the damn thing off," he bellowed. "Now."

The scene continued to roll.

Someone yelled, "Hey, I recognize those people. That's Frank Martinelli giving the hot blonde a blow job."

"Yeah, and look. That's a man latched onto Senator Frankie's joy stick."

"It's that gangster, Luigi Guglione."

As Sam jumped off the stage and started toward the deejay, murder on his mind, the little asswipe yelled, "Hey, lady. You can't do that."

Katie's voice replied, "Watch me."

The screen went dark.

The crowd uttered a collective protest. Over the boos and hisses, someone yelled, "It was just getting good. Turn it on."

Sam raised his voice to be heard over the ruckus. "Please stay calm. I apologize for our technical difficulties. The opening ceremony will continue momentarily."

He was nearing the deejay when a commotion at the entrance followed by a roar of pain caused everyone to surge to their feet.

Switching direction, he elbowed his way toward the sound. The crowd parted to reveal Rooster rolling on the floor clutching his most precious parts.

Sam knelt beside his bouncer. "Rooster. What happened?"

"The blonde bitch kneed me in the balls when I tried to block her attack on Martinelli." Rooster squeezed his eyes shut and whimpered.

Sam winced in sympathy. "Where did she go?"

Rooster sat up gingerly and pointed a shaking finger. "There. She grabbed the senator's dick while he tried to sneak out. She has a thing for a guy's parts."

Sam moved quickly. Sure enough, a woman with wild blonde hair was gripping Frank by his package. He took a closer look at her face. "Deanna? Better loosen the grip, sugar, or you'll tear off Martinelli's favorite body part."

"That's the idea. He tried to murder me on the bondage bed. If it weren't for you and Katie, I'd be dead."

Behind Deanna, Eleanor looked as though she was holding it together by the thinnest of threads. "Frank, is it true?" his wife asked in a quiet voice. "Attempted murder as well as everything I saw on the video?"

Frank's face twisted in agony as Deanna gave a good twist. After he stopped screaming, he caught his breath and said, "No, Sweetheart. She's lying."

"You tried to murder me," Deanna shrieked, letting go, only to haul a handgun from her purse and point the business end at Martinelli's crotch. "You lousy, lying, snotty, slimy rat-bastard. The only reason I didn't tell the cops is because I'd rather shoot your balls off." She cocked the weapon with a metallic click.

The spectators surrounding them backpedalled in a hurry.

"Whoa. Don't do anything you'll regret." Sam scanned the room for reinforcements. The security staff had their hands full with the crowd.

Deanna laughed. "Regret? Hah. This'll be the best day of my life."

Aware of Katie materializing beside him, Sam positioned himself between her and the gun. "Leave," he ordered, never taking his gaze off the gun. "It's too dangerous."

She stepped beside him.

His fear for Katie's safety growing, he tried again with Deanna. "No wonder you're angry, darlin'. Why did Frank try to kill you."

Martinelli spoke over Deanna. "It was an accident. She likes it rough."

Deanna flipped Martinelli off. "The hell I do. I only let you do those things because I believed you loved me. It was no accident. You tried to strangle me, you sick bastard."

Martinelli ignored Deanna and shot his wife a pleading look. "You know how much I love you, Ellie. You mean everything to me."

From Eleanor's stony expression, Sam figured if she were the one holding the gun, Martinelli would be a dead man.

Deanna's face twisted with rage. "You deserve to die. You let me believe I'd be a U.S. senator's wife. You tied me to the sarcophagus, then said you were sick of me. I warned you I'd go public about our affair unless you divorced your wife and married me like you promised. That's when you tried to choke me. The only reason you'd pretended to care was so's I'd help you find a stupid DVD the former owner hid before she went to prison."

A light went on in Sam's brain. "You trashed my office."

"Yeah. Twice. The HR powder room too. Once good old Can't-Keep-His-Pants-Zipped talked you into hiring me, I looked everywhere for the DVD. If that thing ever surfaced, his political career would be over." Deanna's face broke into a vindictive smile. "I'm guessing it's now officially washed-up."

Martinelli's lips twisted with hatred. "Bitch. I can't believe you thought I'd give up my home, my wife, my chance at the White House, everything for a slut like you."

In response, she raised the gun, pointed it at Martinelli's crotch, and squeezed the trigger. The explosion was deafening.

Martinelli's bloodcurdling scream tapered off into a screech and ending in a gurgle, but Sam couldn't see any blood.

The shots alarmed everyone, including, apparently, the security detail, because Rex, joined the commotion, his leash trailing behind him.

While Sam tried to assess Martinelli's wounds, Katie blocked Deanna's escape. Caught off-guard, Deanna said an unladylike word, stumbled, and grabbed a handful of Katie's skirt in an effort to regain her balance.

The gun flew in a graceful arc, landing at Sam's feet. He seized it. Simultaneously, several hundred beads pinged onto the wooden floor and skittered in every direction.

Katie stood perfectly still, disbelief painting her face. "My dress," she whispered. She recovered her voice and yelled at Deanna, "You wrecked my beautiful gown. You're going to pay big-time."

Shit. Katie intended to carry out the murder Martinelli had botched.

Beads crunched as Deanna took a couple of tentative steps to distance herself from danger. Flailing wildly to keep her balance, she landed on her ass. "You stupid bitch. I should have taken you out as soon as Frank's eye wandered in your direction."

Katie's simultaneous cry of indignation ended in a squeak as she too went down, strings of beads entangling her ankles. With narrowed eyes, she started crawling, presumably to get a piece of Deanna.

Katie said, "You attacked Hiram and locked him in the crypt, didn't you? You're the only person I know who's vindictive enough to harm an old man. Hiram said his assailant was big and strong. With those linebacker shoulders, you fill the bill."

"The old goat called me a conniving slut once too often. He needed to be taught a lesson." Deanna regained her feet first, and picked her way toward the exit, her purse clutched to her chest.

Holding the gun, Sam stumbled after her. Not that he'd shoot, but Deanna didn't know that. He was within arm's length when she said, "Put the gun down. I loaded it with blanks."

Dimly aware of a camera pointed in his direction, he stared at the weapon, then at Deanna. "Why?"

Deanna took another cautious step. "I hoped Frank would drop dead from a heart attack. Or at least soil his pants."

She'd reached the exit when a mournful howl filled the air.

Slip-sliding across the floor, Rex skidded straight for Deanna. Flecks of saliva flew from open jaws. He howled again, louder this time.

Sam stepped aside as Rex launched his furry body at Deanna. She went down.

Plunking himself onto her chest, Rex stuck his head into her purse and emerged with a pepperette. It disappeared in a single gulp. He dove in again and rooted around.

"Good dog," Sam said, as Rex withdrew his head from the purse, another pepperette in his jaws. It was justice for terrorizing his granddaddy.

Since Deanna wasn't going anywhere, Sam looked around for Martinelli and found him lurching toward the deejay, presumably to grab the DVD. Between the slippery beads and Eleanor gripping his arm while kicking his shins, he wasn't making a whole lot of headway.

Being as how Sam had an aversion to blood, especially his own, he didn't try to take Martinelli down, no siree. He merely cleared a path through the beads with his boot until he was close enough to jab the gun in Martinelli's ribs. Hard.

Martinelli settled down nicely. Presumably he didn't realize the gun contained blanks.

Sam drawled, "After tonight, I doubt you'll be running for much of anything. This was all caught on camera, and is probably being broadcast as we speak."

A flash of rage crossed Martinelli's face. "If the building inspector I sicced on you had closed *Kinki* like I paid him to, I'd have found that fucking DVD sooner or later, and none of this would've happened."

"How did you know about the DVD?" Sam asked.

"Remember the slimebag who was one of *Kinki*'s former owners? Well, he and Luigi Guglione shared a cell in the New Jersey State Prison. Guglione learned of the DVD and was blackmailing me. I knew if the damn thing ever surfaced, I was screwed, so I had to find it."

Absorbing Martinelli's news, Sam headed for the stage. Microphone in hand, he surveyed the crowd and waited until everyone was silent.

"I hope y'all enjoyed the first instalment of tonight's excitement," he said.

The crowd buzzed, then everyone started talking at once.

"Was it an act?" "What about the gun?" "That was Senator Martinelli. I saw that gangster sucking his—"

Sam interrupted by yelling, "Please stay calm, folks. There is no danger. Senator Martinelli is unhurt. I repeat, unhurt." He didn't dwell on the fact that Martinelli's dick might need a lengthy recovery period after Deanna's attack. Gripping the microphone in both fists, he shouted to the crowd of people shuffling to the exits, "We'll take a brief intermission during which, drinks are on the house. Don't go far. You won't want to miss the rest of the opening ceremony. Guaranteed."

From his vantage point onstage, Sam scanned the crowd for Katie. His heartrate accelerated when he found her. She was on her feet and scowling at her skirt, which had lost several strands of beads. She'd removed her mask. Her face was flushed, her hair rioting around her shoulders. Never had she looked more desirable.

For the first time in his life, he craved a woman. One specific woman. Katie. He even enjoyed talking to her—*talking*, for chrissake—as in telling her things like hopes and fears and dreams, listening to her opinions and advice. Hell, he *needed* her, and it no longer scared him.

He'd finally clued in to what he must do to make things right.

***

The janitorial staff swept up hundreds of beads and went away. In the sudden silence, Katie realized that, except for the camera crew at the far end of the room, she and Sam were alone for the first time since she'd broken up with him.

Suddenly tongue-tied, she shifted from one foot to another. Hey, it wasn't every day a guy stepped in front of a gun to protect her. The gesture meant something, right?

As an icebreaker, she asked Sam, "Did you notify the police?"

"Nope. Both Martinellis and Deanna have left. They can press charges against one another if they want." He tucked a strand of hair behind her ear, trailing his fingers down her neck, as if he cared. The shockingly electric brush of his caress left her quivering with hope.

"But Frank took out a contract on Luigi. I heard it."

"Don't worry. Martinelli will face justice. I heard on the news the Jersey State police picked up the Allegrettis while they tried to dump two bodies, one badly decomposed, but suspected to be one missing Vinnie Constantine, while the other was identified as Luigi Guglione, a well-known criminal recently released pending his appeal."

"The police acted on your anonymous tip."

"Yeah. The Allegrettis implicated Martinelli in Luigi's murder."

Relief washed over Katie, but she persevered. "Frank tried to kill Deanna."

"No proof. It's his word against hers. But I'm sure everything will come out in his trial."

She tried again. "Deanna was Hiram's attacker. Didn't you hear what she said."

"I heard. But she hedged that confession with a 'maybe'. As much I'd like to see her punished for that, it's a he-said, she-said. There's no proof, and my granddaddy wasn't hurt."

"She shot at Frank. That's attempted murder."

"Turns out Deanna had loaded the gun with blanks."

Katie thought about it. "But you didn't know that when you shielded me," she said slowly. "You thought it was loaded." She wanted to tell Sam she loved him, but it felt too risky.

"Katie, I—"

"No, let me go first. I had to break up with you to save your life, Sam. And when that didn't work, I implied you were an addict to make it stick. I didn't want to, and I never believed it, not for one second, but Luigi—"

The doors banged open. Rooster stuck his head in. "We're ready for action," he yelled.

The spotlights flicked on and the theme from *Rocky* blasted from loudspeakers. People filed back inside.

Sam said, "I get it. We're okay, Katie, you'll see. This time, I need you at my side up there." Before she knew it, he'd tucked her hand into his elbow and headed for the stage, giving her no choice but to accompany him.

"I hope my butt doesn't show," she whispered as they climbed the stairs. "The back of my skirt is missing half its beads."

Her reward was his sharp intake of breath. She studied his face with mock concern. "You sure you're okay?" she inquired in her most solicitous tone.

"Couldn't be better," he whispered, blatantly checking out her butt. "Coverage back there is fine. Don't bend over and you'll be good." He gripped the microphone and called for silence.

She wasn't sure what to expect.

What she had not anticipated was that Sam would make her the star of the evening. Who knew he'd present her as the moving force behind the grand opening? He listed her accomplishments in embarrassing detail, taking obvious pleasure in her agitation. She was still blushing when he took both her hands.

"What are you doing?" She eyed him warily, struggling to extricate herself.

He tightened his grip. "Katarina Deluca," he said.

A little shiver that might have been hope ran down her spine. She quelled it in a big hurry. Sam wasn't a permanent relationship kind of guy.

In a swift move, he unhooked the microphone and dropped onto one knee. Her mouth wobbled, but hard as she tried, no sound emerged.

He spoke into the mike, enunciating clearly. "I always believed there was something wrong with me, that I was somehow defective because I couldn't fall in love. But obviously, I was dead wrong. In front of witnesses today, I hereby declare that I'm deeply, dizzily, head-over-heels in love—the forever kind of love—with you."

Her heart pounded in her ears. "This can't be happening. Not here, not now, not in front of hundreds of people. And definitely not when my butt's hanging out."

"Yeah, I hardly believe it myself." The corner of his mouth kicked up a notch. "But I've come to my senses. I'm more than ready to settle down with one woman, and like it or not, you're my one woman."

She stood there, incapable of speech. She was afraid to believe she and Sam would have the happy ending she longed for.

The audience buzzed with excitement.

His smoky drawl enveloped her in warmth. "See, until you came along, I believed a loser like me didn't deserve a real relationship. But you helped me believe in myself in more ways than you can possibly realize."

"Speak up," someone yelled.

He spoke directly into the mike. "You make me want to be a better man. Hell, you make me want so many things that used to terrify me, things like buying a house, having a family of my own, even changing diapers."

Her pulse scrambled.

His eyes pleaded with her to understand. "Don't say anything until you hear me out."

Katie nodded.

A muscle in his cheek bunched as he held the microphone to his lips. "Katie, I love you with all my heart. Hand to God, I've never felt this way about any other woman. I don't know why it took me so long to figure it out."

Her heart ricocheted off the walls of her chest and lodged in her throat.

Hiram's voice roared, "Don't stop now. Spit it out."

Sam smiled. "Will you marry me?"

A collective intake of breath rose from the audience. She looked into this wonderful man's eyes, certain she detected love, hope, and yes, vulnerability.

"Say yes, for God's sake," someone yelled. She recognized Bella's voice.

Katie ignored her sister. "What about my son? We're a package deal."

"I thought that was obvious. I want to marry you both."

A surge of heat sizzled through her body from the top of her head to the tips of her toes. "In that case, yes, yes, yes." By then, her heart felt so full, she could barely form the words to make him understand. "You defend me, Sam. You support me. You're the only man who ever made me feel safe. You treat Josh like a father already. I love you so much, I can't imagine my life without you."

The entire audience rose to its feet, cheering, hollering, whistling. Someone, likely Hiram, gave an ear-piercing cowboy whoop. She expected Sam to stand and embrace her but he merely waited, still kneeling, until the audience quieted.

When everyone settled down, he continued, "I'm not finished. I have a few stipulations and I hope you can handle them."

Katie's stomach lurched. If he hadn't been gripping her hands so tightly, she'd have made a run for it. "Now you tell me," she whispered. "What if I can't deal with your dumb stipulations?"

That made him smile.

The audience chimed in. "Speak up." "We can't hear you." "Yeah. What stipulations?"

Sam raised his voice. "First, I want us to be a real family. I love your son and hope he'll call me 'dad'. I want to adopt him, but only if you and Josh agree. Is that okay?"

Her eyes burned. "Oh, Sam."

"I'll take that as a yes."

She swallowed the huge lump in her throat. "Of course it's a yes."

"Good. My next stipulation is that we have the family that's right for both of us. If it means only Josh, or an entire baseball team, that's fine with me. Agreed?"

Hot tears rolled down her face. "Lots. I want l-l-lots of kids."

"Excellent. Baseball team it is. I have witnesses." He addressed the audience. "Right?"

"Right," they hollered.

"My next stipulation is something I've already set in motion, so you could say it's more of an announcement. I hope you don't mind, but I've sold *Kinki*."

"I think that's a w-wonderful idea." By then, the tears gushed harder.

He handed her the silk puff from his breast pocket. "Here, take this."

She took it and dabbed her cheeks, trying to avoid smudging her mascara. Never in a million years could she have foreseen such intense happiness. He smiled at her, and she found herself giving a watery smile back. "So far, I'm liking your stipulations."

"I hope what I say next won't turn on the waterworks again, but I've found a small ranch in Texas that looks perfect for us."

"Oh, Sam."

"San Antonio is nearby, so you won't feel isolated. We'll be near my family, with a swing set in the yard, a wide porch, and the property is surrounded by a fence." Lovely smiley lines crimped the corners of his eyes. "It's a split-rail fence, not a white picket one."

That had her laughing through her tears. "All my life, I've dreamed of finding a man who gets me the way you do. But I have a stipulation of my own."

Forgetting the lack of butt coverage, she bent and whispered in his ear.

"Hey, we want to hear it too."

Sam got to his feet and wrapped his arm around her shoulders, pulling her tight to his side as he listened. When she stopped talking, he turned to the audience. "My beautiful wife-to-be wants to issue an invitation to someone real important to her."

Katie shielded her eyes from the spotlight and searched the audience until she found her mother. Ma was sitting between Rico and her friend, a nice-looking man with a friendly smile.

"Ma, you're welcome to visit us for as long as you want," Katie shouted, "any time you want. We don't want you to feel abandoned."

Ma yelled back, "Now that I know both my daughters are safe, it's time for me to live my life, have some adventure."

"What kind of adventure?"

"A round-the-world cruise. I've always wanted to see Fiji and Tahiti. Australia too."

"Alone?"

"I'll have company." As Katie squinted in disbelief, Ma patted her friend's hand. Holy crap. The nice-looking man was more than a mere friend. Ma had a boyfriend.

Katie pointed two V-sign fingers at her own eyes, then one at Ma. "You. Me. Later."

Ma merely smiled and nodded.

Katie's last worry evaporated, leaving her lightheaded. Everything she'd dreamed of her entire life was within reach, and all she had to do was reach out and grab it. Turning to Sam, she flung her arms around his neck and kissed him, giving herself up to the certainty of his love and their future together.

The audience showed its appreciation by erupting. Clapping, cheering, and shrill whistles filled the air.

Dimly aware they were making a spectacle of themselves, she didn't give a damn.

With a soft nip to her lower lip, he whispered, "Katie?"

"Yes, Sam?" she whispered back. "Why are we whispering?"

"We're onstage."

"Oops."

He brought the microphone to his lips and spoke. "That's it for now, folks. Eat. Drink. Take in some free entertainment. I hope y'all enjoy the rest of your evening. I know I will."

To thunderous applause, Sam replaced the microphone and linked his fingers with Katie's. He said, "Let's find somewhere more private. There's a couch in our office and a lock on the door. I believe that's where it all began." He pulled her toward the stairs.

She laughed. "It seems fitting. I'll give you the best massage of your life. Unless, that is, you prefer to get started on creating that baseball team you mentioned."

Heat and laughter filled his eyes. "A baseball team has nine players. So far, we only have one. I think we should get started on the rest."

Hand in hand, they slipped out the door.

# # #

Keep in touch with Maureen using the following links:

Website: **http://booksbymaureen.com/**
Twitter: **https://twitter.com/AuthorMaureen**
Facebook: **https://www.facebook.com/MaureenFisherAuthor/**
Goodreads: **https://www.goodreads.com/author/show/845094.Maureen_Fisher**

Other Books by Maureen Fisher

Fur Ball Fever (The Fever Series, Book 1)

The Jaguar Legacy

Fur Ball Fever
(The Fever Series: Book 1)

Romance, mystery & dogs with personality, all wrapped up with humor

An impulsive pet spa owner in big trouble...

Grace Donnelly outdoes herself in the screw-up department when a client's poodle, a shoo-in to win the annual Fur Ball, goes AWOL in her custody. Sadly, the only man who can help is her former flame, Nick Jackson, the most domineering male on the eastern seaboard. With money, careers, and lives in jeopardy, Grace straps on the leather to go undercover in a fetish club looking for clues. Too bad her helpers consist of an aging hippie aunt, a renegade schnauzer, and a drag queen.

A smokin' hot bodyguard with his own agenda ...

Unless security specialist, Nick Jackson, nails a murdering con-artist, his granddaddy will take justice into his own hands. But Grace's amateur investigation threatens the covert operation, an unsettling reminder of their history. To salvage his case, his sanity, and his ex-lover's velvety skin, Nick joins forces with the sassy crusader who rubs him the wrong way— and so many right ways too.

Together, they weather murder, mayhem, and mystery ...

Action bounces from a Jersey Shore beach harboring washed-up corpses, to a fancy yacht and the bawdiest nightclub in Atlantic City. Hazards multiply like bunnies, culminating in fun, danger, romance, and a Fur Ball extravaganza the locals will never forget.

Praise for Fur Ball Fever

"This laugh-out-loud, sizzling hot story had me hooked right from the start and didn't let go until the end." ~ *Amazon.com*

"There were so many lol moments by the time I finished reading I had a cramp in my cheeks and my butt went numb." ~ *Amazon.com*

"Maureen Fisher wrote a book with a great plot, strong characters, a sense of humor and a good mystery. Fur Ball Fever is a perfect blend of good reading." ~ *Readers' Favorite*

"Addictive Prose! Funny, witty, fantastic read!!! LOVED IT!!!!" ~ *Amazon.com*

"I hate to use the often over-used review phrase but the book was a page turner for me and made me read on when I should have been doing other things. It is that good." ~ *Christoph Fischer*

"There were so many lol moments by the time I finished reading I had a cramp in my cheeks and my butt went numb." ~ *Amazon.com*

Excerpt from Fur Ball Fever

The door opened soundlessly. A dark figure slipped into the corridor, and faced Grace, blocking her exit. She fumbled with the pepper spray, trying to flip the safety clip. A steely grip numbed her arm. The canister slipped from her hand to clatter on the floor. The impression of a powerful physique imprinted itself on her brain.

She bunched up a fist and let fly. The punch bounced off naked pecs, eliciting a muffled grunt from the masked intruder. Encouraged, she aimed a kick. A jolt rattled her teeth as her boot connected with his shin. She curled her fingers into claws. He pre-empted a slash at the eye-holes of his mask by holding her at arms-length and sniffing the air like a bloodhound.

Next thing she knew, he'd clamped both her wrists together using one hand. As she struggled, a flashlight clicked on and shone in her face, forcing her to scrunch up her eyes. The beam took a long, leisurely journey down her body, slid back to her boobs, where it lingered.

He made a grim sound in the back of his throat. "Aw, hell. I should have guessed." The iron hand gripping her arm fell away. "Can't you stay out of trouble for one night?" A sleeveless vest constructed of black leather and decorated with cut-outs and metal studs parted to reveal a naked torso.

Anger strengthened her knees. "Dammit, Nick. You nearly gave me heart failure." She shoved him away, flexing her fingers to encourage blood flow. "How did you recognize me?"

He picked up the pepper spray and handed it back. "Besides how good you smell? Darlin', some attributes can't be disguised."

The Jaguar Legacy

Paranormal Romance with Mysticism and Reincarnation

Where Ancient Danger Stalks the Jungle on Velvet Paws...

A journalist determined to unveil the truth ...

Journalist Charley Underhill invades a Mexican archaeological dig, bent on sifting rumors from truth about the curse of the Olmecs. She has serious doubt it was an ancient curse that killed the men. If it means keeping a watchful eye peeled for hairy, hungry predators or lying to the no-good womanizing archaeologist with a sexy Scottish accent, brilliant scientific mind, and penchant for gaudy Hawaiian shirts, so be it. Only the juiciest of exposés will fund her mother's life-saving treatment.

An archaeologist hell-bent on preventing a premature press leak ...

Uncovering the past is archaeologist Dr. Alistair Kincaid's purpose in life. Still smarting from a ruthless betrayal, he guards his latest discovery, an ancient Olmec city buried deep in the jungles of Oaxaca, in the hopes of making a comeback. He won't let a snoopy reporter, even one with a quirky sense of humor, smarts, and a heartwarming smile, destroy his last chance at success. Or steal his heart.

Together, they uncover long-buried secrets best left untouched ...

Strands from past lives intertwine with the present, drawing the couple deeper into a legacy of shapeshifting and danger, romance and evil, reincarnation and karma. Torn between saving her mother's life and betraying the man she loves, Charley must make an impossible choice.

Praise for the Jaguar Legacy

"Hilarious banter, scorching sexual tension, gripping suspense, mysticism – The Jaguar Legacy has it all! Page-turning paranormal romance as hot and steamy as the jungle setting." ~ *Sharon Page, NYT and US Today Bestselling author*

"I read this quickly because the action is non-stop. I liked it so much I immediately bought another book by this author." ~ *Amazon.com*

"Maureen Fisher has redefined paranormal romance, breathing life into magnificent characters and scenarios that demand to be applauded. The Jaguar Legacy creates images of what could be and what could've been in the mind's eye. Thoroughly researched, highly entertaining and well written, this one is DEFINITELY a keeper!" ~ *Euro Reviews*

""The Jaguar Legacy" by Maureen Fisher had me hooked from the first word to the last. Fisher has woven ancient mysteries, past lives, and pure evil, into a story that left me begging for more." ~ *Cheryl Malandrinos*

Excerpt from The Jaguar Legacy

The morning was brilliant with a whisper of breeze to offset the heat. As Charley walked shoulder to shoulder with Kincaid along the rough trail that was barely wide enough for a vehicle, she discovered she was enjoying herself immensely. Branches interlaced overhead, forming a tunnel of alternating shade and sun. Scarlet and blue flashes in the trees revealed a pair of painted buntings hunting for insects.

The boots refused to bend. They were so heavy, they felt like cement blocks attached to her feet. Kincaid was right. They should have driven to the dig.

She glanced up and caught the wicked glint in his eye. "What are you staring at?"

He slowed his pace to accommodate her shorter strides. "Is it my imagination, or are you limping already?"

"Of course not. The boots just take a little getting used to. That was a distinct gloat. Didn't your mother tell you it's not nice to gloat?"

"I wouldn't dream of gloating at your expense. I hate to tell you, but we have a climb ahead of us. The ancient city's built on top of a hill."

"I'll be fine."

"I admire stoicism in a woman."

"My boots are as comfy as bedroom slippers."

"Ah-ha. You're talking about bedroom attire already and it's not even our first date. Is this a come-on?" he asked, leaning closer and sniffing the air near her neck. "Mmmm-mmm, you smell delicious."

It was too easy to enjoy him. "No, it's not a come-on, and leave my neck alone." Charley swatted at him, though her heart turned a somersault. She dragged her mind back to the purpose of her visit. "Do you mind answering a few questions about your dig?"

About Maureen Fisher

Transplanted from Scotland to Canada at the tender age of seven, I now live with my second husband in Ottawa, Ontario. After spending eons in the I.T. consulting world, I grew weary of wearing snappy power suits, squeezing into panty hose, and fighting rush hour traffic. I made a life-changing decision—I would write books. Not dry, boring, technical treatises, but fresh, funny romantic suspense novels.

How do I spend my time? Besides writing, I'm a voracious reader and volunteer for an addiction family counseling program. In addition, I'm a bridge player, yoga practitioner, seeker of personal and spiritual growth, pickle ball enthusiast, and an infrequent but avid gourmet cook. My husband and I love to hike, bicycle, and travel. I've swum with sharks in the Galapagos, walked with Bushmen in the Serengeti, sampled lamb criadillas (don't ask!!!) in Iguazu Falls, snorkeled on the Great Barrier Reef, ridden an elephant in Thailand, watched the sun rise over Machu Picchu, and bounced from Johannesburg to Cape Town in a bus called 'Marula'.

As an author, my goal is to transport readers into a world of romance, adventure, and fun. My sassy romance novels always contain a kick-ass heroine, smokin' hot hero, tons of humor, and an animal or two.

Keep in touch with Maureen using the following links:

Website: **http://booksbymaureen.com/**
Twitter: **https://twitter.com/AuthorMaureen**
Facebook: **https://www.facebook.com/MaureenFisherAuthor/**
Goodreads: **https://www.goodreads.com/author/show/845094.Maureen_Fisher**

www.ingramcontent.com/pod-product-compliance
Lightning Source LLC
Chambersburg PA
CBHW072211170626
46813CB00003B/897